BLOOD RELATIONS

SHIRLEY ESKAPA

BLOOD
RELATIONS

M

MACMILLAN

LONDON

First published 1993 by Macmillan London Limited

a division of Pan Macmillan Publishers Limited
Cavaye Place London SW10 9PG
and Basingstoke

Associated companies throughout the world

ISBN 0–333–56974–1

1 3 5 7 9 8 6 4 2

A CIP catalogue record for this book is available from
the British Library

Typeset by Cambridge Composing (UK) Limited, Cambridge
Printed by Mackays of Chatham, PLC, Chatham, Kent

To Rhona Beck, my sister
and
to Rodney Barnett, my brother

ACKNOWLEDGEMENTS

Once again, my endless gratitude to my agent, James Hale.

The lively interest and perceptive comment of Jane Wood of Macmillan and Suzanne Baboneau of Pan Books are greatly appreciated.

I should like to express my deep thanks to Susan Cowley and Margaret Marshall for the skill and charm with which they typed and retyped this manuscript.

I owe a special debt of gratitude to Patrick Cosgrave and David Elliot for their unwavering support.

The librarians of the London Library, the Victoria Library of the Westminster Library Service, the Fishhoek Library, the Reform Club and the Royal College of Physicians were especially helpful.

I would particularly like to thank Sahra and William Lese for their invaluable assistance.

I am enormously indebted to Dr Mark Bushnell, Susie Elson, Diana Espinoza, Reeva Foreman, Harris Pharmaceuticals, Lisa Kaye, Colonel Ferguson, Richard Grosse, Barbara Howell, Barbara Leser, Judge Cecil Margo, Admiral Edward Martin, Jane Noel, Professor Mark Pepys, Dr Philip Press, Ruth Rosen, Charles and Shirley Schneer, Halina Szpiro, Bea Tollman and Margot Walmsley.

The strong backing, tender support and generosity of spirit of my children, Roy, Linda and Robert, and my sister Rhona, mean more to me than they can ever know or I can say.

And of course it is impossible to thank my husband Raymond, whose magical role in all this is known only to him.

A little hurt from a kin is worse than a big hurt from a stranger.

Moses de Leon
c. 1250–1305

PART ONE

Chapter One

Six nights after Liberation, Cecilia Tortelli ran barefoot and bleeding through the streets of war-torn Rome. Running for her life, she was as fast as an Olympic athlete instead of a girl of sixteen whose childhood had passed her by. Her face was beaten and bruised, her breasts punctured by his teeth, but the adrenalin of fear and shame protected her from physical pain. The sound of his boots grew dimmer; she did not slacken her pace, nor unclench her tight fists. Her lips moved in hopeful prayer – for only eleven months earlier she had been blessed by the Pope after the basilica of San Lorenzo had been bombed. Why, the Holy Father had even laid his hand on her head.

Cecilia had no doubt that it was that blessing that now gave her the strength to streak across the city, and the courage even to take the short cut past the dreaded prison, Fort Brauselta. She prayed too that her stepmother Maruccia would allow her to heat water to cleanse herself of the filth and devil-slime of Vincenzo, the American soldier.

It was past midnight, and she knew she would incur her father's inevitable beating which, after all, she certainly deserved. If only Maruccia would let her boil some of her precious water. Water was more scarce than wine. Just a little water, scalding hot water to burn him out of her. Maruccia's shrill abusive scolding would sound like music.

Her father, like many Romans, hated and distrusted Americans as he had hated and distrusted Germans. Amongst the rubble surrounding their battered apartment building it was still easy to read the writing on the remains of a wall: *We do not want Germans or Americans. Let us weep in peace.*

She clenched her fists still tighter; although she was only

3

sixteen she knew that proof of her assailant's identity lay in the palm of one hand.

The other hand still clasped the precious gift for her hated stepmother – a bar of chocolate.

At last she reached the crumbling Trastevere tenement in which she lived. She climbed the stairs slowly, on tiptoe, hoping against hope that they would be asleep. But they called out to her and, as she entered their feebly lit bedroom, she raisd imploring eyes to the ornate crucifix hanging above their bed.

'*Mama mia!*' her stepmother shrilled, breasts heaving above a belly bulging with pregnancy, as she came in through the door. 'What's happened to you? What have they done to you? Your dress is in pieces. Where are your shoes?'

It was only then that Cecilia began to sob. The harsh animal sound that tore from her throat silenced her stepmother.

'Bastard! Murderer!' her father, Pietro, thundered. 'Who is he? Tell me who he is and I will kill him with my bare hands.'

'First, you will help me lift her on the bed. Then you will call the doctor and the *carabinieri*. After that, you can murder him,' Maruccia told him.

Usually Cecilia slept on a crumbling couch in the living-room. Now, however, her stepmother helped her on to her own bed. Once she was lying on the bed, Cecilia's terrible sounds died down. She managed to point her fist between her legs. 'Water,' she whispered. 'Please, water. Boiling water.'

'Pietro,' Maruccia commanded. 'Use the pitcher. Boil the lot!'

He looked at her with wild, uncomprehending eyes.

'At once, do you hear me? Boil the water for your daughter.'

'Poor one,' Maruccia crooned as she stroked Cecilia's burning forehead. 'It is better that your poor mother is not here to see this.'

Her fists still clenched tight, Cecilia bit her lip. How dared this woman talk about her dead mother? While her mother was dying, her father had brought this woman, this witch, into the very house where his wife lay suffering.

Her father returned with the pitcher of hot water. He had

4

removed his belt and slung it round his neck. 'Who was it?' he asked again.

Pietro began to strike the table with his belt.

'Get out of here!' Maruccia ordered. 'This is no place for a man.' Suddenly the starving woman saw the gleam of the Hershey bar. 'What's that in your hand?' she asked, lifting Cecilia's fist. 'Show me. Open your hand, I tell you – open your hand!'

'NO!' Cecilia said with a finality that was dumbfounding. 'No!' she said again. 'This is for the *carabinieri* to see.'

The tender ministrations of her stepmother surprised her, proving that, besides mutual hatred, they had in common that primeval fear of all women, everywhere – rape!

Suddenly the reaction to the violent assault hit her, and she began to shake. That she and Vincenzo had met at St Peter's somehow made it all the more shocking, all the more painful.

Cecilia and her friend, Anna, had joined the huge, early evening crowds that assembled in the Piazza of St Peter's to give thanks to the Pope. The American general, Mark Clark, had entered Rome, the *Cité Éternelle*, only hours before.

On that golden evening of June 5th, the day all the bells of Rome rang out, together with hundreds of thousands of fellow Romans, she and Anna and Vincenzo and his friend, Mark, had gone down on their knees to give thanks before the Vicar of Christ. It was amazing to Cecilia and Anna that Vincenzo and Mark, far from being the savages and murderers they had been warned to expect, were Catholics. In that emotion-charged atmosphere, festive yet serious, awesomely holy as well as joyous, it would have been impossible for the two young Roman girls not to have responded to the two American soldiers who, incredibly, spoke Italian. Their American accent made them especially – and unexpectedly – exciting.

'What will you do, now that the war is over?' Mark had asked Cecilia.

5

'Find work, I hope,' she answered promptly.

Vincenzo laughed. 'The war is over and she doesn't want to go dancing. No, she wants to work!'

'She has a stepmother,' Anna explained loyally.

'What sort of work would you like to do?' Mark asked sympathetically.

'Whatever I can find,' she replied simply.

Then they had delightedly accepted Hershey bars and agreed to meet at St Peter's in two days' time.

Cecilia had gone away, dreaming of Mark. It was disconcerting because, with his huge rolling shoulders and twinkling, flirtatious eyes, Vincenzo was far and away the better-looking of the two. Mark seemed serious, perhaps even shy, and though he was even taller than Vincenzo his shoulders were slight. Behind his horn-rimmed spectacles his eyes were sad, even pained. As if the war had wounded his soul, she thought. His Italian was soft and musical, with an accent she could not decipher, whereas Vincenzo's had the harshness of the South.

Suddenly she understood why Mark seemed so weary. He was old, she decided, twenty-five or so; Vincenzo was probably no more than twenty.

At their next meeting at St Peter's, which the girls were careful to keep secret from their parents, Vincenzo and Mark seemed to be in a constant state of laughter. They'd been billeted at the Grand Hotel, where they had taken long, gloriously hot showers, and where the beds were feather-soft.

'The Major here wants to take us to the Grand Hotel bar,' Vincenzo said. 'I'm only his junior lieutenant, so how could I disagree?'

Cecilia was wearing the best dress she had but felt certain it was not good enough for the Grand Hotel. It was silk and because it had once belonged to her mother she felt protected by it, though she remembered when it had been a shining emerald green. It was faded now; to brighten it she had added a white collar and white cuffs. As she walked the skirt swirled slightly, yet hugged her hips. The silk felt smooth and lovely, luxurious and sensuous against her bare legs. She pulled her blouse tight into her slim belted waist, which emphasized and outlined her full breasts. As soon as they were a safe distance from home, she and Anna had put on their previously illicit lipstick and coloured their cheeks. Cecilia's flawless milky complexion and her flashing midnight black eyes with their brave gaze reminded Mark of a Modigliani painting.

Now she and Anna exchanged anxious glances.

Intercepting the girls' silent exchange, Mark said quickly, 'You're the prettiest gals in Rome.'

'Like I always say,' Vincenzo said triumphantly. 'My boss has the best taste.' He grinned persuasively. 'These two officers of the US Infantry would be mighty proud to have you accompany us.'

To two war-starved girls who had been impoverished even in peacetime, the plush, glittering foyer was a shock of unimaginable splendour, a vision of forbidden magnificence. But for the war, such a place would have been as inaccessible to them as New York. In a daze, she and Anna found themselves seated at a small table in the bar.

'A carafe of Chianti, *per favore*,' Vincenzo called out to the waiter. Turning to the girls he added, 'Chianti okay?'

Cecilia and Anna giggled nervously.

The waiter brought the wine and they clinked glasses and said, '*Salute!*' Vincenzo seemed to down his glass in a single gulp and quickly poured himself another. As Anna chatted happily to the American soldiers, Cecilia's eyes strayed round the bar. Like countless young girls she had long since accepted her father's low opinion of her and believed herself to be worthless. Consequently she had no idea that she was beautiful; and it was all too easy for her to interpret the stares of the soldiers and the appraising glares of the sleek, sophisticated women as signs that she was out of place and had no right to be there. She wanted to rush away – but then remembered that there had been that promise of chocolate for her pregnant stepmother. She turned her attention back to the table and took small sips of her wine.

7

Mark smiled at her and asked her questions about her family to put her at her ease. He was a nice man, she decided, and found herself responding with warmth.

After about half an hour Vincenzo raised his glass and said, 'To the end of the war!' His American accent gave his Italian an exciting glamour.

'It will end soon, this war?' Cecilia asked anxiously. 'In a month perhaps?'

'Soon,' Mark said. 'But it will take a bit longer to get the Germans to surrender.'

'Cecilia and I,' Anna said, 'we, too, have been fighting the Germans in our own small way, Marco.'

In Italy it made Mark feel great to be called Marco.

'Girls like you fighting?' said Vincenzo with a brash laugh.

'We have been letting out the air from the tyres of German cars and trucks,' Cecilia said proudly. 'It is not much, of course, but it makes them very angry.'

'But dangerous!' Mark said. 'Very, very dangerous.'

'Another toast!' Vincenzo said, raising his glass. 'To two brave girls fighting the Germans!'

Suddenly he looked at his watch. 'Jeez, girls, we have to leave,' he said in his high tenor voice. 'The Major here made a date with his uncle, the General, and he's ordered me along too.'

'Oh, I'd never order Vincenzo to do anything he didn't want to do. I've never had to *order* him to do anything at all, and he knows that,' Mark said seriously. 'I merely told him my uncle would like to meet the man who saved my life. If that sounds like an order, then I'm Mussolini!'

The girls giggled, and Vincenzo laughed. But a laugh has no accent, and to Cecilia it sounded cruel. It made her feel uneasy.

Vincenzo rose. 'Aw, quit the speeches, buddy,' he said smoothly. 'Well then, ladies, it's goodbye.'

'Goodbye?' Cecilia echoed doubtfully.

'That's American for *arrivederci*,' Vincenzo said quickly. 'Stick around, sweetheart, and I'll teach you American.'

Just before they reached the revolving door at the dauntingly lavish foyer, Cecilia summoned up her courage. 'Excuse me,' she said shyly, 'but did you bring the chocolate? Excuse me for asking.'

'Sorry, we forgot,' Mark said apologetically. 'If you'll wait a moment—'

'We're right out of chocolate,' Vincenzo cut in quickly. 'Come back the day after tomorrow, and you'll get as much as you want. We can promise that. Okay, buddy?'

'Sure,' Mark said.

'But I can't come the day after tomorrow,' Anna said regretfully. 'I must go to my grandmother.'

'Cecilia will get yours for you. Okay, Cecilia?' Vincenzo grinned.

'Yes.' Cecilia nodded. 'Of course I will.'

'I'm sorry,' Anna said again. 'I would love to come, but, you see, it's my grandmother.'

'We already agreed it's okay,' Vincenzo said impatiently. 'Hell, I've had a grandmother myself.'

In the hot, airless bedroom Maruccia lay on the double bed that filled the small room. Cecilia roused a slight breeze as she fanned her stepmother.

'Again? You're going to help Anna with her sick grandmother *again*?' Cecilia's stepmother shrilled.

'Please, Maruccia, please,' Cecilia said. 'Anna practically begged me—'

'A liar is worse than a thief.'

'I'm not lying. I *swear* it—'

'Swear it on your mother's grave.'

'On my mother's grave,' Cecilia said evenly, hoping her stepmother could not hear her thudding heart.

Afraid to take the chance of arriving earlier than Mark and Vincenzo, Cecilia was deliberately ten minutes late.

As soon as Vincenzo saw her, he rose to his feet and made the lavish gesture of kissing her hand. She blushed with confusion and pleasure. Her anxious eyes sought Mark.

As if reading her mind, Vincenzo said smoothly, 'Marco couldn't make it. Dinner with his uncle, the General.'

'Oh,' she said nervously. 'I'm sorry.'

'Sorry! Why be sorry? Marco's uncle is one of the most important generals. We Italians have a lot to thank him for. You should be grateful to him, Cecilia.'

'I am grateful to every American,' she said hurriedly.

'We've had the luckiest break, Marco and me,' he said excitedly. Beckoning to the waiter, he ordered two double Scotches for himself and a glass of champagne for Cecilia. 'Letting out any more air from German tyres?' he asked, roaring with laughter.

Their drinks arrived. 'Bet you've never drunk whisky in your life,' he said, slurring his words.

Too shy to tell him that she liked his American voice, and too afraid to admit to herself that she thought he was drunk, she said, 'You're right. I've never tasted whisky.'

Moving closer to her, he pressed his glass against her lips. 'Have a sip,' he suggested.

The fumes of his whisky breath made her turn her face away from him.

Grasping her chin tightly between his thumb and forefinger, he said, 'Taste it.'

Instantly obedient, she took a sip and spluttered. 'Ugh!' she said. 'It's too bitter.'

He laughed. 'Anyway, this lucky break . . . We've moved out of the hotel!' he said proudly. 'A *contessa* invited all us Americans billeted here to a party at her place. She calls it an apartment. I call it a palace.' He went on, sounding awed, 'She was scared the Communists would come into power and take it for themselves, so she agreed to rent it to us. Vincenzo Parsini living in the Contessa de Primidini's palace. Who would believe it? I already wrote home. My sister will go crazy.' He looked into the distance, his eyes glittering. 'Such paintings – it makes even me want to learn about art.' Returning his attention to Cecilia, he said reproachfully, 'You haven't taken even a sip of your champagne.'

Hurriedly she raised the glass to her lips.

'I'm sorry,' she said at once. 'I was listening to you.'

'Drink up,' he ordered. 'I'm taking you to see it.'

'You are very, very lucky,' she said, playing for time.

'Are you afraid of me?' he asked kindly. 'Surely you trust me?'

Forcing a smile, she answered nervously, 'Yes.'

He rose. 'Good,' he said. Taking her hand, he drew her gently to her feet. 'It's good you trust me. I like you very much.'

The apartment was not far from the Grand Hotel.

He slipped his arm about her waist as they walked side by side at a fairly brisk pace. Light though his touch was, her body felt as stiff and as rigidly unyielding as a drainpipe.

'But this is the Piazza Navona,' Cecilia said, astonished.

'You know the place? You've been here before?'

'Which floor is your apartment?'

'The first,' he said shortly. 'Why?'

'I don't like being too high up. It makes me frightened,' she answered, improvising hastily.

Once, and it seemed so long ago now – she had been about ten at the time – her mother, Bella Tortelli, had worked as one of Signora Paravichini's many maids on the fourth floor. Among her duties she had been in charge of the flowers, and sometimes came home with the discarded roses and gardenias, the only flowers the Signora permitted in her home. She cut the stems and steeped them in boiling water and made them bloom again. Happy, safe days of endless love. She felt as if her mother's spirit was protecting her, guarding her, and her lips curved upward, smiling of their own accord. He felt her body relax and gently and skilfully tightened his hold.

In the vast, ornate salon, a bucket of champagne awaited them. 'Compliments of Marco's uncle, the General.'

The champagne, a Lanson, had been randomly and casually stolen from the Contessa's fabulous cellar. With a raucous chuckle he poured two glasses.

Her eyes alighted on the Hershey bars on the sideboard.

'*Mama mia!*' she said, clapping her hands and then holding them to her cheeks. 'So much chocolate.'

'I guess you'd rather eat chocolates than drink champagne,' he said with a sour grin.

'Oh, yes,' she said enthusiastically. 'I love chocolate. I still remember the taste of the chocolate you gave us at St Peter's.'

In the high-ceilinged, noble living-room, with the Contessa's coat of arms sculpted into the wall, his coarse, high-pitched voice seemed to make the crystal chandeliers tremble. Engorged, the arteries in Vincenzo's scrawny neck bulged; his lips peeled back from his teeth in a snarl.

She could smell her own fear.

'Drink your champagne.'

'Excuse me?'

'I said, drink it.'

Alarmed, she put the glass to her lips and drank as if she were slaking a midsummer thirst.

'You should have said *salute*! People say *salute* before they drink. I bet the Germans gave you chocolates!'

'Excuse me?'

'You heard me!' Now very drunk, he suddenly stood up.

At that moment she knew she must escape. Frantically her mind searched for a way out . . .

'*Ja wohl,*' he said, mimicking the Germans. '*Ach so* . . . You kissed the Nazis and opened your legs and grabbed their chocolates.' He paused. Then his voice was heavy with contempt. 'Whores! All broads are whores!'

Bewildered, she shook her head.

'Sorry,' she said. '*Salute!*'

He poured more champagne into her glass. 'Drink up,' he ordered.

'Thank you – no.' She grimaced. 'It seems it doesn't agree with me. I feel a bit sick—'

'Shit!' he half roared, half shrieked. 'It's the best French champagne money can buy, and she says it makes her feel sick!' Pressing the glass against her lips he roared again, 'Drink!'

'No!' she cried, pushing the glass away. 'I'd like to go now.'

12

'You want to go? Just who in the hell do you think you *are*?'

'Yes, I want to go, please,' she said, whimpering.

In answer, he flung the glass across the room and slapped her on both cheeks, flinging her to the floor. Kicking, screaming, scratching, she fought back hard. Breathing heavily, partly in English and partly in Italian, he repeated over and over again, 'So this is how you do it – hey – dirty *stupid* cock-teaser.' He held her down and twisted her right hand; with her left she tore a handful of hair from his head. Ripping her buttons apart, he bit deep into her breasts. For a merciful moment she blacked out with pain.

Now he was spent and silent.

It was all over for him. She lay still, feeling as if her lungs had been crushed by ribs broken under his weight. She tried to slide from under him but he was too quick for her and forced her back.

'Please,' she begged. 'Please, Vincenzo. Let me go now!'

'Lieutenant Vincenzo!' he corrected, his face suffused with hatred.

'Lieutenant Vincenzo!'

'Go then,' he shrieked, pulling her to her feet. 'But leave your shoes.' He gave a brutal chuckle. 'A souvenir from Rome.'

Obediently she kicked them off. Seizing her hand, he commanded, 'Open it, bitch! Open your hand.'

'I can't.' She winced, lying instinctively. 'It feels broken.'

Numbly she watched him button his fly, grab a Hershey bar, thrust it into the open palm of her right hand and squeeze her fist around it. Then he yanked off his belt and whipped it against her buttock. 'Get out of here!' he roared. '*Run!*' She was already running when the belt whipped her again.

Which was how, with a Hershey bar in one hand and a clump of thick black hair in the other, she reached home.

13

Chapter Two

Mark was not to know, as his shoes crushed the splintered glass window of a Fascist shop that had been looted shortly after Liberation, that only a few minutes earlier some of those very fragments had cut the bare soles of Cecilia's feet.

Now, after that intimate dinner with his uncle, he felt closer to his family, and it was pleasant to walk the streets of his mother's childhood. The clamour of his longing for his wife, Fran, and their children, Rufus and Amy, became a hush instead of a shout.

He had spent three summers in Italy – but that was before the war, before the death of his grandmother. It seemed an eternity away now. Those long-ago summers had been in Tuscany, at his grandmother's summer home; he had spent little time in Rome.

Because his uncle was a general, his undisguised pride over the Silver Medal Mark had been awarded for valour in combat had been especially meaningful. Their intimate tête-à-tête dinner had therefore been more of a pleasure than a duty. Previously, his uncle had been the stiff and forbidding general his rather frivolous Aunt Sally had chosen to marry. As her legal guardian her eldest brother, Theodore Cartwright, Mark's father, could hardly have been more approving of his orphaned sister's choice.

It had been neither easy nor secure to be the son of a man as strong, as powerful and as rigid as Theodore Cartwright. He could not recall ever having heard a word of praise from his father, but the Silver Medal would surely ring the bells of approval Mark would have done almost anything to hear.

Theodore Cartwright's patriotism was absolute – just as he

believed in the inferiority of women, so he believed in the superiority of America. At Cartwright Pharmaceuticals every single one of his employees knew that he was a descendant of Abraham Lincoln. Indeed the company motto was *Pro Patria et Scientia* and, since he had founded Cartwright Pharmaceuticals, he made damn sure that everyone lived up to it.

Theodore had always said he would not marry until he was thirty, and his wedding took place on his thirtieth birthday. And because he was known to be the kind of man who carries out his plans – as well as his threats – his wedding had been keenly anticipated for years. His unbridled patriotism made it certain that his bride would be an all-American beauty of distinguished Yankee lineage; which was why his engagement to Lucia, the beautiful Botticelli-type daughter of the Italian Ambassador to Washington, was, if not a scandal, a source of delicious gossip. Those who hinted that marriage to a foreign girl – a Catholic, to boot – might compromise his patriotism were quickly silenced. 'Hell,' he boomed. 'No patriot is a bigot!'

The truth was that though he had expected to marry a beautiful young girl on his thirtieth birthday, falling in love had not been on his agenda. Helplessly in love, he had asked, 'My dear, could you transfer your loyalty from Italy to America?'

'If this is a marriage proposal,' she had replied, 'the answer is that, of course, my husband's country will be my country.' She paused. 'And my children's country,' she added, blushing.

For a moment he did not speak but smothered her face with kisses.

Gently, she withdrew her hand and said gravely, 'If I allow myself to have American children, you must allow them to be Catholic Americans.'

'American Catholics, you mean,' he said, smiling with relief. Looking her fully in the eyes, he seemed to draw her into himself. 'How many American Catholics do you want?'

'As many as our Lord sends us,' she answered quietly.

They had two children.

Although it had been taken for granted that Mark would follow in his footsteps, Theodore had acceded to his wife's desire

15

that their son should first read law at Harvard before joining Cartwright Pharmaceuticals. For even if Lucia was a female – therefore a member of a lesser species – the education of the children had been designated her responsibility, a responsibility to which she had been wholly dedicated. Until she was eight, her own childhood had been attended by an English nanny, and she had been educated by French and German governesses; she spoke all four languages with equal ease.

She had been ruthlessly determined to make her American children as familiar with the language and culture of Italy as they were with their own. And it was to this determination that Mark owed the easy familiarity with which he now walked the streets of Rome, the Eternal City, the city he had barely even visited but knew and loved so well.

Ah, yes, he thought. He had spent an enjoyable evening with his uncle, Rome had been liberated, the end was in sight and, for the first time in this long, long war, he was suddenly sufficiently at peace. He could forgive himself, if only momentarily, for the failure of courage that, but for Vincenzo's heroic intervention, would have killed him on the minefield.

And then he came home to the Contessa's apartment and found Vincenzo passed out cold, and saw his scratched and bleeding face, and his inner peace was shattered; he knew at once that nothing would ever be the same again. For a long moment he stood watch over his friend and saviour. He gave an angry sigh. The entire weight of American military justice would descend on them, and in its merciless quest for the truth his own cowardice would be swept into the open. Nervously he fingered his Silver Star – the decoration that only Vincenzo knew he had not earned.

No matter what the circumstances, Pietro Tortelli raged, his daughter, Cecilia, had no right to tell him – her own father – what to do. How dared she instruct him not to go to the doctor but to the *carabinieri*? Well, he would bring his shame to neither the *carabinieri* nor the doctor – he would go instead to the

16

legendary foreigner, the Irish priest, Father Donnelly. There are moments in life, he decided, when a man can feel not only more comfortable but more safe with a complete stranger, a foreigner of the likes of Father Donnelly. It was well known that Father Donnelly had hidden young men from the Gestapo, had saved them from being sent to forced labour camps. It was equally well known that the good Father was not afraid of a glass or two of wine. The main thing was that the American military would pay more respect to one who spoke their own tongue.

A graceful, elderly nun admitted him into the seminary where Father Donnelly lived. She left him to wait in the echoing silence of the great hall and went to fetch the foreign priest. The minutes dragged by and he felt increasingly nervous, increasingly angry. Now that the Allies were in control, Father Donnelly could afford to take his time answering an urgent night call.

When at last he appeared, he immediately put Pietro at ease.

'Forgive an old man for keeping you waiting,' Father Donnelly said. 'Come in. Come in – please,' he added, taking the two bottles Pietro held out to him. 'Spoiling an old man like me,' he continued in that lilting Irish foreign accent of his. 'A million thanks, my son.'

He drew Pietro into the kitchen, uncorked the wine and, as he filled two glasses, said, 'And who, my dear son, may I have the honour of addressing?'

'Pietro Tortelli.'

Satisfied that the poor man's trembling had lessened and that he appeared to be more in control of himself, he asked gently, 'And how may I have the honour of helping you, Signor Tortelli?'

'It's my daughter,' Pietro began, his mouth twisted in anguish. 'My daughter. My innocent – daughter—'

'Might I ask you, Signor Tortelli, to tell me your daughter's name?' Experience had taught him the value of asking a distraught man a direct question to which there was a simple answer.

'Cecilia.'

17

'Ah, the good Saint Cecilia. One of Rome's most celebrated martyrs.' Father Donnelly crossed himself. He poured himself a second glass of wine. 'And what has befallen your daughter, whom you named so well?'

'Americans! Anglo-Saxon barbarians!' Pietro hissed, his face churned with hatred. 'We warned her, we all warned our daughters. We knew – every one of us knew all about the Anglo-Saxon barbarians!' He let loose an ugly sound – part gargle and part cough – which produced a large gob of glistening spittle.

Father Donnelly was all too familiar with the lies put out by the Fascist press – the propaganda that succeeded in spreading terror in the hearts and minds of the people. They dreaded the Anglo-Saxon barbarians no less than they dreaded the Gestapo, the Nazi–Fascisti rabid dogs. The smallest hint of disagreement would be both useless and counter-productive, so he said nothing. His soothing sounds – like his comforting, sorrowful gestures – assured Pietro that he had his heartfelt sympathy. He made no attempt even to try to calm Pietro, but waited until he was sure his rage had been spent.

'My dear Signor Tortelli,' Father Donnelly lamented. 'Words cannot express my great sorrow, my deep disappointment and my anger. My heart is heavy with the cruel and terrible fate that has befallen your innocent daughter and your only child.' He paused to drain his glass and added, 'You are a brave man, and a wise one, too, to have come to me.'

Pietro nodded. A nervous, self-conscious smile played about his lips.

Rising from his chair, Father Donnelly began to pace the small book-crammed room in which he both worked and slept. 'I believe I know what to do, I believe I do.'

'How do I begin to—'

'I've no water, no electricity,' Father Donnelly interrupted. 'What I do have, however, is as precious as whisky. I have one of the great wonders of the twentieth century – I have the telephone, and what is more, a telephone that works.'

'A telephone, Father?'

'And I shall use it.'

He began at once to telephone, speaking rapidly.

Pietro could only marvel at the manner in which he switched from language to language.

After his third call, Father Donnelly said quietly, as if he had read Pietro's mind, 'You came to the right man, Signor Tortelli. I have friends in high places – the right places. They will meet us here and we will go to your daughter Cecilia.'

After pouring the last of the wine, he said, 'I can guarantee you, Signor Tortelli, that you will be avenged and your honour restored.' He shook his head for a moment, for he needed time to put the complexities of military law, of a court martial, as clearly as possible to a simple man. 'The American soldier will be punished by his own general. He will be treated like a war criminal and not like a soldier. He will be put to death.'

He looked at Pietro and saw a man radiant with satisfaction.

The priest was more than a little crazy, Pietro thought, but he had made it possible for him to keep his dignity. And the law, and the American general, would make it certain that justice would be done. He would be avenged. The honour of his family would be restored. And all because he had had the brains to come to the right man, the foreigner. Pleased with himself, he sighed a long sigh of satisfaction.

For a long moment Mark did nothing to disturb Vincenzo's unconscious stupor. All sorts of thoughts crashed against his skull, but surprisingly the one that dominated his mind was of the inevitable – and wholly justified – disgust and contempt his uncle would direct toward him.

Of course he had always known that war makes strange comrades but who, he wondered, would have thought Vincenzo would be his room-mate? Vincenzo, whose first pair of shoes had been army issue. Vincenzo, whose rough English was almost as poor as his Italian, his mother tongue. Vincenzo, whose deftness with a needle could repair a torn shirt so neatly that you could hardly see the stitching. Vincenzo, whose natural appreciation of beauty had given him an infallible eye for the finest examples of Roman architecture. Vincenzo, whose loyalty was equalled only by his courage – Vincenzo whose account at the debriefing held in the presence of the Major's uncle, General Timothy Byrne, had ensured that the decoration which was rightfully his would go to his superior officer, his buddy Mark.

Reliving again the tragic events in the minefield at Anzio, he broke into a cold sweat.

'The Sergeant got it, sir.'

It was then that Vincenzo had leapt to his defence and lied: 'The Major here, he went in and got the wounded, sir.'

'Major Cartwright?'

'Yes, sir. Major Cartwright, sir.'

Frozen with horrified disbelief, he had lost his voice and allowed Vincenzo's lie to be accepted as the truth, thereby compounding his own cowardice.

It was true that the Sergeant had been mortally wounded – it was also true that he had obeyed Mark's order. Perhaps, if he had not given the order, he would not have become overcome by fear, shameful, paralysing, unforgivable fear. In which case it would not have been necessary for Vincenzo to lead him through the minefield, searching and testing the earth as he did so.

Vincenzo stirred, and Mark's mind sprang to the present. 'Okay, buddy,' he said out loud, 'I owe you—'

His legal mind went into action, noting the evidence that would be more incriminating than the angry scratches on Vincenzo's cheek. Rapidly he collected Cecilia's pitifully worn shoes, her torn panties, and laid them at the back of an antique armoire. Then he up-ended a jug of water over his friend.

'Goddam it,' Vincenzo shouted, waking with a splutter. 'Cut it out, man! Cut it out!'

'You dumb son of a bitch, you. Can't you see you're in deep shit?'

'What d'you mean, deep shit?'

'Get dressed, and do it quick,' Mark said sharply, pulling Vincenzo to his feet. 'Do you think Cecilia will know where you brought her?'

'I dunno,' Vincenzo said, suddenly afraid, 'but I sure as hell hope she doesn't.' Touching his hands to his cheeks, he said, 'Jesus, this burns.'

'That's too bad,' said Mark.

'My whole face feels as if it's on fire.'

'You'd better neaten up,' Mark said soberly, 'before they come here to get you.'

'Shit, what can they do to me? I'm *American* – an officer of the United States Forces. They can't touch me.'

'Sure *they* can't,' Mark said harshly. 'It won't be their police. It'll be our police.'

'What? The Military Police—'

'Now listen to me real good,' Mark said firmly. 'Concentrate, man, concentrate!'

'Okay.'

'Do not admit to anything, you hear? Tell them nothing. That means nothing, zero, zilch. But demand a lawyer – you have the right to a defence.'

'Je-*sus*.' Vincenzo moaned. 'If they nail me, what'll happen? What'll they do?'

'There will be a court martial.'

'Christ,' Vincenzo said. 'What a way to go. To get so far through the war, and then be put away by my own people.'

'They wouldn't put you away, man. They'd hang you,' Mark said under his breath.

'What's that?'

'I will do all I can for you,' Mark said. 'Goddam it, man, I owe you my life.'

'Sure you do,' Vincenzo drawled. 'So what good is that now?'

'I think I know of a way out,' Mark said, drumming his fingers against the armoire in time with each word. 'You could marry her.'

'Marry her?' Vincenzo echoed faintly.

'A marriage would mean that all charges against you would be dropped.'

Chapter Three

Cecilia stared fearfully at the uniformed American.

Maruccia sat guard at the foot of her stepdaughter's bed, her shoulders thrown proudly back, forcing her pregnancy into greater prominence. The American sat at her bedside, stethoscope in both hands, and said, 'I am Dottore Abrahams. I won't hurt you, Cecilia—'

Cecilia shook her head faintly.

'I promise you, I will do my best not to hurt you. Do you believe me?'

Cecilia made no response.

Maruccia snorted bitterly. 'What more can you Americans do to her?'

'Close your eyes if you want to, Cecilia. You will feel better if you do that.'

With a large, shuddering sigh, she obeyed and shut her eyes.

'Will you tell me the name of the man who did this to you?'

'Vincenzo.'

'Vincenzo who?'

'I don't know.' She moved her clenched fist closer to the doctor.

Dr Abrahams laid his stethoscope aside and took her hand – or rather her fist – in both of his. He stroked her hand and asked, 'Will you permit me to open it?'

She nodded.

Slowly, as if he were unwrapping the bandage from a severe wound, he undid her tightly clenched fist, exposing a clump of thick black hair.

'This is his?'

'Yes,' she whimpered.

22

'Good.' He reached for his medical bag, withdrew a sterile dressing and carefully rolled it around the hair. 'We will find him. This will help us find him. You are a smart girl to have kept this.'

'He lives in the same palazzo where Mama used to work.'

Dr Abrahams turned questioningly to Maruccia.

'Her mother is dead,' Maruccia said sharply. 'I am her father's second wife. I'm her mother now.'

Cecilia gave an involuntary shudder.

'Do you know, Signora Tortelli, where that building is?'

She told him.

'If you will excuse me for a moment, I'll use the field telephone in my jeep to let the others know.'

When he returned he said, 'They will arrest him very soon. They are already on their way.'

'He was going to give me some chocolate,' Cecilia said heavily. 'For Maruccia. For the baby—'

'Bastard!' Dr Abrahams said in English. Reverting to Italian, he said apologetically, 'I will have to examine you now. You know that, don't you?'

Cecilia was silent.

'But I have examined many, many young girls before you. Hundreds, I suppose. Try not to be frightened.'

It was a lunatic world, Dr Abrahams thought. Here he was, a captain in the US Fifth Army, but a doctor sworn to save life, long opposed to the death penalty, now part of a killing machine, wishing – hoping – co-operating in the punishment that would undoubtedly result in the hanging of an American soldier.

At the vicious sound of the dreaded, expected knocking Mark's hair stood on end and he broke into a violent sweat. Vincenzo bit frantically on nails that were already down to stumps.

On his way to answer the door, Mark wheeled round and said tersely to Vincenzo, 'On your guard, Lieutenant. Three points. Answer no questions, give no statements, ask for a lawyer. And a fourth one – stop biting your nails.'

Soon the Contessa's apartment swarmed with the military police of the Fifth Army.

Within less than an hour, a handcuffed Lieutenant Vincenzo Parsini was escorted to room number 164 at the Hotel Romulo, where he was held, under armed guard, to await proceedings.

By nine the next morning Captain Abrahams' official medical report was on Vincenzo's commanding officer's desk.

Colonel Fergusson, Vincenzo's commanding officer, read it quickly and let out an ugly laugh. '*Jee-sus*,' he said out loud. 'The man's an animal.'

As far as he was concerned, Lieutenant Parsini was scum – he had disgraced not only himself, his brigade and the Fifth Army, but his country. America could do without the Lieutenant Parsinis of this world.

For scum like Parsini, hanging was not good enough.

For two days and two nights, Mark wrestled with his conscience and his intellect. Clarity, it seemed, was not helped by his legal training and he became more and more convinced that there was little connection between law and justice and, for that matter, humanity. There are no absolutes, he told himself again and again. There are only concepts. Yet he believed in one absolute – every form of gratuitous cruelty was evil. His entire being was repelled by Vincenzo's savage, cowardly attack on a defenceless, innocent young girl.

Thanks to military law, only marriage could save Vincenzo from the firing squad. And marriage would be a licence to rape Cecilia again and again. Obviously Cecilia could not tolerate the sight of him, much less marry him.

He would have to find another way to save Vincenzo.

Yet he himself was guilty of extreme cowardice, on two counts. Cowardice in combat, and cowardice before his uncle.

On the morning of the third day following Vincenzo's arrest

Mark's investigations led him to call on the legendary Father Donnelly.

After a few discreet meetings with Captain Gordon of Intelligence, he had learned of the dangerous missions Father Donnelly had willingly risked in the Allied cause, of the ingenious methods with which he had outwitted the Italian Fascists. It was said that behind their steel-rimmed spectacles his humorous, sympathetic eyes betrayed a worldliness that was almost saintly.

The truth was that, if he was to help Vincenzo, he would need to know more about the Tortelli family. Because first an idea – then a plan – and, finally, a strategy – had taken shape in his mind.

He knew, of course he knew, that Vincenzo deserved the maximum punishment. But Vincenzo had saved his life . . .

And it was just possible that his new plan might not only save Vincenzo, but lead the poor suffering girl to a better future, a better life . . .

Mark had no idea when he went to call on Father Donnelly that he had only just returned from a visit to the bewildered, grieving Tortellis. However, thanks to a few judicious enquiries, he had a very shrewd idea of the priest's earthly likes, and the first and, according to his informant, the most important was a bottle of Scotch.

Father Donnelly took up the bottle as soon as it was presented to him, saying, 'Indeed, we'll not be waiting for what you Yanks call the cocktail hour.'

'Indeed not,' Mark replied.

He poured them both a glass and took a long draught. The way he savoured it lifted Mark's heart and hopes enough to make his smile a genuine one. It was so cool and easy in the book-lined room that Mark felt relaxed enough to ask, 'Do you mind if I smoke, Father?'

'Indeed, if you offer me one I shall smoke myself.'

25

'With pleasure,' Mark said, rising at once to hand him the pack of Camels. 'My apologies – I didn't know you smoked.'

'Now, Major, perhaps you will tell me what brings you to see a priest on a day as fine as this?'

Debating how to put things, Mark was silent. His eyes strayed to the window.

'Perhaps you'd care for a walk, my friend. A little air would do me a power of good, I know. Walk with me and tell me what's on your mind.'

As they strolled through the ancient piazzas and the narrow *vicoli* leading off them, the priest pausing frequently to point out statues and buildings and relate their little histories, Mark's thoughts took shape and he was ready to speak. He assembled his story thoughtfully, pausing at a street corner to elaborate, or by a fountain, and all the while Father Donnelly listened. As Mark spoke his game-plan grew and became clearer. It was after eight when he seemed to have finished. They had reached the Borghese Gardens.

Seating himself on an elaborately carved stone bench under the canopy of a leafy tree, the Monsignor withdrew a silver flask from under his soutane. He took a swig and handed the flask to Mark. 'There are times when it is better to be drinking from the neck,' he chuckled. 'Now, my son, you want to know what I think, is that it?'

'Yes.'

He took another swig. 'Well, before I give you my thoughts, I must ask you one question.'

'Sure.'

'A half-truth is greater than a half-lie. It's an honest answer I'm after, and an honest answer I'll get.' He spoke with an authoritative air. 'Why would a major of the United States Fifth Army wish to help his junior officer get away with murdering the soul of the innocent beauty of Cecilia?'

'Lieutenant Parsini saved my life.'

'In the line of duty?'

'Above and beyond the line of duty. Lieutenant Parsini saved not only my life but my face.'

'And you wish to discharge your debt?'

'I would if I could,' Mark said with a helpless shrug. 'Some debts can never be settled.'

'True, my son. True.' He removed his spectacles and took his time polishing them on his soutane. At last he said, 'I saw the poor darling this morning. She was so silent. On that rough, shapeless couch, her purity shone through her bruised, broken face. It was as if she had been cut from the purest marble statue of the martyred Saint Cecilia herself.'

'Oh, I know it's sordid to bring money into this,' Mark said wretchedly.

'There's nothing so sordid as needless poverty,' Father Donnelly retorted. 'You have the resources to buy that young girl a whole new life.' He paused and rolled his tongue against his inner cheeks. 'But how, might I ask, in the midst of war, will you be bringing this magnificent ambition of yours to fruition?'

'Well, I guess it helps that General Byrne is my uncle.'

'And when a general chooses to pull strings an entire army marches at his pleasure,' Father Donnelly growled. ''Tis fortunate indeed that General Byrne is your uncle.' He stood up and folded his arms across his chest. 'I'll be putting your proposal to the stepmother with some confidence. I've little doubt she'll be turning her stepdaughter's adversity to her own advantage.'

Mark closed his eyes in relief. Things had gone much better than he could have dared hope.

He had not expected Father Donnelly to take charge of the negotiations. To persuade an innocent, wounded girl to brand herself a liar and a temptress, when she had told nothing but the truth, would require the skill of a diplomat, the faith of a priest and the nerve of a surgeon.

All the same, Mark felt uncomfortable; he was a Harvard-trained lawyer and he was guilty of inducing a young girl to commit perjury. Because of him, she would lose her honour.

He felt corrupt. True, Vincenzo had saved his life. He felt corrupt, he realized, because he was using Vincenzo's victim to pay off his own debt.

Chapter Four

General Timothy Byrne regarded his nephew with something closely allied to suspicion. Narrowing his eyes, he barked, 'Why you would want *me* to put my neck out for that man beats me.'

'I've told you before, sir. Lieutenant Parsini saved my life.'

The phone shrilled. The General snatched it up and, holding his hand over the mouthpiece, said, 'We're fighting a war, not running a social welfare agency.'

Truth to tell, the General had always had his doubts about this nephew of his, this son of his wife's sister who was no blood relation. His great height notwithstanding, there was something too sensitive, too disconcertingly delicate about him, like a reed grown too high that could easily snap. He seemed all too breakable for a major of the US Fifth Army.

Replacing the receiver, the General continued blandly, 'You take your loyalty – your misguided loyalty – too far into the line of fire.'

'It is anything but misguided loyalty, sir,' Mark persisted stubbornly. 'In fact loyalty does not come into it.'

'Explain yourself, Major!' The General's lips curved scornfully. 'Let me remind you, when I met Lieutenant Parsini I was distinctly unimpressed.'

'I do realize, sir, that I am presuming on *your* loyalty to your wife's sister, my mother. I apologize for that—'

The General waved his hand dismissively.

'—but it is only because I have an unpayable debt that I dare presume in this way.'

'Well, I certainly wouldn't have seen you if you weren't my nephew, that's for sure. But come on, Major, you'll have to be more explicit.'

And so, in a voice as calm and expressionless as he could make it, Mark told his uncle the truth. He explained that he had given Sergeant Mulligan the order that had resulted in his horrible death, punctuated by his unearthly cries; he had frozen with panic. In a state of hysterical paralysis he dumbly surrendered to his junior officer's leadership, following him as he picked and scratched a safe path through that murderous minefield. Pressing his hands against his ears, he said, 'I can still hear that screaming, that animal shrieking.'

For a long while the General didn't speak.

Mark, unable to endure the silence a second longer, pointed to his Silver Medal and burst out, 'Vincenzo deserves this medal, not me. It belongs to him.'

The General winced. 'You can substantiate this, Major Cartwright, can you?'

'I can't; Vincenzo is the proof,' he said emphatically. 'But even off the battlefield I was too cowardly – and too proud – to admit that the medal should be awarded to him and not to me.'

Suddenly Mark flung his head back and raked his fingers through his hair. It was an unconscious gesture, a gesture so characteristic of almost everyone in the General's wife's family that it had grown into a joke. The General came suspiciously close to softening. After all, soldiering was not Mark's vocation; he had graduated from Harvard Law School. How was it possible, he wondered, that a healthy young man of Mark's height could look so small, so reduced?

'Either your uniform's grown or you've shrunk,' he growled. 'Stand upright, my boy. Stand like the son of Theodore Cartwright, stand tall!'

Mark straightened at once. The General's mention of his father hinted at a certain sympathy.

'Misguided loyalty is false thinking,' the General said unexpectedly, 'and false thinking brings false conclusions.' He gave a short, mirthless laugh. 'You're too noble for your own good, Major. I want you to know that I would have organized things for Parsini, if only because you asked me to. But to invent such an improbable story and put yourself in the wrong, merely to save the hide of a common criminal, would be beyond all understanding.' He stood up to indicate that the interview was over. 'I'll issue and sign the appropriate orders tomorrow. Paperwork, that's all it is, paperwork.'

Mark rose, saluted smartly, and said, 'I can't begin to thank you, Uncle Tim—'

'No need,' the General said stiffly, waving him away with a practised salute.

As Mark reached the door, he called out, 'By the way, I'm glad Father Donnelly's involved. His credentials – in my book – are fine. Had *he* asked me, it would have been an honour to have assisted. The good Father helped one of my men, Captain Formsby, to escape.' He grinned with sardonic amusement. 'Captain Formsby owes *his* life to Father Donnelly.'

When Mark left the General's formal, martial office he felt an inexpressible lassitude, as if his life's force were being drained out of him. His body relaxed, all tension spent, as in the moments after love-making. Dazedly he walked the streets of Rome, seeing neither the cadaverous beggars nor the wild flowers that had sprung up in the cracks between the paving stones.

At last, he reached the Gianicolo, with its statues of Garibaldi and his sad wife Anita, the park with the magnificent view of Rome laid out in honour of those who fell in a desperate attempt to overwhelm the French troops guarding the Vatican. We make gardens out of men murdered in war, he murmured to himself.

And all that waste was sixty years ago, he calculated; part of his Italian grandfather's folklore. Heroes all, all wasted, heroes of whom his grandfather had so often boasted.

Glancing at his watch, he realized he would have to hurry for his meeting with Father Donnelly, and he set off briskly for the church of St Cecilia in Trastevere. When he got there he knelt in front of the serene white marble figure of St Cecilia and a curious calm stole over him – a serenity of a kind he had not known before. He thought of the simple white church near his parents' country home in Prestyn, Connecticut, the almost-new church that seemed always to have been there, as if it had grown

30

out of the land. He was reminded of his baby son's christening, Fran's radiant recent motherhood, the rise and fall of her soft, milk-swollen breasts, of her dreamlike seriousness.

Still kneeling, he took Fran's photograph from his pocket and drank it in once more.

Aware of a presence behind him, he looked up and rose at once. 'Father Donnelly,' he said, relieved.

'You've been at prayer, my son?'

Mark glanced down at his photograph. 'I wish I could pray, Father.'

'The wish to pray is a prayer in itself.'

'Perhaps.' He returned his photograph to his pocket.

'Indeed, I've a message to bring to you, my son. So I'll be giving it to you now.' Behind his steel-rimmed spectacles, his eyes twinkled. 'If you wish to hear it, that is. It's up to you.'

'I certainly would appreciate it, Father, if you would—'

'The message is simple. Tomorrow, at noon, I'll be able to give you Cecilia's answer. Come to my lodgings.'

'*Tomorrow?*'

'I'll leave you now,' said Father Donnelly, gliding away as soundlessly as he had come.

Mark was punctual – the church bells were still pealing the hour when he arrived. Handing over the bottle of Scotch he had brought, he felt a surge of unexpected relief. Father Donnelly accepted it with a frown, placed it on the sideboard and gestured him to a seat. When he finally spoke it was abruptly.

'Rape, as the Tortellis see it, is one of the spoils of war. And they are right, indeed. For it is victorious armies that most frequently commit the crime.' Squeezing his clasped hands until the knuckles turned white, he added with a touch of violence in his voice, 'It seems men have the licence to rape when they have the licence to kill.'

'It was Cicero, was it not, who said that laws are silent in times of war?'

'Indeed it was,' Father Donnelly said, nodding vigorously.

31

'I am to tell you that Signor Tortelli accepts your offer with gratitude.'

'With gratitude?'

'With gratitude. This morning I doubled the offer I made yesterday.' Mistaking Mark's look of amazement for alarm, he added quickly, 'But it's exactly what you said it should be, not a penny more, not a penny less.'

'Unbelievable,' Mark said with wonderment. 'Unbelievable.' Suddenly, he smiled a wide open smile. But then his mouth fell in anxiety. 'They don't know it was from me, do they? I mean, you let them think it was from Vincenzo, didn't you?'

'The family know nothing of you,' Father Donnelly assured him. 'I think I need not have doubled the offer; they would have given their consent anyway. After all, what choice do these poor souls have?' he said, glaring at Mark. 'But you know that, don't you?'

'I—'

'It's my own conscience I've been searching. Sometimes, for the wrong reasons, the power of money can go a long way toward turning evil into good.'

'I'm not sure—'

'Of course it can,' Father Donnelly said scornfully. 'To lie that she had lied is dishonest. But it is the kind of white lie that compromises no one's honour but her own.'

'I see what you mean.'

'Indeed, and why should you not? So she will tell the *carabinieri* that she had tempted the American officer. She will also say that someone else – an unknown man with a rough Calabrian accent – beat her up.'

Mark said humbly, 'I am more grateful to you, Father, than I can ever say.'

'And you might be interested to know, my son, that it was you she was asking after.'

'Me?' Mark said, alarmed.

'The tall fair one with the kind eyes, she said. The one who gave her all his chocolate.' He smiled with weary resignation. 'An old peasant woman once told me that she believed there were two types of people who make up this world of ours,' he said. 'The decent and the damned. The decent give candy to children to do good. The damned give candy to children to do evil.' He took off his glasses and rubbed his tired eyes. 'The good understand evil, she said, but the evil never understand good.'

Father Donnelly stopped speaking and replaced his glasses. Instinctively Mark knew that he had not said his piece, and so sat, silent and patient, and waited.

At last Father Donnelly rose. 'We must pray, Major, that America will be half as good to her as she deserves.' Dropping his voice, he added, 'Or meet just one-tenth of the poor darling's hopes.'

Hoping that for once the ornate solid gold taps would yield enough water for a long soak, Mark strode purposefully along the long baroque corridor towards the Contessa's opulent black onyx bathroom. In his haste he tripped over a pair of military boots strewn carelessly in his path. As he fell, he heard a familiar sound, looked up and saw Vincenzo bent double in hysterical mirth.

'Vincenzo! What the hell—' A burst of his own laughter overtook him; he rolled about the cold, marble floor, his entire body heaving with one great snorting, shouted laugh. When at last he regained control, he sat up and said flatly, 'They released you.'

All humour drained from Vincenzo. 'I didn't do nothing,' he said guiltily.

Stemming the feelings of contempt mixed up in his relief, Mark rose to his feet and let out a yell. 'Attaboy! Attaboy!'

'*Jee-sus*, Marco, what the fuck did you do? I didn't say nothing, and the guards tell me I'm a free man – how come they sprang me?'

'They worked quickly.'

'They told me she came clean. She *lied*, they said; she's guilty. I'm innocent.'

33

'Yeah—'

'And they're shipping me out, I'm joining a new command.'

'Where to?'

'I dunno.'

'When do you go?'

'I'm to report to Colonel Saunders at 1600 hours today.'

'Okay, Vincenzo, let's go. I'll buy you a drink.'

'I quit the stuff,' Vincenzo said softly. He put out his hand to Mark. 'Thanks, buddy. You sure saved my life.'

It was only with the greatest difficulty that Mark managed to meet his eyes. 'Think nothing of it,' he said gravely.

A little later, when Mark stepped out of the bathroom, Vincenzo was waiting for him.

'See here, buddy,' he said, coming to the point at once. 'You and me – we make a date, okay?'

'Sure thing. When and where?'

'June 'fifty-four. Rome.'

'Okay, Lieutenant. Report to the Grand Hotel on June 22nd, 1954, at 1600 hours.'

That evening Mark sat down to write to his wife, but after only a few sentences he stopped, unable to go on. Perhaps, he thought as he folded the tissue-thin paper on which he was writing, perhaps he was merely too inhibited – too shy – to tell her what was uppermost in his mind.

Suddenly he stood up and restlessly paced the long baroque corridor in which he had tripped over Vincenzo's boots.

How could he tell his wife about the way he had been stirred by a young girl's beauty – about the purity of it and the waste of it, and the shame of it? Could he expect of his wife – or for that matter, any wife – an understanding of the tenderness, the insufferably chaste tenderness he knew he would always feel for a young peasant girl whom he had met only twice? How could he tell his wife of the painful wrenches of his heart when Father

Donnelly had told him she had '*asked after the one with the kind eyes*'.

But Father Donnelly had also said, '*We must pray, Major, that America will be half as good to her as she deserves.*' The words echoed in his mind ominously.

Chapter Five

Wrapping her regulation scarlet Red Cross cloak about her like a security blanket, Cecilia Tortelli boarded the hospital ship that was to carry her to New York.

Cecilia Tortelli – a nurse's aide! Who would have thought it possible? Yet here she was, wearing an official uniform which gave her status even in her own eyes. Her stomach churned with excitement and fear, with happiness and hope – and with sadness that she felt as little sorrow at parting from her father as from her stepmother.

In the two weeks before embarkation, she had spent many secret hours in front of her small, cracked mirror, nervously gazing at her magically transformed style. The starched, sparklng white uniform lifted her out of the hopeless poverty that surrounded her, the poverty she had been bred to accept. America had seemed as distant as heaven – indeed, all she had heard made her believe that heaven was probably another America.

Her stepmother's baby had come too soon and was stillborn. Shrieking curses, the grief-stricken Maruccia Tortelli had immediately laid the blame for the tragedy on the evil eye her stepdaughter had brought into the household the night she had been with Vincenzo. Maruccia cursed the world and everything in it, including even the money that they all believed had come from Vincenzo.

'Blood-money,' she spat at Cecilia. 'Blood-money, bought with the blood of my womb!' But neither her grief nor her curses prevented her from accepting Cecilia's gift of 300 dollars, leaving her a total of 200 dollars in her pocket – a fortune in lira, Cecilia calculated; she would find work in America and it would be more than enough. Maruccia Tortelli at once began to quarrel with her husband as to how the money should be spent. They were arguing on the day Cecilia left – her father dreamed of a vineyard in Tuscany, while her stepmother already saw herself as the *padrona* behind the cash register in the grocery store she would own.

All these, and many more memories besides, Cecilia carried with her as she walked the gangway at the beginning of her new life.

The hospital ship was called *Harton*. It had once been a luxury liner on the Bermuda run, and reminded Cecilia of a large, floating palace.

Ever since it had been decided that she would travel to America everything had been a source of wonder and astonishment to her. To begin with, Mark had arranged English lessons for her, which would continue while she was on board. Nurse Gardener, RN, had undertaken to give her as much time as possible. Her stepmother had been against the idea of English lessons, but Father Donnelly's implacable insistence had won the day. It turned out that she had a musical ear. 'She's a gifted girl, and it's a linguist she might have been,' Father Donnelly had told Mark with some sadness, 'if the poverty hadn't got her.'

Cecilia certainly had a gift for sustained hard work. A nurse's aide was a euphemism for a cleaner. Nurse Billington had only given her one job to do in the two days before the boat sailed – scrubbing the sluice room, and already she could tell that Cecilia could not be faulted. Not that it was easy to please a martinet of the likes of Nurse Billington . . .

She stood on the boat deck, watching the last of her native country. She waited until the land was out of sight before turning her eyes to the distant sunset. Away from the port and out to sea, the ship's lights went on, illuminating the giant red crosses on each side of the *Harton*. The ship seemed to skim the sea with its strength. She felt safe.

She had been told that hospital ships were not attacked. Somewhat simplistically, the Geneva Convention had been

37

explained to her. And she understood that, according to the rules of war, hospital ships were neutral and safe. But everyone on the *Harton* knew of the ship that had sailed out of Naples one afternoon only to be deliberately attacked by a formation of nine German aircraft.

She knew, too, that no one on the hospital ship was armed. Captain Winter and his crew were civilians. Not even the Captain carried so much as a revolver. However, Colonel Smollen, the commanding officer and physician-in-chief, had two guns in his safe – both kept to prevent mutiny or cannibalism, and not to be used against the enemy.

The *Harton* carried 300 military invalids, and a medical corps of about forty. Though less than half of the invalids had been wounded, many were in body-casts. And there were several cases of shell-shock; some of them screamed with a cry that was not quite human. A few of the sick were recovering from infectious hepatitis – a viral disease of the liver. Others had fallen victim to malaria and typhoid. Now, aboard this majestic ship, in an infinity of free ocean space, it was hard to conceive of the million or more refugees struggling to survive in Naples, where an epidemic of infectious hepatitis was on the rampage.

The operating theatres were in the well-insulated heart of the ship, for a considerable amount of surgery would be necessary.

It was known that the *Harton* was not to sail directly to New York. In fact, the voyage would be close on four weeks before the *Harton*, with its single escort, the destroyer *Fordyce*, would land in New York. The ship would be compelled to zigzag through the seas to avoid U-boats and the speed of advance would therefore be far slower than the usual eight to twelve knots.

Besides that, it was likely that the *Harton* would first make for Gibraltar – a four-day voyage from Naples. From there they would sail to Monrovia, and that journey would probably take six days. Although an additional two days would be spent at the port of Monrovia taking on supplies, it was unlikely that shore leave would be granted at a foreign port. Their next port of call would be Brazil, Fort Recife, where there was a US submarine base, and it would be nine more days before the *Harton* would arrive at its final destination – New York.

Cecilia took her meals in the doctors' and nurses' mess. At their first meal, everyone was served a two-pound chicken that had come out of a tin. She'd never heard of tinned chicken. The very idea was revolting, and yet it was delicious. As she ate, she realized she had been even more hungry than she had thought she was. She was given a strange – but pleasant – drink called a Coca-Cola. Before leaving New York the ship's morgue had been filled with Cokes – but the chef had made a point of keeping enough for their first night at sea. She ate too quickly and too much, and had to rush to the bathroom.

Late on the second night at sea, Cecilia decided not to try to sleep. All her pulses throbbed with wonder and excitement. Why, she had even watched a movie called *Gone with the Wind* and, what was more, she had understood some of the English. She was furious with Scarlett and in love with Rhett Butler. For the first time in too many years she felt young enough to have the right to feel hopeful. And she was still only seventeen . . .

Some of the crew had formed their own small band. Only two days away, on Wednesday night, there was to be a dance.

Converting the luxury liner into a hospital ship had not removed all traces of its former glory. The grand staircase and the panelled lounge remained in all their incongruous splendour.

If she could not wear her nurse's aide uniform she would refuse to go. She had brought nothing to wear to a dance because she owned nothing suitable. Besides, how could she have guessed there would be a dance?

She went out on the boat deck, taking her English–Italian phrase-book with her. The moon was high and she fancied reading by moonlight. She sat with her back against the wall, trying to get some light from the blue emergency bulb. Suddenly a cigarette-lighter flared and a GI said, 'Berlitz Italian–English phrase-book? You must be learning Italian.'

'No, English,' she said. 'English.'

39

'So she must be Italian, no?' another voice broke in loudly, speaking Italian. 'Allow me to introduce myself. Lieutenant Albert Rizzoli at your service. Call me Al.'

It was a relief to revert to her mother tongue. Soon she and Al were deep in conversation and the GI drifted soundlessly away. She was especially pleased to speak to Al about *Gone with the Wind*.

'You look like her,' he said suddenly.

'Like who?'

'Scarlett O'Hara. Vivien Leigh.'

'No, I don't,' she said, laughing.

'You do. You do.' Taking her book from her, he said, 'Let's go for a walk, Scarlett.'

The moon was high, the night was balmy and from a phonograph the romantic sound of Vera Lynn singing 'I'll See You Again' drifted towards them. It was only natural he should put his arm about her slim waist, only natural that she should rest her head against his shoulder. They moved to the ship's railings and stood looking out at the rolling, fascinating, black ocean. The song changed, and now Vera Lynn was singing 'Yours'. Al sang along, and then quite unselfconsciously Cecilia began to hum with him. She was transfixed – she could not remember when anything like a song had issued from her lips. Ah, yes, when Mama was alive . . . she had not been too afraid to sing, then. She felt hot tears start to her eyes.

When the song ended she said, 'Thank you. That was beautiful. Forgive me, I must go now.'

'Will you be at the dance?'

'Perhaps.'

But she knew she would not go.

Nurse Gardener, a sharp, slim-boned woman, who called herself a bachelor girl, had decided to use the Wednesday night dance as a conversation topic for Cecilia's English lesson.

After a lengthy introduction and many corrections, it emerged that Cecilia would not be going to the dance. It took an even longer time to get her to say why.

40

Nurse Gardener explained that in America it was possible to borrow a dress. She herself had three dresses from which Cecilia could choose.

More difficulties.

In Rome, family members were known to borrow one another's dresses. To borrow a dress from a stranger was unthinkable. Nurse Gardener decided to turn the whole thing around. Laboriously, she insisted that Cecilia's refusal to borrow the dress was a serious matter. Standing up, she concluded her argument by saying, 'Never in my life have I been so hurt, so wounded, so insulted.'

Cecilia capitulated.

The next night there was a movie – *Casablanca*. Al was waiting for her. He'd reserved two seats so that they could watch the film together. It was a romantic movie, and she wept unashamedly.

Later, he told her that he was recovering from infectious hepatitis. His commanding officer was on the ship – he too had this viral disease of the liver. Cecilia thought he sounded as if he were proud to be sharing the same disease as Major Coulter. 'That's him over there,' he said excitedly, pointing to a lone figure staring out to sea. 'Hey, Major,' he called out in English. 'Howya doin'?'

'Not too bad, Lieutenant,' the Major said with glacial politeness.

The nuances of the officer class were lost on Al, a bricklayer in civilian life.

'I'd like for you to meet my gal,' Al said. He took Cecilia's hand and led her towards him. 'Cecilia Tortelli – Major Coulter.'

'How do you do, sir,' Cecilia said, in her faltering English.

'Pleased to meet you, miss. I see your English is excellent,' Major Coulter said politely. 'Very commendable.'

Cecilia turned to Al for help. The translation tripped off his lips with what she thought of as brilliant ease. She admired him because he could speak both English and Italian. She loved his American accent and was sure he must be a highly educated man. In truth, his English was poor, his vocabulary limited and his heavy Lower East Side accent was excruciating.

Al smiled. He was pleased to have a girl as pretty as Cecilia to introduce to his commanding officer. Until this moment, Cecilia had only seen him on deck in the dim light or in the darkened movie theatre. Now she saw the three dimples that accompanied his wide, full smile. He was tall and too thin, but his immaculate uniform lent him an air of elegance. His face was strained with his recent illness.

'Your dress is beautiful,' he told her at the dance the following night. 'But it is not as beautiful as you.' He was tender and kind, and a surprisingly good dancer. The pressure on her back was subtle and yet it was powerful enough to direct her body in a rhythm that exactly matched his own. She was grateful for all the secret hours she and Anna had spent practising the waltz. Her body felt light and at one with the music. He drew her close and, gently resting his cheek against hers, drew her still closer. He whispered that he loved her, and she believed him.

Overwhelmed by a gratitude powerful enough to be mistaken for love, Cecilia closed her eyes. Al did not look upon her as a leper as she looked upon herself. According to the rules of the society in which she lived, her shame would follow her wherever she went: she would have been a social outcast. Therefore, as Father Donnelly had explained, exile from her own country would be far less painful than exile from her own community. She had understood him too well.

Ever since Vincenzo she had believed that, because no man would ever want to marry her, she would be doomed to a life barren of children and barren of respect. All her life she had been waiting for this moment. Even as a little girl she had been in love with her future husband.

She had expected to fall in love with her heart but not with her whole body. Now she pressed her body against his, and he danced her away from everyone and away from the music. Still dancing, he sang to her in his soft tenor voice. He went on kissing her, singing to her, stroking her. His head brushed the long stem of her neck. His touch was light against her neck, and strong against her breast.

At once she pulled away.

'What's wrong?' he asked.

'This,' she said, flustered. 'This is wrong.'

'But I love you, Cecilia.'

'And I love *you*, Al,' she replied, her voice soft and full of wonder. 'But I must keep myself for my husband.'

His lips tightened furiously. His body was rigid. But every single cell of his cried out for her. He would have to have her. He was going to have her. Nothing in the world could stop him from having her.

'You are right,' he said, his voice thick. 'You must keep yourself for your husband.'

Pressing his lips to her hand, he said, 'Good-night, little one.'

He turned on his heel and left her, and she felt strangely lonely. Heavy with desire, her body ached for his caresses. Already she missed the smell of him, missed the feel of his smooth, clean cheek, missed his warm, mobile lips.

Maruccia had broadcast her shame to the entire neighbourhood. When she had boarded the *Harton* she had felt both an exile and an orphan. Now she would have a husband, and she would begin her own family, and never feel lonely again.

The next morning they were at Gibraltar, and the air was thick with tension – the area swarmed with German submarines. It was now five days since they had left Naples, but it was the very first time Cecilia had experienced that piercing fear she had known during the terrible Allied air raid on July 19th the year before. That was when the basilica of San Lorenzo had been badly bombed.

Cecilia and Al did not meet while the *Harton* was in port. But as soon as the ship was safely out to sea, two days later, Al was in the dental chair. He had faked a toothache because the dental surgery was close to the ward on which Cecilia worked and he

43

hoped to see her. She came into view only once, but it was worth the painful injection he had been given. Her starched white uniform served only to emphasize her voluptuous shape.

Undressing her with his eyes, he gasped out loud.

'Hold on,' the dentist said. 'It will be over in a minute.'

His mouth full of dental equipment, Al could only nod. He returned to his thoughts. Cecilia was a real Italian girl from the old country, where men were kings and women were slaves. They knew how to treat their men, these women who had not been spoilt by America.

Telling him that she had to keep herself for her husband had been the biggest turn-on he had ever experienced. This meant that she was a virgin, and the thought of being this close to one made him mad with ambition to have her. Other than that whore in Naples, he reflected, he hadn't had a woman in years, not since his last leave in New York, since Anna . . . And for the past several weeks he had been too ill even to want one. But with her sensual, innocent mouth and firm, full breasts, Cecilia had changed all that. Besides, her needy, vulnerable nervousness boosted his masculine ego and sweetened his sour temperament.

He would do anything in the world to have her. Yes, he would go so far as to marry her.

This was crazy. What man in his right senses would offer to handcuff himself for nothing more than a good lay? But his body, and his mind, burned for her. Men outnumbered women by fifty to one on this ship. Unless he moved quickly, some other guy would get her . . . He felt his very bowels contract with jealousy.

There was no other way. He would have to marry her and make her his wife.

He never stopped to consider whether or not she would want to marry him. All women were broads, he reasoned, and all broads wanted to trap guys into marriage. Why should she be any different?

They had barely spent a total of seven hours together, and already he was a changed man. He wanted to be with her.

44

Friendless, he had been a loner all his life; he disliked almost everyone with whom he came into contact. Which is why the rigid machine-like routine of military life was entirely satisfactory to him. He made no attempt to be friendly, nor did he go out of his way to be antagonistic.

In New York he shared an apartment with his older sister, Tina. Three years ago, on his last leave, he and his sister's friend, Anna, had reached what was known as an 'understanding'. But he had been deliberately vague about this, not least because Anna was sorely afflicted with acne. Thinking about her now he decided that though she was a willing fuck, she spoke lousy Italian . . .

'Two more sessions and I'll be through with you,' said the dentist.

Al made no response; he had not been listening.

The dentist tapped him on the shoulder. 'I said two more sessions, Lieutenant, and we'll call it a day.'

'Great.'

'First patient I ever heard say that!'

Al merely grinned and showed his dimples.

That night, kissing Cecilia in a secluded spot on the boat-deck, Al realized that they were living under the same roof. At any given moment of the day or the night he would know where she was . . .

For Al, it was like living on a floating island. And in many ways he felt as if the *Harton* was a town – a whole town – that had been transferred to the sea.

In peacetime, on board an ocean liner, apart from the sea and the sun it is the sensation of a simultaneous contraction and expansion of time that is the stuff of romances. How understandable, then, in wartime, on a ship, safe from the battle, the devastation and the fear, to plunge into a sea of Utopian love.

The day after they had left Monrovia, when he and Cecilia had been zigzagging the ocean together for fourteen timeless

45

days, he went to see Major Coulter, his commanding officer. 'I'm gonna marry Cecilia Tortelli,' he said, speaking very fast. 'I need your official permission.'

'Cigarette, Lieutenant?' the Major asked in his Boston accent. 'I'd rather offer you a drink. Can't understand why military regulations insist on dry ships, can you?'

'Thanks.'

Drawing deeply on his cigarette, Al had the sensation that he could hear his commanding officer's mind rolling into action.

'Did you know Miss Tortelli in Naples?' Major Coulter asked reasonably.

'Nope.'

'We've been at sea for precisely two weeks—'

'Long enough to know this is the woman for me.'

'Love at first sight and all that?' asked the CO sarcastically.

'Sure,' Al said eagerly. 'I'm nuts about her.'

'Perhaps,' the Major began. 'Perhaps we should talk about this man-to-man. Forget that I'm your CO.'

'Jeez, Major,' Al said humbly. 'Thanks.'

'In that case, I'll be frank, okay?' said Major Coulter quickly. 'You've got the hots for this girl so bad that you think it's love. But you can't think straight. You want to screw her; she's holding out on you. So you think if you marry her, everything will—'

'No, sir,' Al cut in quietly. 'What I'm saying is kinda personal. But I – that is we – ' he paused and swallowed deeply, 'didn't wait for no piece of paper.'

'I see,' said Major Coulter studying him searchingly.

The Lieutenant failed to look him in the eye, confirming his suspicion that he was lying. He was at least two years younger than Al. It made things awkward. What the hell, he thought, it was a personal and not a military matter. And in civilian life he was a surgeon . . . What would he know about Al's kind of love? He'd seen the Lieutenant and the girl together. There were so few women on board that it was easy to remember her. He longed for a woman himself . . . He said briskly, 'I take it you've asked her?'

'Naw,' Al said. 'I hadda ask you first.'

'Go ahead and ask her, then,' the Major said evenly. 'I'll have a word with Captain Winter. If he agrees, we'll have a marriage at sea.'

'I – uh – I – well, thank you, sir.'

They shook hands and had another cigarette.

'You want Cecilia to be Mrs Alberto Rizzoli when you land in New York,' he said shrewdly. 'I can understand why you would want to do that.' He paused to put out his cigarette. 'Mrs Alberto Rizzoli will be a citizen of the United States of America.'

'The United States forces in general and the United States Navy in particular is not in the business of marrying people,' Captain Winter said testily to Major Coulter.

'I guess I goofed, then,' Major Coulter said wearily. 'As his commanding officer I more or less gave my word that Miss Cecilia Tortelli would be Mrs Albert Rizzoli and a citizen of the United States of America before we landed in New York.'

Running his cold, hard, measuring eyes over him, Captain Winter said, 'What the hell made you say that?'

'I thought a captain of a ship had the authority and the power to conduct a marriage ceremony—'

'In peacetime, yes, a captain does have that authority.' Suddenly his fierce expression softened. ''Course, so long as we are at anchor, your lieutenant could get married in Recife. We'd be in port then, and not at sea . . . And Padre Falkson could perform the ceremony—'

Thus it was that on Sunday, December 17th, twenty days after the *Harton* had set sail for New York, Cecilia Tortelli and Alberto Rizzoli were to be married. In the early hours of the morning of her wedding-day, unable to sleep, Cecilia was out on B deck walking in the rain, drinking deeply of the cold night air. It was good to feel the cleansing rain on her cheeks rinsing her past away. For she was sailing ahead, to a new future, a new country, a new family.

Her mind switched back to the commanding officer's question. 'Do you love him?' he had asked via an interpreter.

It had seemed a strange question. Of course she loved him! He was about to become her husband. And she had loved the man who would one day be her husband long, long before she had known who he would be. So, with great dignity, she had answered, 'I am lucky to love a man such as Alberto Rizzoli.'

Chapter Six

Like a birth, a marriage holds out promise of hope. The Atlantic was now largely under Allied control and a marriage on board ship, as Major Coulter and Padre Falkson saw it, was a celebration of both peace and victory. But Franklyn Winter, the ship's captain, had – as he put it – seen too much of life to indulge in sentiment.

In Captain Winter's eyes, Cecilia was a pretty seventeen-year-old kid who ought to have been in high school. That she was a bride instead was bad enough. Worse still was that she would be married to an inferior specimen of humanity, a coarse, vulgar brute of a man. This marriage was, he told himself, one of the many casualties of warfare. And he was powerless to prevent it. The law was on their side.

But the sight of a young couple so wholly absorbed in one another, their faces shining bright with their belief in their love, was in Padre Falkson's view just one of the many evidences of the glory of God.

Despite his misgivings, Captain Winter gave orders for a small wedding reception, and went so far as to arrange a private cabin for the newly-weds.

When they stood before the padre, she blazingly beautiful in the sparkling whites of her nurse's uniform, and he neat and shining in his lieutenant's uniform, he did what he had to do and pronounced them man and wife.

Everyone kissed the bride and called her Mrs Rizzoli, and congratulated the bridegroom. After that, there was a celebratory dinner at the Captain's table, and it was, in wartime, a real feast.

Like most brides of her day, Cecilia was unable to eat.

Al, however, impatient to get the meal over with, wolfed his food. He did justice to the meal.

Cecilia's heart churned with fear and loneliness. She could understand her fear, but not the loneliness. It seemed wrong for a bride to feel lonely on her wedding-day. And then she understood that she was a stranger among strangers. Yet, like everyone else on the *Harton*, she was an American citizen.

Al had done this for her . . .

She only hoped she would deserve to be his wife.

And then at last they were alone in their cabin. It had portholes but was like any compact hotel bedroom. And, wonder of wonders, it had its own private shower and toilet. Motherly as ever, Nurse Gardener had unpacked her few meagre belongings, and placed a tablet of lavender soap on the sink. Luxuries in wartime are given a new order.

No sooner had the door been shut than he yanked off his jacket and began fumbling with her tight white belt.

'Hold on,' she said gently. 'Hold on, wait for me to sit down, and I'll get it undone—'

In answer he took the belt in his two hands and wrenched it open. 'I've been waiting too long,' he groaned. Then, again in a single fluid movement, he ripped her uniform apart.

Her buttons scattered. Still standing, but in a frenzy of haste, he began to tug at her petticoat. She had not yet taken her shoes off, and he was fully clothed.

Her petticoat torn, and her bra undone, he picked her up and flung her on the bed. The next moment he was tearing off her panties, and the harsh, cruel sound of cloth being ripped filled the small cabin. Seconds later, his trousers were undone. Then, his trousers still around his ankles, he entered her. She screamed. In too much agony from her reopened wound even to be embarrassed by the thought of others hearing her, she screamed again. To silence her Al pressed his mouth against her, ramming his tongue against her throat to shut out the sound.

Less than a minute later it was all over. He rolled off her and, shoes, socks, shirt and tie still intact, he fell asleep.

50

Holding her breath, she lay motionless beside him for a long while. Eventually she went to the bathroom, fetched a towel and covered him with it.

Then, longing to have a shower but too afraid to disturb him, she sat at the porthole looking out at the dark sea. She fancied she could feel the vibration of the engine and suddenly, overcome by exhaustion, she returned to lie rigidly beside him. Sleepless, over and over again she repeated, 'This is my husband. I am now married. Alberto Rizzoli is my husband.'

He awoke and, again without a shred of tenderness, took her a second time. Pleased with himself, he had her five times that night.

His only comment to her was, 'Al Rizzoli broke his wife in.' He kissed her roughly. 'If you had not been a virgin, I would have beaten the hell out of you.'

He was thinking of Anna, the girl who thought she was his fiancée. Anna who, if you told her to sit down, she'd lie down. Why, Anna had had more men than he'd had breakfasts. How dared she even think he would marry her?

The next day, strutting on deck, he paraded her. His wife. To his great satisfaction, she kept her eyes downcast. If he as much as saw another man looking at her he'd kill her, he'd kill him, he'd kill them both. She was his, she belonged to him the way his arms belonged to him. True, he had been loving and tender, but that had been the bait he'd used to hook her, made up of gentleness. Sure he'd let her think he was gentle and kind – he was no oil-painting. He'd guessed that she was the kind who'd go for the gentle touch. Now that she was his wife all that sissified gentle crap was redundant.

From the corner of his eye he mistakenly thought he saw Major Coulter staring at her. He jerked her towards him. 'I want you,' he whispered hoarsely. Then he turned her around and marched her back to their cabin.

Because he was her husband, she loved him.

*

All in all, it was a nine-day honeymoon from Recife to New York. Sensing his state of permanent, suppressed rage, she waited for the right moment to ask him about his parents. Someone, she knew, must have hurt him very deeply when he was a small boy. The troubled, pained expression was always with him, and even when he was asleep he was never free of it. The taut, anxious look surrounding his sleeping eyes stirred her to measureless tenderness, and she would have done anything in the world to help him to be less unhappy.

Almost as if it had a will of its own, her hand moved out to soothe his forehead. Though her touch was light and gentle, he roused himself, and said, 'My father broke my nose.' He appeared to stare into space. 'Said I was trying to lay my stepmother.' He sat up now, and his eyes churned with anger. 'I *hated* the whore!'

'That's terrible,' she answered, a catch in her voice. 'Terrible.'

'Yeah,' Al growled. 'He smashed my face with a hammer.' He ran his thumb and forefinger along his nose. 'He's dead now. He sure made it hard for me to forget him!'

She took his head in her arms and rested it against the pillow of her breast. For a long while she held him like that, saying nothing. Some time later he kissed her and made love to her; astonishingly, he was gentle and triumphant and even affectionate.

Her heart swelled with sympathy for him. She, too, had a cruel stepmother. Who knew, if she had been born a man she probably would have been as mixed-up as he was. Her eyes clouded with pain and sympathy – how he must have suffered as a child. He needed – more, he deserved – a good woman. She would heal him. She would help him.

Holding his sleeping head in her arms she felt a certain peace. At that moment she loved him as deeply as a mother loves a son.

And then the honeymoon ended, and the voyage was over and within moments she would be on dry land again. American land. The Statue of Liberty hove into sight. To a young Italian girl, a refugee and an immigrant of war-torn Rome, it was both right and comforting that it was the statue of a woman who would be welcoming her to her new motherland. She stared wonderingly at the figure of a woman holding a torch in her right hand, and a tablet symbolizing the Declaration of Independence and therefore the greatness of America, and said a prayer of gratitude.

Her heart swelled with pride and gratitude.

A magic wand had been waved.

She was an American . . .

Al's sister lived in a tenement on Spring Street. Lined with shops, it was a quiet enough street in one of the thirty-seven 'Little Italies' of the city. Cecilia quickly learned that because over one million Italians and their descendants lived in New York they made up the largest foreign-language group in the city. This only strengthened her determination to speak 'proper' English.

Now thirty-seven, Tina Rizzoli had not gone out to work since Al was fourteen, eleven years ago. Al had earned their daily bread, first as a shoe-shine boy, later as a longshoreman, and finally as a soldier, a GI. From the age of twenty-one, ever since the doctor had told her she had a bad heart, she had stayed at home. While Al was in the war, fighting in Italy, the characters in the radio serials were her main preoccupation. She ate potato chips, drank beer and Cokes, grew heavier and heavier and developed a matching personality.

Tina's reaction to the news of his marriage was infinitely more terrible than anything he had anticipated. 'You bring me a *bride* you met on the *ship!*' she exploded. 'What do you expect me to say?' she shrilled at him when he presented Cecilia to her. 'You bring me this – this thing you met on the ship, and you tell me she's your *wife?*'

'Tina,' he said, throwing his hands in the air. 'Let me—'

'I wasted my life for *you!*' Tina said, drawing circles in the air and then pointing the index finger of each hand at him. 'For *you* I didn't marry Luigi Toraldo!' Raising her voice to the skies and

53

for her neighbours, she added, 'Look at what my only brother brings home – a girl with no hips! But has this wretch of yours at least brought a dowry?'

'No,' he said miserably. 'No dowry.'

Pale, and shaking with fear and rage, Cecilia stood up. 'I will work for my living,' she said with quiet dignity. She looked around the grimy, chaotic apartment. 'I'm a very good cleaner. I could clean your apartment.'

'The place sure could stand a good cleaning,' Al said. 'Come see the bedroom.'

The apartment had two rooms and a kitchenette. The bathroom was along the hall. With many complaints and more sighs, Tina gave them her bedroom. She would martyr herself and use the living-room. The second time Cecilia meekly asked Al if they could look for a small place of their own, he flashed his dimples and slapped her with the flat of his hand so hard that she fell back against the sofa.

It was cold that year, as cold as Tina's welcome. Bitter winter winds shrieked through the rat-holes in the linoleum, and the snow cut across the streets like an icy whip. If she had to live there, she would have to repair the linoleum with the money she had been given before she left home. But though she searched frantically, the money was gone. Tina had a new radio. Cecilia was too afraid to believe that it was her dollars that had paid for it.

Meanwhile, Al had his disability pay. The doctors said he was still too sick to work.

Every day, several times a day, Tina would shriek in English: 'We send our American boys to fight for you in Italy, and what happens? What is our reward?' Here she would stop and clap her hands against her thighs. 'Our boys get stolen by foreign Italian bitches like you!'

On her hands and knees, scrubbing the floor, she had not so far seen a rat, only little black specks in or near the holes. So she decided, if she could, to fill in the holes herself.

'You wanna fix the holes?' Al chortled. 'You need stuff? So go to the drugstore.'

54

She had been in America for two long weeks. She could not live with rats, and she did not have a dime.

Trembling, she forced herself to say, 'Could you give me some money?'

'Goddam it! You gotta get off your ass and go earn it!'

She had been praying for permission to work, but had been too afraid to ask. She said carefully, 'I'll look for a job, Al.'

So she started work in Dee's Drugstore. Despite its harsh, continuous twenty-four-hour lighting, and the constant rush and pressure of its all-day clientele, it was, as far as Cecilia was concerned, a haven of peace. She was away from them, away from the sour smell of their grimy apartment, away from the threat of rats.

At the end of the first week Mr Donatello paid her. She asked at once to buy the material to fill in the rat-holes and a rat poison. 'How much?' she asked nervously.

'For you Cecilia, one dime.'

'One dime?'

'Have it on the house.' Seeing her hesitate he added, 'Just this once I won't charge you.'

Although she and Mr Donatello spoke Italian, many of the customers did not. After only five days, she knew that her English was at least as good as Al's.

Chapter Seven

The quickening of the baby, at first no more than a brief, hushed flutter of an eyelash, infused Cecilia with a new – a strange, almost mystical – strength. At the same time, she was half afraid of this strength she drew from her unborn child, for it seemed to her that she should be giving and not receiving. On the other hand, she took it to be a sign of the child's love for her, and believed that she carried within her the source and the secret of life and love. As the pregnancy wore on, she would hug her stomach in her folded arms, and together, she and the child were their private world. The terrible loneliness – without the privacy of loneliness – was made more bearable.

The truth was that without the consolation, comfort and indeed the nurturing that the pregnancy gave her, there would have been nothing to live for and everything to die for. Sin or no sin, this was how she felt. Her pregnancy was her lifeline and her oxygen and she knew it and exulted in it.

She began to pray that the child would not be born before time, for if it were, Tina's insults would turn into truth.

'You trapped him – forced him to marry you,' Tina had snarled. 'There was only one way to get him, and you knew it!'

'How can you say such a thing?' she had asked brokenly.

'My brother would never have married you unless you were pregnant—'

'That is not true,' she protested fiercely. 'Why are you so cruel to me, Tina? Why do you hate me?'

'Drink more milk,' the older woman said, getting up to pour a glass. 'It's good for the baby . . .'

*

In the event, the baby was not born early. During the last six weeks of her pregnancy, she was the happiest she had been since her mother's death. Tina and Al took care of her, watching over her like devoted parents. She felt cosseted and protected and cherished enough to believe she was neither hated nor hateful. She felt safe and dreamed that her mother was still alive and putting the baby boy – her grandson – to her own aged and shrivelled breast.

Cecilia, Al and Tina – the entire Rizzoli household – shared the unshakeable conviction that the baby would be a boy. Indeed, only several months later Cecilia was to wonder whether their disappointment over a girl instead of a boy was responsible for their renewed and increased hostility towards her. Her daughter was born after a long and cruel labour and she gloried in the child and was not in the least disappointed at having given birth to a daughter. At the very beginning Al hid his disappointment well enough to behave like a proud father; like a true American father he bought a box of cigars for his pals and a bouquet of roses for his wife. When he saw that his daughter had inherited his dimples, he bought her a gold bracelet. Cecilia treasured the roses; hoarding their faded petals, she vowed that she would keep them for her daughter. It was at Cecilia's suggestion that Al allowed Tina to name the child. She chose to call her Giorgina. Naturally, Tina was the child's godmother and Cecilia could not help hoping this honour would go some way towards winning her forgiveness for having married her brother.

It was, however, a vain hope.

Cecilia's milk dried up when Gina was only three months old. 'Punishment,' said Tina, 'for stealing a man from his fiancée!'

By this time Cecilia knew better than to argue, or even to try to defend herself. Al was out of work again, still frittering away his military allowance on gambling, and though he still had the second-hand auto, bought with Cecilia's money, his contribution to the finances of the Rizzoli household was erratic.

As Cecilia saw it, she had no choice.

Besides, much as she resented leaving baby Gina with Tina,

57

it was almost a relief to leave their miserable apartment and their snide backbiting barbs to go back to the drugstore where she could earn her own – and her baby's – keep. Tina had decided to quit the first job she had taken in twelve years – 'I'm too old to slave for *your* board and lodging,' she had shrieked. 'Why should I be a cleaner at my age?'

'You *want* to stay at home with Gina,' Cecilia said flatly. 'But she's *my* baby – she is *mine.*'

'*You've* got no milk,' Tina taunted. 'If you had good mother's milk—'

'I know,' Cecilia said wretchedly. 'I know.' She did not say that the sight of orange lipstick on Al's underpants had dried her breasts just as surely as shock dries saliva. Tina probably knew more about it than she did, including the name of the owner of the lipstick. Sometimes she had the uneasy feeling that Tina knew everything that went on between her brother and his wife. There was a silence.

'Are you trying to tell me that I'm not good enough to take care of your baby? Of my god-daughter?' Tina demanded shrilly.

'Of course not. Please don't—'

'Who do you think took care of Al?'

'You took—'

'My poor mama died bringing him into the world,' she interrupted, wailing as always at the mere mention of her mother. 'I was fourteen – *fourteen*—'

'Gina loves you, Tina,' Cecilia said quickly. 'She couldn't be in safer hands than yours.'

So it was that in January 1946 Cecilia went back to work at the drugstore on Seventh Street, sometimes a saleswoman and sometimes a waitress. A dab-hand at easy-over and hamburgers, she was a friendly waitress who got the orders right and quickly built up a regular clientele. She was a working mother, and knew that she looked much older than her eighteen and a half years.

If it was true that she looked about thirty, it was also true that even in her garish canary-yellow uniform, white cap and apron she was astonishingly beautiful. Profoundly unconscious of the effect of her beauty on others, she made no attempt to exploit her good looks.

Her sad, soft expression set her apart from the usual hard resignation of most waitresses in the neighbourhood. When she got larger tips than the others she put it down to the way she made it clear that she was there to be as helpful as possible. She would hand the tips – as she handed him her salary – to Al and was too tired, sometimes, to count her money. Al always counted it, however, and then it was up to him to decide how much he would give her for household expenses such as food and clothing for Gina. Cecilia was expected to account to him for every dime she spent – if she were the breadwinner, he was the boss. It was a hard life, but there were no more traces of lipstick or cheap scent and Cecilia was grateful for that.

As the months sped by her English improved. She even began to dream in English and, whenever she and Gina were on their own, she spoke to her in English. She was determined that Gina would never speak as badly as her father or her aunt. To think that she had once been proud of Al's English! That he could actually speak a language other than Italian had made him seem glamorous and important and powerful and smart. How ignorant she had been!

The awful realization that he was flabby and insignificant and weak and stupid was a truth she dared not face. Instead she told herself she was lucky. She was a lucky woman because her husband did not beat her. Carmella and Otlia, who worked with her, did not have the same luck. They took their beatings with the same fortitude and resignation with which they accepted the inevitable hardships of a cruel world.

She counted her blessings. She made the most of her life and looked forward to the time when the three of them could be together without Tina. By this time she had made good friends with Miriam Stern, the pharmacist at the drugstore.

A maternal young woman, Miriam Stern was ahead of her

time. For one thing she regarded work as therapy – she had little need of her paltry part-time salary herself, but over the years several families had come to depend on her. Miriam radiated self-confidence and talked in a hearty voice about sex and contraception. Cecilia had only heard these matters mentioned in nervous whispers and embarrassed giggles. But Miriam changed all that. Birth control, she believed, was as natural – and as necessary – as sex itself.

Under the gaze of her clear, honest eyes Cecilia felt safe. It was a while before she realized that she trusted Miriam much in the way she had trusted her own mother.

Miriam was nothing if not direct. The second time in one morning she saw Cecilia return, pale and shaken, from the toilet at the back of the drugstore, she said bluntly, 'I guess he's put you in the family way again.'

'No.' Cecilia blushed. 'I don't think so.'

'Period late?'

'Not yet.'

'When is it due?'

'The day after tomorrow, I hope.'

'But aren't you hoping to have lots and lots of children?'

Cecilia blushed again. 'Yes, but not yet,' she said painfully. 'Right now it would be too bad.' She shrugged. 'It will be different when we leave my sister-in-law's place and get one of our own.'

'Are you afraid of falling pregnant again?'

Shamed, Cecilia nodded. 'Yes,' she said bravely. 'That is my great fear.'

'And does this fear disturb your sex life?'

'Excuse me?' Cecilia said, bewildered.

'Does the fear of another pregnancy prevent you from enjoying making love to your husband?'

'Yes,' she answered, thinking of the sleepless nights she spent praying, making bargains, begging the Virgin Mary not to make her pregnant, not this time, anyway. Suddenly she laughed bitterly. '*Enjoyment* – you speak of *enjoyment*,' she said incredulously.

60

'Have you never enjoyed making love?'

'For a while. After I knew I was pregnant the first time.'

'And if you knew how to prevent pregnancy, would you?' Because Cecilia made no response, she added, 'Contraception is legal, you know.'

Cecilia said, 'Yes, but Al—'

Miriam broke in. 'Forget Al, honey. He doesn't have to know. Look, I'm going to arrange for you to have a diaphragm fitted, and *of course* we won't tell your husband.'

Tormented by endless guilt, Cecilia followed Miriam's advice and disobeyed the teachings of the Church. For weeks and then months, all day every day, even as she worked she prayed to St Cecilia, her name saint, and to Mary, Mother of God, to beg Jesus for mercy.

While it would be too much to say that Cecilia actually enjoyed making love, it no longer held the terrors of pregnancy and was therefore less of an ordeal. Al must have sensed that something had happened to change her, for he became more and more demanding.

As she watched her baby grow into an alert and demanding little girl, the rhythm of her days left her no time for either boredom or discontent. Tina was a nanny of a sort, and like all good nannies refused the household responsibilities that were not directly connected to her small charge. Which meant that the housework, the cooking and the shopping were entirely left to Cecilia. After three years she graduated from waitress to managing the cosmetic department of the drugstore. Al said that now she was the breadwinner, he was the banker.

Her feeling of loneliness without privacy was not nearly as distressing as it had been.

Her friendship with Miriam was precious; it gave her a secret sense of self-respect. Miriam had a positive way of finding something good in all things, including tenements.

'Will you look at the pattern of iron lacework these fire escapes make?' she would add rhetorically. 'If you sniff those

61

fruit carts standing wheel-to-wheel, you can smell a summer orchard.'

'You're nuts, Miriam. Nutty as a fruitcake.' Cecilia laughed. 'Know something? Things are getting much better for me. I'm feeling more like I was born here, like I was a New Yorker. I've never been to a christening or a funeral, but now at last I'm going to a family wedding.'

'Christenings make me hopeful, weddings make me sad, and funerals make me philosophical,' Miriam said lightly. 'You deserve to feel like a New Yorker,' she added emotionally.

Chapter Eight

If it hadn't been for his grandmother, Lucia Cartwright, there would have been no triumphal home-coming party for Mark. At first, Mark's father, Theodore, had found the notion of a celebratory party insensitive; after all, there were too many young men who were never going to come back from the war. In the end, and thanks to Lucia's gentle but skilful persuasion, his brother-in-law General Byrne's seemingly casual remarks had carried the day. 'Five battle stars, a Silver Medal and a Purple Heart deserve the fullest recognition,' he had said with all the authority of his superior station.

The General had been determined not to protect Mark in any way, and Mark had fought in the Battle of the Bulge. Therefore he had more than made up for his earlier cowardice. Not long after his single-handed capture of a German sniper, a shrapnel wound to his head had resulted in emergency neurological surgery in a tent hospital.

Fortunately for Lucia, her son's wife Fran had a sunny, saint-like disposition. This meant that Fran had left the planning of the large party to her mother-in-law. This time, however, her acceptance owed nothing to Lucia's insistence on having her own way. Rather, she was so overjoyed to have her husband safely back home she would have agreed to anything at all. Nevertheless, despite her shy smile and unfailing modesty, her confidence as a wife meant that she was a force to be reckoned with. From the moment Mark had decided to ask her to marry him, he had made it abundantly clear that nothing and no one was – or ever would be – as important in his life as his future wife. Even now, after an absence of four years, his two small children, Amy and Rufus, came a very poor second. Fran was number one.

Generously, Fran allowed her mother-in-law to take over the running of the party. After all, it was to be held at Cartwright House, the Connecticut summer home that had been in the Cartwright family for more than fifty years. Designed by the famed Richard Morris Hunt, it had been bought by Theodore's father, Cornelius, from the Stroud family in 1895, and even before the family had moved in the name had been changed from Stroud House to Cartwright House. Gradually Cornelius had acquired additional land – and it was now surrounded by several hundred acres.

No one in his family would have dared to challenge Theodore's unquestioning belief that Americans had a special destiny, a mandate to reform the world. While he did not go so far as to consider it un-American to be poor, he had little sympathy for those unfortunates he classed as losers. Indeed, the Cartwright Foundation had been established to promote the aim of excellence.

Everything about Lucia Cartwright, from her majestic carriage to her Roman nose, her hands, her distinctive clothes, was the last word in elegance. Indeed her designer, Reginald Bantie, had been heard to declare that she was probably just as elegant naked as formally dressed. For this party she wore a trailing emerald-green chiffon dress that exactly matched the emerald and diamond necklace which had once belonged to Napoleon III's wife, the Empress Eugénie.

Now, on the evening of the party, Theodore, resplendent in white tie and tails, his thick crop of white hair closely brushed, escorted his wife Lucia down the sweeping staircase made of Sienna marble. Everything Italian was meaningful to Lucia; at the foot of the staircase she could not stop herself from looking back at the panelled marble walls and the filigreed brass balustrades. Then, slowly, she and Theodore made their way to the opulent gold ballroom.

Through the windows, Lucia looked at the gently falling snow. The snow pleased her: white and new, it symbolized

64

everything about the country she had so passionately adopted. Besides, coming in out of the snow to the warmth of blazing log fires would create a festive ambience for their guests.

Roederer Cristal, the vintage champagne of the Tsars, stood about in a profusion of silver buckets, and glacial white swans held large tins of Beluga caviare. The orchestra, led by Tommy Dorsey, were tuning their instruments and the gold ballroom shimmered with expectancy.

Soon Mark and Fran were beside Lucia, and the rest of the family followed, to join them for a pre-party family drink. Mark's sister, Betty, and her husband, Montagu Ellis, were there, as well as Theodore's sister and brother-in-law, General Byrne and his wife, Sally. Solemnly, the butler offered each a glass of champagne.

When they all had a glass in their hand, Mark said emotionally, 'May I propose a very private toast to General Byrne, to whom all Americans owe so much? My own debt to him, I may say, is unpayable.'

'Nonsense, Lieutenant-Colonel,' General Byrne said testily. 'I did you no favours when I sent you north to the Ardennes.'

'You were one of those who liberated Rome, your mother's very own city,' Theodore said, his voice gruff. 'Allow us to drink to that.'

The butler refilled their glasses. To change the subject – the atmosphere had become too emotional for his taste – the General added, 'By the way, any news of that soldier you went so far out of your way to help?'

'No, sir. We were separated.'

'Of course. I may have had something to do with that myself,' the General said thoughtfully. 'And the poor girl? Whatever became of her? Cecilia, wasn't she called?'

'Right,' Mark said. 'Cecilia.'

'Cecilia?' Fran said, smiling the confident smile of a confident wife. 'You never mentioned anyone called Cecilia, Mark.'

'She was only a kid of sixteen or seventeen,' he said painfully. 'She was one of those victims – or trophies – you get in every war.'

'I'm not sure I'm with you, darling,' said Fran, sounding puzzled.

'Ironically, she saved one of my men from being court-martialled,' Mark said, a cold, controlled anger in his tone. 'Her testimony saved him from being shot.' Dropping his voice, he continued. 'We asked her to say she had lied, when we knew she'd told the truth. So she co-operated,' he mumbled in a sudden fit of disgust. 'She took our advice and perjured herself.'

'Now you're getting too maudlin for a soldier,' the General cut in roughly. 'If my judgement's worth anything at all, I'll guarantee that the young woman is now a prosperous American wife.' Pursing his lips he added dismissively, 'She was more than well compensated for her trouble.'

Sensing unpleasantness in the air, Theodore intervened. 'There's no more than fifteen minutes before the hordes descend on us,' he said with a twinkle. 'Just enough time for me to propose my own little toast and to make a very special announcement.' Drawing his daughter-in-law close, with his arm about her slender waist, he continued, 'I was going to tell all our guests what I am about to say, but my daughter-in-law, Fran, thought it unseemly.'

Everyone except Fran looked at him with open amazement. With pride and affection he announced that Mark had decided to forsake the legal profession in favour of Cartwright Pharmaceuticals. He reminded them that, like Mark, so too, in 1865, seventy-one years earlier, his grandfather, Harrison Cartwright, had forsaken his chosen profession as a medical doctor to found Cartwright Pharmaceuticals. He had begun by refining citrate of lime to produce citric acid, but it was not until the 1920s that Cartwright Pharmaceuticals discovered how to ferment citric acid from moulds.

'Bear with me,' Theodore said, his voice carrying through the vast gold ballroom. 'This story has a point. Call it luck, call it serendipity, but it was because of those deep fermentation tanks that our fortunes are, shall we say, considerably greater than they were before the war.'

'Go on,' the General said. 'We're all ears.'

66

Theodore maintained his calm. 'Penicillin, discovered in 1928, might have remained a laboratory curiosity if the American government had not challenged companies to devise a technique of mass-producing it. Cartwright's fermentation tanks proved to be the answer.'

'Of course I knew you synthesized vitamins,' the General said reasonably, 'but I'd no idea that you were connected with penicillin! Why, countless numbers of our wounded were saved by penicillin.'

'Including one Mark Cartwright,' said Lucia emotionally.

In a remarkably deep voice Theodore continued, 'Now I don't know when I shall be leaving these earthly shores—'

'Oh, Theo,' Lucia protested reproachfully. 'Don't be morbid!'

'Anticipating that distant day, I am making gifts ahead of bequests,' Theodore went on as if she had not spoken. 'Lawyers of the ilk of my son Mark agree the principle: gifts to one's own before gifts to the people. So far I have not discussed details of this with my son.' Pausing to place his hand on Mark's shoulder, he went on, 'No doubt, Mark, you will be surprised to learn that you have already been given half of the land on which Cartwright House stands. Likewise, Amy, I have made a gift to you and to your husband. You and Montagu will build the house of your dreams in Maine.'

'I knew you'd be the best father in the world,' Lucia said, to lighten the atmosphere. 'That's why I married you!'

'I don't know what to say,' Mark began.

Amy took his arm and stood on tiptoe to kiss her papa.

He smiled fondly at her and then at Mark. 'My children,' he said, 'you are our future. Savour it. Now – let the party begin!'

At that moment the butler sounded the arrival of Senator and Mrs Wayne Fairfield. 'Wayne's always disgustingly punctual,' Cordelia Fairfield complained. 'I hope we're not interrupting a family tête-à-tête,' she said hastily, accepting a glass of champagne.

*

It was one of those successful parties that went on until dawn. The guest list was as sparkling as the menu – champagne and caviare flowed like good conversation. Senators and bankers were closeted together; not a few eminent physicists and pharmacologists settled into serious talk. But even physicists and politicians responded to the call of Tommy Dorsey's orchestra and took to the dance floor.

February 1946 was an era of magical optimism, and the heady perfume of hope, goodwill and faith permeated the great golden ballroom. The talk was of the 1945 San Francisco Conference, at which the United Nations had been founded. Post-Hiroshima and Nagasaki, everyone seemed to believe that the atom bomb's legacy was only the beginning of the era of permanent peace in the world.

Catching a glimpse of Solomon Steiner, the theoretical physicist and German-Jewish refugee, Mark found himself incredibly moved to be in the presence of so great a man.

'It is an honour to meet you, sir,' Mark said.

'I have also heard that you were a participant in the liberation of the *Cité Éternelle*,' Dr Steiner said in his careful English. 'However I am told that, but for penicillin, you and I would not now be meeting.'

'I was one of the lucky ones. I got it in time,' Mark said quietly. On a sudden impulse he went on, 'We are hoping to attract scientists of the calibre of Nobel laureates and potential laureates to Cartwright Pharmaceuticals.'

'Alas! I am engaged full-time at Princeton, or I might myself be tempted to apply—' Dr Steiner said. 'But I do have in my acquaintance one or two candidates who might fulfil your criteria.'

'Any time you could spare to discuss this with me would be wonderful. A half-hour's warning is all I would need.'

At once the distinguished scientist offered his hand. 'It will be my pleasure,' he said.

*

It was dawn when Mark and Fran reached their elegant quarters. The softly lit, intensely feminine bedroom emphasized Mark's masculinity and made Fran feel he was more desirable than ever. The night had ended, and it was too early in the day to go to sleep. Besides, they were wound up and excited and their bodies hungry for one another. They tumbled into one another's arms and made love with a new and almost frightening abandon.

Much later, Mark said, 'I don't think I've ever been so happy.' Shaking his head with wonder, he added, 'Or so grateful to have a woman like you in my life.'

Everyone knew that Fran Roper had fallen in love with Mark Cartwright at their very first meeting. Fran was not beautiful in the conventional sense; her tanned, open, friendly, freckled face was certainly appealing, and she looked like the good sports-woman she was; but for her commitment to fund-raising for charities, she could well have been a champion golfer. Because she was dependable, people liked her. And she was as rich as she was good-natured. Which meant that the Fran Roper Trust could easily have matched Theodore Cartwright's generosity.

All the same Fran said, 'I think your father has been absolutely wonderful. I never thought he would part with an inch of his land—'

'The war seems to have changed him,' Mark said solemnly.

'What was she really like, darling?' Fran asked lazily.

'Who?'

'Cecilia.'

'I hardly knew her.'

'But you said you advised her to perjure herself.'

'I persuaded a priest to act on Vincenzo's behalf.' He sat up and raked his fingers through his hair. 'But I have to admit that the perjury was my idea. I must take sole responsibility for that. Once she said she had lied, there could be no case against Vincenzo.'

'She sure must have been pretty,' Fran said kindly.

'She was only a kid of sixteen or seventeen. I guess you could call her a peasant.'

69

Wanting to obliterate Cecilia from his mind, he took his wife in his arms again. 'I just want to forget about the whole damn war,' he said.

But, as so often these days, sleep eluded him. Terrors and nightmares and sadness poured into his mind. Because the world thought him a hero, he had at last won his father's approval. But the art of self-deception had never been his. He knew the truth of himself. And that truth – or that shame – now resided in the form and the shape of the beautiful young woman with the melting velvet eyes. He had stolen her honour and grasped her shame and exploited her helplessness – all to discharge nothing more than his debt of gratitude to Vincenzo.

When at last he fell asleep he dreamed that many of his wildly painful memories were beginning to subside. He awoke feeling unusually optimistic, unusually carefree. No doubt some time in the future, dissolved in the mists of his own forgotten history, Cecilia would die away.

But the next night the ferocious nightmares began. Before long, he became almost too frightened to sleep. Three weeks later Fran took him to see Dr Fraenkel, a psychiatrist who specialized in wartime traumas.

Chapter Nine

Despite the undeniable misery of her poverty-stricken life, Cecilia blessed the day that she had come to America; here, in this land of opportunity, her daughter would be taught to dream, taught to hope, and taught to expect happiness. Back in the Old Country, in the alleys of her childhood, even the hope of happiness had carried a tinge of sin. Certainly the men went out and sat in their cafés and drank wine and laughed loudly; but that was to forget, to anaesthetize the drab drudgery of their lives.

When Miriam asked Mr Donatello, the owner of Dee's, whether Cecilia could add an extra thirty minutes to her four o'clock lunch-hour one Tuesday, he agreed reluctantly. 'Just this time,' he said truculently. 'The customers will miss her.'

Miriam went at once to tell Cecilia. 'You've got an extra thirty minutes off, so I'm taking you to my place,' she said quickly. Her ever-present bangles seemed to click more rapidly than usual. 'I've got my own home-made coffee cake and coffee.' Then, noticing Cecilia's bewildered expression, she added, 'It's about time you visited with me, kiddo. It'll do you good to see a different neighbourhood.'

Miriam lived in Brooklyn. All the way there Cecilia could scarcely speak for amazement. In Rome the very idea of a qualified pharmacist – a professional – inviting a lowly worker to her own home was unthinkable. Indeed, if she had not had so much faith in Miriam, she would have been more than a little suspicious of her motives.

When they reached the house and Cecilia was shown into Miriam's library, her face glowed with excitement and wonder; she had never been in a room such as this before. Suddenly she was reminded of the Contessa's library on the Navona Piazza and, in a flash, the long-suppressed image of Vincenzo surfaced. Involuntarily she winced.

Her face calm and serene, Miriam asked, 'What's troubling you?'

Cecilia made no reply.

'You'd rather not talk about it?'

'This is a beautiful, beautiful room,' Cecilia said, gesturing towards the knotty-pine panelling and the book-lined shelves. A tall faded velvet step-ladder rested against them. An entire row of shelves had been constructed to house Miriam's considerable collection of record albums. The library doors opened out into a pale, cool living-room whose floors were covered in a beige carpet. It was only October, but a great fire roared in the library and in the firelight the vibrant oriental rugs on the waxed floor shimmered and softened. Books and newspapers were everywhere, but in spite of the chaos – or perhaps because of it – the room was warm and welcoming and affectionate.

'Why do you work, Miriam?' Cecilia asked bluntly. 'You don't need the money.'

'I studied hard to become a pharmacist,' Miriam said with a self-deprecating smile. 'My parents worked even harder to make it possible for me to study.' She hesitated for a moment and continued. 'You see, I grew up on the same street as Dee's. I was raised there, I guess. Then I married Bernie Stern and moved away into his world. Then my folks died, and we split up and I moved back, at least in part, to my world.' She gave a short laugh. 'And the funny thing is, he was the one who couldn't have kids!'

'I'm sorry,' Cecilia said. 'I didn't know—'

'Of course I don't *own* this apartment. It's rent-controlled. I couldn't afford it. But almost every single book you see belongs to me. I guess I work because I need the money. Simple, isn't it?' Cutting a slice of cake for each of them she said, 'You're wondering why I asked you here?'

'I'm glad you did,' Cecilia responded quietly.

She had planned to tell Cecilia about her great mentor,

72

Dr Gerti Theresa Cori, who, together with her husband, were the first husband-and-wife team to receive the Nobel prize. For a very short while they had all worked at the same institute. Those were the days when Miriam had been interested in biological chemistry. Suddenly her plan seemed like a bad idea. Instead she said, 'I asked you here because I like to think you and I are friends.'

'Thank you,' Cecilia said. 'I am honoured.'

Over the next three years Cecilia spent several pleasant after-noons in Miriam's library. Needless to say, none of this was ever mentioned to Al. One day she found herself telling Miriam about Father Donnelly and the English lessons. 'A human saint, Father Donnelly is,' she said, her eyes shining.

'Are you still in touch with him?' Miriam asked.

'I send him a Christmas card every year—'

'Oh, so you exchange Christmas cards?'

'No,' Cecilia said, shaking her head vigorously. 'He doesn't know my address.'

'From now on, give him my address,' Miriam said instantly.

'I don't even know whether he's still alive—'

'Give him my address and, if he's around, he'll write back to you.'

Precisely three years and one month after she had landed in New York, Cecilia received her first letter from Father Donnelly. He said that, though he was much saddened by the thought that she was too afraid to tell him where she lived, he was glad to have a contact address. He looked forward to an ongoing correspondence and unfailingly remembered her in his prayers. He congratulated her on her English, but said he was not in the least surprised. 'You were a promising student,' he concluded. 'You might well become an excellent teacher of the language.'

Cecilia smiled when she read that. Now almost four years old, Gina knew the alphabet. Already she had begun to read from the elementary learning books that Miriam supplied. Gina might even become a teacher . . . in America anything was possible.

Chapter Ten

These nights there was no rest for Cecilia. No matter who brought in the bread, Al *owned* her just as surely as he owned his Ford. These past three or four months Cecilia had seemed less anxious, less afraid; once or twice he had even caught her humming. Something had been making her happier. He could have understood it if a new baby was on the way, and was partly relieved and partly angry that she was not pregnant again. They all needed the dough she brought in.

Cecilia's humming made him distinctly uncomfortable. The long and the short of it was that he did not believe or trust happy wives. The best wives were the frightened wives who were always slightly panicked, wives who knew their place. He'd had to let her know the weight of his fists.

His irrational, jealous rages these past three or four months had left her bruised and beaten. She put it down to Al's resentment over not having steady work. But then, as far as she knew, he had never had a regular job. He was secretive about his work, anyway. Cecilia knew no more than that he was a sometime debt-collector.

Neither of them attended mass the next morning. But, except for Gina, who was in bed with a slight cold, the ritual of the Sunday lunch went on as usual. Cecilia served herself last and was just about to begin her risotto when Al pushed his empty plate forward and got up to go.

'Aren't you having dessert, Al?' Tina wheedled through wine-laden breath. 'Cheesecake's your favourite.'

'If I want cake, I'll ask for cake,' Al said.

'But I got up early to make it for you special, Al. Of course I

74

had to get up early because your wife overslept. Lazy women have all the luck!'

'If I want cheesecake, I'll tell you,' Al said moodily. 'Can't you see I'm late?'

Tina grumbled as Al slammed the door behind him. 'Look forward to Sundays all week—'

'I'm sorry, Tina,' Cecilia said.

'I'm sorry, Tina,' her sister-in-law mimicked unkindly. 'Well, you should be sorry, you should be ashamed of yourself.'

'Now what?'

'Up all night – keeping everyone in the house awake all night – shaking the whole place something terrible. Why'n't you get your own place? My *nerves*—'

Cecilia said nothing. She felt her throat contract with rage. It was impossible to swallow. She made no attempt to eat and wanted nothing more than to leave the table.

'My *nerves*,' her sister-in-law whined. 'Who cares about me? I gotta listen to you two screw till mornin'. Why'n't you leave my brother alone, let him have peace?'

Still Cecilia said nothing.

'*Whore!*' Tina shrieked, her upper lip beaded with sweat. 'You *conned* my brother into jilting his fiancée, my best friend.' Her shrieking turned to a harsh whisper. 'And I gotta live with a whore in my own place—'

The injustice of this hurt too much. 'What did you call me?' she said, desperately calm.

'Whore, that's what I called you. *Whore!*'

With clenched fists and bitter lips, Cecilia fought for calm.

Swaying, Tina left her chair, lurched her unhappy, obese body forward and stood menacingly over Cecilia. 'Just as well the kid sleeps in my room,' she went on wildly. 'Or she'd have to listen to your all-night screwing. And she'd have to hear you moaning like an animal, too—'

At that, Cecilia's control left her. In one graceful movement she stepped forward, ramming her fist right into Tina's bulging belly. Tina's breath exploded out of her and she fell gasping to

75

the floor. Horrified by what she had done, Cecilia rushed into the bedroom.

Tina recovered her breath and banged on the door, shouting over and over again. 'You'll pay for this, you whore.'

Cecilia put her head in her hands and wept with humiliation and self-hate. Humiliation because, if she did *not* moan during sex, Al pinched her breasts to make her cry out with pain. Her moans were false, meant to prevent pain. And she was angry because she had grown weary of fighting them. She was married to both the brother and the sister, and was powerless even to suggest how her money should be spent.

She hated herself because she had allowed them to overpower her, and despised herself for what she saw as her own cowardice. Why, she had been too cowardly – and too ashamed – even to confide in Father Romano. Sometimes she felt her life had become a kind of punishment for the sin of using a diaphragm. But they could not afford to have another child, and besides, she could not have forgiven herself if she had brought another child into a life of pain . . .

Al made up his mind to teach her a long and permanent lesson in discipline. There would be no mistake about who was boss in the Rizzoli family. Every day for ten days he beat her, taking care that not a mark nor a bruise nor any sort of evidence whatsoever would be exposed to view. So he pinched her buttocks, her breasts, her pubis and her thighs until she yelped for mercy.

'So you like to beat up on Tina, huh?' he would say contemptuously.

He never let her forget he had been a champion lightweight boxer. 'I won my dentures in the boxing ring,' he would chortle. People usually laughed with him – they were too scared not to. How could Cecilia stand up to him?

Her tactic seemed to be working – her frightened, subservient apologetic talk and bearing had been impressive enough to win a pardon; for the past five days there had been no beating.

And then, though she was as penitent and as obedient as any tortured prisoner, her luck changed and all the tactics in the world were as useless as a gun without a bullet.

The first Cecilia knew that things had gone badly wrong was when she returned home, as usual exhausted from a hectic day at the drugstore. She'd stayed on, talking to Miriam Stern, for ten minutes longer than she had budgeted, and so was unusually breathless when she walked in, longing for nothing more than to put her feet up for five minutes before preparing the evening meal.

The apartment was ominously quiet. Her heart sank but she said cheerfully, expecting Gina to run into her arms, 'Hi, everyone! Hi, Gina – how's the bestest baby in the whole world?'

But instead of the delighted giggles she was accustomed to, there was only silence. It was then that she saw her husband's face, churning with rage and hate, and her sister-in-law's face glowing with glee and a controlled but undisguisable excitement. The tension was palpable while they waited. And they *were* waiting, she was sure. She managed not to show her alarm and asked apologetically, 'Where's Gina?'

'Gina is with Molly,' Tina said coldly.

Cecilia had learned never to ask why. So she said, 'Is Gina having supper with Molly?'

'That depends—' Tina said.

Snapping his fingers at Cecilia, Al said, 'C'm'ere.'

Nervously she obeyed.

He grabbed her arm and twisted it behind her back. At once she said, 'I'm sorry, Al—'

By way of reply he snorted.

'I'm sorry, Al,' she said again. 'I'm sorry, I don't know what I've done—'

'Tina's got something that belongs to you,' he said with studied indifference.

'I'm sorry,' she said quickly. 'I didn't mean to lose—'

'Can I show it to her now, Al?' Tina asked acidly.

'Yeah,' Al said. 'I ain't saying no—'

The next moment, Cecilia's diaphragm was dangled in front of her like a poisonous spider. Tina flung it on to the floor, spat on it and ground it underfoot.

Satisfied that his sister had done what she had said she would do, he hurled Cecilia across the room and ordered her into the bedroom. He lost no time in throwing her on to the bed.

Pinned down by Al's massive, hairy arms, Cecilia began to pray. But her prayers quickly turned to screams and before long she was unconscious.

Drifting in and out of consciousness, she was nevertheless aware of the cold compresses her sister-in-law applied to her wounds and her febrile forehead. On the fourth day, however, she only pretended to be half-conscious and silently watched her sister-in-law, submitting to her astonishingly tender nursing. She hated this unused obsolete reject of a woman as much as she hated Al.

It was only now that she understood Tina was a pervert who got her kicks out of listening to the sexual activity of others.

But there was no time for hatred now. All her thoughts were concentrated on escape.

Chapter Eleven

Miriam Stern liked to say that she respected everyone's right to privacy, which was why she had made a point of not prying into Cecilia's private life. She sensed, though, that even if she had pried she would have got nowhere – there was an unassailable aura of dignity around Cecilia. Although Cecilia had never been heard to complain, she did not realize that her tragic eyes revealed more than she wanted them to. 'That girl Cecilia has guts,' she would say. 'And I sure as hell admire her for that.'

The following Monday Cecilia returned to work, walking with difficulty.

'I hurt my back lifting something too heavy,' she explained.

'And you've dropped more weight too, kiddo,' Miriam said unexpectedly. 'In fact you look like hell.'

Cecilia burst into tears.

'You can trust me,' Miriam said softly. 'You know that, don't you?'

Cecilia continued to sob.

'I'm only trying to help. I'm not trying to interfere,' Miriam said kindly, 'but you should talk to someone.'

'I'll not only tell you,' Cecilia said at last, 'I'll *show* you what they did to me when Tina discovered where I'd hidden my diaphragm.'

'Let's go to the bathroom,' Miriam said grimly.

She gasped when she saw the ugly weals across Cecilia's back, around her thighs and criss-crossed over her buttocks. 'We'll go to the police.'

'*No,*' Cecilia said urgently.

'If you won't, I will.'

'I beg you,' Cecilia said, 'don't do that. They'll take Gina

79

from me. They told me they would. They'll take her away and I'll never see her again.'

'Who is they?'

'Al and his sister.'

'You must leave him. Your life is in danger.'

'And go where?' She shrugged. 'They'd find me.' She put her head in her hands, covering her eyes in a timeless gesture of helplessness.

'No,' Miriam said forcefully. 'They sure won't find you if I've got anything to do with it!'

'D'you think I haven't thought of asking you to help before? They'll only come to your place and get Gina – or else they'll get her at school—'

'But they won't know where you are,' Miriam claimed triumphantly. 'They'll *never* be able to find you.'

The absolute conviction and confidence in her voice made Cecilia uncover her eyes. 'How?' she asked simply.

'Leave it to me, kiddo,' Miriam said with a grim smile. 'Leave it to me.' She laughed suddenly. 'And if they come to *me* to look for you, I'll tell them I'm looking for you, too. For the money you owe me.'

Chapter Twelve

So it was that Cecilia and Giorgina found themselves at the Children's Place, a Jewish orphanage.

'He might look for you in a Catholic convent, kiddo, but never in a *Jewish* orphanage!' said Miriam drily.

Although Miriam had arranged for Cecilia to be employed in the laundry, the Matron refused to let her work. 'You'll not work until you're healed, Mrs Rizzoli,' Matron Ford said firmly. 'It will take two weeks, I reckon.'

'But where will we go for two weeks?' Cecilia asked anxiously.

'Why, Mrs Rizzoli, you'll live here, of course. Haven't you seen your room?'

'It's a beautiful room, Matron,' Cecilia said, 'but I thought I'd have to be working—'

'Nonsense,' Matron Ford said. 'You'll work as soon as you feel strong again.' Taking Cecilia's two hands in her own, she added, 'We trust you, you see.'

And so she began her new life – a life filled with affection and warmth and compassion, very like the life of emotional security she had known when her mother was alive. Everyone fussed over Gina, the older children especially.

'She's become a real kid just like any other kid,' she bubbled to Miriam on the phone. 'She used to look like a frightened old woman.'

Miriam chuckled. 'I called your husband,' she said.

Cecilia said nothing.

Miriam heard her sharp intake of breath. 'Take it easy, kiddo,' she said soothingly. 'I asked him if he knew where you were. I want my money, I said. I told him that if he didn't tell

me where you were, *he'd* have to cough up the dough you owe
me.'

Cecilia laughed helplessly.

The absence of fear was enough to make her sparkle with
happiness, Miriam thought soberly. And she asked so little of
life.

The very thought of the cruel injustice of it all gave her
heartburn. And yet, though Cecilia seemed to expect nothing
from anyone, she had become stunningly lovely. Her cheeks
glowed and contrasted perfectly against the rest of her creamy
skin. And, set off by her flawless complexion, her black eyes
dazzled with their shine.

But whenever she was within spitting distance of a man, her
loveliness evaporated, emptied like a bowl of water left too long
in the sun. She would void her face until it was an expressionless
mask, her gaze and her shoulders would slant downwards, her
throat would tighten and her voice would constrict.

'She's been deeply, perhaps irrevocably, traumatized,'
Matron Ford told Miriam. 'We see this with some of our new
orphans.'

'We know so little about her, Matron.'

'She said something vague about having emigrated to the
States during the war; apparently she had some terrible trouble
with an American officer.'

'Did she say who it was?'

'I didn't ask her,' Matron Ford said reproachfully. 'You told
me she was a private person. Besides, what difference would it
make?'

'Who knows?' Miriam said enigmatically. Pity you didn't ask
her, she thought.

For the first week after she had left, Al and Tina had absolutely
no doubt that she would return.

'She'll crawl back here where she belongs with her tail
between her legs,' Tina said for the sixth time that morning.

'How many times you gonna say that?'

'It's true, Al.'

'Don't smart-ass *me*, you fat bitch.'

Helpless tears rolled over the humps of fat in her cheeks. 'Nice way to talk to your sister,' she sobbed.

'Quit that quick,' he snarled, his neck swollen with anger, 'or I'll give you something to cry for.'

Obediently she stopped.

Slumped at the kitchen table, Tina wrinkled her nose in disgust. Dirt and chaos were everywhere. They needed Cecilia. She took care of the kitchen. And they were getting short of cash, too. Cecilia brought the bread in.

'The cops'll find her,' she said wearily. 'You better go call the cops.'

'My daughter,' he said brokenly. 'My Gina—'

'Who's been caring for Gina, I'd like to know!' Tina rasped furiously. 'You shoulda married Anna—'

Lunging towards her, he aimed a blow in her direction, but the beer had destroyed his co-ordination and he only succeeded in knocking things off the table.

In the event, however, the police came to them. It seemed the boss at Dee's Drugstore as well as several customers had reported her missing.

Looking at the accumulated filth, one of them growled, 'Lost your breadwinner.'

'My daughter,' Al whispered. 'My Gina.'

'What's with you, pal?' The officer was openly contemptuous.

'My *wife's* gone. Who knows what's—'

Ignoring his outburst, the officer said coldly, 'Beat the shit out of her, huh?'

'Whadyamean?'

'Your neighbours,' the cop said wearily, 'say we should lock you up and throw away the key.'

Officer Santini had seen it all before: the brother and sister exploiting the wife and sister-in-law. Hadn't it happened to his own mother? This poor kid Cecilia deserved to be left in peace;

the people at the drugstore had said nothing but good things about her. Even so, he would have to locate her, if only to make sure she and her child were still alive.

Not long after the police had left, Anna was in their kitchen – pale and sweating, she set about cleaning the filth.

A sly smile hovered around her lips. 'I know when I'm needed,' she said.

Still terrified of being recognized, Cecilia never removed her large dark sunglasses. Inside them, she felt as protected as if she were hidden behind a barrier. There were a few small girls at the orphanage, which meant that Gina was less conspicuous than she might otherwise have been. All the same, it was five days before Cecilia could control her trembling.

Whatever little security she had was shattered when she was called to Matron's office to take Miriam's call.

'Listen, kiddo, I'd better not come tomorrow,' she said hurriedly.

'Anything wrong?'

'The cops are looking for you. Al reported you as missing.'

Cecilia's answer was a nervous gasp.

'I didn't want to tell you—'

'You *had* to tell me. What choice did you have?'

'No choice.' Miriam laughed feebly. 'It occurred to me that they might follow me. People at the drugstore told them we were friends.' She did not say that she was sure she was being followed. She had darted in and out of the traffic, taken little-used roads, but the same green Ford was on her tail. In the end she had stopped at a Binnyon Nursery and bought a huge azalea she didn't need. Then she and the green Ford returned to her apartment.

'At least we got the phone. We can talk.'

'God bless Alexander Graham Bell.'

Miriam did not tell her she was calling from her sister's phone. She might be paranoid, but why take the risk of having her phone bugged? 'We'll stay in touch on the phone, okay?' It

84

occurred to her that Cecilia might call her, and that the call could be traced. So what if she was paranoid? Better safe than sorry. 'Don't call me. I'll call you. Okay?'

'Okay, Miriam.'

'Take care of yourself, kiddo.'

Cecilia put down the phone and began to weep. Years and years of stored-up tears came in torrents. The weeping turned to a long howl of terror and frustration.

The cops were looking for her. Instead of protecting her, they were looking for her. And they would find her – what was she against the cops? Who was she, anyway? The cops would hand her back to Al and Tina. She could see them now, grinning malevolently, two gaolers filled with power at having her back under their control.

The unspeakable injustice of it all was too much for her to handle.

Only two days after she had arrived, she had insisted on working. And she had worked harder than hard in the laundry, darning torn sheets, restoring urine-yellow sheets to a healthier-looking shade of white, removing the coarse feel of institutional starch from them.

Matron had understood that, for Cecilia, work was a matter of pride. Anything like time taken off for physical recovery would have smacked of charity to her. She needed the work as much as she needed the salary. The hard physical labour was a balm to her soul. Still a devout Catholic, the mere thought of the sin of divorce meant that she would surely go to hell. By leaving Al, by deserting her husband, she had, as she understood it, defied the teachings of the Church.

Her wrestle with her conscience was as long as it was lonely. She became more and more convinced that she had been born with something deeply evil in her nature. Had not her step-mother told her so often enough? 'Born evil, born bad,' she had shrieked, crossing herself. And Cecilia had not been able to forget that her stepmother had blamed her for the dead child that had issued from her womb.

Sleepless, she would leave her bed and sit for hours at the

85

window, saying her rosary, reciting her devotional prayers and staring from her dark room into the darker night. What was there in her that incited men to violence? First Vincenzo, and then her husband. She had heard talk of women like this, poisonous women who brought out the worst in men. Because it was well known that women are more susceptible to the devil than men. Therefore it must have been her evil, seductive powers that drew – and deserved – the hatred and the lust of men such as Vincenzo and Al. Everyone knew that it was Eve who had unloosed the devil on the world: only a woman could have done that . . .

She, too, was evil. After all, she had practised contraception. Had she not used a spermicide to murder his sperm the way a pesticide is used to exterminate vermin? True, Al had discovered her pesticide, had beaten her within an inch of her life, but had she not deserved it? Because she had defied not only Al, but the Church as well, the appropriate punishment had been meted out.

During these three months she grew thinner, then she became an indistinct shadow of herself. Her large brown eyes sank back into their sockets, and her fine high cheek-bones appeared ready to pierce through her flimsy flesh.

There, in that Jewish institution, the warmth and the compassion notwithstanding, everything was alien. Though she had feared that an attempt to try to persuade her to change her faith would be made, nothing of the kind had happened. Indeed, after consultation with her, little Gina was excluded from all Jewish religious ceremonies.

Divorce, however, was out of the question. She was married to Alberto Rizzoli, and would be until the day she died.

What if he were to find her?

It was only three months since she had left him . . .

Constantly afraid, the tiniest sound was enough to make her jump.

Even now, waiting for Matron in her cosy, book-lined office, she felt as afraid as if she had outworn her welcome at the Children's Place. Overtaken by an unexpected storm of weeping, she was unaware that anyone had entered the room.

Holding a large bouquet of golden daffodils in his huge hands, Mike O'Connor, the head gardener, stood behind her. Hoping she had not noticed him, and not knowing what to do, he placed the flowers on Matron's desk and made to leave the office. At that moment Cecilia looked up and saw him.

She blushed furiously and laid her swollen, tear-streaked face on her arm. She fought for control but lost. As a further fit of crying took over, her shoulders heaved.

They had exchanged a few pleasantries but scarcely knew one another. He was normally a shy man of few words, and her ragged beauty had made him still more shy, more silent. In spite of himself, he knelt beside her and awkwardly patted her back. 'There, there, Miss Cecilia,' he said huskily. 'It will be okay. Things are going to get better.' His voice was deep, calm and soothing.

Her crying ceased abruptly. No man had ever called her Miss Cecilia. It was the kind of tenderness she had experienced on the hospital ship. Al had been so kind then, so loving . . . Miss Cecilia sounded infinitely more gentle than Mrs Rizzoli.

'I'm sorry,' she said haltingly. 'I don't usually let go.'

'Crying is nature's way of sorting things out,' he said simply. 'Don't apologize. You got troubles, you're entitled to cry.'

A silence fell between them.

'Come on, I'll take you out for a coffee.'

'Oh, no,' she said, shuddering. 'I can't go anywhere. I might be seen—'

'Well, then, we'll go to the kitchen. Mrs Stimon's coffee is good enough for me.'

The kitchen was deserted, but Mrs Stimon always had a pot of coffee on the stove.

He brought a steaming mug of coffee and set it before her. 'Want to tell me about it?' he asked in that quiet voice of his.

'Yes,' she said, surprising herself. 'Yes, I do want to talk about it.'

87

And so she told him about having been married at sea, about the job she could have had in Boston, about the tenement life and Tina and Al, and Tina taking over her small daughter, Gina. She told him how Miriam had saved her, how she went in fear not only for her own life, but for Gina's life too. But she did not tell him about Vincenzo. She had never talked with anyone about Vincenzo.

He listened carefully and, when she had done, he placed his large hand over hers and said, 'You must not worry, Miss Cecilia. I don't want you to worry any more.'

She shrugged and made a vague gesture with her hands.

'Have you thought of seeing Father Cummings?' he asked unexpectedly.

'Matron and my friend Miriam have talked about him,' she said shyly. 'Do you know him?'

'I certainly do,' he responded stoutly, 'and a finer man would be hard to meet.' Their eyes settled searchingly on each other. 'He's wise, he's kind, and he's understanding.'

'It is many months since I went to mass – ' she said, her voice faltering. 'And now I cannot go, even if I wanted to.'

'That's because you can't leave the Children's Place?'

She nodded dumbly.

'But he would come here. You could take communion right here in Matron's office.'

She sprang up and rushed towards the window. At the same moment, without realizing it, she withdrew her rosary from her pocket. Then she looked up and saw that he was studying the movement of her fingers. 'Communion right here in Matron's office?' she whispered.

'I will talk to Matron and I will talk to Father Cummings.' He fumbled with his cap and frowned. 'But only if you are absolutely one hundred per cent certain that you would like me to.'

'Thank you,' she said softly. 'I am certain.'

*

88

The following Sunday Father Cummings heard her confession and gave her communion. Though he could not entirely approve of her having left her husband, he appeared at least to understand why she could not return to him. He seemed to understand that, though she had lost some faith in the teachings of the Church, she still believed in its rules. When he left, she knew that the unbearable heaviness of the sin on her soul had been lightened.

Then she went out into the garden to look for Mike. She found him seated under a fig tree. The figs were plump and luscious, and so tempting that she reached up and picked one from the tree. She took a bite from the fig and signalled for him to take one too. Behind the tree a wall covered by heavily scented, brightly blooming honeysuckle shielded them from view.

'It's a fig tree,' he said, smiling. 'We are Adam and Eve.' Then he asked, 'Did you see Father Cummings?'

'Yes.'

'That's good,' he said.

Too emotional to speak, she merely nodded.

'I have to check on the greenhouse,' he said awkwardly. 'See you around.'

Feeling strangely disappointed she watched him until he was out of sight.

A week later, Mike requested a meeting with Matron. 'It is a matter of some privacy,' he said.

'Well, of course, Mike. Come to my office and we'll have a talk.'

'Right now?'

'Sure.'

'But do you have enough time?'

'I've always got time for you, Mike. You should know that.'

As he followed her to her office, he marvelled yet again at the gifted way this woman managed and mothered the children of the orphanage. She seemed to have a special smile, a special word for each child.

When they were both seated in her office, she asked, 'What will you have Mike? Tea or a Coke?'

'Nothing for me, thanks,' he said, twisting his cap in his big hands.

'How can I help, Mike?' she said, coming to the point directly.

'It's about Miss Cecilia.'

'Mrs Rizzoli?'

'She prefers me to call her Miss Cecilia,' he said defensively.

'A very special young woman,' Matron said seriously. 'What's the problem?'

'No problem, Matron,' he said, awkwardly moving his cap from one hand to the other. 'It's just—' he paused and sighed.

Matron smiled at him. It was best to let him go at his own pace. The silence between them grew uncomfortable. At last, she said, 'I have the greatest respect for Miss Cecilia.'

Rising from his chair, he said, 'I would like your permission to take her out, Matron.'

With difficulty Matron suppressed a smile. 'I see,' she said. 'Why are you asking me, Mike?'

'Well,' he said anxiously, 'when I asked her to go out with me she said, "But what would Matron say?" So I thought I'd better come and ask you myself.'

'It would do her the world of good,' Matron said enthusiastically. 'She needs to go out.' Suddenly her face dropped. 'Oh, but she refuses to leave the Children's Place. She's terrified her husband will discover where she is.'

'I think,' Mike said carefully, 'that if you gave her permission, she might just make it through that gate with me. I'll take it step by step.'

'That's probably an excellent way to proceed, Mike O'Connor,' Matron said admiringly.

'Thank you for seeing me,' he said appreciatively.

Chapter Thirteen

Slowly, Mike won Cecilia's confidence and people got used to seeing the two of them with Gina.

Eight months after his chat with Matron, Mike was offered the job as head gardener and greenkeeper at Monk's Bay Country Club. Justly famed in Long Island, it was a once-in-a-lifetime opportunity for a dedicated gardener.

The night after Mike had decided to accept this new position, he took Cecilia to Franco's for a spaghetti dinner and asked her to marry him.

It had been a long and slow courtship. She was nervous of him, nervous of all men, and he understood that and kept his longing for her well hidden. After about three months of going to the movies and taking Cecilia for walks along the beach, he ventured to kiss her. She did not resist him, nor did she respond. He sensed that she was not yet ready for a physical relationship, so he lowered his lips to her hand, on which he dropped a light kiss.

'I'll wait for you, Ceci,' he said gravely. 'I've got all the time in the world.'

Only a few days later, during another long walk along the dunes, she stopped suddenly and threw her arms about his neck and then covered his face with kisses. 'I'm ready, Mike,' she said. 'I'm very ready.'

She had grown accustomed to the faint aura of freshly turned soil that clung to him. Now, closer to him than ever before, she found it wildly attractive, and her body shuddered with the kind of longing she had never before experienced.

'Come with me,' he said.

Together, moving slowly, in a hush of passion they made their way to his apartment. In all this time she had never been there before. It was filled with all manner of exotic plants but the furniture was stark and functional. At the doorway to his bedroom he picked her up and kissed her and pulled her down with him on to the bed.

Slowly, almost leisurely, he began to remove her clothes. His touch was light and delicate as his undressing hands roamed her body, stroking, soothing, now speedily, now maddeningly slowly until at last she was naked. In a swift and seemingly single movement his clothes were strewn about the room. Still he continued his gentle caress. Again and again he whispered his love for her, and their confidence mounted along with their desire, and she beckoned him towards her and received and locked him into her deepest embrace.

Afterwards, the world returned and she heard the sounds of the traffic and for the first time in years felt peace instead of fear.

However, much as Cecilia cherished the idea of being respectably married, her religion meant that divorce was out of the question. Besides, serving papers would have disclosed her whereabouts. And she would always be too terrified of Al to dare risk him finding out where she and Gina were.

Although marriage was not possible, she would take Mike's name and they would live together as man and wife. And so it was that, by the simple legal act of changing her name, Cecilia Rizzoli officially became Cecilia O'Connor on 17 November 1951. Then Matron Ford could not let the decision go by without at least giving them a celebratory lunch. Ever since she had been a small girl Cecilia had been nifty with a needle and thread. Now, for the lunch party, she copied the design from *Vogue* magazine – a flower-printed cotton dress chosen as a tribute to Mike. At the centre of the deep white-collared *décolletage* she wore a corsage of real violets grown by Mike in the hothouse.

She was so happy, she was too happy, she was afraid.

Miriam and Matron Ford clubbed together and bought her a Mix-Master and a sewing machine – she was as talented at cooking as she was at sewing. Just before dessert – a flaming baked Alaska – Miriam handed her a second beautifully wrapped gift. Cecilia read the card and gasped. It said: 'Giorgina O'Connor's college fund'. Her fingers fumbled as she undid the wrapping to reveal a savings book in the name of Giorgina O'Connor showing a deposit of 200 dollars.

Struggling to control her tears, she said, 'I'll never be able to thank—'

'Giorgina O'Connor will get there, kiddo!' Miriam interrupted. 'She'll be a college graduate. Why, if we start planning and dreaming ten years ahead, who knows? She might even make Vassar or Radcliffe.'

'With a man like Mike for a father, she's got a good start in life,' Cecilia said, smiling into Mike's eyes.

Miriam and Matron Ford exchanged a conspiratorial smile. Mike was so ordinary, they thought, so dull, as they had said to one another so many times. And Cecilia was so stunningly beautiful that she could have married anyone. She could have really gone places. The rarity of Cecilia's peaceful radiance was glaringly obvious to anyone who cared to look.

Mike had bought a small bungalow near Monk's Bay Country Club. At the club, word of Cecilia's skill with a needle spread quickly, and she soon became the local seamstress to the members.

It would not have occurred to either Miriam or Matron Ford that she had deliberately chosen an ordinary stable man because she wanted to give her daughter the benefit of a stable father.

She was twenty-four years old, and already she had achieved her greatest ambition for herself – she had provided her daughter with a suitable father and an adorable man.

She had taken effective control of her own life – but she had no control over her ambitions for her daughter's life. Greedy for Gina's success, Gina's happiness, Gina's power, she would become even more ruthless, even more cunning in her drive to make certain that her daughter would have the world at her feet.

She was yet to learn that, beside Gina's limitless aspirations, hers would be modest, for her daughter was to become the very definition of ruthlessness.

PART TWO

PART TWO

Chapter Fourteen

On Monday May 4th, 1954, the Cartwrights were on their way to Rome. It was a day short of ten years after Liberation, but they had decided to get there ahead of time. 'Just in case Vincenzo keeps the rendezvous,' Mark had said to his wife Fran.

'Do you think he will?' she had asked. Mark almost never mentioned the war.

'Frankly, I don't know him well enough to say.' His face tightened.

She glanced sideways at him.

He lit a cigarette and inhaled deeply.

'You know, Vincenzo always called me Marco. Almost everyone in our outfit called me Marco.' His mouth tensed. 'I never liked it much.'

She wanted to ask him if he'd feel let down if Vincenzo did not come, but said nothing. Although Mark was a member of the Officers' Club, he never went there. It was as if he wanted to hide everything connected with his part in the war.

Suddenly she said, 'I hope he won't come. I hope he's forgotten.'

'He won't have forgotten, Fran,' he now said mildly.

Laying her hand on his knee, she said, 'It will be a second honeymoon, anyway.'

'An extended honeymoon,' he corrected.

'Right now,' she said, her voice soft, 'I'm going to take a nap. I'm going to forget for a while that I'm the mother of a fourteen-year-old boy and a twelve-year-old girl.'

'They're great kids,' he chuckled. 'You go right off to sleep now, honey.'

She sank back into her seat and shut her eyes.

97

Mark found himself thinking about the past, with the kind of intensity he had last known when he returned home from the war. Since then, he had succeeded in putting most of the horror out of his mind. He had wanted to put his entire war experience behind him.

Yet here he was, flying all the way to keep a date with the sort of man he never would have met in civilian life. It was as if he were obeying some elemental force; as if there had been no choice. Fran had gone along with him. Sensing how important it was to him, she had arranged for the children to stay with her parents before they went to summer camp. She and Mark were to have a week in Rome and, all told, a month in Europe. Though European trips had been an annual event in their lives, they had previously instinctively avoided Rome.

Looking at his sleeping wife, her serene, trusting eyes closed to the world, he suddenly realized he was hoping Vincenzo would not turn up.

That night in Rome they did all the things tourists do; they even threw coins into the Trevi Fountain. When they returned to their hotel they checked for messages, but there was nothing. The next day, the real anniversary of the liberation of Rome, they went to mass at St Peter's.

At the end of the second day, although there was still no word from Vincenzo, Mark was dressed and ready to meet him. He was tying his shoe-laces when there was a knock on the door. 'Room service, Signor Cartwright.'

'We didn't order anything,' Fran said.

The next moment the door opened and two waiters were wheeling a snow-white table towards them.

'Signor Parsini presents his compliments—' the waiter began.

'How imaginative of Vincenzo,' Mark chuckled. 'The master of the flamboyant touch.'

'Is Signor Parsini also staying at the hotel?' Fran asked gently in her faltering Italian.

'Excuse me, Signora, the *signore* is not in Italy,' the waiter said in English.

'Not in Italy?' Mark said, his voice rising in disbelief.

'Until two days ago, he was here in Rome, staying in this very suite,' the waiter said with an expansive wave of his hand. 'But, alas, he was called back to the United States on urgent business.'

Intercepting the glance exchanged by the Cartwrights, the waiter continued. 'These past few years, Signor Parsini has been one of our most important customers. He personally selected this champagne for you. Lanson 1933, I believe it is.'

'It is Lanson 1933,' Mark said drily. 'Signor Parsini and I drank that champagne together ten years ago.'

As soon as the waiter had left, Fran said, 'What an insufferable man.'

'The waiter or Vincenzo?'

'Both,' she said with a wry laugh. 'I'm glad he can't come.'

'I've never been so pleased to be let down,' Mark grinned. 'I'll open his card before I open the champagne.'

'Go ahead, darling. I'm dying to hear what he says.'

'"A thousand regrets. Suggest reunion be delayed until 1964 – same place, same time. Cordially, Vincenzo."'

'If there's one word I hate, it's "cordially",' she said irrelevantly.

'I'll tell you what,' he said with a wide, slow smile. 'We'll dine up here. Champagne, caviare and anything else you fancy.'

'I'll tell *you* what,' she said, moving closer towards him, until her body was pressed tight against his. 'We'll have the champagne and caviare later.'

They spent every moment of the following four days together, as if, like two people who have narrowly averted a catastrophe, they couldn't bear to let each other out of their sight.

On the fifth day she left him to do the things that women do on their own – facials, massage, tinting, cutting, waxing – all at Salon Eve.

For five uninterrupted days, Mark and Fran had revelled in one another's company and one another's bodies. Even so, the prospect of time to himself was wholly pleasing. He would go on his own to the church he had been waiting to visit for ten years.

99

Unfortunately, the church of St Cecilia was closed; permission to visit it was required from the ecclesiastical authorities. Unused to red tape of any sort, Mark had not thought to make advance arrangements.

He and Father Donnelly had exchanged Christmas cards these past ten years, so he knew that the good Father had not yet returned to Ireland. He had the strongest feeling that Father Donnelly would have up-to-date news of Cecilia. Now that he was only about five minutes away from the monastery where the priest lived, he felt a surge of adolescent-like excitement at the very possibility of asking about her. A guilty smile hovered about his mouth – Fran had often accused him of being a hopeless romantic, and it looked as if her assessment had been all too accurate.

Only moments after the heavy, carved oak doors of the monastery had been opened to admit him, he was seated in Father Donnelly's study.

Clasping Mark's hand firmly in his own, Father Donnelly said, 'I've been expecting your visit these past ten years, my son.'

Mark saw at once that the priest was seriously ill. His eyes still twinkled but it was immediately apparent that time and illness had done their terrible work.

'It hardly seems that long.'

'Time,' said Father Donnelly, 'is to be measured in intensity rather than duration.'

'I guess so,' Mark answered thoughtfully. 'When I look back on my time in Rome it feels as if I was here for years rather than weeks.'

'Nostalgia lengthens time,' said Father Donnelly with a faint smile. 'Nostalgia gives the past a face-lift.' A sudden fit of coughing overcame him. ''Tis my vice, the cigarettes,' he said when he could speak. 'As long as one suffers, one lives.'

'Have you seen a doctor?'

'Doctor Sartelli calls here regularly and uselessly,' he said with an air of finality. 'I've not much longer—'

'That can't be,' Mark protested.

'It's unavoidable, my son,' the priest said briskly. 'All the same, curiosity can be more powerful than pain,' he added unexpectedly. ''Tis news of Cecilia you're after, isn't it?'

'You're right, I am,' Mark said, abashed.

'She married, you know. She was married on board the hospital ship on her way to New York.'

'I'd no idea,' Mark said. 'That probably explains why she never made contact with my aunt in Boston.'

The priest coughed again. 'Could you pass me that foul-tasting medicine?' he asked when he had recovered.

'You ought to be in hospital, Father.'

'Not yet, my son.' The priest shrugged. 'Soon, perhaps, but not yet.' He threw back his head and poured some of the liquid down his throat. 'Cecilia's stepmother, Maruccia, came to see me, you know. She wanted to show me her poor dead husband's last will and testament in which he had left whatever he had to her—' He shook his head sadly. 'Cecilia gave them almost every penny you gave her, you know. She must have kept only a pittance for herself, and probably got to New York with nothing in her pocket—'

'I wish I'd known that,' Mark said regretfully. 'I wish you had told me. I believed she had financial security, at least.'

'But, my son, you did not ask me,' Father Donnelly said gently. 'And in the absence of any mention of her I could not be giving you news of her, could I?'

'Where is she now?'

'In New York, I believe.'

'Who did she marry? Do you have an address?'

'She doesn't live at the address to which I send my letters,' Father Donnelly sighed and gathered up his hands, like a pair of lighted candles. 'But I can give you that.'

He withdrew a small black address book from the folds of his cassock, opened it and handed it to Mark. 'There you are. There's no need for you to write it down,' he added. 'You'll not be forgetting it.' He tried to laugh, but coughed. 'I'm not the tease I was.' He grinned weakly.

They chatted on for a short while longer and Father Donnelly told him that he thought he was about to discover where time itself came from. Presently, Mark took his leave.

As he reached the doorway, the priest called out in a harsh whisper, 'She had a disturbing purity, my son. Even now, an old priest like me is still haunted by her beauty.'

Mark made his way back, and on the winding Via Garibaldi, beside a flight of steps leading to San Pietro in Montorio, where St Peter was said to be crucified, he chanced upon a begging monk. Bereted and wearing a voluminous black habit, he carried a big pocket-book in which he was collecting contributions.

Mark shuddered. The crippled monk was not a good omen. Hoping to nullify the portent of the monk, he gave a huge donation, and was once again reminded of the way all those years ago he had paid off Cecilia.

Walking along a shady avenue, bordered by plane trees, a strange and comforting peace took over. For the first time since his confirmation he actually wanted to go to the confessional.

He had an address and he had a name. Father Donnelly had hit the nail on the head – he had not needed to make a single note – he had Cecilia's married name and he had an address, and he knew what he must do.

Chapter Fifteen

It was only a few months short of the tenth anniversary of Cecilia's arrival in America. They usually celebrated the anniversary in a small Italian restaurant. Afterwards, Mike would tell her that their lasagne could not hold a candle to hers.

Sometimes it seemed to Cecilia that her life was too good to be true. Her happiness made her nervous – there was bound to be a terrible price!

They had made their little home into something like a jewel-box. Only this morning Cecilia had finished hanging the soft-pink and white gingham drapes she had made for their living-room and dining-room. Mike had painted the walls pink, and even the carpet was pink. 'Like blossoms,' he said proudly. 'Like you, Cecilia.' The bedroom was full of roses. The wallpaper, the drapes, the coverlet and the chair all bloomed with roses. Cecilia was most proud of the hand-painted roses in the centre of their bedhead, and she loved her dressing-table with its skirt of pink roses on a white background. 'It's a garden-room,' Cecilia said. 'For you, Mike.'

There was no disputing that Mike was the kind of gardener whose talent was backed up by dedication. He had a photographic memory, and knew each and every one of his plants. He reorganized the rose garden, and included herbs such as basil, thyme, tarragon and chives among the flowers. In the spring he edged the beds of tulips with a wide blue ribbon of grape-hyacinth, and in the summer the roses were framed by a border of heliotrope. The club became famous for its cut flowers. From early April to late June drifts of snowdrops, crocuses, daffodils and tulips, and cascades of crab-apple and cherry blossom, were in endless supply.

Cecilia went into the small conservatory to take one last look at it before Mrs Courtney's arrival. Mike had created it out of a small back porch. He had tiled the floor himself in black and white marble offcuts, and set a tiny goldfish pool into the floor. Only when it had been filled with scarlet geraniums did he add masses of lavender hyacinths and pink tulips. It was, he said, 'a perpetual spring, like you, Cecilia'.

It was only because Mrs Courtney had decided to call on her this Monday morning that Cecilia was not arranging the flowers at the club. She was always ready to help at club parties and receptions and the members liked and respected her. 'Cecilia's a real gem,' they would say. She was also a sort of agony aunt. After listening to their problems, she would present them with an uncannily accurate analysis. Many a discontented woman came to depend on her simple advice that carried the authority of peasant-like, real wisdom.

'Cecilia O'Connor is as safe as the confessional,' Charlene Standing, the reigning golf champion, told her lover. Cecilia had supported several alibis.

To be sure, Cecilia was much loved at the club. Seated on white raffia chairs, on the high, graceful porch front of the clubhouse, overlooking the woods, the polo field, the glittering grass courts with their white-clad players, and the rolling acres of the golf course, they would discuss Cecilia as if she were a valuable communal possession, like the club's swimming-pool. Why, in addition to all her other virtues, in an emergency, Cecilia had even been known to handle the most complicated alterations from a designer gown to a golf skirt.

Those customers who remembered to ask after her daughter, Gina, would receive special attention. Frequently, after hearing about her college ambitions for Gina, they would contribute to her savings book. Mrs Courtney had been particularly generous. Cecilia had no doubt that the alteration of her ball gown was only an excuse – Mrs Courtney was coming to complain to her about Mr Courtney. It was the usual sort of thing; Mr Courtney was involved with another woman who was older, this time, than Mrs Courtney. Cecilia gave her her standard advice

– he'd get over it, don't bitch at him, don't bitch about the other woman.

Eventually, Cecilia skilfully brought her daughter into the conversation. 'Gina's only nine,' she said grimly, 'but by the time she's fourteen, I'm going to teach her what *not* to expect from a man.'

'What *not* to expect?'

'She must not expect fidelity,' Cecilia said, sounding like a doctor. 'Only if you *work* for fidelity can you expect fidelity.'

'But how do you *work* for fidelity?'

'For one thing, you must appreciate your man. Let him think he's *important*, like he's the boss—'

'You're going to teach that to Gina when she's only *fourteen?*' Mrs Courtney asked incredulously.

'Sure thing. Why not?'

'*Fourteen!* But that's when the girls go off to Talbot.'

'Talbot Hall?' Cecilia asked. 'Oh yes, I remember. Moira Dalgleish, Conrad Dalgleish's daughter, is there now—'

'I'm one of the trustees of the school. I helped the Dalgleishes to get Moira accepted at Talbot.'

Though she managed to respond mechanically, the rest of the talk passed over Cecilia's head. Her mind was in a turmoil. For when Mrs Courtney had said, 'Fourteen – but that's when girls go to Talbot,' she had decided then and there that that was where Gina would go, too. After all, Gina was a girl, just as Moira Dalgleish was a girl . . .

'But, Ceci, are you sure that sort of place would be right for Gina?' Mike asked when she told him about Talbot Hall.

'You know the Dalgleish girl, don't you?'

'Conrad Dalgleish's daughter? Sure I know her, but—'

'Is there anything wrong with her?'

'Moira Dalgleish is a fine girl.'

'If Talbot is good enough for her, it's good enough for Gina O'Connor.' By now Cecilia was familiar enough with the school to call it merely Talbot, the way everyone else did. Since Mike had taught her to write English, it was not difficult to write to schools for prospectuses. She now had several and had chosen Talbot for three reasons. Firstly, the school's College Board exams were consistently high enough to achieve a higher than average acceptance with the Ivy League colleges. Secondly, she liked the setting: the photographs showed rolling lawns, hedges and stately elm trees. The ornate architecture of the building reminded her of Rome, and she was particularly drawn to the chapel, whose high tower symbolized strength and glory. And finally, and perhaps most importantly, Moira Dalgleish was a student there. Moira, with her fresh cheeks and fresher complexion, her shiny eyes and pert nose – and, above all, her effortless self-confidence – was everything Cecilia aspired to for Gina.

'But the fees, Ceci? It's way out of our range,' Mike said anxiously.

'We could always get a second mortgage.'

For a while neither of them spoke. What Cecilia had come up with was too momentous for speech. They were both violently opposed to borrowing and yet here she was, suggesting it.

'Does Gina know about this?' he asked quietly.

'Not yet.'

'But surely you should tell her?'

'I'm waiting for Mrs Courtney's letter of recommendation.'

'You asked Mrs *Courtney*?'

As respected as she was envied, there was something forbidding about Constance Courtney. For one thing, her father had been Felix Stuart, one of the Stuarts who had been in Monk's Bay for five generations, and for another she had been President of the Student Senate at Talbot. Her present – and only – husband, Dwight Courtney, was a descendant of the founder of Courtney General Insurance, one of the most powerful companies in the insurance industry. Constance Courtney had acquired a reputation as a hostess who despised philistines and those who were invited to Penfield Manor believed that they had indeed arrived.

'I couldn't think of anyone better than an ex-head girl of Talbot,' Cecilia said cheerfully. 'I showed her Gina's reports.'

She paused for a moment and, sounding awed, added, 'Those straight As are amazing.'

'But what did she *say*, for gosh sakes?'

'She said she would help,' Cecilia replied simply. 'She said—' Cecilia's voice broke, she could not go on.

'What is it, Ceci?' Mike asked urgently, rushing to comfort her with his big hands.

Regaining herself, she spoke slowly and deliberately. 'I'll tell you exactly what she said, exactly in her words. "I've always been a stubborn woman, Cecilia," she said. "I've never had too much patience with people who spend their time trying to choose which of Grandmother's paintings they should sell to pay the butcher." When I told her that I wasn't sure what she meant, she said it meant that she hated snobs.'

'What a wonderful woman,' Mike said fervently.

'Of course she had to meet Gina before she could promise to help.'

'Did she meet her?'

'Yesterday.' Again she stopped, unable to go on. Dabbing her eyes with a handkerchief, she continued. 'She was invited to tea at Penfield Manor. Mrs Courtney gave her a chocolate malted sundae and cookies. And after she came home, Mrs Courtney called me to say that Gina was a credit to both of us.'

'And what did Gina say? Why didn't she tell me about it?'

'Mike, you weren't feeling too well yesterday, remember? By the time Gina came home you were fast asleep, and I wouldn't let her wake you.'

'Damn those aspirins. They knock me out cold.'

'You do look pale, Mike.'

'I'll be okay when I get out in the garden.' He shook his head with admiration. 'I got to hand it to you, Ceci. I got to. Next thing you know Gina will be riding.'

'Do you want to hear what she said when the chauffeur brought her home? She said she liked Penfield – she'd own something like it herself one day.'

*

To say that Cecilia and Mike were besotted with Gina is to understate the case. Too often this sort of love affair with a child is motivated by some kind of disappointment with the marriage. It could be a secret. The child is the repository of all and more of the unfulfilled hopes, ambitions and dreams of the parents. But Mike and Cecilia cherished one another – there was not a trace of discontent in their relationship. True, Gina was an unusually lovely child – her sparkling black eyes, wide forehead, dancing dimples, infectious laugh and perfect manners saw to that. It may have been that it was because Gina was not his child that Mike believed that through loving her, his love for his wife could be demonstrated again and again.

Often, when Gina and Mike were deeply engrossed in their jigsaw puzzle, Cecilia would stop everything just to watch them. The three of them were a real family.

'I love looking at the two of them together,' she said to Miriam, who was helping with the preparations for their Sunday barbecue.

'They belong together,' Miriam said softly. 'Mike is a perfect father.'

'Do you think she ever remembers Al?' Cecilia asked in a nervous whisper.

'Never,' Miriam responded firmly. 'She's obviously repressed all memory of him.'

'Repressed?'

'Let me explain,' Miriam said, her eyes flashing with intelligence. 'Children force dangerous memories out of their consciousness. It's a defence mechanism which protects them from pain.'

'Freud again?' Cecilia said eagerly. Freud was one of Miriam's pet subjects.

'Who else?' Her friend shrugged. 'Freud always makes sense to me.' She paused reflectively and, in ringing tones of conviction, continued, 'Gina believes Mike is her father. More than that, she *knows* she is his daughter.'

Cecilia found herself letting out a long breath. It was the sort of anxiety she had been too afraid to express. She looked at her friend with a mixture of gratitude and even awe. Miriam was so knowledgeable, so educated.

'How lucky we three are to have you in our lives, Mirrie!'

His wife and his stepdaughter were his life.

About six weeks after Gina's application and supporting references had been sent to Talbot, Cecilia and Mike were invited to Penfield Manor.

If nothing in the world could have prepared them for the invitation, they were still less prepared for Penfield. The gardens were legendary, of course. Even so, as they drove up the winding, graceful, elm-lined driveway, the sight of 20,000 daffodils, orange, red and pink azalea bushes and dogwood trees planted along one sweeping lawn made them catch their breath in wonder. Part of the legend was that one hundred and fifty vases of fresh flowers were changed each day. The effect of all this on a dedicated and professional gardener such as Mike is not difficult to imagine.

The residence itself was of classic Italian style. A butler conducted them through the lofty hall with its cool Travertine marble floors to the terrace looking on a seemingly endless path of shaped hedges. Moments after they were seated at the café-styled table, Mrs Courtney joined them. Ever the gracious hostess, she presided over the huge pitchers of orange juice and iced coffee as well as the array of traditional cookies and tiny iced cakes that awaited them. Her subdued dress clothes were of high fashion, high quality and pronounced elegance. After exchanging a few pleasantries, Mrs Courtney set them at ease.

'The rose garden you're working on at the club looks good,' she said encouragingly.

'I had wanted to put in older, foreign varieties,' Mike said eagerly.

'I love the old make of rose myself,' she said, pleased with her little joke. 'Especially the climbers.'

But Mike's involvement with roses was too intense to permit humour.

He pronounced the words in phonetic English.

'I guess you mean "Gloire de Dijohn".' Turning to Cecilia he added, 'It first made its appearance in 1833.' The history of roses was a hobby of his, and he could never resist an opportunity of showing something that he knew.

'Ah, yes, Gloire de Dijon.' Mrs Courtney smiled. A passionate rose gardener herself, she was delighted to find a professional *aficionado*. 'I've been thinking of creating a new sunken rose garden on the west lawn here.'

'That's what I wanted to do at Monk's Bay,' he said wistfully.

'If you would like to work on one at Penfield for me, I could ask the committee if you could be a consultant.' Since her husband was the president of the club, the answer was certain.

'There's nothing I would like more,' he said simply.

'Well, that's fixed, then.' Then with a delicate wave of her hand, she introduced the matter of Talbot. 'Miss Armstrong, the headmistress, would like to meet with Gina before a final decision is made.'

'Is that normal?' Cecilia asked nervously, her Italian accent more pronounced than usual.

'Why, certainly. It's standard practice,' Mrs Courtney said warmly. 'My own daughter went for an interview.'

This last was not true, but Mrs Courtney wanted to reassure them. As it was, they had no idea – and she was never going to tell them – how many strings she had pulled, how many favours she now owed . . . But for her own clandestine reasons she was heavily indebted to Cecilia O'Connor. Leaving that aside, however, she would have gone out of her way to help, for from her quiet dignity to her peasant wisdom everything about Cecilia commanded respect. Which was why she felt constrained to raise a matter of some delicacy.

'Gina will be – uh – living a very different sort of life at Talbot.'

'She'll fit in,' Cecilia said. 'She's got a strong personality.

She's always known what she wants. When she was less than two years old she already let me know which dress she wanted.'

'I've no doubt she'll fit in at Talbot,' Mrs Courtney said cautiously. 'But she may not fit in when she's back at home.'

'Not fit in with us?' Mike asked, raising his big hands in disbelief. 'She's the best daughter anyone could ever have wished for.'

'She'll probably speak differently when she comes home. Dress differently, too.' Mrs Courtney thought of telling them that Gina would be taught to speak correctly by practising with a pencil clenched between her teeth, but decided against it.

'That's what we *want*,' Cecilia said. 'That's why we're sending her—'

'Gina is a fine girl. Talbot will bring out the best in her,' Mrs Courtney said, smiling. One of her mother's warnings flashed into her mind – 'No good deed ever goes unpunished'. Suddenly she felt less than comfortable.

'On my daughter's behalf, and on my wife's behalf, I would like to thank you,' Mike said quietly.

'It has been a privilege,' Mrs Courtney replied. Deftly changing the subject, she said, 'Cecilia, I've decided what to wear to the costume ball. You'll be able to handle it, I'm sure. A similar colour to this, I thought,' she said, pointing to her beige-pink suit.

Accepting a glass of iced coffee Cecilia said, 'It's a wonderful colour, a wonderful cut.' She spoke in the voice of a true dressmaker, half admiring and half envious. 'Who made it?'

'A designer who is quite new to me.' Mrs Courtney smoothed the silk fondly.

Huddled in the front seat of the new car of which they were so proud – a sea-green Studebaker that looked like an aeroplane – Cecilia felt her world opening up before her. Both she and Mike had been more than apprehensive about Mrs Courtney's invitation. They had put so much into it. Mike had bought a grey pinstriped suit, which, except for Gina's distant graduation, he would probably never wear again.

And Mrs Courtney had received them so well – like ordinary guests instead of, well, not exactly servants, but underlings. But then this was America and, making the sign of the cross, Cecilia blessed the country that had given her life, liberty and love.

Yet she did not feel a foreigner. Indeed in the shops and at the supermarket she melted in with other, fairly affluent matrons, except that she would not have been caught dead in a supermarket with her hair in curlers. After all she was American, with an American passport too.

At the beginning of April, when the lilac trees seemed to swallow the sky with their fragrant purple blossoms, Mrs Courtney took Gina to her interview with Miss Armstrong at Talbot.

The headmistress pronounced her an excellent candidate for Talbot Hall, noting in her file that 'Gina's independence of spirit combined with her ambitions and discipline is a sure-fire recipe for success. An unusually impressive pupil'.

Later, looking back on that time, Cecilia would conclude that Gina had discarded her childhood, like a used straw, on the very day that she spent with Mrs Courtney at Talbot Hall.

But in truth, Gina had not so much discarded as replaced her childhood with something better – youth. From the time she was ten, Cecilia would say Gina's policy had been never to give anything away unless there was some profit in it.

Chapter Sixteen

Mike's determination to make the Courtneys' rose garden the finest in Long Island became his mission in life. It was going to be to the left of the croquet lawn, every inch of which was measured with a leveller. He pored over books borrowed from the library, making heartbreaking decisions over which roses to leave out. Mrs Courtney sent him with her driver, Riley, to visit several nurseries and horticultural gardens. Sometimes he would come back with an exquisite bloom, a 'Reine des Violettes', a smooth assembly of Parma-violet petals, with paler, pinker petals around the eye of the rose.

If Cecilia had begun to feel a mixture of peace and panic about her life having become a bed of roses, the arrival of a letter from a Los Angeles lawyer gave her a shock that was almost too much to be borne. However, she followed the instructions carefully; indeed, it might even be said that she went according to the letter of the law. Consequently, she said nothing to anyone, nor was she even tempted to tell Mike.

It was a secret no less sacred than her mother's grave.

It was almost a year before the rose garden at Penfield Manor had been laid out. But by the spring of 1956, it was already impossible not to gasp at the dense roses cascading into the rock pool below, while the fountain in the centre threw the water high into the air.

The scent of the roses and the sound of the water made it into what Mrs Courtney called 'a sort of celestial retreat – a place of bliss'. Close to the pool, an ancient wrought-iron bench enticed people to be seated. But at the very edge of the water, Mike had cunningly placed a large flat rock. This is where he preferred to sit, as if at a river bank. The goldfish he had chosen grew into plump, burnished orange flashes darting in the clear cool water.

Though his work at the club meant that he could only spend one full day a week at Penfield, he was there long after working hours, staying until it was late enough to flick the switch that lighted the fountain.

At last the main body of the work was over, and any extra time and work that Mike now put in was for his own account, for the pure luxury of savouring what he had created. For the O'Connor family, the summer of 1956 was a fine summer. It was the summer of the rose garden, of Jack Kennedy's vice-presidential nomination, and of Gina's winning of the diving trophy.

'The summer of the rose garden,' said Mike, the romantic.

He and Cecilia were in the middle of one of those long, life-giving cuddles. It was Mike's ability to express and to receive affection that Cecilia found so uplifting, so precious and, above all, so very safe.

'When I die I want my ashes to be buried in the rose garden,' he said, with the hopeful smile of one who believes he's talking nonsense.

'Oh, Mike, my *caro*, don't make jokes.'

He kissed her full on the mouth, breathing her, inhaling her as if he could never have enough of her.

Chapter Seventeen

Spring moved into summer, and the roses grew large and lush and lovely. At Penfield preparations for a wedding were in full swing. Constance Courtney's niece was to marry Chuck Redfern and the press were hailing it as the wedding of the decade. A dance hall had been set up in the tennis court; vast quantities of palm trees had been brought up from Florida. Trellises decorated with gardenias and tiny pink lights covered the walls. The pianist of the famed Jackson Watson orchestra, who had been given the use of the priceless Louis XV gold piano, shocked the Courtneys by declaring that its tone was too thin for dance music.

The huge Courtney family had all assembled at Penfield – Constance and Dwight Courtney's five-year-old granddaughter, Mary-Lou, was to be the bridesmaid. It was said that her dress, made by Dior to her measurements, had been flown in from Paris.

Mike had been asked to inspect the palm trees to see what arrangements, if any, could be made to keep them at Penfield. There was therefore no reason – other than his love of sitting on his large, flat rock – for him to be at the rock pond at that crucial moment. But he was there and, peering into the pool, lost among the goldfish and the pink water-lilies, he saw something white flapping in the water. He bent down to look and, realizing it was a small child, cried out and threw himself into the pool. Then, in his desperate haste to get to the child, his head hit against the jagged rocks at the bottom of the pond. He grasped the child and hurled her out of the water, and saw that it was Mary-Lou.

By then Mary-Lou was found to be missing and everyone

spilled out into the gardens looking for her. The first to think of the rock pond, it was therefore Constance Courtney who was the first to hear Mike's anguished roar for help.

Things happened with astonishing speed. All was confusion and chaos. Constance Courtney screamed hysterically. Her cousin, Monica, pushed her aside and instantly applied mouth-to-mouth resuscitation. After a seemingly inconscionable time little Mary-Lou was breathing normally. Feeling dizzy, and more than a little confused himself, Mike sat back on his favourite rock.

Suddenly Constance Courtney reached up to him and threw her arms against his still dripping chest. 'You saved her,' she wept. 'You saved her life! You saved my granddaughter's life!'

Gently, Mike disentangled himself. 'Anyone would have done the same,' he said quietly.

By the time Mike got home Cecilia, who had already heard what had happened, had a hot bath waiting for him. The wedding went on as scheduled, and later the O'Connors heard that the bridegroom's speech had made mention of 'Mike's great heroism, without which this great celebration would have been ruined'.

Three days later the Courtneys presented him with a gold watch. 'With everlasting gratitude from the Courtney family' read the engraving. Bemused, he went about his work.

And then, only four days after that, and exactly one week after Mary-Lou's accident, face down and lifeless – Mike O'Connor was found at the bottom of that very same rock pond.

*

'There is a very good chance that he hit his head when he dived into the rock pond,' Doctor Bushnell told an anguished Constance Courtney when he was called. 'Subdural haemorrhage does this sort of thing.' He would be with Cecilia O'Connor just as soon as he could. There was another emergency.

*

Ten minutes later, Constance Courtney was on her way to Cecilia. The family tried to dissuade her from the terrible task of breaking such bad news.

But she was adamant. 'Cecilia O'Connor is my friend,' she said. Ten minutes away from Cecilia's bungalow it occurred to her that, though she thought of Cecilia as a good friend, she had not as much as thought of asking her to her niece's wedding. No, not even after Mary-Lou's accident . . . But what sort of a friend was she, Constance? Thinking of her friendship her memory jogged. Of course Cecilia had a friend – a good friend – called Miriam.

Miriam who?

She realized she had never known Miriam's last name. But Miriam worked at a drugstore called Dee's. Praying that Miriam would be there she ordered Riley, her driver, to stop at a pay phone. Riley raised his eyebrows, gave a quick shrug, and did what he was told. He was amazed to discover that she even knew how to use a pay phone.

She was put through to Miriam, and slowly and very distinctly she told her what had happened.

There was a sharp intake of breath and a long silence.

'Could you go to her?' Mrs Courtney said.

'I'll leave at once.'

'Thank you,' Mrs Courtney said politely. But Miriam had already hung up.

Back in the car a flash of panic overtook her. What would she say? How would she say it? A long, dry sob escaped. Then she lit a cigarette and regained her composure. Never one to flinch from her duty, she would be strong.

She found Cecilia in the garden watering the roses. The afternoon was ending and, in the light breeze, the scent of the roses was strong.

'Mrs Courtney,' Cecilia said, smiling. 'What a lovely surprise!'

'I – uh – I'm sorry, I – uh—' Constance Courtney began, her face ashen.

'There's been an accident? Mike?'

'I'm sorry,' Mrs Courtney said. 'So terribly, terribly sorry.'

'Oh God,' she said, closing her eyes. 'What happened?'

But Mrs Courtney could not speak. She swallowed and cleared her throat, but still she could not speak.

'He's not dead is he?' Cecilia cried. 'Not dead?'

Mrs Courtney nodded and moved closer, putting her arms about her, guided her towards the house, knowing instinctively that Cecilia would need to be physically helped to walk.

'He was forty-five,' Cecilia said, when they were in the kitchen. 'Forty-five—' Her staring, bewildered eyes bored into Mrs Courtney. 'Gina,' she whispered. 'Oh, my Gina, Gina, Gina—'

She broke down.

Beating her hands against her head she flung herself to the kitchen floor. Her whole body rolled and thrashed and the ancient, terrible sound of her keening filled the room.

Mrs Courtney felt helpless. Cecilia seemed to show her body no pity. Mrs Courtney was suddenly afraid that she might do serious injury to herself.

Mercifully the doorbell rang and she answered it and let Dr Bushnell in and he took over.

As soon as Miriam arrived, Mrs Courtney left. Seated in the back seat of her Cadillac – quite out of character – she made no attempt to discipline her emotions and wept long and loudly.

It was Miriam who saw to all the funeral arrangements, and it was Miriam who broke the news to Gina. Taking leave from the drugstore, she stayed in the O'Connor household for two weeks, sleeping in the living-room, always ready to serve but never to intrude. When Cecilia was calm enough, Miriam moved out quietly, leaving the depleted O'Connor family to take up the reins of their life.

But it was not Miriam who broke the news to Gina that Mike O'Connor had not been her natural father.

Chapter Eighteen

For the first month or so after the accident – as they all called Mike's death – Gina received even more than the usual attention from her class-mates. She was, after all, something extraordinary – as if having become fatherless at eleven was as distinctive an achievement as winning the tennis championship.

And then one day, during break, she noticed a certain coolness, a turning away from her as if from a foul smell. The chill persisted, but she said nothing, and pretended not to notice. The following day, the chill turned to silence. As she approached all talk stopped as surely as if the teacher had commanded them to be silent.

It was during one of these silences that she heard Lucy Harrison's high whisper. Lucy had been absent from school for a few days – one of her asthma attacks had kept her at home. In a raspingly clear whisper, Lucy said, 'Mike O'Connor was not her real father!'

'Shut up,' someone said urgently. 'Can't you see she's here—'

Gina affected indifference and the moment passed. But the chill continued. Years and years later, the image of that moment was with her still. She would hear again Lucy's spit and the whisper, 'Mike O'Connor was not her real father!' and feel again the unspeakable horror, the sudden gathering and surfacing of sunken, repressed memories of the hideous sounds and ugly shouts of her earliest childhood. And then she would tell herself that if she had survived the rest of the day with nothing more than a pretence of indifference, she could survive anything.

*

She arrived home in a storm of weeping, and flew into her mother's arms. 'Tell me it's not true,' she begged her mother. 'Tell me it's not true.'

'But what are you talking about, *tesoro mio?*' Cecilia asked, bewildered.

'They say Daddy was not my real daddy.'

'Who told you that?'

'Lucy Harrison.' Detaching herself from her mother, she said, her voice hoarse, 'What difference does it make who told me?'

'No difference,' Cecilia said bleakly. 'No difference.' Even in her worst moments she had never imagined it could be like this, so sudden, so sharp and so impossible to deny. She sat down at the kitchen table, praying for the right words, and briefly laid her head on the table. As if it were not already too much, losing Mike like this. Tragedy begets tragedy, she thought. And now she would have the tragic fate of telling her daughter the truth.

The silence gathered a horrible momentum.

Clearly alarmed now, Gina sat down beside her. 'Mama,' she pleaded anxiously. 'Why don't you answer me?'

She's so unhappy, she's calling me Mama again, Cecilia thought desolately. What to do? Even as a wild battle raged inside her, she knew what she must do. Seconds were passing. She must summon the courage to be strong. 'You could not have had a better daddy, could you?' she began, taking Gina's hands in both of hers. 'You had the best daddy in the world.'

'I know that—'

'He loved you more than anything in the whole world, *cara*. He wanted you to be his daughter – his own daughter.' She raised one hand to stroke Gina's cheek.

'But I *was* his own daughter—'

'You are going to have to be very, very brave, *tesoro mio*. For his sake. You loved your daddy.' She stopped speaking, and rose from her chair. 'Here, come with me, *cara*,' she said firmly, gently. 'You are probably too big to sit on my lap, but let's do it one last time, okay?'

When they reached the living-room, she took Gina on her lap and in a slow, level voice told her the truth.

As she drew to an end, she said, 'So you see, *cara*, Daddy is your *real* daddy, he would never have dreamed of hurting you, he would have killed anyone who tried to touch you. He was the exact opposite of the man I met and married on the hospital ship.'

She paused and, fighting for self-control, went on. 'He loved you so much, and I loved him so much for loving you so much, that I even believed he was your father.'

Her whole body shook with a great sigh. Gina felt it. 'Is my real father still alive?' she asked, her voice lifeless.

'I don't know.'

'What's his name?'

'Alberto Rizzoli. Everyone called him Al.'

'And I also have an aunt? What's *her* name?'

'Tina.'

'Well, I never want to see either of them as long as I live.'

'You'll never have to, *tesoro mio*.'

For a while longer they remained quietly together, saying nothing. Then Gina stirred herself and got up. 'I'm going to my room, Mother,' she said bleakly. 'My brain hurts. But I'm going to think about all this.'

When she left, Cecilia stayed rooted to her seat, unable to move. Mike would have helped her, of course. But Mike was dead – Mike, who had never ever wanted Gina to know that she had not sprung from his loins. Mike, who had taught her that life could be beautiful. Mike, who had died an unsung hero's death in a pool of lilies. Sure, she had her widow's pension, and she had Mike's insurance, and Gina would go to Talbot thanks to the Courtneys, and she had something of her own, and things could be worse. But nothing – *nothing* – could be worse than the churning, curling, twisting pain over this gaping, this ever-widening loss, this multiplying bereavement that had now turned Gina into a double victim.

Her real father was alive, but her true father was dead.

Later, when she called Gina for supper, Gina asked to be left alone. 'I'm still thinking,' she said.

'Okay, *cara*. Come out when you're ready,' Cecilia replied, following her instinct to go gently.

It was close to midnight when Gina appeared in her mother's kitchen. She seemed changed, very changed. Her eyes were no longer the eyes of a healthy American eleven-year-old who lived in a house behind a sparkling white picket fence, and a garden overflowing with roses. She did not look older, only different. With a start of pain, her mother concluded what it was that had changed. Gina had lost her innocence – the trustingness had gone from her eyes.

Standing in the middle of the glitteringly white kitchen floor, Gina said, 'I want you to see Miss Henderson.'

'Miss Henderson? The principal of the High School?'

'I want you to tell Miss Henderson about this story that is going on about me. I want you to tell her it's a lie.'

'But, Gina—'

'Will you do that for me? Please, Mama, do this for me. Miss Henderson will *have* to listen to you.'

'*Cara*—'

'You must tell her to tell the kids to stop telling these horrible lies about me.'

'I will tell her, *cara*. And she will listen to me.' She crossed the kitchen to where Gina was standing and took her in her arms. 'Miss Henderson will do as I say. This I *promise* you—' Of course Miss Henderson would have to be told the whole truth. It was the best and the only tactic to get her to lie for Gina.

But her daughter, no longer her little girl, stiffened unyieldingly in her arms. 'Why didn't you tell me yourself?' she said painfully. 'You should have told me.'

Chapter Nineteen

On an early autumn afternoon three years later, in 1959, Cecilia and Gina were on their way in a hired chauffeured limousine to registration day at Talbot Hall. Gina had paid perhaps even more attention to her mother's clothes than to her own. Consequently, Cecilia was wearing a simple beige and white soft wool dress under a classic beige trench-coat.

Reaching up to touch her mother's hair, Gina said, 'You look lovely, Mother. Just right.'

'The bandeau's a little too tight,' Cecilia answered, smiling at hre daughter's compliment. Gina approved because the black bandeau had been her idea. She had seen it in a *Vogue* sketch of Princess Grace.

But Gina had lapsed into silence. Her confidence about how her mother looked did not extend to herself. She was not entirely certain whether her delicate, shell-pink tweed suit styled by Chanel, and exactly copied by her mother, was right. She longed for the moment when she could wear her grey and navy school uniform that was as elegant as Talbot itself.

'You look just right, *cara*,' Cecilia said reassuringly, reading her mind. 'Even your valises are perfect.'

Monogrammed tan leather suitcases had been a last-minute gift from Mrs Courtney. The luggage *was* perfect – but Gina hated it just as she hated the fact that it had been given by Mrs Courtney, who was hateful to Gina. She had given serious thought of refusing to use it but, even at fourteen, that had seemed childish. She would have hurt no one but herself.

The silence between mother and daughter was not uncomfortable.

Cecilia well remembered the first time she had heard of

Talbot. Years of planning had gone into this moment. It was Cecilia, and not Gina, who had thought of hiring a limousine. She had known that her daughter's nervousness would increase as they drew nearer to the school. Her own heart thudded, and though she knew she would miss Gina, and feel lost without her, she rejoiced for the realization of the ambitions of both of them.

Suddenly Gina said, 'It's scary, Mama. Real scary.' Her voice broke. 'You are so good to me, Mama. The best mother in the whole world.'

Mama again, Cecilia thought with some inescapable elation, even though she knew Gina only used it when she was afraid and distressed. So far, everything was as she had anticipated – including Gina's nervousness. But Cecilia's planning had included even this contingency. Plunging her hand into the pocket of her new trench-coat, she brought out a small velvet box.

'I've got something for you, *cara*. A sort of good-luck token.'

'But what is it?'

'A surprise.' So saying, she slipped the tiny box into Gina's hand. 'Big surprises come in little boxes,' she said.

Gina opened the box, gasped and then squealed with delight. 'Pearls!' she exclaimed. 'How did you know I was dying for pearls?'

'You'll wear them on weekends, *cara*.'

'They look real! They really do look real!'

Cecilia smiled enigmatically. 'They might even be real.'

'Gosh, Mama. You're too good to me,' Gina said soberly. 'I'm really, really happy.'

'Here we are, Mrs O'Connor,' the chauffeur interrupted. 'Talbot Hall.'

Cecilia had only seen pictures of it and Gina had described it in detail, but neither had done anything like justice to the long, sweeping, elm-lined driveway or the brilliantly white colonial-styled building that glinted in the distance. Her breath caught in her throat, but she succeeded in keeping tears at bay. 'If anyone deserves to be at Talbot Hall, it is Gina O'Connor,' she said firmly.

Too soon, she had kissed her daughter on both cheeks and left her to begin her new life. Then she was back in the limousine. Shutting her eyes, she knew her daughter would make it – that she would rise into her mother's image of near-aristocracy was undoubted. But there was no telling quite what she would do with it when she had it.

If Gina's first night at Talbot Hall was the most exciting of her young life, it was probably no less disturbing for Cecilia. But the expected anticlimax for which Cecilia had prepared herself was not to be. Now that she had briefly met and seen Kate Hills, the room-mate to whom Gina had been assigned, her hopes – already high – soared. Kate Hills, the great-grand-daughter of Ogden Hills, the founder of the Ogden Hills Bank. Why, Cecilia's own checking account was at the Monk's Bay branch of this great bank. Gina and Kate were to be together for at least a year. Gina would be well and truly mixing with the best.

Towards dawn, still sleepless, Cecilia went to the kitchen and sat at the table munching cookies and drinking milk. She needed Mike more than ever. Over these past three years the anguish of grief had blunted somewhat, but now it became an acutely raging physical pain. Mike had made this moment possible – he had deserved to share it with her.

Despite her mixed feelings about Mrs Courtney – after all, Mike had drowned in her rock pool – she found herself looking forward to their meeting that day. She half suspected that Mrs Courtney had deliberately planned the meeting for the day after Gina had started at Talbot both to fill Cecilia's time and to hear about how things had gone on registration day.

Early the next morning, Cecilia was once again in a chauffeur-driven limousine, this time accompanying Mrs Courtney to Manhattan. They were to choose the fabrics for the fancy dress she was to wear to the Wainwright Ball. Mrs Courtney was to go as the Tsarina Alexandra, and Mr Courtney as Rasputin, the Russian mystic, the mad monk. Rasputin's outfit, like Mr

Courtney himself, presented no problems. A flowing chocolate-brown cassock would be easy enough. The Tsarina, on the other hand, needed more thought, more imagination. The dress would have to be intensely feminine, dignified and, at the same time, subtly sexy.

'And what did you think of Gina's room-mate, Katie Hills?' Mrs Courtney asked.

'I liked her,' Cecilia said promptly.

'She's a shy girl, Katie. Very modest, all things considered,' Mrs Courtney declared. 'Ogden Hills, her great-grandfather, I think it was, built his own school on his own property to keep the riff-raff away from his nine children.'

'What happened to the school?' Cecilia asked curiously.

'It didn't take more than a generation for the whole thing to vanish.' Mrs Courtney shrugged. 'There was no more frugal a man than Ogden Hills. If he knows anything about his descendants he must be turning in his grave right now—' She gave a delicate shudder. 'Poor Katie's father, especially. You must have heard the story. It was only about eight years ago.'

'No, Mrs Courtney. I can't say I know anything about it.'

'Well, the family managed to keep it out of the papers.' Leaning forward towards the chauffeur, she said, 'Drive more slowly, Paul.' Turning back to Cecilia she continued. 'It happened in Amsterdam. Apparently he made friends with a woman of the red-light district while he was over there, got into a fight with her pimp and was murdered.' Shaking her head in puzzlement, she added, 'Murdered, just like that. Murdered.'

'Sudden death,' Cecilia said sadly. 'Same as my poor Mike.'

'But Kate's father was murdered. Deliberately murdered.'

'They are two teenage fatherless girls. They will understand one another.'

'That's what I thought, so I told the headmistress.'

'You arranged it?'

'Girls who room together should have as much in common as possible.'

Cecilia sat back in the car with a feeling of profound relief.

Gina, at Talbot Hall, would be thoroughly transformed into

a society lady. Apart from that, she could be educated, thoroughly educated. Why, the headmistress had one of the finest reputations in the land. Only last week she had read a profile describing Talbot Hall's headmistress as 'a serious educator who enriched young minds in the great classic tradition'. Undoubtedly one of the greatest names in New England secondary education.

Yes, Gina was safe now. It was a terrible pity she had ever had to learn about Al Rizzoli's existence.

Chapter Twenty

'Could you come a little earlier and stay a little longer, Mrs Courtney?' Cecilia asked on the telephone some months later. 'I'd like to talk with you.'

'Why, of course, Cecilia,' she responded unhesitatingly. 'I'll come at two instead of three.'

Feeling slightly unnerved, Mrs Courtney put down the phone thoughtfully. Only once before had Cecilia O'Connor asked something of her and that was to help her with Talbot Hall. She wondered what Cecilia could want of her.

She picked up the telephone and immediately called Diana Thornton to cancel their lunch date. She was more than a little relieved not to have to wait a whole day to find out what it was that Cecilia wanted.

'In four weeks' time it will be parents' day at Talbot,' Cecilia explained even as she helped Mrs Courtney off with her coat.

'Is she in the diving team?'

'Yes, yes,' Cecilia said agitatedly. 'She wants me to be there.'

'Well, of course she wants you to be there,' Mrs Courtney chuckled good-naturedly. 'That's only normal.'

'But not on my own,' Cecilia said faintly.

'Sorry, I'm not sure I understand.'

'She – that is, I—' Cecilia floundered. 'I don't want to go there on my own. All the other mothers will have their husbands with them, and the girls will have their fathers, and I have no one.' Her voice broke. Still struggling for control, she continued, 'But, of course, if you could—'

'And you'd like me to accompany you?' Mrs Courtney interrupted kindly.

'I know it's a lot to ask—'

'Was this Gina's idea?' Mrs Courtney asked, still in the same good-natured tone.

'She thought it would be easier for me. Having you, I mean,' Cecilia said defensively.

'Of course, of course,' Mrs Courtney said smoothly. She stopped to light her ever-present cigarette. 'You've got to admire your daughter,' she said unexpectedly. 'She's one smart cookie, your Gina.' It was obvious to Mrs Courtney, as it was perhaps to Cecilia, that Gina's status would be augmented by her presence, just as it would be decreased by her mother's presence. Clearly, Mrs Courtney would appear to be an old family friend . . . 'She's a smart cookie, your Gina,' she said again. What a schemer, she thought to herself.

'There's only one Gina,' her mother said proudly. 'Only one Gina.'

Cecilia had not exaggerated when she had told Mrs Courtney that she was very much on her own. These past three years without Mike she would have preferred to wear black. She had wanted to go back to her origins, back to the perpetual, traditional black that widows wore. The truth was that, now she had been widowed, she never wanted to change her status. She'd rather be a widow to Mike than wife to any other man. She would have liked to have proclaimed her grief for everyone to see.

But this was America, and all that would have been bad for Gina.

Neither happy nor unhappy, she was slowly beginning to come to terms with Mike's death.

She had thought that once Gina was away at school, the strength of her maternal feelings would diminish somewhat. After all, she would not be cooking and shopping for her. Instead, her maternal instinct seemed to have grown even stronger. She could sit for hours thinking of her daughter, imagining what she was doing and who her friends were and what she was wearing.

129

Somehow, thinking of her love for Gina as measureless, yet always expanding, gave her a certain solace, but also a sense of wonder.

Brooding on what her life would have been if she had not escaped from her Roman slum, she would count her blessings. She was an American, her daughter was an American and, thanks to Talbot, the fulfilment of the American Dream was already under way.

Perhaps, if her childhood had known less sadness, less poverty and less cruelty, she might have been sorry for herself.

After all, she had been only twenty-seven when she had been widowed. She was not yet thirty-four, yet felt ageless.

So ageless that she had not yet felt the lack of men in her life.

For all that Gina was her life, she was an undemanding mother.

According to Miriam, she was far too noble . . .

And so parents' day came and went, and Mrs Courtney's presence was a great success. Gina's regular letters were full of news, full of love. She had made the merit list and she and Katie were now best, best friends.

But Gina's most recent letter both surprised and delighted her mother. '*Katie Hills has invited me to join the family on their yacht,* Clarissa, *for a month-long Mediterranean cruise in the summer. She said I could fly direct to Monte Carlo from New York when they do, on August 2nd. First-class tickets get booked way ahead of time, so I should book now, she said. Of course, I told her that you and I had made our summer plans months ago. I said I was sorry, but I couldn't possibly make it.*

'*I miss you, Mama. I miss you so much. I simply could not spend the summer without you.*'

In fact, Cecilia's savings could well have financed a first-class ticket to Monte Carlo. But that was thanks to the secret trust that had been set up for her, and she did not want Gina to know anything about it. When the time was right, Gina would be told.

When Gina returned to Monk's Bay for the summer vacation, her entire being was given over to the campaign to elect John

Fitzgerald Kennedy President. Which meant that far from regretting that she was not cruising the Mediterranean, she was positively delighted. Already her mother had come to conclude that Gina was the sort of person who would turn a necessity into a virtue.

And so Gina set off every day for the local campaign office. In common with countless thousands of volunteers, she saw Jack Kennedy as the romantic light in the sky, the visionary, the Harvard scholar with the Boston accent whose sense of mercy for the weak outdistanced his concern for the counting-house men. Her sense of mission matched her idealism, the meek would indeed inherit the earth. At the same time she was sure she was on the winning team. Privileged, she would yet have the power to have others benefit from that privilege.

She would work at the Monk's Bay campaign office until three in the afternoon. At four she would take up her duties at Martha's Hamburger Haven, a cheerful, spotlessly clean restaurant whose walls were decorated with huge blow-ups of the young senator from Massachusetts. Which meant that Gina's volunteer work and her waitressing became one. It was like belonging to a rather exclusive club whose members all wore an inner badge of social conscience. If social justice was their commitment they could not be wrong about anything.

It was Miriam Stern who had made it all happen. Miriam's recommendation could not have been more concise. 'Gina is an attractive, unusually adult fifteen-year-old, with a winning telephone personality.'

The youngest of the volunteers, Gina did not let Miriam down; everyone loved her. It was only natural, therefore, that both Cecilia and Miriam would join her at the campaign office on the day Senator Kennedy and his cavalcade were to address a rally at Monk's Bay. Which was how Cecilia and Gina were photographed with Senator Kennedy, covered in confetti, leaning forward from his platform to touch the hands of his supporters. Although several others were in that photograph, the camera seemed to focus on Gina and her mother. Somehow the camera turned their very obvious mother-and-daughter resemblance into a silent, immensely moving vignette of their involvement, their hopes for the presidential candidate.

When the first editions of the *New York Times* were on the street, only a few hours later, Cecilia and Gina found themselves on the front page.

In an airless, crumbling apartment on the Lower East Side, a bull-necked man in a vest slurped a long swig of beer and stared at a newspaper.

'It's her,' he growled. 'It's them.'

'Who's her?' the woman asked suspiciously. 'Where's them?'

'My wife,' he said, emotionally. 'My kid.'

The woman shuffled towards him and squinted at the paper. 'She's a pretty girl, your daughter.'

'The bitch didn't change the kid's name,' he said heavily. 'She's still Gina.'

The woman stared at him open-mouthed. 'What you gonna do?' she asked curiously.

'Forget what I said,' he snarled. 'Forget it! You heard me.'

'Yeah, yeah. I heard you.'

'I'm still married to the bitch! We ain't never divorced. I'm going to find her one day.'

But it would be months before he would even come close to seeing her.

PART THREE

Chapter Twenty-One

By midsummer, when Senator Kennedy was finally nominated the Democratic presidential candidate, Gina, like everyone else in the campaign office, was jubilant. All around the United States, following his rousing acceptance at the Los Angeles Coliseum, his audiences grew, sometimes up to half a million people hurling confetti, waving banners and flags and paper streamers. It was in that atmosphere of confident optimism, bordering on euphoria, that Gina received the phone call from Katie Hills that was destined to change her whole life.

'Hi, Gina, it's—'

'Kate – where are you calling from, Monte Carlo?'

'No. I'm back in Connecticut, at our country place.'

'What happened to the cruise?'

'That's still going on,' Kate giggled. 'But my mom – well, thing is, she and Ned are on a kind of honeymoon, so I decided—' She hesitated, drew in her breath deeply and continued, 'I decided not to be in the way.'

'Oh, *Kate*. How—'

'Who needs a sixteen-year-old daughter near your twenty-four-year-old guy? It's kind of embarrassing.'

'To say the least,' Gina said feelingly.

'She said I should ask you to come up to spend the rest of the summer here at Severn Woods.'

'Gosh, I'd have to ask my mom,' Gina said uncertainly. 'I don't know if she'll let me—'

'So ask her, Gee. I'll call you tonight to hear what she said.'

Gina fully expected her mother to refuse, but decided to ask her anyway.

Her mother's reply astonished her. 'What sort of place is it?' she asked.

'It's a farm, I guess. It's got its own private lake, and horses and sailboats. Kate showed me a few photographs of it at school.'

'It sounds like paradise,' Cecilia said softly. 'But who'd be in charge, if you did go? I'm not leaving you in the care of no maids—'

'*Any* maids, Mother,' Gina interrupted, automatically correcting Cecilia's grammar.

'Any maids,' Cecilia amended rapidly and good-naturedly. 'I don't go along with two young girls on their own like that.' She shook her head sympathetically. 'Poor Kate,' she said softly. 'I can imagine how she feels. I always felt I was in my father's way when he married Maruccia—'

'If she's got an aunt or someone staying with her, will it be okay for me to go?'

'We'll see, honey,' Cecilia said firmly. 'We'll just have to wait and see.'

A short while later the phone rang and, after a hasty conversation, Gina put down the receiver.

'She says her sister and brother-in-law will be there—'

'Kids,' Cecilia said doubtfully. 'A couple of kids.'

'But they're a married couple, Mother!'

'Still—'

'She said Evelyn – that's her sister – is going to call you herself.'

Moments later the phone rang again. Evelyn was so polite and respectful that it was almost impossible to refuse her. Cecilia was about to hang up but asked suddenly, 'How old is your baby boy, Evelyn?'

'He's three months.'

'And how old are you, Evelyn?'

'Twenty.'

'Only twenty?' Cecilia repeated dubiously.

'Mature enough to take my responsibilities very seriously, Mrs O'Connor,' Evelyn said.

Reluctantly, Cecilia agreed to think about it. Then she extracted a promise from Gina that she would never – under any circumstances – get on a horse. First she had a quick telephone conference with Miriam. 'It's an opportunity you can't afford to let her refuse,' Miriam said.

Five days later, Gina and her skirts, jeans, shirts and sweaters were on the way to Severn Woods, the Hillses' country place.

Severn Woods turned out to be a thirty-roomed house in eighty acres of woodland, with a lake and stream. A wooded driveway scattered with persimmon leaves led up to a grey-shingled, white-shuttered house sitting high on the hill. Kate took Gina through a stately entrance hall with inlaid marble on the floor, polished marble columns, up a wide, graceful double staircase into the guest-room that had been made ready for her.

Gina took one glance at her bedroom, gasped with wonder and squealed with delight. Her eye went from the cool, still, blue silk hangings on the four-poster bed to the valance above the bay window and came to rest on the two wing chairs on either side of the fireplace. It was a huge room, but the blue silk somehow brought it all together and made it cosy. A glass table held several of her favourite books – their pristine jackets told her that *Pride and Prejudice*, *Jane Eyre* and Robert Frost's poems had all been especially acquired for her. Bowls of daisies stood beside the books, on the mantelpiece and on the night-tables.

Still squealing with delight, she rushed over to Kate and hugged her. 'My favourite books,' she said. 'Oh, Kate—'

'Let me show you the bathroom and then we'll go down for a swim, okay?'

A huge sunken bath under a white pleated canopy to match the white marble, and bathrobes in the same cool blue, and stacks and stacks of fluffy white towels, and a collection of delicate shells, made her long for the moment she would luxuriate in soft warm water.

'Let's go down to the pool,' Kate said.

'Okay. I'll unpack quickly, get out my swimsuit.'

'Oh, Donna *always* unpacks for us. She'll be upset if you don't

137

let her do that,' Kate said easily. 'The pool-house is stacked with swimsuits—'

'Lead the way,' Gina said confidently. Now I know why you're so disorganized at school, she thought. I guess you don't know how *not* to be untidy, if servants do things for you, she said inwardly, filing this new insight away for future use.

Still spotty, still too skinny, it has to be said that Kate was a plodder. She tried hard at everything, but no amount of effort seemed to help. Because chocolates caused skin eruptions, she couldn't eat them to help her gain weight. She'd had a private swimming coach since she was eight, and though she could swim, her style was too clumsy to be competitive. Years of piano lessons, and musical notation remained a maze of hieroglyphics, so she stopped trying to be a musician. Successful orthodontistry had straightened her teeth, but an unsuccessful plastic nose-job had left her nose more crooked than it had been to start with.

The house was grander than grand, but from the very outset Gina made up her mind that she would not be intimidated by it. When they were not swimming, or sailing on their private lake, or playing tennis, they fell into the habit of using the wicker tea-house. There they lounged about on yellow wicker chairs on light red floorboards. To get to it they passed weeping willows and bamboos, crossed wooden stepping-stones curving across a floor of pebbles, and a trickling fountain.

Chapter Twenty-Two

Soon after their first swim, Kate had whispered urgently, 'Don't mention anything about the baby to Evelyn. Pretend he doesn't exist—'

'Why? That's weird.'

'Evelyn said she didn't want to talk about it. The baby's gone to Jake's parents. They didn't want it with them on their vacation.'

'I brought him a teddy—'

'Take it back. Give it to someone else.'

'Sure,' Gina said. Inwardly she thought it was crazy. What sort of mother was this? Yet Kate had always told her that Evelyn was like a mother to her.

'This sometimes happens to new mothers,' Kate said, reading her mind. 'Miss Hamilton told me.'

'Miss Hamilton?'

'You know, our housekeeper. She's been with us for yonks. She says Evelyn will get over it. Right now it would be too dangerous for the baby to leave it with her.'

'What's its name?'

'Theodore.'

'Poor Theo. Poor, poor Theo.'

'Maybe it's because she's worn out with mothering me. She's been doing that since she was ten and I was five.'

Upstairs in her bedroom, Evelyn watched her sister's clumsy efforts on the tennis court with mounting irritation. She turned away from the window.

'Kate's had one of the greatest tennis coaches of all time,' she said to her husband Jake. 'And what does she do? She either misses the ball or falls over her own feet.'

'Quit nagging,' Jake answered, sounding bored. 'You're always picking on her.'

In answer, Evelyn flounced off to the bathroom, opened a cupboard, removed a small bottle and hastily swallowed two Valium tablets.

'You're getting to be a junkie,' he said pleasantly. 'Who's Kate's new friend?'

'A *nobody!*' she said angrily. Snatching up a cigarette, she brought it to her lips with a vicious movement. Her lighter clicked on obediently and instantly. 'She's no one you would want to know. Her mother's a seamstress, I hear—'

'A seamstress?'

'You heard me.'

She returned to the window and watched in silence for a minute or two. Suddenly flinging her head out of the window, she called out, 'Keep your eye on the ball, Kate! The ball, not the trees.' The next moment she slammed the window shut and, for the second time that day, went to wash her hair.

Down below, on the court, Kate's game went to pieces. After a series of double faults, she threw down her racquet and said quietly, 'I am never going to play tennis again as long as I live.'

'Let's go swim,' Gina said quickly. 'I'm boiling.'

'Okay,' Kate mumbled, kicking the surface of the court.

Without thinking, Gina picked up both racquets.

'Leave that racquet where you found it,' Kate said angrily. 'I told you, I'm finished with the game.'

'You mean you're never going to use it again?'

'Right.'

Gina shrugged. 'It's a neat racquet,' she said airily.

'It's yours.'

'No, thanks,' said Gina, who would dearly have loved to have had a racquet as expensive as Kate's. Nothing in the world would have made her show it. One day she too would be in a position to throw away her racquet, only she never would . . .

*

140

Apart from the glimpse of Evelyn's mane of flaxen hair through the window, Gina did not see her for three days. Once, from her bedroom, she saw Evelyn's husband, Jake, standing beside the pool. Tall, dark with rolling muscles, a strong jaw and bushy hair, he reminded her of Jack Kennedy. Since the Senator was on her mind so much, this was hardly surprising.

Almost without thinking, she called out, 'Hi.'

He looked up. 'Hi,' he answered, quickly diving into the water.

She felt rebuffed, and went in search of Kate. 'When am I going to get to meet your sister and brother-in-law properly?' she asked bluntly.

'Tonight. We're having a barbecue.'

Wearing blue jeans and a white shirt Gina joined them at the pool.

It was going to be a simple meal, they said. The scene of that simple meal that Gina took in on the early summer's night was permanently imprinted on her mind.

The barbecue gave off the delicious scent of hickory smoke, and the banks of hibiscus and azaleas were discreetly lit, and the cook hovered over the charcoal. Even before Gina was formally introduced, she was handed a glass of champagne. Everyone, including Kate, wore sparkling white trousers. And yet Kate had told her to wear blue jeans.

'Welcome to Severn Woods,' Evelyn said. 'I'm Evelyn and this is my husband, Jake. My sister Kate ought to have introduced us before.'

With a seemingly assured smile, Gina answered, 'Hi, Evelyn. Hi, Jake.'

'Kate tells me you don't ride.'

'Well, I promised my mom—'

'So Kate said,' Evelyn said pleasantly. 'But tomorrow you can come and see me take Clover over several jumps.'

'I've seen Clover,' Gina said. 'He looks such a beautiful animal. Such shiny black fur, too—'

'Coat.' Kate interrupted to correct Gina.

'Coat?' Gina repeated.

141

'We don't speak of a horse having *fur*, Gina. It would be like talking about a Labrador's fur. Horses and dogs do not have fur. They have coats.'

'Next to the white fence, his coat really—'

Again, Kate interrupted. 'Never speak of a white fence when you mean post and rails,' she said with a shudder of distaste.

'Thank you for that lesson, Kate,' Gina said, flushed with rage and embarrassment.

'What's going on here?' Jake said. 'The champagne's flowing like concrete.'

Evelyn and Jake kept to themselves, which meant that the following ten days were given over to talking, gossiping, whispering. Gina took care not to trounce Kate at every game. Thanks to Miriam Stern, Gina knew a great deal of the history of the area, and they went into the town and visited the church.

It was at the Art Institute in Williamstown, on the day before Gina was due to return to Monk's Bay, that she was introduced to Rufus Cartwright. It was only a very brief meeting, but it was long enough for a teenage girl to fall in love. Permanently.

Chapter Twenty-Three

At first Cecilia believed Gina's fretfulness and her headaches were the result of having had to quit the splendour and the luxury of the place she had been vacationing in and to return to their little cottage. But when she developed a temperature and a light rash, Cecilia took her to the doctor. The diagnosis was German measles and Cecilia was overjoyed.

'Every girl should get it before she gets married,' she exulted. 'Miriam and I tried to get you to catch it when you were a kid, but it just didn't take.'

'Oh, *Mother*,' Gina said irritably. 'I was counting on going back to the campaign office.'

'It'll only be a few days – four at the most, *cara*.'

The next day Cecilia had to go to Mrs Courtney's home. The arrangement had been made weeks before. Mrs Courtney had bought a sewing machine so that all the alterations to her wardrobe – newly acquired in Paris – could be attended to in three or four days in her own home. Which meant Cecilia would not be there to minister to Gina and her German measles.

'It's the third day already, Mother,' Gina said impatiently. 'Doctor Bushnell said it would only take four days.'

'Even so, I hate leaving you, *cara*.'

'Mother, *please*. I'm going to have the greatest time watching *As the World Turns*.'

But when her mother left, she found it difficult to concentrate on the endless heartbreak of the main characters in the serial. Indeed, it was hard to concentrate on anything. She went over and over the events of the last few days at Severn Woods – everything had been done for her, the bed turned down, all her clothes and even underwear washed and ironed. The washing and ironing was done in the space of a single morning, so that all her clothes would be in perfect readiness all the time.

She switched on the radio and listened to the *Fortune Chat Show*. At the same time she began sketching on a note-pad, scarcely aware of what she was drawing. Suddenly, as it took shape she saw that she had sketched Rufus Cartwright. It seemed so powerfully like him – she'd got it all. The shape of the chin, the high cheek-bones, the clear honest gaze, and even the small irregular scar on his forehead. Anyone would have recognized him. Of course, she was too young for him; he would never look at her. After all, he was a Harvard Junior, and he certainly didn't date schoolgirls who were still in their school uniforms.

The half-smile that hovered about her lips made all three dimples dance. She was thinking that she knew exactly why she had fallen for him, and it had nothing to do with his looks. True, he was a handsome young man, tall, muscular – as the image of John Kennedy, how could he not be?

It was his voice – the music of his voice. It was a quiet, soft voice, but musical; a sensitive, intelligent voice. Just listening to it made you feel cherished and protected. Yes; it was above all kind, but equally it was a voice that could have played Hamlet.

So it was that, in the midst of a teenage daydream, she closed her sketch-pad and went to answer the doorbell.

The man who stood on the doorstep held up a newspaper clipping with a photograph of her on it.

'When I saw your picture, and those dimples, in the paper I knew it was you,' he said gruffly.

Gina shrank back. Her rash prickled, and she actually felt her temperature soar. Instinctively, she tried to shut the door, but the man's foot prevented her from doing so. She felt quick hot tears sting her eyes and covered them with her hands.

'Gina? Don't be afraid,' the man said. 'I'm your *daddy*. You're my little girl. Hasn't your mother told you about me? I'm Al Rizzoli, your daddy.'

'No!'

'Look,' he wheedled. 'I'll smile. You'll see; we have the same dimples. You're my daughter.'

Whereupon he smiled.

She gasped and felt so weak she had to prop herself up against the wall.

'See,' he said, smiling ever more hugely.

She felt a wave of nausea.

'I looked for you, *cara*,' he said brokenly. 'For years and years I looked.'

'Come in,' she said reluctantly.

He came in, taking off his baseball cap so respectfully she felt even more revolted. He followed her into the pink and white living-room, sat down awkwardly, and twisted his cap in his hands.

Immediately only one powerful need consumed her. She must get rid of this horrible, disgusting man. He must never, never, never see her again. *Never!* She left to fetch him a Coke – he'd asked for beer but she told him there was none in the house.

She sat opposite him and watched him gulp it down. At least he's not dirty, she thought. Nor does he smell. But she'd rather be dead than have anyone know this coarse man – with the kind of thick Italian-American accent that was the stuff of ethnic jokes – was her father. Her flesh and blood. Her blood relation.

Her mother was so different, so elegant. So very American. Mrs Courtney's hand-me-downs were perfect for her. True, she had an accent, but it was so slight that it was distinctive and her English grammar was now perfect. The image of what her life would have been if her mother hadn't left him made her shiver.

Suddenly tears sprang to his eyes. Leaning forward in his seat, he said passionately, 'I've missed you so much.'

She felt the bile rise up within her. Her body convulsed, and she rushed to the bathroom, where she vomited.

As soon as it was over she returned, but remained standing by the door. 'I've got German measles,' she said weakly. 'I'm sick. I really should be in bed right now.'

'Poor kid. German measles, huh?'

145

'Can you come back tomorrow, when I'll feel a bit better? At around the same time?'

He got to his feet and hugged her. 'Aren't you going to kiss your daddy?' he crooned.

'Put me down at once,' she said coldly. 'I'm sick. I told you, I have German measles.'

He set her down instantly. 'It must have been a shock for you, seeing me. It'll be fine when we get to know each other better. The same time tomorrow?'

'The same time.' She walked to the front door and he followed her obediently. 'Tomorrow,' she said.

Gina raced upstairs to take a scaldingly hot bath. She felt sullied, dirty, as if she'd never be clean again. With such a man for a blood relation, how could she ever, ever be clean again?

Suddenly she felt a hatred so powerful, so all-consuming, that it was literally difficult to breathe. She had thought she had hated Evelyn, but compared with what she felt now, that was merely a vague minor annoyance.

It was a hate born of instinct – it was the key to her own survival. She felt murderous . . .

There was less than twenty-four hours to formulate a plan. Meanwhile, one unwavering decision. She would not tell her mother about this. Perhaps her mother would never have to be told that the man of her deepest nightmares had surfaced . . .

When Cecilia came home Gina insisted that she was much, much better – merely tired. She would like to be in bed by seven.

'But you should have been in bed by the time I came home, *cara*,' Cecilia protested.

'It seemed stupid to be staying in bed when I felt so well.'

In a way the German measles was a blessing. Her insane inner tremble, inner sickness, and her flushed, feverish face could all be attributed to her illness. Her knees felt weak, but if her mother suspected that anything was less than it should be, she would cancel Mrs Courtney. Which would mean that she would meet that animal. So Gina was sweet and kind, and disarmingly affectionate.

She sat up throughout that night trying to devise a plan, but by morning nothing – not one good idea – had come to her.

And yet the moment her mother left for the Courtneys' a spring was released in her mind and a possible plan began to take shape.

But the hatred had strengthened, had grown murderous.

Chapter Twenty-Four

Cecilia hated to admit this to herself, but she actually looked forward to the time she spent with Mrs Courtney at Penfield Manor. Strangely, she and Mrs Courtney had become firm friends, even though Cecilia was the only one whose first name was used. Of course, long before the tragedy, Cecilia had always been Mrs Courtney's confidante. It ought to have been an unequal relationship, between employer and employee, but because the respect on both sides was so sincere it was a good friendship.

'How did Gina get on at Severn Woods?' Mrs Courtney asked over the first of the many cups of coffee the two women would stop for during the day.

'There's something weird about the older daughter, Evelyn,' Cecilia began. 'She refuses to have anything to do with her own baby.'

'Post-partum depression – that is sad.'

'I've never heard of it.'

'It happens,' Mrs Courtney said briskly. 'It seems to be happening more and more often, too.' Launching into a gossipy sigh, she added, 'It must be so hard on Kate, what with her mother's latest adventures.'

'Poor thing. What's she up to?'

'She was stoned out of her mind. They had to throw her out of the Hôtel de Paris in Monte Carlo. The gossip columns are full of it. She stripped off in front of everyone.'

'When did this happen?'

'It's reported in Knickerbocker's column this morning.'

'That's going to be very rough on Kate. She's a shy girl anyway, Gina says.'

148

'In my day, the other parents would have insisted that the daughter of such a mother should be expelled,' Mrs Courtney said primly. 'A school like Talbot cannot permit any lowering of its moral tone.'

'Poor Kate. I hope that won't happen to her. It would be so cruel—'

'It's not altogether out of the question,' Mrs Courtney said flatly. 'Nor should it be.'

Seated beside the telephone, Gina reread the notes she had prepared. She had been over the notes again and again – in fact she knew almost every word by heart, but she dared not risk getting a simple word wrong. She dialled the number of the Monk's Bay police station and hung up before it was answered. She had never been as nervous, because she had never had to defend her life. How she wished Mike O'Connor were still alive. He would have known exactly how to handle this.

At last she dialled the number, got through, and asked for Lieutenant Fowler. She knew him fairly well. It was Lieutenant Fowler who had attended Mike's accident and he had been particularly kind to her – and to her mother – after Mike's death.

'Hi, Gina,' he said, sounding pleased to hear from her. 'What can I do for you?'

She found she could not speak.

'Is there anything wrong?' he asked into the silence.

'Yes. Yes, there is.'

'I'd like to help you, Gina, but I can't do anything unless you tell me what's wrong.'

Crumpling up her notes, Gina whispered, 'This man – he – tried—' Once more she tried and failed to speak.

'Gina?'

'Sorry, Lieutenant Fowler,' she sobbed.

'Where are you calling from?'

'Home—'

'I'll be right over. Hold on till I get there.'

149

Now that she had talked to him, now that help was on the way, she let herself give way to the heartbreak and rage and shame over having met this terrible man who said he was her father. By the time Lieutenant Fowler arrived, she was still crying hysterically. She rushed up to him, and he tried to comfort her – this teenage girl whom he knew so well, and for whom he had such great respect. Flushed with distress, and feverish from her illness, her rash was even more pronounced. He scarcely recognized the flushed and swollen girl. 'There, there,' he said, patting her back. 'Sit down, and I'll get you a glass of water, and you'll tell me all about it.'

Obediently, she drank from the glass he had brought her. Then, after struggling for and gaining enough control of her voice to speak, she told him her well-rehearsed version of what had happened. She went on to say that she must protect her mother from ever knowing what she had experienced. She explained the way she had found out that Mike O'Connor was not her real father. 'I *had* to let him in,' she explained brokenly. 'When I saw those dimples were exactly the same as mine, I just *had* to.'

'You had no choice, Gina. I understand that,' he said sympathetically.

'*Ugh!*' she exclaimed, beginning to sob again.

'Try to tell me what he did—'

'It was terrible.' She clasped her hands tightly, and in a low, scarcely audible, voice said, 'He touched me. He put his arms around me. Then he kissed me. Then he—' Again she broke into sobs. 'He's coming back. He's coming back.'

'When?'

'At lunch-time—'

'I'll be here when he comes.'

'But I don't want anyone to know about this,' she begged. 'I couldn't face talking to anyone else. I won't have to go to court, will I?'

'I won't tell anyone, Gina, I promise. And you certainly will *not* have to go to court. But I will have to call in and say I'll be delayed.' He called the station and asked for information on Al Rizzoli.

Now that she knew she would not be alone when he came, and that her mother need never be told about it, she felt much calmer. So she told how he had picked her up, and carried her and hugged her. 'He touched me everywhere. He tried to tear my jeans—'

'*Bastard!*' he said, unable to contain himself. 'Slime. Pure slime.'

'I don't know what I would have done if you couldn't have been here. Please help me. I just couldn't tell my mother about any of this.'

'I'll wait in the kitchen, so he won't know anyone's with you.' His voice was matter-of-fact. 'The second you need me I'll be right in there with you.'

At last the doorbell rang. Lieutenant Fowler slipped quietly into the kitchen, and Gina went to answer the door to her father.

He was carrying a bunch of red roses, and reeked of after-shave.

'Roses for my *bellissima*, my Gina,' he said emotionally. 'My daughter, my little girl.'

'Thank you,' she said coldly, adeptly leading him into the living-room, where she took the roses from him.

'Aren't you going to kiss your poppa for bringing you roses?' he said hoarsely. Scooping her – roses and all – into his arms, he covered her face with kisses.

That was when she screamed and screamed. Instantly Lieutenant Fowler was at her side, grabbing her out of her father's arms.

'Go to your room, Gina, and lock the door,' he commanded.

When she had left the room, he said coldly, 'Al Rizzoli, you're under arrest.'

'What do you mean?'

'I'm gonna put you inside and throw away the key,' the

Lieutenant said. In one fluid move, he stepped forward and plunged his fist right into Al's protruding belly. Al's after-shave assailed his nostrils. 'Christ, you stink,' he said, his voice heavy with disgust.

'You can't arrest me, she's my daughter.'

'Don't try to smart-ass me, scumbag,' the Lieutenant said, his neck swollen with rage. 'Ever heard of incest, scumbag?' So saying, he whirled, grabbed Al's wrist with contemptuous ease and twisted his arm behind his back. 'You two-bit toad, you leg-breaking son of a bitch,' he snarled, bending Al's arm still further.

Al screamed.

'Quit squawking. Look at me when I talk to you, scumbag,' he said, thrusting his face so close to Al's that they were almost nose to nose. 'Stay away from her,' he said softly. 'You come near her again and you'll be dead. Get it?'

'I got it,' Al whined.

'Let me even see you and I'll let the blood out of your head,' he said stonily. 'Get your ass off someplace else, like Miami.' His voice rose to a roar. 'Get the fuck out of New York State!' Then, with the edge of his hand, he gave Al's arm one final, expert chop, breaking it. His voice a whiplash, he said, 'Beat it!'

Whimpering pathetically, Al scurried out.

When he had gone, Lieutenant Fowler said quietly, 'I understand why you don't want to let your mother know, Gina. But don't you think you need a counsellor to help you? I could arrange for a psychologist, and it wouldn't cost you.'

'Thanks,' she said with a wan smile. 'I'd rather not talk to anyone about this. I just want to forget the whole thing.'

He looked at her. Already that wan, beaten look was hardening into a look of stunning strength and determination. She sure was a cool customer, this one. For a moment, he even wondered whether her father had, in fact, tried to rape her . . . She might have just wanted to frighten him out of her life. But then he heard her tearful voice saying a dignified thank-you, and her radiant innocence reasserted itself, and he knew that his inner thought had been unforgivably unjust.

Chapter Twenty-Five

The academic year had scarcely begun when Gina overheard Joanna Sullivan telling a group of three curious girls about Kate's mother. 'Mrs Hills was naked as a newborn babe, so they threw her out.'

'What *are* you talking about?' asked Felicity Russell, who had just joined the group.

'Kate's mother, naked, at Jimmy's Club, Monte Carlo. The papers were full of it.'

'I thought you said it was at the Hôtel de Paris,' someone said.

'I meant Jimmy's. I mean, what difference does it make where it was that Kate's mother decided to strip off and make a spectacle of herself?'

'I guess we'll have to ask her to resign from Friars, won't we?' Joanna said gravely. 'We will have to call a special meeting.'

Friars was a small, secret club of eight, that had only been created in the final week of the last semester. It was nothing special, only exclusive. Once in two weeks the Friars girls would meet in one of their rooms for a midnight feast.

Gina's immediate reaction was to interrupt and offer her own resignation. Almost in the same instant, she decided not to do anything until she had had a chance to persuade a few others to resign with her. She knew instinctively that she was the sort whom others followed. This had been confirmed by her latest report card where the headmistress praised her, among other things, for her leadership qualities.

Quietly and efficiently Gina set about her campaigning. In the end it was *she* who invited Joanna Sullivan, Felicity Russell and Stephanie James to the extraordinary meeting that she was convening. Since Kate was the business of the meeting, it was to be held without her knowledge. Marjorie Phillips had been deputed to keep Kate occupied while the meeting was in progress.

Honest enough with herself to recognize how strongly she identified with Kate, she wondered whether she would have felt so deeply if she had never seen Al Rizzoli (she thought of him only as Al Rizzoli, never as her father). She made a brief, incisive, emotional speech. 'Those who are for expelling Kate from Friars,' she ended emotionally, 'are those who, by actively visiting the sins of the *parent* on the children, would play God.'

'I guess we're going to vote on this?' Felicity asked.

'Of course,' Gina smiled serenely. 'Those in favour of expelling Kate raise their hands—'

Not one hand was lifted.

'Unanimous,' Gina said, smiling. 'One last thing. We will all of us have to swear on this bible that we will never say a word to Kate about any of this.'

The oaths were taken, and were not broken. Much, much later, however, when Kate did learn about it, the unexpectedness of her informant would make it seem trivial.

In January 1961 John Fitzgerald Kennedy became President, and Gina took his inspiring words to heart; 'Ask not what your country can do for you, but what you can do for your country.' The first and best way to go about this was to give every last inch of herself to her school.

So she made the most of all her years at Talbot. In her third year she played Ophelia in the school production of *Hamlet*, and she was on the debating team. She was also captain of the tennis team, and in her senior year she made a monitor. Her headmistress's remark on her most recent report card had absolutely thrilled Miriam Stern: 'All-round excellence.'

No matter how crowded her hours, she wrote regularly to both her mother and Miriam. She looked forward to the day she would be a Radcliffe freshman, but at the same time dreaded the thought of leaving.

It was during the spring recess of 1962, in her senior year, that she went with Kate and three other girls to the Biltmore Hotel in Boston. Felicity Russell's brother Brett had arranged a date for each of the girls.

Cecilia, anticipating just such an event, had a ball gown ready. It was a dress made by Cardin that Mrs Courtney had never worn because she thought it too young for her. Even if Cecilia had not had a vested interest in that stunningly simple creation she would not have made merely polite and tactful noises. The full-length sophisticated dress was of the uncluttered, simple style that Jacqueline Kennedy had adopted. To begin with the colour, a fondant-pink, was stunningly suitable for a young girl. The softly draped top was plain pink, but the checked gingham skirt in varying shades was the perfect contrast. It also had a subtle modesty; tight-waisted, it emphasized Gina's slender, reed-like shape. She felt good in the dress, and confident too. She could not have said how, or why, but she had no doubt that she was the best-looking girl that night. It may have been the fact that she was constantly surrounded by young men, or it may have been the sidelong envious glances of almost every girl, but perhaps it was because so many men alluded to her looks – her eyes, her hair, her dress. She exuded confidence and radiated energy and there was nothing brash about either.

Whatever it was, she felt beautiful.

And when Rufus Cartwright came to talk to her, she felt even more beautiful. Rufus was a Harvard Junior, and she was still at high school – what a triumph! Since meeting him at the Art Institute, she had read extensively on the history of Harvard luminaries such as James Russell Lowell, Oliver Wendell Holmes and Henry Longfellow. It therefore seemed only natural to talk about them.

'You might not look a bluestocking, but you certainly are one,' he said admiringly.

'I take that as a compliment,' she answered gravely.

'Are you going on to college?'

'Radcliffe.'

'You know that already?'

'I took early placement.'

'I suppose you've decided on your course-load?'

'For the freshman year only.' She laughed.

'Since you work so far ahead I'm going to make a date with you now – for the ball at Elliot in September.'

'Thank you,' she said softly, a smile brightening her face like a spotlight. 'I'd love to be your date. But September seems too far ahead, even for me. Couldn't we meet before then?'

They both knew he could not have accepted an invitation to the Talbot Hall Commencement Ball. Neither junior Harvard men nor even, for that matter, freshmen dated high-school girls. So he said, 'Have you ever been to the Frost Museum? It's on Birley Street, right next to Birley Pizzas.'

'They're the best pizzas in New England.'

'So you *do* know it,' he said, pleased. 'Could you meet me for lunch? Are you allowed out?'

'Miss Fotheringham knows I'm working on an extended essay on New England furniture. And Birley's *is* open on Sundays.'

'Next Sunday?'

'Next Sunday.'

As she spoke she felt a *frisson* of the sort of anxiety that is born of the fulfilment of a long-awaited dream.

Chapter Twenty-Six

'She's going out with a boy called Rufus,' Cecilia said to Miriam over lunch at Bloomingdales. 'His family is Cartwright Pharmaceuticals.'

'Cartwright Pharmaceuticals?' Miriam demanded, her bracelets clicking. 'Wow! Remember, CP for the smile of happiness? That was Cartwright's toothpaste, baby formula, CAP. You must have used that for Gina, right?'

'And she did really well on it.'

The two women smiled affectionately.

Some thought it strange, this seventeen-year-old friendship between a highly qualified pharmacist and a little-educated Italian immigrant. And yet they were as close as sisters. The friendship was important to both of them, not for what one could or could not do for the other, but rather because it was *there*, as tangible and as sheltering as a well-built house. Even so, Cecilia had never told Miriam about the trust.

'She doesn't usually make such a thing of going on a new date,' Cecilia offered. 'This time she even wrote telling me what she's going to wear.'

'Me too,' Miriam grinned. 'Her black and white checked skirt with a white sweater and matching muffler.'

'So this Rufus must be important.'

'Sure he's important,' Miriam chuckled. 'He's a Harvard man, isn't he?' The subject changed swiftly, as it always did when they were lunching together or merely talking on the telephone. 'Your new hair-style suits you.'

Cecilia's hands flew to her hair. She'd always worn a chignon, but a new stylist had persuaded her to wear it long and straight

– the sixties look, she said. 'I'm not used to it yet.' She giggled. 'It's *so* heavy.'

'That's because it's wonderfully thick. I wish I had hair like that, instead of my rats' tails.' Then, with a mischievous wink, she asked, 'Is there a new man in your life? I bet there is.'

'No,' she said emphatically. 'Mike O'Connor was and always will be the only man for me.'

'I know,' Miriam said kindly. 'You always were a one-man woman.'

Then they laughed together in the manner of those who have a profound understanding of one another.

Still astonished that he had actually made a date with a schoolgirl, Rufus Cartwright decided to keep it to himself. He simply wasn't in the mood to put up with the kind of friendly ribbing that would automatically follow. 'Sugar-daddy' and 'cradle-snatching' came to mind. He could see no good reason why he should put himself in a defensive position.

Schoolkid or not, the guys had all been knocked out by her. But besides being stunningly beautiful, she had the sort of quick, intelligent mind he had all too rarely encountered. He had sensed that the first time they had met at the Art Institute – she had been so alert then, so receptive to learning.

Had he been asked, he would have denied it, but he was a born romantic. He had a habit of tugging his thick, curly chestnut hair that gave it a touchingly boyish look. In short, he even looked like a romantic intellectual.

Certainly he would not have denied that he lusted after knowledge in the abstract. His consistently top grades proved that he was not ashamed of being an intellectual.

He found himself unaccountably anxious for the week to end so that Sunday would come. And then he chastised himself for being stupid – time can neither be lengthened nor shortened, he told himself.

He reminded himself that there was no shortage of women in

his life. Indeed, often, embarrassingly often, he was the one who was hunted. If he found the notion of lust without love somewhat primitive, it nevertheless conformed to his idea of masculinity. And although he indulged – rather more frequently than he liked to admit – in this there was something repugnant about that sort of primitive physicality, as he put it.

So why go overboard? Gina was obviously a virgin. Surely he did not aspire to be a lusting, conquering male?

That she was virginal was not in doubt. That she had depths of undreamed-of sensuality was not in doubt either. What was it – one chemistry sparking off another? He couldn't say. He only knew that he wanted her more than he had ever wanted anyone else.

The electricity of Gina's brief exchange with Rufus meant that she too had uncovered a long-hidden aspect of her personality. She was definitely *not* the sort who went in for daydreaming during the history class, but her concentration, it seemed, had taken wings. Her mind was everywhere but on her books, and, very unusually, she had been reprimanded for her inattention.

But she found herself imagining the women in his life – those in his past, those in his present and those in his future. Wave after wave of incomprehensible jealousy assailed her. If this was the passion and the pain of first love, she could do without it. Meanwhile, all manner of erotic thoughts invaded her brain.

And then, at last, it was Sunday, and on their way to the museum they met one another at the traffic-light. They stopped and regarded one another with undisguisable delight, then, walking close together, made their way to Birley's Pizza Place.

Facing her across the standard red and white gingham cloth and the empty Chianti bottle smothered in candle-wax, Rufus hoped she didn't think it corny. Coming from a back room, a taped, sugary rendering of an aria from Puccini's powerfully emotional *La Bohème* drifted over to them.

They made a great show of studying the large, colourful menus.

'What will you have, Gina?' he asked.

'You choose for me.'

'A pizza Margarita?'

'That sounds great.'

'Wine?'

'Uh, no wine for me, thanks,' she said awkwardly, not wishing to draw attention to the fact that at seventeen she was still below the legal age for drinking anything alcoholic.

'I'm not having any wine either,' he said easily. 'Coke?'

'Thanks.'

'Well,' he said after the waitress had taken their order. 'Now that that's settled we can talk.'

'Yes,' she said. But what about? she wondered, her mouth suddenly dry. Desperately casting about for something to say, she asked, 'Are you a Kennedy man?'

'How could I not be,' he said with a chuckle she found delicious, 'when I worked my butt off during the campaign?'

'I worked in the Monk's Bay office.'

'You did? Good,' he said seriously. 'I divide the world into two groups: those who are for Kennedy and those who are against him.'

'So do I.' She laughed suddenly. 'Only I hadn't realized it until this very minute.'

From then on the talk and the laughter flowed as merrily as a country brook. They leaned forward in their seats, their faces close together, taking their eyes off one another only to fork pizza into their mouths. When the meal was over she fiddled, quite unselfconsciously, with the thick layers of wax on the Chianti bottle. 'I love fooling with this stuff,' she said.

In answer he took her right hand, laid it on the table, and covered it with his. They stared long and deep into one another's eyes, and she placed her left hand on top of his, making a pile of three hands. It was an instinctual invitation to intimacy, the first one she had ever made. Her mind seemed to throb with her body; she had never experienced anything like this before.

Because there seemed to be a mutual need to project themselves into the future, they talked about their summer plans. He was going to Europe, the family had a place in Cap Ferrat; she was going to be a counsellor at a summer camp in Maine.

Meanwhile he had some tough exams in jurisprudence and, since he was after the Clarence prize, every waking second would be taken up with study. As an honours student who had made the merit list, and who would graduate *summa cum laude*, she understood.

Already, their harmony was such that it was accepted that serious dating would begin in the fall, by which time she could be a college student.

Until then they would write very, very often. Perhaps daily?

Chapter Twenty-Seven

It was a glorious excitement, this courting by letter. Gloriously old-fashioned, too. And stimulating. For it made him probe, get in touch with his private thinking. And, in getting to know himself, he was getting to know her. Slowly, almost without their awareness, their letters multiplied, for they wrote to one another even before it would have been possible for them to have a reply to a previous letter.

It was he who began to write twice a day – even if he only scribbled a few words on a postcard. Of course, the postcard would only be safely private in an envelope.

Sometimes he would write on snapshots: *Water-ski'd this morning. Exhilarating surf and sun.* For some reason this was the one that stayed in her mind. She would imagine him winging through the surf, his muscles rippling, his seductively broad shoulders gleaming, his chestnut hair water-darkened and glinting, all of him spattered by the sea.

Her letters would give accounts of the problems the children had in adjusting to a prestigious summer camp. Some were extraordinarily neglected, others over-protected and over-loved. She was pleased, she wrote to him, she'd been given the opportunity to have this sort of experience – it certainly made her appreciate the strength and the selflessness of her own mother.

She was becoming something of a respectable canoeist, she wrote. By chance, a junior tennis champion was another coun-sellor. The champion probably suffered at having to play with one as mediocre as she, but her tennis had benefited enormously. Best of all was the play she was producing. She'd opted for *Death of a Salesman*, and to her astonishment the snobby camp director had agreed. She had chosen it – she said – because she had

162

thought this was an ingenious way to get privileged kids to identify with the realities of economic hardship.

She was anxious about Dr Martin Luther King – there were reports that he would be arrested in Albany if he dared to hold a prayer meeting on the steps of the city hall.

Holidaying on the Riviera, Rufus became interested in French politics and saw parallels between the Algerians in France and the American blacks. Both Rufus and Gina were passionately committed to the National Association for the Advance of Coloured People, the NAACP. But he did not tell her that his source of information was Yvette, a French student whose fiancé was in Algeria. There was no need for her to know that he and Yvette were lovers, for they did not even try to be in love.

One blistering hot day, they stopped for lunch at Beaulieu. They ordered *moules marinière* and a bottle of chilled Chablis. While they were waiting for the *moules* he searched in his pockets for the letter he had not yet opened.

It was not a long letter, and took only a minute or so to read. He was folding the pages to return them to the envelope when he became aware of Yvette's intense stare.

'A letter from your *amoureuse*?' she said reproachfully. 'A man does not read a letter from another woman in front of the woman he had been making love with all morning.'

'Forgive me,' he said at once. 'But the letter is not from an *amoureuse*.'

'But it is from a woman, no?'

He nodded.

'You are wondering how I know it is from a woman,' she continued in the French voice he found so sexy. 'I saw you smile.' She went on after a pause, 'It was your smile, the certain smile I have myself seen you smile at certain times.'

'But she's still at high school,' he said, sounding angry.

'So?'

'Well, I'm a Harvard Senior.'

She broke into peals of laughter. Seeing his stricken face, she stopped and took his hand. 'You are too conventional,' she said gently. 'Too naïve. But that is because you are an Anglo-Saxon.' Quickly she added, 'She is about eighteen, I suppose. If you were twenty and French, you would not be ashamed to be passionately in love with a high-school girl of eighteen!'

'I'd be the laughing-stock of all the guys at Elliot—'

'A Frenchman does not care what strangers or his friends think about his love-life.' She looked out at the sparklingly white yachts moored a few yards away from the restaurant. The Mediterranean was as calm as a sheet of glass, too calm for a real sea, she thought. That is why she preferred the Atlantic. 'You will wait, I suppose, until she is a college student?'

'Yes.'

'Don't,' she said urgently. 'Don't keep her waiting. Allow yourself to be her first love, and you will be her greatest love.' A tender smile hovered about her lips. 'Besides,' she began. But stopped.

'Besides, what?'

'In you she will be getting a superbly experienced man to be her first lover,' she said, now unashamedly sentimental. 'Most young girls suffer at the gauche hands – the nervous speed – of their first man.'

'It seems as if you speak from experience.'

'But certainly I speak from experience.'

'Your Stéphane is a lucky man.'

She gave a Gallic shrug. 'I hope he knows that.'

Yvette's influence must have been very considerable for his next letter suggested they meet for lunch again at Birley's. 'I think of Birley's as our place,' he wrote, 'but it would probably be politic to keep our rendezvous to ourselves. If, by any chance, you are free on September 12th, I'll be a lucky man,' he wrote, surprised at his own humility.

That letter brought a smile to her lips, making all three dimples dance.

*

164

So the summer of 'sixty-two came to an end. The trees seemed to sing with the colour of their leaves, in myriads of subtle grades of yellow, moving from orange through to strawberry, crimson and scarlet.

Seated opposite her at Birley's, Rufus was aware only of her. Although the high windows had been constructed with views of the New England fall in mind, Gina's presence totally eliminated the landscape. Seated opposite her grave, flashing eyes, he felt, as he looked at her, as if he had been hit, physically, by a tangible yet hypnotic force. He knew he had never felt anything like this before. He felt foolish and excited and guilty. How could he feel so riotously tantalized by a high-school kid?

Staring into the glinting whites of her eyes, aware at the same time of her high pointed breasts under the soft cream sweater, he knew he would have to see her again and again. Surely he could not have fallen in love?

Lost in his own emotions, he found it a great effort to focus on what she was so earnestly saying. 'Miss Phipps, my history mistress, says we're living through a revolution in terms of black civil rights.'

Suddenly, with a warm chuckle, he said, 'I bought you a present.'

Her face shone, as if lit by a thousand-watt searchlight. 'A present?' she said, delighted. 'For me?'

'You sound like a little girl.'

'But I'm not,' she replied seriously. 'I'm not a little girl. And I'm not a big girl.' Tapping her fingers against the table-cloth, she added, 'I like to think of myself as a woman.'

'Don't you want to know what my present is, woman?' he asked.

Laughing, she nodded.

'Joan Baez singing "We Shall Overcome".'

'How did you know I wanted it?' she asked, her voice husky.

'Because I love you,' he wanted to say. But he said, 'You told me you liked Joan Baez.'

*

165

Towards the beginning of October they were again at Birley's. He found her waiting for him. 'You're beautiful, Gina,' he heard himself saying. 'You're the most beautiful girl – uh – sorry, I mean – woman that I've ever dated.'

In answer she leaned forward and took his hand.

Unexpectedly, he added, 'I need to kiss you, Gina.'

'And I need to kiss you.'

'Shall we go?'

'Yes.'

'Would you care to take a ride with me?'

'I'd love to,' she said, smilingly.

Those dimples of hers, he thought, they drive me crazy. But she's too young for me.

He helped her into his car, a chic, sleek, blue Alfa-Romeo sports.

'I just love this car,' she said admiringly.

'Did I tell you it was a present from my grandmother?' he said as he helped her into her seat.

'What's she like, your grandmother?' she called above the roar as they took off.

'What did you say?'

'I said, what's your grandmother like? She must be something special to give you an Alfa. I guess she's nuts about you.'

'She's a real powerhouse. She's not like anyone else's grand-mother, I'll tell you that,' he said, almost boastfully, she thought. 'She belongs to another century. In her own way, she's the real head of the family.'

There would be a time when Gina would wonder what it was that had made her ask him about his grandmother. For it would be this woman who would change Gina's attitude, her aspirations and even her personality – just as surely as if she had been a real witch, waving a real wand.

At last the Alfa-Romeo slowed down, and he turned into a quiet, leafy lane of elms.

'This is the Six Chimney Inn. We've been coming to the

restaurant for years. No one's here now, they go back home to Austria for the winter. So we've got the place to ourselves.'

'You mean, they leave the place *unlocked?*' she asked, astonished.

'Only the gardens,' he said with that warm chuckle she had come to know so well.

He moved forward and drew her to him. Their faces brushed against one another, and his cheek came to rest against the silky swirl of her hair, and though she had never been kissed before, she thought it one of the most beautiful moments she had ever experienced. He buried his face in the soft pillow of her hair, moving his head from time to time to kiss her cheek.

Slowly, softly, his lips approached, until they were full on her mouth. She did not resist. Instead, her lips came alive with a life of their own and parted for him and they breathed one another, so that his breath became her breath and her breath became his. Still not taking his lips from hers, his hand crept up under her sweater, under her bra, until he found her breast and its hardened nipple. At that moment she felt herself swoon with longing.

The gear shift came between them.

At last he moved his lips from hers, and she rested her head against his shoulder, and they stayed there in his car under a canopy of elms. She felt she had become her body.

After a while he gently disentangled himself and said gruffly, 'I think I should take you home.'

She made no answer. Her lips felt bruised. For a terrible moment she remembered being sullied by that man's foul embrace – that man who called himself her father. She shuddered. In an instinctive need to obliterate that memory, she pressed her mouth tighter against his, breathing him deeply, as if breathing for life.

Abruptly, she ended the kiss. 'I said I'd be back in the dorm by six. It wouldn't do for me to be late.'

'A monitor is expected to set a good example to the rest of the girls,' he teased.

They laughed then, and it was an ecstasy of laughter for they both knew that before long their togetherness would be complete.

Chapter Twenty-Eight

Three successive Saturdays of heavy necking in his uncomfortable car left Rufus trembling with frustration.

'After Thanksgiving, Lane Foster wil be spending his weekends with Charlotte in Princeton,' he said hoarsely. 'He said I could use his apartment. I only have to tell him if I want it or not.'

'Tell him yes,' she said, feeling bold and brazen and full of longing. 'Tell him you do want it. Tell him you want it very much.'

He wanted her to continue to be his secret. It was not only because she was still at high school; true, it made him reluctant to face the mockery of his fellows, but it was not the entire reason why he wanted no one to know about her. Somehow she had aroused his masculine protective instinct; he sensed that she felt that what they had between them was sacrosanct. He felt the same way.

'Does Lane know?' she asked softly, her voice slightly nervous. 'About us?'

She nodded.

'He thinks I'm involved with a married woman!'

At that they both fell about laughing. Their laughs seemed to combine with one another – his a hearty shout, and hers a musical explosion. Suddenly, at exactly the same moment, their laughter ended and they moved together, and he buried his face in the cloak of her hair, and they felt joined together, as close as if they were in the act of love. And he knew that Gina was the most important girl in his life, and that his agenda had been changed and that, all plans to the contrary, he had fallen in love.

Chapter Twenty-Nine

That Thanksgiving of 1962 was the first that Cecilia and Gina had not spent together.

Miriam's friends, the Maddoxes, lived in a typical gracious Southern home of whitewashed brick with a shingle roof, a pair of classic columns and a veranda. Their bedroom looked out on a cedar drive. A four-poster bed hung with antique lace had been in the house since it was built, well before the Civil War. Years ago, Miriam had given Cecilia *Gone with the Wind*; it was the first full-length English book she had ever read, and she had never forgotten it. She was also reminded of Scarlett O'Hara's bedroom, which overlooked a cedar drive so she could see anyone who might be coming to visit. She had been so desperately unhappy then. And afraid, as only those who are in fear for their lives can be terrified. It was when she and Gina had first been given shelter at the Children's Place, before she had met Mike O'Connor . . .

Now, looking at the cedar drive, she hugged herself as she always did when she was alone and suddenly emotional. She reflected on the distance she and Gina had travelled since then. Gina was in Connecticut with Kate Hills, waited on hand and foot by a house full of servants, while she was here, warmly welcomed by Miriam's friends, both of whom were university professors. As always, her thoughts turned to Mike – if only he could have lived to enjoy this with her. She had urged Gina to spend Thanksgiving with Kate – she would learn so much about how other people lived. Gina, of course, had not wanted to leave her and, if she had not decided to go away with Miriam, Gina would not have gone to Kate. Remembering the way in which Gina cared for her when she came home from school, Cecilia smiled. The waffles that girl could make! If only Mike could have lived to have Gina make him waffles . . .

Gina was with Kate at Severn Woods. So far, amidst all the opulence and splendour of the place, it was the worst Thanksgiving of her life.

Also the most terrifying.

She picked up the telephone and dialled the New Orleans number her mother had given her. There was no answer.

She returned to Kate's room, where she resumed her vigil at Kate's bedside. Kate looked even paler now, so white that her face was positively luminous. Again, she checked to see whether her chest was moving. Of course it was. The pain must have stopped. But she was growing more and more nervous. Kate needed a doctor, but Gina did not have the courage to ask anyone among the staff for help. Throughout the long night, she had wrestled with her conscience. But she had sworn on the Bible that no matter what happened, she would not tell anyone.

A short while ago she had decided it would be all right to tell her mother. Mama will tell me what to do, she had thought with relief. But there had been no reply. Just when she needed her most, her mother was not at the other end of the telephone. Tears of disappointment and anxiety sprang to her eyes, and she gave a soft sob. Pulling herself together, she rinsed a cloth in cold water and applied it to Kate's burning forehead.

'I don't need a doctor. I only need you,' Kate had insisted. 'Once it begins – *if* it begins – it will be over in a few hours.'

But it had begun. Whatever she had done to herself had worked. And the cramping contractions had been going on for an eternity, or so it seemed to Gina. She checked out her watch; three hours had passed.

'Thanks,' Kate whispered.

'You should have a doctor!'

'You promised.'

'Please, Kate.'

'It's harder on you than it is on me,' Kate said, her voice sounding weak. 'I can tell, it's almost finished.'

Gina rinsed yet another cloth in cold water. She placed it against Kate's forehead, which seemed even hotter, as if it had reached boiling-point. Kate moaned.

Gina slipped out of the room, found her address book, and with shivering hands dialled the number Rufus had given her.

Almost at once the phone was answered by their English butler, Alec. 'The Cartwright residence,' he said.

'May I speak with Mr Rufus Cartwright, please?'

'Certainly. Who shall I say is calling?'

'Gina O'Connor.'

'Mr Rufus is at Thanksgiving lunch,' the butler said, mild reproach in his voice. 'Do you wish to leave a message, or shall I call him to the telephone?'

'*Please* call him,' she said firmly.

'One moment, Miss O'Connor.'

Sighing, the butler made his way along the long panelled corridor towards the dining-room. It seemed wrong to disturb Mr Rufus. He went straight to him. 'I'm sorry to disturb you, Mr Rufus,' he said quietly, 'but you're wanted on the telephone.'

'Could you take a message?' Rufus asked, vaguely annoyed.

'It's a Miss O'Connor. She says it's urgent.'

'I see. Thank you, Alec.' Turning to his grandmother with his habitual politeness, he said, 'Excuse me, Grandmama, but I'll just have to take this call.'

Tilting her head and smiling gracefully, Lucia Cartwright, daughter of the Contessa de Salavincini di Capolli, said, 'Of course, my son.'

As he left, she raised her eyebrows. 'An urgent call?' she said to her son Mark.

She looked down the length of the table, noting with approval the embroidered Florentine banquet-cloth that had been a part of her trousseau fifty years earlier. She was well pleased with the floral centre-piece of yellow and white roses which made a ribbon of colour down the full length of the table. The heavy

Baccarat cut-crystal water-goblets, wineglasses and champagne-flutes shimmered under the vast crystal chandelier. The intricately sculpted silver formed a perfect frame for the late-eighteenth-century navy-blue Sèvres porcelain. The initialled silver cutlery glinted in the lamplight. The eighteenth-century Beauvais tapestry on the walls represented something of a triumph. Her daughter-in-law had been against the idea of hunting tapestries, but had agreed to experiment with them. In the end, she had fallen in love with them too.

Everything on this table was as beautiful as it was valuable. And every single piece of it would one day belong to Rufus.

A phone call in the middle of Thanksgiving was a highly unusual event. If she wanted more detailed information, she would have to have a word with Alec. Nothing could be simpler.

The butler's footsteps echoed across the wires. He must be walking on marble, Gina guessed correctly. But did he have to walk so slowly?

Perhaps she ought not to have called. In fact, she knew she was doing the wrong thing. Interrupting a Thanksgiving meal meant committing a social gaffe of the worst sort. But, she argued with herself, what choice did she have? Their farm at New Prestyn was not too distant from the Hillses' place. Surely they knew of a doctor?

She felt as if she were drowning in terror. She was lost and afraid and ignorant. Of course she was terrified for Kate, but her own overwhelming ignorance was a different kind of terror. She struggled to recall everything she had read about miscarriages, but her mind appeared to have registered nothing but the unearthly screams of women in agony.

Kate had refused to name the father, or she would have been able to contact him. But the mere mention of who the father might be had sent Kate into hysterics.

Desperate, she began to pray. 'Mary, Mother of God, she must not die. Don't let Kate die—'

It was at least two minutes before Rufus reached the library, where he could take his call in private.

'Gina, honey, what is it?' he asked, concerned.

'It's Kate—' She found she could not go on.

'Kate? Hello? Gina?'

'Yes.'

'Gina, if you don't tell me what's wrong, I can't help.'

Forcing self-control, she said, 'Kate needs a doctor. We're at her summer place.' Her voice broke down. 'She's seriously ill. She's having a miscarriage.'

Abortion, Rufus corrected mentally. But he said, 'You're asking me to call our family doctor and—'

'If I had his name I could call him myself.'

'Hang in there, Gina honey. I'll get right back to you. You're at Severn Woods, right?'

'Right,' she murmured.

'Let me have your phone number.'

Speaking very quickly, she told him.

Hours ago, when it had all begun, Gina had automatically picked up the telephone to call an ambulance. 'What are you doing?' Kate had yelled.

'Why, I'm calling an ambulance,' Gina had answered reasonably.

'You idiot! I'll be sent to prison if you call an ambulance.'

It seemed an age before the phone rang again. 'Dr Streckels has called the Parkside Clinic and they're expecting her.' Rufus's voice was clear and concise and authoritative. 'Dr Streckels and Dr Dexter will be waiting for her at the Parkside Clinic.'

'Kate'll go crazy if I call an ambulance.'

'An ambulance is already on the way. I called it myself,' he said gently. 'Go get Kate ready.'

Kate made no comment when Gina returned to her bedside. She had already lost consciousness. Her heart pounding in her own ears, Gina hastily grabbed Kate's wrist.

*

173

'That was rather a long call, dear,' said Lucia to Rufus when he returned to the table. 'Nothing serious, I trust?'

'Nothing too devastating,' he replied absently.

From the far-away look in his eyes, it was obvious to Lucia that his thoughts were elsewhere. He seemed tense and excited, and at the same time deeply troubled. Lucia's serene eyes were quickly shadowed by distrust. Up until this moment, she reflected, she had been sure that Rufus would not lose his heart any faster than his head. Now she was not so certain.

She wondered who the girl was. An outsider, of course. She had long since compiled a list of eligible families from which Rufus would choose a suitable wife. Lucia was not unduly alarmed. 'Power,' an old Chinese proverb states, 'is wealth.'

The Cartwrights therefore had their own powerful way of dealing with outsiders.

At the Parkside Clinic Gina willingly surrendered Kate to Dr Dexter. Now that the terrible burden of responsibility for Kate's life had been lifted from her, she fell into a sudden storm of weeping. Although it passed as quickly as it had begun, Gina was compelled to struggle for control. This time it was laughter that threatened to get the better of her. She wanted to laugh because Dr Dexter had told her how tragic it would be if Kate's haemorrhage could only be stopped by drastic surgery such as a hysterectomy.

'Is her life in danger?' Gina had asked.

'There is an element of risk in all surgery,' Dr Dexter had answered.

Because the doctor had not denied that Kate's life was in danger, her life was the only thing that counted. What did it mattter if she had to lose her uterus in order to pay for her life?

Restlessly pacing the small waiting-room reserved for the family of patients in surgery, she did not hear the nurse come in. The first she knew of the nurse's presence was when her name was called. 'Miss O'Connor?' the nurse said in that tone of professional sympathy that is always so frightening.

Her voice a rasp of terror, Gina answered, 'Yes. How is she?' The words tumbled out so quickly that it sounded as if they were all joined together.

'Miss Hills is still in surgery. The – uh, surgical procedure takes more than two minutes, you know.' She clicked her tongue reprovingly. 'There was a call for you. Mr Rufus Cartwright would like you to return his call. He left his phone number.' Gina moved towards the phone on the coffee table. 'The phone company is coming to check that phone. It's not working. There's a pay phone along the corridor.'

Dazed, Gina followed her directions only to discover that in her anxious rush to get Kate to the hospital she had left her purse behind at Severn Woods. She had no money to pay for the call. She had no choice. She would simply have to call collect. No doubt she would be asked if her call was urgent.

She placed her call and almost at once, to her absolute joy and limitless gratitude, Rufus answered the phone himself. Years and years later she would know that it was at that moment that she had accepted that she was well and truly and hopelessly and permanently in love with him. Full of strength and support and sympathy, he was there for her, and she would willingly have died for him. But for this emergency, she never would have had to turn to him and it was for this reason that Kate became an inextricable part of her life.

'How is she?' he asked.

'She's still in surgery,' she answered.

'How much longer will it be?'

'I don't know.'

'I'll meet you at the hospital. I'll be there within the hour.' His tone a mixture of confidence and humour, he added, 'Don't go away, honey. Wait for me!'

Thanksgiving was perhaps even more important to Lucia than it had been to Theodore; it was vividly indisputable proof that she had indeed brought up her children to be patriotic American Catholics.

175

Thanksgiving at the Cartwrights was also a house party. No one was expected to leave until after Sunday lunch, when the long weekend would come to an official close.

It is therefore not too difficult to imagine the uproar that followed Rufus's apologetic – but determined – departure.

He had been heard to mention a meeting at a hospital. Grandmother and mother communicated silently. An anxious knowing look was exchanged. Decoded, the look meant: could Rufus have got a girl into trouble?

Looking out at the gentle falling snow, Gina sat at the window, waiting for him. Kate had come round from the anaesthetic and was now safely tucked into a bed in a private room. Gina had been frightened by Kate's pallor, and was greatly relieved when a nurse had explained that it was due to the anaesthetic.

He saw her at once as he entered the foyer. She had not heard his approach and was startled when she heard him call her name.

'How is she?' he said.

'Fine,' Gina said. 'She's sleeping now. She'll be okay.'

'Let's get out of here,' he said. 'I hate hospital smells.'

He helped her into the car and they drove off. For a while neither spoke. She felt faint, and realized she had not eaten since breakfast, ten hours earlier. 'I'm starving,' she said.

'Here,' he said, flipping open the glove-box, 'have some chocolate.'

She ate it quickly and said, 'Thanks. Boy, did I need that.'

They stopped at a traffic-light, and he turned left. He should have made a right here to get to the Hillses' place, she thought. 'Where are we going?' she asked.

In answer, he pulled the car off the road and took her in his arms. He kissed her deeply. 'You taste of chocolate,' he said. He took a great clump of her hair in his hands. 'Do you want to go back to Kate's house?'

She shook her head.

'Will you come with me to a very special place I know?'

176

She nodded. She'd go anywhere with him – surely he knew that?

'I'll call them,' he said quickly. 'We'll stop at a pay phone – I'll check if it's okay.'

He switched on the ignition and the engine roared back to life. Minutes later he stopped the car and made his call. 'It's all arranged,' he said quietly. 'We're going to the Elm Walk Inn.'

'I'm glad,' she said. She loved his old-fashioned way of speaking.

A delicate electric current seemed to flow between them. The silence was delicate, too. A steady rain was falling, and she felt safe in the cocoon of his car. Suddenly he swung the car into a long curving driveway that reminded her of Kate's country house.

He stopped the car in front of the colonial-styled house and went inside. Moments later he returned triumphantly, carrying a key on a large wooden holder. 'The manager is a friend of mine. He's given us the guest-house,' he said. He drove up to the guest-house and let her in. Then he left her to park his car.

She was nervous and excited. Standing at the threshold of the bedroom, dazed, she was aware of every detail of the way in which it had been decorated.

It was more like a doll's house, she thought. Bright floral chintzes decorated the minute living-room. A huge, raised four-poster bed took up most of the bedroom. A stepstool stood in front of the bed, which fitted snug against the walls.

Then he was back and they were together, swaying in one another's arms. Then, still kissing her, he lifted her off her feet and set her down gently on the tall bed.

And then he was beside her, unravelling her clothes, unravelling the quilt. Afterwards, she never knew how he had managed to undress her, and himself, and the bed, and even protect her from pregnancy. She was nervous and wanting, but not at all shy. All was natural. All was right. All was inevitable. Along with their bodies, their souls soared dizzyingly, reaching heights, moderation too, and he was gentle and caring and experienced.

177

After it was over they lay together quietly, touching, kissing, exploring, nibbling. He whispered that he loved her body, her high pointed breasts especially, and she pressed herself closer, closer to him.

She forgot about Kate, and the horror and pain of the long day, and opened herself to him.

The dawn came suddenly. And, just as suddenly, Kate came into her mind and she felt guilty.

'I must call the Parkside Clinic,' she murmured, slipping out of bed.

When she came back Rufus asked, 'How is she?'

'She's doing well, they say. She's been asleep all night.' Then, although she had not planned to say anything of the kind, she said, 'I wish I knew who the father was.' She shook her head and added, 'I didn't even know she had a boyfriend.'

'She's okay and that's the main thing,' Rufus said, taking her in his arms again.

Exhausted and spent, they fell asleep. By the time Gina awoke, she saw that it was already nine o'clock. Rufus was nowhere to be seen. Then she heard the sound of running water, and knew that he was in the bathroom. She got up, knocked on the door, and when there was no reply guessed – correctly – that he was in the shower.

She needed a shower too, and went to join him. He washed her, and soaped her everywhere. And they raced to the bed, and left the shower running, and much later, when they remembered it was still running, they laughingly returned to it and showered once more.

Then it was time to leave, so he towel-dried her hair and gave her coffee in the little kitchenette.

They held hands on the way back to the Parkside Clinic. 'Would you like me to come in with you?' he asked.

'I wish you would,' she said, 'but that would be wrong. I wouldn't want Kate to have even the slightest hint that the night that was so terrible for her was the most beautiful night of my life.'

'Where will you say you've been all night?'

178

'If she asks me, I'll say I was at an all-night diner. If not, I'll say nothing.'

'How will you get back to Kate's place?'

'I'll take a cab, of course.'

'I knew you'd say that,' he said, looking at her adoringly. 'You didn't bring a purse with you, remember?'

'You're right. I haven't got a single dime.' She laughed suddenly. 'I guess I'll just have to ask you for some money, just like a call-girl.'

'Here, take this,' he said, handing her two twenty-dollar bills.

'I'll give it back to you,' she said, her tone unexpectedly serious.

'Sure you will,' he said, his mind elsewhere. 'Will you call me and tell me how she is?'

'No one must ever know about her—' she began.

'And no one will ever know about our magical night.'

'I love you for saying that, Rufus.'

'You'll call me?'

She did not relish the thought of speaking to that daunting butler again. But she said nothing about that. 'When's the best time?' she asked.

'Any time. I'll be home all day.'

As soon as the antiseptic hospital smells assailed her, she felt guilty and afraid. She was convinced that something terrible must have happened to Kate.

Chapter Thirty

Tall, slender and unusually fit, Theodore Cartwright at seventy-five was still as handsome as he was elegant. Though not as powerful on the tennis court as he had been in his youth, he was by no means a weak player. The indoor court he had built at Cartwright House meant that tennis was a year-round sport. Whenever he was there instead of in New York – as was more and more frequent these days – Peter Anderson, his tennis coach, was there to keep him up to scratch. His self-discipline was as relentless as his need to dominate his family. But if he was a tyrant, he was at least a courtly tyrant.

His sense of conservative patriotism had strengthened with the years, which was only one of the reasons why both his affection and his respect for his son, Mark, had steadily diminished. Perhaps if Mark had not gone as far as to be a conspicuous contributor to Jack Kennedy's presidential campaign, things might have been different. For if Mark, and for that matter his wife, Fran, had had enough common sense to keep quiet about it, their relationship would not have deteriorated into a state of undeclared civil war rather than an armed truce. As Theodore saw it, while Franklin Roosevelt was a traitor to his class, the Kennedys were plain dishonest. In any case, the Kennedys had no class.

Theodore could find little or nothing of either his wife's or his personality in their son. Where his parents were confident and commanding, he was courteous and considerate, almost as if he felt there was something manifestly unjust about having been born to so much power. Theodore and Lucia kept German shepherds; Mark and Fran kept lurchers. Sometimes it seemed to Theodore that these coarse cross-breeds were just one of the many weak messages his son sent out to signal his independence of thought. The fact that Mark and Fran chose to support repertory theatre, two obscure literary journals, an avant-garde art gallery and a non-commercial radio station when they could equally have endowed a chair at Harvard or Yale or Princeton, was as maddening as it was childish.

Where Theodore sought fierce competitiveness, Mark preferred cosy amiability. How, he wondered, could he have sired such a son? And yet Mark had a Purple Heart and a Silver Medal. It seemed to him that Mark was more of a liberal than a businessman – a do-gooder who put prestige before profit. Still, if Theodore Cartwright could stay at the helm just long enough for his grandson, Rufus, to take over from him, Cartwright Pharmaceuticals would be safe. Satisfied that his grandson's quick brain was equal to his ruthless sense of reality, Theodore had always believed that no woman would ever get the better of him.

There was nothing to be done about it: Mark – his own son – lacked the killer instinct.

Fortunately, however, Rufus, his grandson, had inherited it; it had skipped a generation, that was all. But he had not yet put it to the right sort of use. He had all the makings of a shrewd businessman, yet he chose to dice with death. Rufus and his fast cars. Rufus, the gifted scuba diver, hang-glider and champion of the Aspen ski runs. Rufus, who had the strength to believe in his own immortality.

He admired Rufus's daredevilry, but was afraid of it too. He thought sometimes that Rufus was too handsome for his own good, and yet he would find himself irresistibly drawn to feast his eyes on him.

With his head of tight chestnut curls, blue, humorously intelligent eyes, graceful long legs and generous lips, Rufus's relaxed kind of animal sensuality was as attractive to men as it was to women. He had a hearty infectious laugh for everyone, and a low, intimate laugh for women. But he was also given to wild whoops of laughter that sounded like shattering mirrors.

Whether he felt contempt or admiration, affection or dislike for his father and grandfather, not even he could say. For all that, leaving Cartwright House on Thanksgiving was as shocking and even as offensive – not to say unforgivable – to him as it was to the rest of the family. Indeed, it was as great a lapse in manners as if he had chosen to go skiing instead of to his aunt's funeral . . .

'Who is she?' Mark asked Fran when they were quite private in their soothing sitting-room. As it was Mark's policy as well as his inclination to live and let live, his curiosity over a mere telephone call could only have been motivated by something as strange as his son's abrupt departure from the Thanksgiving table.

'According to Alec, she's called Gina O'Connor,' Fran replied with a shrug. ' "She sounds young," he said. "Younger, madam," he told your mother, "than the usual young ladies who call." '

'How on earth does Alec know that?'

'Apparently she said it was extremely urgent. An older woman would not have been so frank, Alec feels. He tried to dissuade her from interrupting our Thanksgiving lunch. Alec was very put out, your mother says—' She paused for a moment to examine her Thanksgiving present, a simple, gold Patek Philippe watch, before continuing. 'Your mother is sure that Gina O'Connor must be a very determined young woman.'

'What's all this fuss about?' Mark said, as reprovingly as if he had not been the one to draw Fran's attention to it. 'The boy's not yet twenty-one and everyone reacts as if a call from a girl on Thanksgiving can only mean bad news!'

'I'm sure you're right,' Fran said, moving closer to lay her head on his shoulder. 'It's just that your father certainly gave me a hard time about his Thanksgiving being disturbed by a stranger.'

'Christ!' Mark exploded. 'Why shouldn't Rufus have a girlfriend if he wants to? And who the hell gives a damn what his grandfather thinks?'

But they were not nearly as independent of Theodore as the

182

world believed them to be. True, they could support the charities of their own choice, but that was only because tax considerations had compelled Theodore to set up an additional foundation in Rufus's name. There was a time when Fran's family could have all but bought and sold the Cartwright family, but a disastrous real-estate investment or two had put an end to that.

Why, even the country house on the Cartwright land that had been given to them after Mark had returned – as a hero – from the war did not, in fact, belong to them. It was part of a trust, and the trustees were beholden to Theodore Cartwright and not to his son.

At precisely 7 a.m. the following morning, Theodore was – as always – on his way down to breakfast. A few feet from the head of the elegantly curved, wide staircase he was stopped in his tracks for there, outside Rufus's room, lying in a dismal heap, was Caesar, the German shepherd who had made Rufus his own. It was only when Rufus stayed over with his grandparents that Caesar deserted his habitual kitchen basket for Rufus's room. If Rufus had been in his room, Caesar would not have been outside the door – a huge hunk of misery – waiting for him. Clearly Rufus had not returned home last night, and this was Thanksgiving weekend! Even so, he decided to check. He turned the handle and flung the door open. Rufus's bed was untouched. He was with that girl who had disturbed their Thanksgiving dinner.

Lucia, who had spent the entire night waiting for Rufus to come home, was (very unusually) at the breakfast table ahead of Theodore.

'I thought that just this once we'd forget about cholesterol and so I ordered bacon and eggs for you, dear,' she said soothingly.

Even as she spoke, the steaming plate was set before him. 'Nothing quite like sinning early in the morning,' Theodore said gruffly. Suddenly he pushed his plate away. 'I have no appetite today,' he growled.

At a glance from Lucia the maid removed his plate.

'Mr Cartwright will have some grapefruit,' she said.

'He didn't come home last night,' Theodore said in an ominously calm tone. 'Who is this girl whose call was urgent enough to take my grandson away on Thanksgiving?'

'I believe she's called Gina O'Connor.'

'You'd better get to know a little more about her than her name.'

'Of course, dear,' Lucia said impassively. 'I'll take the matter in hand.'

They looked at each other across the wide breakfast table. It was a look of utter harmony, of complete understanding of their lifelong partnership: Theodore shaped the bullets, and Lucia fired them.

When Rufus arrived home, he came in quietly through the kitchen door. He had planned to go up to his room, freshen up and then come down apparently as naturally as if he had spent the night in his own bed. But when Alec saw something in his expression, a youthful sort of dreaminess and wonderment, it moved him to say, 'Your grandparents are at breakfast. I suppose you'll be joining them, Mr Rufus?'

'Thanks for letting me know, Alec,' Rufus replied, with a hearty, infectious laugh. 'I believe I will join them.'

The large, colourful and cheerful breakfast-room could well have been a dining-hall. A log fire made of pinewood blazed at one end; lunch and dinner were served in the vast brocaded dining-hall.

Rufus approached his grandparents with his usual enthusiastic smile and, after dropping a kiss on each tired cheek, said, 'You're up early, Grandma. It's almost worth the kind of rough night I had last night to have breakfast with you.'

'What happened?' asked Lucia, careful not to turn her immaculately coiffed head towards her husband. 'You must be exhausted if you've only just got in.'

'A fraternity brother of mine got into a tight corner,' Rufus said, amazed how easily the quickly invented lie tripped off his lips. 'Got his girl-friend to call me to bail him out. I wasn't all that happy about having to interrupt our Thanksgiving, but what could I do?'

'I take it you solved the problem?' Theodore said nonchalantly.

'It took some doing, I can tell you,' Rufus said, shaking his head. 'He got into a brawl. He can't hold his drink.' Downing a glass of orange juice in a single gulp, he continued, 'I'll sure have one reformed character on my hands.'

'I'm glad you did your duty, son,' Theodore said warmly. 'Always do your duty by a friend.'

'I'll say,' Rufus replied.

Of course it was understood that to have mentioned his friend's name would have broken the code of gentlemanly conduct.

The talk turned towards Theodore's newest philanthropic project – a new chair of Astrophysics at the University of Bridgewater.

It was outside visiting-hours, but as Gina claimed that she was the closest to Kate's next-of-kin in America at this time, she was allowed to see her. She sat quietly beside her friend, watching the life-giving substances from the IV – the blood and the saline – dripping down into her arms. As she took Kate's white and fragile-looking hand into her own, she seemed to go even paler. Frightened, but fighting for calm, she manoeuvred Kate's wrist into a position where she could feel her pulse. Her own mouth was dry with fear. She could feel nothing, no sign of life, and yet she could see the regular rise and fall of her chest. She leapt from her chair and raced out, calling loudly for a nurse.

In a flash Nurse Osborn was at Kate's bedside, taking her pulse. For Gina there was something surreal in the waxen look on Kate's face in that still, white room. She felt as if her own brain had been divided in two, one half watching and keenly observing, the other frozen in a state of acute denial.

And then the nurse looked up and smiled. 'She's going to be fine,' she said firmly. 'She's doing very well.' She busied herself with the fine plastic tubing. 'Your friend is a lucky young woman, a very lucky young woman. She had a narrow escape.'

Gina felt an insane urge to jump up and kiss the nurse's hand. Instead she heard herself saying, 'Then she's not going to die?'

'Oh, you poor child,' Nurse Osborn said sympathetically. 'This must be a terrible time for you, too.' Leaning over Kate, she said, 'Kate, say hello to your friend. Tell her you're okay.'

Kate's eyes fluttered open. She shut them quickly.

'See?' Nurse said, satisfied. 'She's doing great.'

'My name's Gina O'Connor,' Gina said. 'And I'd like to thank you.'

Nurse Osborn regarded her with sympathy. 'It isn't easy to be a woman,' she said quietly. 'It never has been, and it never will be—' And then, in her flat, sturdy white shoes, a vision in white, she reached the doorway. 'But I guess it's worth it.'

The day wore on and the anaesthetic wore off. At last Kate spoke. 'Promise me you'll never, never tell anyone about this,' she said in a fierce whisper.

'Of course I won't. I already promised you, didn't I?'

'Promise me *again*!'

'I promise—'

'Say I promise I'll never never tell anyone or God will strike me dead.'

With a heavy heart, but knowing there was no way out, Gina repeated the words.

Satisfied, Kate drifted back to sleep.

But Gina knew she had betrayed her. She had told Rufus. What else could she have done? In point of fact it was Rufus who had saved Kate's life. Still, she *had* promised. It was all so very confusing – where she had expected to feel guilt, she felt nothing but a mixture of relief and exaltation.

Chapter Thirty-One

Early in May, in the unseasonal heat, when the air was still moist and warm even though the sun was gone, Tina Rizzoli lay on her bed quite naked. The hill of her stomach obscured her fat toes from her view. She had just returned from visiting her brother, Al, at St Luke's Hospital. Slow, fat tears travelled over the mounds of her cheeks and down her throat. Staring at her limp, unused breasts, she cupped one in each clammy hand.

Al was dying. A massive heart attack meant that there was no hope for him. They had connected him up to a machine with a moving red light flashing numbers to tell them what his heart was doing. Oxygen-giving tubes had been fed into his nose.

One thing and one thing only was keeping Al Rizzoli alive, the little girl he spoke of over and over again. 'My little girl. My sweet little girl. I must see her,' he had whimpered again and again. 'It's my last dying wish.' His weary but intense eyes burned into her. 'At least let me die in peace—'

'You're not dyin', Al,' she had whispered.

'Quit kiddin', it's too late for that.' His weak voice trembling, he added, 'I want my little girl from the *Harton*.'

Which is why she lay on the bed now, contemplating the outsize maternity dress she was going to wear to go to see Gina at her school. Until Al's illness and her visits to the hospital, she had almost never ventured from the apartment. He had bought her the few clothes she needed. Now she had even made the huge effort to go out and buy this new vast orange and black floral dress, as well as a pair of shoes.

After choosing the dress, she had bought herself a bag of caramel corn. She reached a fat hand into the bag now, and quickly crammed a fistful into her mouth. It was delicious, and for a brief moment or two she felt a little better about the world at large and her life in particular.

It was four years since her brother had returned home after seeing Gina for the first time in more than ten years. He had come back with a bruised and swollen arm that had turned out to be broken. Although he had never told her what had happened, she had, of course, had her own suspicions. As far as she knew, he had not seen her again face to face, yet he had somehow kept track of her doings, and knew that she was a student at this fancy school, Talbot Hall.

To be sure, Gina could not be ashamed of an aunt who was wearing such a lovely clean new dress. These days lots of men and women were overweight. The only thing Gina might be ashamed of were her shoes. The only shoes that would fit her were men's moccasins that looked more like slippers than shoes; come to think of it, they probably were slippers . . .

Gina would be shocked, of course. She probably didn't even know she had an aunt.

Tina had never seen Al like that, so weak, as dependent as a baby. He was worn out, probably too sick even to be angry with her. It gave her a funny feeling, this change in him. The constant talk about his innocent young girl, the beautiful young girl of whom he was so proud. All the festering pus of hate had gone out of him like a lanced boil.

These past several years Al had got himself a job working nights, cleaning doctors' offices. That was lucky; a nurse had found him. They said he had probably collapsed only about an hour or so before . . . Even the doctor had said he'd been lucky – a little while longer and it would have been all over.

Her eyes took on a cunning look. They'd given her the money Al had had on him, and she was going to use it now. She had a small secret emergency fund of her own too. She had already paid for the dress and the shoes, and now she would have to spend still more money to get to Gina's fancy school.

She could not face heaving herself on to buses, then climbing out of subway cars. She was terrified of standing, caged in the

188

crowd, or of being squeezed too tight in a seat. It was kind of suffocating in the trains.

So she had hired a limousine and a driver. As the car-hire company had rather contemptuously told her, all limousines were air-conditioned. Then, when the girl at the other end of the phone at Limo-Lux heard where she lived, she'd immediately insisted on a cash deposit. What could she do? She'd had to spend on a taxi to get there.

Tomorrow morning the limo would collect her.

Tina felt more than a little ashamed of herself. Her poor brother was dying, and she was looking forward to riding in a limo . . .

The next morning she was ready at least an hour before the limo was due to arrive. She sat patiently on the sturdy kitchen bench, staring out at the black fire-escape, as absorbed in it as if she were looking at the sea and the froth and the movement of the waves. At last the limo arrived and, for the first time in her life, she saw the spacious interior of a stretch Cadillac.

Fortunately the driver, a tall, powerful man called Gerry, who used to work in a Ford assembly line, had no difficulty helping her in. Once she was seated, he gently removed the large tote bag and an equally large paper bag from her clutched hands and offered her a drink. Then he opened a cupboard inside the door and a miniature bar with crystal decanters and glasses was revealed.

'I'd like a beer,' she said quickly.

'Schlitz or Schlotz, ma'am?'

'Schlitz . . .'

She took a sip and then thought it would not look right, arriving at this fancy school with beer on her breath. Gerry shut the door. She opened it. 'I guess I'll have one of my own Cokes this early in the morning,' she said, pushing her glass of beer towards him.

He took the glass and she immediately removed a Coke-bottle and an opener from her paper bag.

189

'But, ma'am, if anybody wants Cokes we got Cokes,' Gerry said, sounding annoyed. Taking the Coke from her hands, he continued, 'Allow me to offer you one of ours. It'll be colder.'

'Thanks,' Tina said. 'Can we go now? I don't want to be late.'

The car moved off smoothly and she sank back into the amazingly comfortable leather seat. The only just discernible scent of a Havana cigar clung to the leather and it reminded her of someone. It was highly pleasurable. She tried to recall who or what it was, but gave up and contemplated Gerry's elegantly cut grey uniform instead. Here she was, Tina Rizzoli, riding in a fancy limo with a fancy driver, all paid with her own private money. It was so good, looking through the smoked-glass windows that screened her from everyone else, that she removed the dark glasses that she habitually wore.

She sank her hand into her bag of caramel corn, put less than usual into her mouth at one time, and ate more slowly.

Frankly, she was nervous about meeting the headmistress, Miss Armstrong. Marvelling at the words that had come into her mouth at the time, she went over their conversation again.

She had left her name and telephone number with Miss Armstrong's secretary. She had asked for the principal, but the secretary had said that she assumed Tina meant Miss Armstrong, the headmistress. 'Yes,' Tina had replied. 'I need to speak to her urgent,' she had said. 'Somethin' personal.'

'In connection with?' the secretary had asked smoothly.

'One of her students.'

She had just returned from the hospital and vowed that she would sit beside the phone until it rang.

About an hour later, Miss Armstrong was on the phone. 'Miss Rizzoli?'

'That's me, Miss Armstrong.'

'I believe you wished to speak with me on a personal matter?'

'Personal *and* urgent,' Tina replied, her voice shaking with emotion, 'or I wouldn't waste your time—'

'Could you give me some indication what it's about?'

'I need to see you to tell you, ma'am,' Tina said respectfully.

'Very well, then,' Miss Armstrong said briskly. 'Tomorrow morning at 11.30.'

The car-hire company said it would take two and a half hours. Just in case it took longer, Tina reserved the car from 8.30.

She was glad the head teacher was called *Miss* Armstrong. It meant she wasn't married either. An old maid, just like me, she thought with more than a little satisfaction . . .

As the car drew into the long elm-lined driveway leading into Talbot Hall, Tina gasped. She had seen this sort of sumptuous environment before on television, on *As the World Turns*, but – as she put it to herself – she had never thought of entering such a place in person. Rolling lawns, towering trees, tennis courts – why, it was like being on a film set. It was far more beautiful than she had imagined it to be. Al's description had been very vague. 'Big,' he'd said. 'Hundreds of acres.'

Posing as a delivery man, Al had driven right in, getting as far as the kitchens. Then he'd pretended he'd gone to the wrong address . . . It was cruel, real cruel, the way his own daughter, his flesh and blood, had been kept from him.

Now he was dying, and he had begged to see her. His blood coursed through her veins – he was Gina's father, her blood relation.

Bitch or no bitch, Gina was his daughter and he had every right to see her.

They drew up to the portico and stopped the car. As Gerry helped her haul her massive body out of the car, he saw that the large tote bag was still clamped in her hand. Automatically polite – and practical – he attempted to remove the bag from her tight grasp: she would be able to move more easily without it.

'Don't touch that bag!' she snapped.

'But, ma'am, I'll give it to you just as soon as you're out the door.'

'Thanks for nothin'!' Tina said irritably. 'I'll keep it myself.'

191

Gerry sent his eyes to the sky and gave a shrug. 'As you wish.'

At last, breathing heavily, her moccasins slapping against the flagstone corridors, she was directed towards Miss Armstrong's study. She bludgeoned her way past the spluttering secretary and barged into Miss Armstrong's study. Seeing her huge bulk negotiate the doorway, Miss Armstrong rose from her desk and went forward to meet her. Because it was at once obvious that the chair in front of the desk would not accommodate her uninvited, unknown and bizarre guest, Miss Armstrong led her towards the leather couch that had been in the mahogany-panelled study for about eighty years – ever since the school was founded.

Sinking into her seat, Tina wrinkled her nose in distaste. This was a very different kind of leather from the limo's, she thought. The couch belonged in a junk-yard.

'How can I help you?' Miss Armstrong asked pleasantly, coming directly to the point.

Patting her tote bag, Tina said, 'I'm here to see you about one of your students.'

'I see,' Miss Armstrong said, lifting her brows. 'May I ask the name of the girl?'

'Gina Rizzoli. My niece.'

'We've no one of that name here, I'm afraid.'

'You'll recognize *this*, I reckon,' Tina said triumphantly. Her puffy, broad hands surprisingly nimble, she deftly removed the large blown-up photograph of Cecilia and Gina taken during the Kennedy campaign. After wordlessly handing it over to an increasingly aghast Miss Armstrong, she withdrew yet another poster-size photograph from her bag. This one showed Gina and her father laughing into the camera, the three distinctive dimples the undeniable stamp of their blood tie.

Ready for the attack, Miss Armstrong stiffened and said nothing.

Now Tina spoke the words she had so often rehearsed. 'Gina O'Connor is Gina Rizzoli and you can't deny it!'

'There must be some mistake,' Miss Armstrong began.

Tina cut in roughly. 'Her father is my brother and dyin'. It's

192

his heart. Al is going to *die*, the doctor told me,' she sobbed. She took out a man-sized Kleenex and blew her nose loudly. Her great shoulders shook as a fit of weeping overtook her. She covered her face with her hands.

He heavy legs reminded Miss Armstrong of the trunks of oak trees. 'I'm very sorry to hear about your brother's illness,' she said sympathetically.

'He's beggin' to see her. His doctor told me I should come here to tell you.'

'You were right to come,' Miss Armstrong said tactfully.

Tina's weeping stopped abruptly. 'I want to see Gina *now*,' she said, her voice shrill.

Twenty-two years as headmistress of Talbot meant that Miss Armstrong was more than a little familiar with the emotional turbulence of young women. Nothing in the world would have induced her to expose Gina to this lump of weeping flesh who claimed to be her aunt. Her blood relation! Why, the very idea of a Talbot girl being connected with anything like this common blob of inferior humanity was nothing short of preposterous. All the same, she would have to inform Gina's mother of these strange events.

'I do wish you could have informed me of your intended visit,' Miss Armstrong said politely. 'Unfortunately her seminars are not on the campus this week,' she lied easily. 'They're on a field-study expedition in Colorado.'

'Well, then, call her and tell her to get her ass back here real quick!' Tina commanded.

'I most certainly will do as you ask,' the headmistress said, smiling one of her diplomatic smiles. 'Now, if you would be kind enough to leave us your telephone number, we'll call you just as soon as they return to their base tonight.'

'You do that,' Tina said, her voice now ominously calm. Pointing towards the photograph of Cecilia and Gina, she continued, 'Y'see, they were in this newspaper, and so that's how my poor brother found his daughter again. Ten years he don't seen her, his own flesh and blood.' Her voice broke. 'He finds her, he goes to see her on a Wednesday. Thursday he's so happy, he's like a kid in a tub of ice-cream. Then he goes to see her again.' Stopping to slap her thighs in disgust, she went on, 'That Thursday he went to Monk's Bay, she called the cops.' Now her voice dropped to a horrified whisper. 'And what do the cops do? They beat him up so bad his arm broke. His own daughter set the cops on him. And now he's on his deathbed in the hospital and he wants to see her one last time.'

'I can understand that,' Miss Armstrong said. She stood up and put her hand out to help Tina heave herself from the couch.

'You sure could do with some new furniture,' Tina said. Casting a lingering, suspicious look around Miss Armstrong's office she handed her the photographs. 'Keep them,' she said. 'You'll need 'em.'

'Why – that's very kind,' Miss Armstrong began.

'I've got duplicates, or I wouldn't give you them,' Tina said fiercely.

After having conducted Tina to the waiting limousine, Miss Armstrong returned to her study immediately and examined the photographs again. Her severe, calm face was pulled into a tight, deep frown: beyond all reasonable doubt these photographs were genuine. It was all too obvious that Tina Rizzoli was genuine too. She rolled the photographs carefully and, after encircling them with an elastic band, she hid them behind her thirteen-volume Oxford Dictionary.

What to do?

The whole thing was outside her experience. There was, however, one person whom she could consult. Gina's mother, Cecilia O'Connor.

Chapter Thirty-Two

Above all Miss Armstrong did not want to frighten Cecilia, but she knew that her very name would set the alarm bells ringing. Consequently she chose her words with great care.

'Mrs O'Connor?' she began.

'Speaking,' said Cecilia.

'I'm Miss Armstrong from Talbot Hall and I'm calling to let you know that Gina has been an excellent head girl. The whole school will miss her when she goes to Radcliffe.'

'Why, thank you for saying so,' Cecilia said, her voice high with pleasure.

'However, if it is at all possible, Mrs O'Connor, I would like you to come to see me at Talbot Hall.'

'You're sure Gina's okay? I mean, she's not sick or anything?'

'You have my assurance that Gina is perfectly well and an excellent student.'

'Does Gina know you're calling me?'

'No, she doesn't. I – uh—'

'Please, Miss Armstrong,' Cecilia said, making no attempt to hide her nervousness. 'Please tell me what the problem is—'

'It would be better to see you face to face.'

'*Mama mia!*' Cecilia wailed. 'So there is a problem!'

'Gina's done nothing wrong.'

'Miss Armstrong, if you're calling me it's something serious. I'll leave right away and I'll get to you as soon as I can, if you want me to. Only please, *please*, give me an idea of what it's all about.'

Miss Armstrong decided that she had no choice. Speaking quickly, she said, 'This morning a woman called Tina Rizzoli came to see me. She told me that her brother, Al, is dying, and begging to see Gina.'

After a sharp intake of breath Cecilia said only, 'Oh, my God—'

'She brought photographs. She left them with me—'

'I'll come right over,' Cecilia said slowly. 'And Gina doesn't know anything about it?'

'Not yet,' Miss Armstrong said, relieved. 'I'll wait for you—'

About two hours later, Cecilia and Miriam were on their way to Talbot Hall. As always, Cecilia had turned to Miriam for help.

'I don't know what I would have done if you hadn't been able to drive me, Mirrie,' she said again, beaming her huge, helpless eyes on Miriam.

'We go back a long way, kiddo,' Miriam said gruffly, her bangles clicking.

Indeed they were staunch allies. It was one of those deeply sincere friendships where trust was absolute. Instinctively each knew when the other needed quiet. A shared silence fell between them as Miriam concentrated on her driving. Fortunately the traffic was light; they would be at Talbot Hall at least thirty minutes earlier than they had expected.

'I always knew he'd find us,' Cecilia said finally, 'but I never thought of what would happen if he died!'

'No more did I,' Miriam said, ruefully.

'It was bad enough Gina had to find out that Mike wasn't her father,' Cecilia said, hugging her arms about herself the way she always did when she was distressed. 'And now she's got to find out that she also has an aunt,' she said, pulling in her lips.

Miriam merely sighed; there was nothing helpful to say.

'It was that photograph in the paper,' Cecilia muttered. 'Miss Armstrong said Tina had brought photographs—'

When Cecilia and Miriam turned into Talbot Hall's elm-lined drive Miriam parked the car. As they made their way towards Miss Armstrong's study, she asked once more, 'Are you sure, kiddo, that you want me in Miss Armstrong's study with you?'

'Very sure.'

'I think we're a little early.'

196

'We left it that I would come as soon as I could.'

For the second time that day, Miss Armstrong found an unexpected visitor.

'I hope you don't mind my intrusion—' Miriam began.

'Not at all,' Miss Armstrong responded warmly. 'Goodness me, you're hardly an intruder! You're a *friend*. We at Talbot certainly believe in friendship. Indeed, lifelong friendships begin here.'

Although Talbot Hall and all it stood for went entirely against Miriam's principles, she had done nothing to discourage Cecilia from sending Gina there. After all, Gina would get an excellent education. But Talbot Hall made no secret of the fact that competitiveness was a dominant feature of the school. Friendship and competitiveness, it seemed to Miriam, cancelled one another out.

Which may not have altogether been a bad thing, Miriam reflected. For it seemed to her that common sense, not compassion, was what was needed now.

'Seeing her father for the first time in more than ten years, dying in a hospital bed,' Cecilia exclaimed. 'What would it do to her?'

'You will readily appreciate why I wanted her mother's opinion,' Miss Armstrong said. 'It is an unhappy situation.'

'To say the least,' Miriam put in scornfully.

'It would, of course, be Gina's decision, wouldn't it?' Miss Armstrong went on, as if Miriam had not spoken.

'Do we *have* to tell her?' Cecilia asked simply.

'Do we have a choice?' Miss Armstrong said.

'If you do have to tell her – which I myself doubt – does that also mean that you have to advise her to go?' said Miriam, her voice rising indignantly.

In the end, after nearly an hour of agitated debate, it was decided that Gina would have to be told. And, needless to say, once she knew that her father was dying she would feel obliged to go. Here again, Miriam disagreed. 'Wild horses wouldn't drag her there,' she said.

*

197

Miss Armstrong's secretary was dispatched to fetch Gina. By the time she joined them, the study was thick with Miriam's cigarette-smoke.

'Hi, Mom, hi, Mirrie,' Gina said, kissing them each in turn. 'What's the problem? Has something happened to Kate?' she asked anxiously. Kate had been sent home with a severe case of mumps.

'Kate's doing well,' Miss Armstrong said.

'We had some unexpected news this morning,' Cecilia began. Her voice broke. 'I don't know how to tell you this—'

At that moment raised voices were heard outside the study door.

'I tell you, Miss Armstrong can't be disturbed,' the secretary shouted angrily. 'You can't go in!'

'The hell I can't! She thought she'd seen the last of me—'

The next moment Tina Rizzoli crammed her body into the doorway.

Seeing her, an uncontrollable scream escaped from Cecilia.

'What's going on?' Gina asked nervously.

'I'm your Aunt Tina. Your father's dyin' and beggin' to see you on his deathbed.'

'*You're my aunt?*' Gina shrieked. '*Never!*' And she ran from the room.

Later that evening, with Miss Armstrong in her study, Gina found herself saying wildly and irrelevantly, 'Can you imagine? When I was told you wanted to see me I thought it was because of Kate. I was so afraid she'd had a bad turn.'

Miss Armstrong said kindly, 'No, there's no news from Kate. I'm sure everything is just fine. Bad news travels fast.'

'Yes, yes, of course. I'm so stupid. I don't know *why* I'm so stupid!'

'But how on earth could you have possibly imagined what it was that made me send for you?' Miss Armstrong said heatedly.

'I'm almost sorry it wasn't about Kate. That man calls himself my father!' Gina cried, her lips curving scornfully. 'Why, if I saw that man drowning and a rat drowning, I'd save the rat!'

'Have you seen him recently?' Miss Armstrong asked unexpectedly.

'Yes.' She nodded dully. 'But I've never told anyone about it. I don't know how you guessed—'

'I understand, Gina. I wish I didn't understand, but I do. You see, my dear, I understand because I've been there, too.'

'You've been there?'

'I've been there.' Miss Armstrong nodded, twisting her hands. 'So you will understand why I can't talk about it.' Never affectionate with the girls in her charge, she leaned forward now and took Gina's hands in hers. Choosing her words very carefully, she continued, 'What happened to you and to me was, and always will be, evil. But good triumphs over evil. It has in my life, and it will in yours.'

Gradually, Gina's expression changed from churning hatred to astonishment. Casting her eyes over the cosy, softly lit, book-lined walls, over the thick Baccarat vase filled with the delphiniums that had come to be known as the school flower, and finally over the elegant, scholarly, classy headmistress, a mixture of sadness and relief swept through her.

Strange, Miss Armstrong thought. Here we are in 1963, the age of Betty Friedan, Women's Liberation and the pill, and still there are some words that even fellow victims cannot bring themselves to utter. The pain and the shame are still too deep for speech.

Wrenching herself from her reverie, she said, 'They can't make you see him, you know.' Then with exquisite timing she turned the talk towards Commencement, only three weeks away.

Miriam drove slowly. It was safer to plod along, she reasoned, sticking closely to the right, simply focusing ahead, driving as if she were being towed. Her head was spinning and she wanted to follow the traffic and not negotiate it. For a long while they drove in silence. It began to rain, and the squelch of the tyres on the road was a welcome sound. The squeak of the wind-screen-wipers made the silence in the car less oppressive.

At last Miriam said, 'No one can make Gina see him, you know.' Her bangles suddenly clanged against the steering-wheel.

'I know that, Mirrie,' Cecilia said mildly. 'I will go and see him myself.'

'You!' Miriam exclaimed. 'You, go and see that monster!'

'He's dying, Mirrie,' Cecilia said simply. 'What harm can he do me now?'

'But—'

'I couldn't live with myself if I didn't go. Maruccia, you know, my stepmother, she used to say that he who refuses to visit the deathbed when he is sent for will travel more speedily to his own end.'

'But he wants Gina, not you.'

'He also wants me,' Cecilia said, somewhat shyly. 'I know that.'

'But how do you know that?'

'Because Tina kept repeating that he wanted his little girl from the *Harton*. That was the hospital ship where we met—' She made a confused movement and swung her bewildered, tortured face towards her old friend. 'Could you take me to the hospital and wait for me?' she asked supplicatingly.

'I'll go right with you to his very bedside, kiddo.'

'Thanks, Mirrie,' Cecilia said, her voice trembling. 'I knew you'd offer.'

'Yes, but you'll get a good meal in you before you see him. I'm starving.'

Towards midnight Miss Armstrong broke one of her strictest rules. She gave Gina a mild barbiturate, a phenobarbital, and a drink of cocoa and sat with her until she fell asleep.

It was exactly midnight when Cecilia and Miriam arrived at the hospital. Tina had not lied – Al was dying.

But for the whirr of the medical equipment and the fiercely

200

laboured sound of his breathing, an eerie sense of quiet filled the small room. Only a few hours earlier he had been moved from a large curtained-off cubicle so that he could at least die in privacy.

The harsh lighting had been turned down, but even in the half-light Cecilia saw at once that the woman kneeling against the bed was none other than Anna, the girl Al had been supposed to marry all those eighteen years ago. It was easy enough for her to work out; Gina was going on eighteen.

As she slowly approached the bed, Anna stalked from the room. Suddenly Cecilia was standing right beside the dying man. At that moment she felt that it was right that she was there, sharing his last moments with the man who, after all, had been responsible for the most important event in her own life: the birth of her daughter. An almost mystical sense of serenity overcame her. Through their coming-together, she and this man, this other human being, the glory of a new life had been begun. For too many years, Gina's three dimples notwithstanding, it had seemed not only irrelevant but impossible that Gina had ever had anything to do with anyone's genes but her mother's . . .

Drawing still more calm from the calm of the room, she reached his bedside. Placing a cool hand on his febrile brow, she said, 'It's me, Al. It's Cecilia.'

His eyes fluttered open questioningly.

'It's Cecilia from the *Harton*,' she went on, moving into Italian. 'You remember the *Harton*, the ship that brought you back from the war?'

He made the vaguest movement, but it was a nod.

How delicate he looked, Cecilia thought, now that all the savage anger and violent hatred was out of him.

Deep in thought, she was entirely unaware of the efficient male nurse's activities at the bedside. 'If you'll excuse us,' the male nurse said. 'We're about to aspirate his lungs.'

'Certainly,' Cecilia said nervously. 'Certainly.'

'And if you don't mind, we don't want to tire him after this, do we?' the nurse said, casting a meaningful look in the direction of the door. 'One *regular* visitor is all we can handle at this time. I dare say his sister will join us soon enough.' Clattering his syringes against their aluminium tray, he signed deeply. 'You may come again tomorrow.'

But there was no tomorrow.

Al Rizzoli's was no more commonplace and no more mysterious than any other death.

As far as Cecilia was concerned, she had made her peace with the man who had stained her soul with so much hate.

And it was only now that it was gone that she knew what a measureless burden of poison her own hate had been.

Chapter Thirty-Three

Strange, how the ending of the life of a man she had not seen for fifteen years resulted in Cecilia's own personal redemption. Now at last she felt not only free of the sin of him, but of herself sinning against the Church. For, in the eyes of the Church, she had been his wife; her marriage had endured . . .

It seemed, however, that even in the eyes of the law she had been his wife right up until the moment of his death. Al died intestate, which meant that his pension would go to her.

'Legally, you're entitled,' Miriam explained.

'I know, Mirrie, but I don't feel too good about it.'

'That's because what is legal is not necessarily moral,' Miriam assured her. She had been waiting for the opportunity to tell her that Gina did not want her to touch a single cent of her legal entitlement. 'It's dirty money,' she had said. 'Too dirty even to give to charity. Give it to his sister. Let her roll in the filth, like the hog she is. Only don't let Mama talk to me about it!'

Believing this to be the right moment, Miriam seized it. 'Gina wants everything to which the two of you would be entitled to go to Tina.'

'Gina is too generous for her own good,' Cecilia said tartly. 'I hope you're not encouraging her to throw all this money away.'

Without bothering to reply, Miriam continued, 'You never dreamed you would inherit, so you won't really be losing anything you even thought belonged to you.'

'I guess I need to see a lawyer,' Cecilia said. 'I'll have to find some way to protect Gina from herself.'

That afternoon she went to alter Constance Courtney's newest Yves Saint-Laurent pique ball gown with guipure-stitched sleeves after the Empire style. She decided to put the matter to her. After all, it was Mrs Courtney who was funding Gina's tuition at Talbot Hall . . .

Constance Courtney was the kind of woman who had a talent for listening. Because she believed that, as much as a problem deserved sympathy, it needed attention even more.

Getting to the point at once, she said, 'Your sister-in-law really needs the money? Would her life be much harder without it?'

'Yes.'

Surprisingly, Mrs Courtney came up with a ready answer. 'You keep his army disability pension. But only for as long as you so wish it—'

'For as long as I wish it?' said Cecilia, sounding puzzled.

'It's simple, really, Cecilia,' Constance Courtney said eagerly, opening and closing her silver cigarette-case. 'The moment you or Gina feel you need the money, you take it right back.'

Then suddenly, almost abruptly, Gina's career at Talbot Hall was at an end. All through the month of May, she felt as if her life were being lived in cramped segments of time, trying to schedule all the major events of the semester in which she was invariably a major player. As director of the school play, *Sandy Snows*, and class president, Gina's administrative skills were sorely tested.

Far from being found wanting, however, her many commitments floated easily, as if her every move had been choreographed.

'How do you manage it?' Kate asked enviously. 'You look great, you're never in a panic and you keep smiling.'

'There is so much to look forward to,' said Gina enthusiastically. 'I feel as if my whole life is about to begin.'

PART FOUR

Chapter Thirty-Four

Even before graduation, Rufus made sure to reserve the family cabin in the Adirondacks, in the wilderness but not too far from Balsam, a tiny town north of Saranac Lake.

He discussed his plans with his grandfather. Theodore Cartwright believed that he and his grandson had a close, honest relationship and it was only to Rufus that he had confided that for several years after his marriage he had continued with his secret hobby – collecting women. If Rufus had told him that he was going to the cabin with a young woman, his grandfather would not only have understood but applauded. Instead, because Rufus wanted everything about Gina to be kept secret, he lied and said his friends John Thayer and Clyde Bartlett would be going with him, fishing and living rough. 'Living rough' notwithstanding, Jim Hawkins, their man at the camp, would be sent to the cabin to make up the beds and get the place in working order.

He and Gina were going to have two whole weeks – fourteen whole days and fourteen whole nights together. He would wake early every morning and she would be beside him, in the clean Adirondack air scented with balsam fir. At the moment, late night thoughts of their future unlimited love-making kept him awake. She was only a girl, not yet eighteen, yet she dominated his mind; his very brain felt tight, as if it had lost its elasticity.

What was it about her that made her so very different from the other women in his life? It was simple, really. Besides her quick mind and her stunning beauty there was a courage, a strength, a determination and a confidence like nothing he had ever encountered before. She beamed an elemental power as potent as lightning, yet at the same time she could be as feather-soft as her low, rippling laugh. In some ways she reminded him of his grandmother, Lucia; and then he would think of Gina's uninhibited fearless love-making and she and his grandmother would become worlds apart.

By 1963 the sexual coming of age was, for a young woman, easier than it had been for centuries. Gina was on the pill. She had thought of discussing it with Mirrie, who was, after all, a pharmacist; but like Rufus her need to keep it secret was as great as the sexual need itself. So, again like Rufus, she practised deception and told her mother she was going away to a log cabin in the Adirondacks with her friends Harriet Sanders and Monica Canfield. The three of them would be going on to Radcliffe, so it made sound sense. That the cabin had no telephone was hardly surprising. She promised to call her mother every other day, and went off with a back-pack to take the train to New York, where she was to meet Rufus.

They drove slowly, for the choice wilderness of mountains and lakes was as awesome as their feelings for one another. When at last they reached the cabin they stepped out on to the deck and took in the view of the jagged sweep of mountains rising out of the forest. The grandeur of it all was breathtaking; there was something forever wild about it. Wordlessly they made their way to the bedroom, whose large double bed was made up and waiting for them.

They made love slowly and delicately and perfectly, until together they rocketed high, beyond light, beyond dark, flashing into a magnetic storm, and then they floated in a glow of calm fulfilment.

Later, naked in the kitchen, they ate bread and cheese and drank rough red wine that Rufus had thought to bring along.

'You know what?' she said, stretching her arms voluptuously to the ceiling. 'I didn't even think of bringing anything to eat. I only thought of—'

'Of what?' he interrupted quickly, knowing what she was going to say.

'Of fucking,' she said.

He had expected her to say that she had thought only of making love, and yet the fervent musicality of the tone with which she said 'fucking' turned it into a word of near-mystical loveliness.

For all his macho style, he felt himself incomprehensibly close to tears. He left his seat on the bench opposite her and, sliding between her bench and the table, he laid his head against her firm, pointed breasts, shamelessly gave way and allowed his emotion to spill into tears.

She responded at once by putting her head to his head, while at the same time she grasped his tight chestnut curls with her fingers, and suddenly they were in one another's arms weeping together, weeping for the enormity of their emotional experience. Instinctively, but understandably, they both feared that things might not work. Like the mountains surrounding them, their experience had sprung from eternity.

'I'll be twenty-one next month,' he said when he had regained himself. 'And I'm going to marry you, you know.'

'I know,' she said, her voice clear and strong. 'I know you want to marry me.'

'But I *will* marry you!'

'Your family will not be too pleased. They would want a far more socially acceptable wife for you than the daughter of a seamstress and the stepdaughter of a gardener!'

'Nonsense,' he said, his voice hollow.

She said nothing, but merely sent an openly quizzical gaze in his direction.

After a short silence he said, 'I don't give a damn what they think!'

The next day he took her hiking, and showed her his secret places. He took her to a white-birch parkland with seven tiered ponds. He took her to his favourite well, and they drank the cool, clear water, and she told him she had never tasted anything so pure.

'I have,' he said. 'I have tasted a purity greater than this.'

'What was it?' she asked.

'You,' he said. 'You are purer than the purest well-water.'

He drew her closer then, and kissed her, and their bodies thirsted for one another. Moments later he had carried her into the woods and there, on a carpet of pine-needles and mushrooms, they made love as urgently as if it would never happen again. The moon was high that night and she made him scrambled eggs on toast and they talked the night away, regretting that they would be forced to go to the produce store to buy some provisions.

'Couldn't we fish for our food?' she asked suddenly.

'Do you want me to teach you fly-fishing?' he said.

So they fished, successfully, for rainbow trout, and picked mushrooms. At the end of the afternoon she remembered she had not yet called her mother as she had promised. He drove her to Hilltops and she lied to her mother and felt no twinge of guilt.

On the fourth day, however, they were compelled to go to the store. They stocked up with cereals, pasta, rice and canned fruit and decided to leave their paradise only to make phone calls. Laden with their purchases, they were about to leave when Gina remembered they had forgotten to buy candles.

'Wait for me and I'll get them,' Rufus said, putting down his bulging packets.

And if it hadn't been for those candles, they would have been in his car, at least five miles away from the Balsam Store, and they would not have run into Senator and Mrs Dick Powell, Lucia and Theodore Cartwright's oldest friends. Just at the moment Rufus was presenting Gina with the candles and a very long kiss, the Powells recognized him.

'Rufus Cartwright,' Veronica Powell called. 'Your grandfather told me you might be up here with—' But then she stopped. It was all too clear that Rufus was with Gina and not with any of his Harvard friends.

After an awkward silence, Rufus said proudly, 'Senator Powell, Mrs Powell, allow me to introduce Miss Gina O'Connor.'

'Delighted to meet you, Miss O'Connor,' the Senator said.

'Well, since we're all here, we might as well have a cup of coffee or a beer together,' Veronica Powell said, gesturing towards the small rustic restaurant that adjoined the Balsam Store.

It would have been ungracious to refuse and, almost before they knew it, they were drinking the strong brew of coffee for which the restaurant was justly famous. They chatted about Radcliffe and Harvard, and then President Kennedy's name came up.

'I helped campaign for him,' Gina said innocently.

'Pah! Are you aware that John Kennedy was the only Democratic senator not to vote for the resolution to condemn Senator Joseph McCarthy?' Senator Powell asked frostily.

'No, sir,' Rufus replied staunchly. 'I was not aware of that.'

'Well, our President actually contributed 3000 dollars to McCarthy's campaign in 1952—' the Senator persisted.

'Senator Powell is a Republican,' Rufus explained to Gina.

'Have you been here long?' Mrs Powell asked deftly.

'About four days, I guess,' Gina replied.

'Making a long stay?'

'Another ten glorious days.' Gina smiled.

'We almost never get to spend as much as two whole weeks up here,' Mrs Powell said enviously.

'This is my first visit,' Gina said, her eyes shining. 'I've fallen in love with the wilderness.'

'I wish we hadn't run into them,' Rufus said as they were driving away. 'Still, it can't be helped.' His expression seemed strained; he sounded uncomfortable.

'Is that because you were with me?' Gina asked fearlessly.

He didn't answer. It would not be long, he knew, before Mrs Powell would be on the phone to his grandmother to report what she had seen. Listening to Gina's astonishment over President Kennedy's involvement with Senator McCarthy, Rufus soon forgot about the ill-fated encounter with the Powells.

*

'You're not calling Lucia Cartwright already,' Senator Powell said to his wife, who had rushed to the telephone even before unpacking their provisions.

'And why not?' his wife responded tersely. 'Why wait to tell Lucia Cartwright that I've just met her future granddaughter-in-law.'

'Women!' Senator Powell said, shaking his head. 'A guy goes away with a gal and already she's a bride—'

'I never saw a young man so blindingly in love as Rufus Cartwright,' his wife said, sighing with satisfaction. 'Lucia would want to know about it—'

No use trying to stop her, the Senator decided: Veronica Powell was a dedicated gossip. Any attempt would have only made her all the more determined. Besides, the girl was a Kennedy supporter, and therefore of no account. She seemed a bright girl, though. He wondered idly which O'Connors she came from – the oil O'Connors, he concluded. Then, like Rufus, he put the entire matter out of his mind.

'Lucia!' Mrs Powell exclaimed, when finally she was put through. 'Such a surprise meeting today I couldn't resist telling you about it.'

Lucia shook her head and smiled her regal smile. Really, but Veronica Powell was such a character. A gossip but a charming, witty one. 'Tell me,' Lucia said. 'I'm all ears.'

'I believe I met your future granddaughter-in-law today.' Her plain face suddenly lively, she continued, 'They're too young, of course, both of them, but it's perfectly obvious – at least to these old eyes of mine – that they belong together. Even as we speak, I hear the sound of wedding bells.'

'Veronica, dear, I don't know who or what you're talking about.'

'Why, Rufus, of course. So like his grandfather, too. And his girl, Gina O'Connor. Stunningly beautiful, such an open, honest face.' She stopped and sighed and launched into her favourite topic – her daughter-in-law. 'Now if only my Gordon could have found himself a real all-round American girl instead of that foreign, illiterate—'

Lucia had heard it all before. 'Gina O'Connor?' she interrupted.

'Have you met her? Dick thinks she must belong to the oil family. A smart girl, too; she's going to go to Radcliffe.'

Forcing herself to keep control, Lucia said, 'So sweet of you to tell me about Rufus, darling. But he's not yet twenty-one and he is, as you say, like his grandfather – a chip off the old block. He won't tie himself down until he's at least thirty—'

'I hate to contradict you, Lucia, but I'm on a high from just being with those two kids. They just seem to fit together, like they melted into one another.'

The conversation over, Lucia rested her throbbing head against the back of her tall *bergère* chair. *Gina O'Connor* – she ransacked her brain, but could not remember the exact context in which she had heard the name before. Her head continued to throb; it felt as if someone was tightening a vice around her temples. Lucia Cartwright was sixty-four, and the wife of the President of Cartwright Pharmaceuticals, but nothing in the world would have induced her to take an analgesic to relieve the pain. Instead she went to the vegetable garden and selected the salad greens for their lunch.

Picking vegetables or cutting roses were activities reserved for special occasions such as Thanksgiving or Christmas or a family birthday. Suddenly she was reminded of cranberries she had herself selected from the greenhouse last Thanksgiving.

She laid down her secateurs.

She had remembered.

Gina O'Connor was the girl who had called Rufus away from their Thanksgiving lunch. She had meant to make enquiries about the girl then. Theodore had asked her to look into the matter, but somehow she had delayed things. Theodore must have assumed she had gone ahead with the investigations.

Well, it was not too late. Marriage at twenty-one – even to the right girl from the right family, a family known to the Cartwrights, was out of the question.

Rufus was too young.

And the Cartwright family did not believe in divorce.

An hour later she was having an interview with the chief of security at Cartwright Pharmaceuticals. That afternoon a plain-clothes man was dispatched to the Adirondacks to photograph the young couple. How could you fight your enemy if you did not even know what they looked like?

Two days later the investigator brought her the photographs, some of which he'd had enlarged. One of the photographs showed Gina with a fishing-rod in one hand and Rufus's hand in the other. How the investigator got it was anyone's guess, because they appeared in full frontal view. The smile on Rufus's lips, and the love in his eyes – his expression of limitless happiness – dazzled her, and she turned the photograph face down, for she could not bear to destroy it.

Thus was the thorough investigation into Gina's background begun.

Too soon their fourteen days came to an end. Rufus went off to join his parents at the Hôtel de Paris in Monte Carlo for ten days, after which he was to go to Geneva, Switzerland, where a six-week course had been arranged for him at Cartwright Pharmaceuticals' main European subsidiary. It was at least a year since these plans had been laid down, and the fact that he was desperately in love made it all the more crucial for him to begin his career at once.

Once again, Gina and Rufus were in daily correspondence. Like Rufus, she refused all dates. Mark and Fran quickly realized that he must have a serious girl-friend – he spent so much time waiting for letters. It was only when she sent him advance copies of the magazines in which she appeared during the vacation that he told his parents about her. He simply could not resist showing her off.

'You'll meet her at my twenty-first,' he said proudly.

'Why wait till then, son?' his father asked.

'I think I want to keep her to myself, Dad,' Rufus answered. Something suspiciously like a blush crossed his face.

'That's fine by us,' Fran said softly. 'We can understand that.'

'She *is* lovely,' Fran said to Mark when Rufus left. 'Gina O'Connor. Do you think she's from O'Connor Oil?'

'I've no idea,' Mark said. Picking up the photograph Rufus had left with them, he stared long and hard at Gina's perfectly proportioned body, at the enigmatic smile that hovered about her generous lips. 'She reminds me of someone,' he said, puzzled. 'But I'm damned if I remember who.'

Meanwhile, back in Connecticut at Cartwright Farm, Lucia had received her private investigator's detailed report on Gina. Wrinkling her long, Roman nose in disdain, she laid the report down. She decided to read it again, the better to take in all the facts. Bad enough that the girl was the daughter of a seamstress, and the stepdaughter of a gardener; it was worse that she was the daughter of an out-of-work disaster called Al Rizzoli. It had always been understood, acknowledged and accepted that Rufus would make the right marriage: he would marry into the right family. Any girl without the right credentials was out of the question. Indeed, Lucia had long since compiled a mental list of the right families.

'It is believed that Alberto Rizzoli had a minor connection with the Mafia,' (she read this part out loud to herself) 'which may or may not explain why his daughter refused his last, deathbed request to see him before he died.'

Beside the fact that she had refused to see the dying father who had begged to see her, the rest of the report that concerned Gina's scholastic career at Talbot Hall, as well as the glowing character references, was irrelevant.

After all, what greater crime could there be than turning your back on a blood relation as close as a dying father who was begging to see you? Whatever the circumstances, Lucia could imagine nothing worse.

For the moment, however, she would keep the report strictly private, under lock and key. When the time came, she would show it to Theodore and, if necessary, to Rufus as well.

And there could be no doubt that it would become essential reading for Rufus. The report safely locked in the secret drawer of her secretaire, she turned her attention to the menu for the twenty-first birthday ball that she and Theodore were hosting for Rufus. Lately, the decision over whether or not to serve hot caviare blini to one hundred and fifty guests was exercising her mind.

Lucia sighed. Menu decisions were unfailingly troublesome . . .

Chapter Thirty-Five

Miriam could not help feeling that there was something particularly touching about the way Cecilia glowed when she talked about Gina. She was telling Miriam it was the first time she had ever seen her daughter nervous about going to a party.

'It's absolutely natural for her to be a little nervous. After all, she is the birthday boy's date,' Miriam said.

The two women were seated in Miriam's comfortable library. Cecilia had recently taken up needle-point, and she was busily stitching a cushion cover for Miriam. Their sixteen-year friendship was as good as it was thorough, and neither could have imagined life without it.

'No, I don't think she's afraid of being Rufus's date,' Cecilia said speculatively. 'It's more like she's afraid of being a house guest, of spending three days with his family.'

'They'll adore her,' Miriam said staunchly. 'Everyone does.'

'I've often seen the grandmother on the society pages. I saw her picture yesterday. She looked kind of regal.'

'And more than a little smug,' said Miriam, who had seen the same photograph.

Cecilia laid down her sewing. 'I almost forgot to show you the dress,' she said. 'It shows you how excited I am!'

She took the dress from its tissue-lined box and spread it out on Miriam's cobalt-blue couch. It could not have been more simple, or more demure. Ice-white peau-de-soie, three-quarter sleeves, a low back with roll collar, and a full-length skirt. Gina's shape would be shown to perfection.

'It's beautiful, kiddo,' Miriam said, fingering the silk. 'What's more, it looks *haute couture.*'

'Thank you,' Cecilia said. 'It turned out better than I had

hoped.' Lovingly folding it back into its box once more, she added, 'She's going to put her hair up in a chignon.'

'She's not a little girl any more,' said Miriam with the half-sad, half-proud tone people use when they speak of children who have suddenly become young adults. 'She's a young woman, I guess.' Placing her hand on her friend's shoulder, she added, 'And so very beautiful too.'

'I feel afraid for her.' Cecilia shuddered slightly. 'I don't know why.'

'What do *you* think of Rufus?' Miriam asked suddenly. 'You haven't said.'

'I think he's charming,' Cecilia said. 'And he has perfect manners to go with his looks. I met him about a week ago, when he came to collect Gina, just after his return from Switzerland.' She stopped suddenly. Then, her voice trembling with emotion, she went on, 'But I must confess, Miriam, that most of my attention was on Gina. It was so obvious that she couldn't take her eyes off him. The shine in them was so bright it bored right into my heart. She glowed with love. I guess you could say she was in a state of grace.'

Miriam had been listening to her friend in total stillness. She could not recall when – if ever – Cecilia had talked for so long without stopping. She lit a cigarette and her bracelets clashed the silence, but she said nothing and waited for Cecilia to continue.

'Oh, I wanted to try to sum him up, to get a feel of what he was like, but seeing my own child so unspeakably happy, so recklessly in love, blinded me to everything else.'

Once again a silence fell between the two women. Each was lost in her own thoughts. Miriam's main focus was on Cecilia, for she knew that she lived for her daughter. Although Cecilia was not a clinging, demanding mother, both she and her daughter took it for granted that the dominant force in her life was Gina.

Sometimes, thought the childless Miriam, sometimes mother-love is awesome to behold.

218

'I *hope* Rufus is a good man,' Cecilia said almost prayerfully, 'because my daughter sure is crazy about him.'

'Gina is a strong girl,' Miriam said forcefully.

'True,' Cecilia said with a wan smile. 'But Rufus is her weak point.'

The ball was to be on Saturday, July 30th (the actual day of Rufus's birthday) but the house guests arrived on Friday. These were the more intimate friends and relations, amongst whom were Rufus's closest friend and former room-mate, Howard Wright, and Edward Bruce, his oldest school-friend from his Groton days. General and Mrs Timothy Byrne, Rufus's great-uncle and his wife, Senator and Mrs Mark Powell, and cousins and aunts and uncles brought the number of house guests up to twenty. Since Cartwright House had twelve bedrooms and just as many bathrooms they would all be accommodated easily enough.

Lucia inspected every guest-room and bathroom herself. Three of the guest-suites included small sitting-rooms and these were assigned to Rufus's parents, his uncle the General, and Senator and Mrs Powell. Baskets cascading with fruit and vases filled with roses were in each room. Lucia made a slight adjustment to every single vase. Next she checked the bathrooms to see if the toiletries and bathrobes were all in order. After that she went back into the bedrooms and sitting-rooms to make sure that current magazines, *Vogue, Town and Country*, the *New Yorker* and *Time* magazine were all in place.

Satisfied that all was as it should be, she hummed quietly to herself. She had never made any secret of the fact that Rufus was her favourite. She believed the bond between herself and her grandson was the strongest of all; greater, even, than the tie with her own children. Consequently this ball celebrating Rufus's twenty-first was one of the great landmarks in her own life.

At the same time she had her own and very cogent, if secret,

219

reasons for believing that this party would be one of the most meaningful events in Rufus's life. She would see to that with the same thorough efficiency with which she had checked the bathrooms.

Vigilance was the hallmark of Lucia Cartwright's life: she left nothing to chance. If she had, she could never have been the kind of wife that Theodore expected her to be. Strangely, she didn't in the least mind being subordinate to him, because she felt protected by him. It suited Lucia that Theodore was the undisputed leader of the family. Everyone except a leader needs a leader, she believed, for it could not be denied that under his leadership both Cartwright Pharmaceuticals and his family were a spectacularly successful example to follow.

Gina packed her bags with the same meticulousness that Lucia would have packed hers. Given to her by Constance Courtney when she had entered Talbot, her leather baggage was comfortably shabby. So far, except for Senator and Mrs Powell, she had not met anyone in Rufus's circle. Her mother's judgement had been accurate – she was nervous of being in such close proximity to his family for four days. She had listened carefully when Rufus spoke of them, and understood that, though he loved his parents, he revered his grandparents. It seemed to her that it was his grandfather and not his father who was his role-model.

Folding her sparkling tennis togs, her mind slipped back to its usual place – the world of Rufus; or rather, her world with Rufus. When Rufus had returned from Switzerland she had not left her mother's home to stay with him. Instead, they had met one another every day and gone to the hotel in New York in which he was staying. They had been apart for six weeks and, when they came together again, their love-making had risen to a peak of untold perfection. It seemed as if her skin still vibrated with the purity of it and the wildness of it. She longed for him and not for the first time wondered what would happen at Cartwright House. Would they be able to get together? She had wanted to ask Rufus about this, but had long since understood that he liked to take the lead in such matters.

When the suitcase was done, she checked her bag of toiletries, the soap and other luxury bath-care oils and creams that her mother had given her. The soap had a strong smell of lavender; it reminded Cecilia of her own wedding-day, on the *Harton*, when Nurse Billington had presented the unbelievable wartime luxury of a tablet of lavender soap. She almost never talked of that period of her life, but suddenly found herself telling Gina about it.

'Wartime or no wartime, I'd never dreamed that that sort of soap could possibly exist. I kept the wrapping for years. I think I still have it.'

'Were you very very poor, Mama?'

'Dirt poor,' Cecilia sighed. 'But worse than the poverty, worse than the bombs, was my stepmother.'

'I know. Maruccia,' Gina murmured. 'Oh, Mama, thank God I've got you,' she said in a burst of emotion.

'How ignorant I was! What a dumb fool! To think I thought Al Rizzoli was smart just because he could speak American!'

At once Gina's face darkened. The mere sound of her father's name filled her with an almost uncontrollable rage. Half furious and half sad, she said, 'I'll make it up to you, Mama. One day you will have your own personal maid and a marble bath with real gold faucets. Nothing will be too good for you. You deserve the best. Better than the best!'

Jerking her mind into the present again, it suddenly occurred to her that the Cartwrights might have gold taps themselves. She went to take a shower and wash her long, luxuriant raven hair. She would wear it in a chignon to the ball. Her heart lurched upward. In less than two hours she would be in Rufus's new Mustang – a twenty-first birthday present from his mother – and on her way to Cartwright House.

Chapter Thirty-Six

As soon as Rufus turned his car into the mile-long, winding driveway leading up to Cartwright House, Gina fell silent. Courtesy of her American Architecture Course, Gina easily placed it as neo-classical Georgian. Gracious linden trees softened the approach to the entrance courtyard. Almost before she knew it, she and Rufus were standing in the majestic oak-panelled reception hall towering up three storeys to a vaulted stained-glass ceiling. She recognized Alec the butler's voice from the time she had spoken to him when Kate was almost at death's door. She understood why Rufus had taken so long to get to the telephone.

'Alec, I'd like you to meet Miss O'Connor,' Rufus said genially. 'Alec has been in our family for years.'

'How do you do, Miss O'Connor?' Alec said politely. 'I believe we once talked on the telephone.' Then, with an infinitesimal gesture, he led them to the library where Lucia and Theodore were waiting to receive them. The introductions over, Theodore told them that Rufus's parents would be joining them very soon.

'We decided to have a real English tea,' Theodore said with a twinkle. 'Scones, cucumber sandwiches, everything.' Then, turning his distinguished, leonine head towards Gina, and looking her directly in the eye, he remarked, 'I applaud your taste, Rufus. Miss O'Connor is a very beautiful young lady.'

'I knew you'd think so, Gramps,' Rufus replied. 'You and I have the same taste.'

'Oh, Mr Cartwright, please call me Gina.'

'If that is what you wish.' Theodore smiled. 'I assume Gina is a contraction of Georgina?'

The talk turned to the ballroom and the Jim Davies orchestra that had been engaged for the evening. Recently, Jim Davies had become something of a hero in the Cartwright circle. The Guy Harrisons had been giving a party in a marquee over their swimming-pool, which had been especially covered with a sprung dance-floor. Suddenly, the dance-floor caved in and several people fell into the pool. At once Jim Davies had leaned back and disconnected the electricity, leaving everyone in darkness, but a terrible tragedy had been averted.

'We've had no refusals,' Lucia said contentedly. 'Not one.'

It was a beautiful room, and their collection of rare books gleamed in the light of the roaring fire. Rich, burnt-sienna panelled bookshelves covered three sides of the room. To the left of the fireplace the panelled wall was without bookshelves; it was dominated by a portrait by Sargent. Gina had tried not to stare, but now, almost as if they had a will of her own, her eyes strayed to the portrait.

'Why, that's a John Singer Sargent,' she exclaimed, delighted. Again, without meaning to, she left her seat to study the painting. 'How very beautiful,' she said. 'He certainly was a virtuoso with pigment.'

In a flash Rufus was at her side. 'Allow me to introduce you to Agnes Williams Cartwright – my great-grandmother.'

'He painted my mother in 1909,' Theodore said proudly. 'One of the last portraits he ever painted, you know.'

Looking at the portrait, Gina and Rufus had their backs to the Cartwrights and, even as he spoke, he and his wife exchanged one of their brief but meaningful glances. 'She's smart,' the glance said, 'very smart. But we'll continue with our strategy. And how right we were to devise it.'

And at their black-tie dinner for twenty that night, in keeping with their strategy, Gina was treated like a particularly honoured guest. Theodore's daughter-in-law was always seated on his right; no guest in the world had ever been important enough to make Fran give up her seat. But even though Maud Prescott, the wife of the Harvard professor who was one of the White House advisers, should have been seated on his left, that place was given to Gina. Like Professor Greenburg, the elegant, creative scientist who was one of Cartwright Pharmaceuticals' 'backroom boys', Professor and Mrs Prescott were not house guests. Any awe Gina might have felt for Professor Prescott was rapidly overcome by her boundless intellectual curiosity. She and the Professor found themselves united by their delight that the White House finally had an intellectual President who had had the imagination to invite Robert Frost to read a poem especially written for the inauguration.

Purely for fun, Theodore decided to test her ability to handle a tricky situation. 'Kennedy pretends to be a devout Catholic, and yet it is common knowledge that he has a wandering eye.'

'The President does have great charisma, which makes him a very attractive man. People envy his style. Rumours are bound to spring up,' she replied seriously. Shyly, she added, 'Rufus is a bit like him. I guess that's why he is such a great hero of mine.'

Theodore's hatred of Kennedy was equalled only by his distrust of him. Gina should not have been so open about her feelings for his grandson. Little wonder that she had no real understanding of the niceties of life – she was, after all, the daughter of a seamstress. Lucia had done well to heed his instruction to investigate her background: Gina O'Connor was, and always would be, a nobody.

Much later, to drown out the sound, Gina and Rufus turned on her shower at full blast. They made love quietly and urgently on the bathroom floor.

Shortly before he left to go to his own room he said, 'Gramps thinks you're just one hell of a smart girl—'

'Have you always cared more about impressing your grandfather than your father?' she asked.

'But I thought you knew that grandfather is the head of the family,' Rufus replied, somewhat coldly. 'He and I are close. Very close.'

'Oh, I see,' Gina answered just as coldly. 'King Theodore. You should have told me.'

If this was a quarrel, Rufus decided to make peace at once. Giving a wild whoop of laughter, he took her in his arms. 'Grandfather's name is on the building, and on his house. He's not King Theodore, he's Big Chief Hawkeye.'

She laughed with him, and they made love again, and the tension was over.

Many years were to pass before she would recall this incident. But once it was back in her mind she would drive herself crazy asking herself why she had let him off so lightly. If only she had paid the proper attention to this seemingly insignificant little episode, she would have understood what a heartless opportunist he was.

But the very moment that it happened she had allowed his love-making to erase it from her mind just as surely as if it had never been.

On the day of the ball the young people were instructed to play tennis, or go swimming or riding – in short to do whatever they wished except get in the way of the team of caterers who had arrived and pitched a marquee merely to house their own kitchen, even though the Cartwright kitchen was unusually large. The menu they had designed made a large kitchen essential.

Dinner would begin with seafood-stuffed artichokes. Encircled by artichoke, and mounted on the thistle's heart, the shrimps, bay scallops, oysters and succulent morsels of lobster accented by thin rounds of black truffle would be nothing if not original. Lucia was especially pleased with the entrée: tiny, boneless quail stuffed with veal sweetbreads, goose liver, shallots and wild mushrooms baked in golden pastry, would without doubt become legendary. Dessert: individual Grand Marnier soufflés – the perfect finale to a flawless dinner.

So Gina and Rufus and all the other young people went

swimming in the huge, half-sized Olympic pool. The high diving-board was, of course, irresistible to Gina and those who observed the way Rufus lusted after her perfectly proportioned body diving through the air felt like an audience of voyeurs. She went to him after each dive and they hugged one another, and their wet bodies clung and curved into one another, fitting so perfectly and in such a practised way as to cause a sudden, irrepressible sexual stirring in the loins of their circle of spectators.

Upstairs in his bedroom, Theodore trained his binoculars on the scene. Spellbound, even from that distance, he was shocked by the effect on his own body. It was both frightening and exciting to witness the sheer physical force of his grandson's sensuality.

Even before nightfall, the trees lining the mile-long drive up to Cartwright House glittered with a thousand blue lights. Gina was expected to join the family at eight o'clock in the ballroom, where she was to be part of the receiving-line. 'We want Rufus to believe she has our total acceptance,' Theodore had told his wife.

Ready and dressed well before she needed to be, Gina looked out at the scores of flaming torches that bathed the gardens in an ethereal light. At the far end of the garden she could just make out the swans gliding in a reflecting pool.

She turned away and went again to the full-length mirror to inspect her appearance. Her raven hair gleamed in a chignon, and although she had learnt a great deal about make-up during the short time she had been a model, she had gone in for the natural look, using nothing more than mascara and a pale lipstick. No need for rouge – her cheeks glowed with summer. Her ice-white dress was in brilliant contrast with her tanned skin and set it off perfectly. On impulse, she removed the pearl necklace her mother had given her before she went to Talbot Hall and put it in its velvet bag in her cosmetic bag beside her birth-control pills. She knew instinctively that, unadorned, she would be more startling, more distinctive. She did not want to appear pushy, and so decided that it would be appropriate to join the family ten minutes later than she was expected.

She was not wrong. In spite of themselves, Lucia and Theodore cast approving glances in her direction. Glamorous and elegant, her serene, assured beauty could not but draw stares of admiration. As she took her place beside Rufus, Lucia cringed. She was convinced that Gina would kiss him full on the lips. Instead Gina left a discreet distance between them, and did not as much as hold his hand.

'Whatever else she is, she doesn't look common,' Lucia murmured to Theodore.

'She doesn't have to look common. She *is* common,' retorted Theodore, who had not yet recovered from the impact she had made on him that afternoon. And through binoculars, too. Needless to say, he blamed her for having turned him into a peeping Tom. 'Brazen hussy,' he said under his breath.

As usual, Senator and Mrs Wayne Fairfield were the first guests to arrive. As usual, Cordelia complained about her husband's disgusting punctuality, signalling that yet another fabulous Cartwright party had begun.

Everything seemed to shimmer that night: the orchid centre-pieces on each table, the flaming torches in the garden, the candle-light, the guests. Even the plain-clothes security men in their evening dress appeared to have absorbed the glitter of the evening.

Except for the lobsters, which Lucia had pronounced over-cooked and therefore too tough, the food was perfect. At last it was time for the dancing to begin. Despite the contrast between Rufus, with his tight chestnut curls, and Gina with her sleek, raven-black hair, they were – as they waltzed – the very definition of harmony. At the same time they were a vision of loveliness.

Fran and Mark, Rufus's parents, were certain their son and this girl had been made for one another. Although they knew very little about her, they liked her and approved of her so much that they felt they didn't need to know more.

Mark's uncle, General Timothy Byrne, made his stately way towards him. Goodwill and even excitement radiated from him. 'She's a smart young woman, Gina O'Connor,' he grinned. 'She's read my book.' His book, entitled *Anzio*, had only been published about two years before. 'She told me she read it for an extended essay she wrote on the Allied landings in Italy.'

'I hope it won't turn out to be a case of meeting the right young woman when you are too young,' said Fran soberly. 'After all, he's only twenty-one. And yet I'm sure he'll never find anyone like her if he lets her go.'

'Of course they are too young, both of them,' the General agreed. 'Marriage is a long way away for those two.' Then, with a flourish of his hand, he added, 'May I have the pleasure of this dance, Fran?'

Mark decided to ask his mother to dance. The relationship between them had always been somewhat strained, probably because his father had never entirely approved of him. His political affiliations, his support for Martin Luther King and the like were highly irritating to Theodore, who had no time for 'bleeding hearts'. Lucia's allegiance was first to her husband and then to her son. As Lucia saw it (or wanted it), her husband's opinion was law. Theodore had no time for bleeding hearts and she, of course, went along with him. There was absolutely no doubt in her mind that Gina's background would make Mark and Fran think more – and not less – of her.

Lucia declined her son's invitation to dance, however. One of the security men needed to speak to her, she said. A good conversationalist and a master of the sudden quick witticism, Mark moved among the guests offering champagne and dispensing laughter wherever he went.

A while later Fran joined him and, with an imperceptible movement of her eyelid, indicated that she wanted to speak to him. He understood at once and laughingly led her to the dance-floor.

'Have you any idea what has upset your mother?' she asked anxiously. Unusually, she was smoking a cigarette.

'Why?'

'She told me she's waiting for the lighted birthday-cake to be brought in and then she's leaving the party.'

'She could be tired,' Mark offered. 'She's not so young any more.'

'She said she had something important to attend to,' Fran said, puffing deeply. 'It's unlike her to leave one of her own parties.'

They were interrupted by Rufus, who wanted to dance with his mother. Even though he took great pleasure in watching his son and his wife dancing together, his mother's wholly uncharacteristic behaviour had left Mark feeling decidedly uneasy.

As good as her word, Lucia left the party. Then, to Mark's unspeakable astonishment, his suddenly stern-faced father came to tell him he was leaving too. 'No,' he said testily. 'I'm in perfect health and so is your mother.' He gave a thin, mocking laugh and added, 'Your mother and I have a rather awkward problem on our hands.'

'Can't I help?'

'I think not,' Theodore said decisively. 'We can't have all the Cartwrights leave the party!'

Mark knew that his father had long since dismissed him as a 'bleeding heart'. Theodore had done little to conceal his disapproval of him. But since he approved of Rufus, he thought this gave him the right to take him over. Mark had been forced to accept that whatever respect Rufus felt for him was far outweighed by the respect he felt for his grandfather.

Theodore turned on his heel and rapidly walked up the stairs to meet Lucia. She and the security man, Jim Nilson, were in her small and delicately coloured sitting-room waiting for him.

He found both his wife and Jim Nilson staring at the open cosmetic bag which lay on the marble coffee-table. Beside the cosmetic bag, on a crumpled paper tissue, was Lucia's dragonfly brooch. Made by Lalique, its wings covered by opalescent enamel veined with gold and heightened by diamonds, the dragonfly was startlingly realistic. When Rufus was about ten, he had been allowed to hold it in his hands.

Chapter Thirty-Seven

'It went missing and so I had Jim Nilson and his assistant, Dave Henning, systematically search every single guest-room,' Lucia said, her voice hard and cold.

'And where was it found?' Theodore was neutral.

'In Gina O'Connor's room.'

The room was silent.

Then, in a harsh whisper, Lucia broke the silence. 'The brooch was found next to her birth-control pills.'

'What are we going to do?' Theodore asked rhetorically.

'That's for you to decide.'

'You will press no charges,' Theodore replied, his tone businesslike. 'And there will be no publicity.' Turning towards Jim Nilson, he said, 'Need I remind you, Mr Nilson, that our contract stipulates absolute privacy?'

'Naturally, sir.'

'Might I then ask you to resume your duties until we send for you?'

Once Jim Nilson had been dismissed, Lucia was free to speak her mind. 'I do not expect the last guests to leave much before 4 a.m. Doubtless, Mark and Fran will have already left the party – they never stay up much beyond midnight. I want you to send Alec to Rufus close to 4 a.m. or earlier, if he sees that only ten or less guests are left.'

'I see. You want to inform Rufus directly,' he said easily. 'In other words, Fran and Mark will only be told about this several hours after Rufus.'

'And then it will be up to Rufus to decide when to confront her.'

'It won't be easy for him,' Theodore said bleakly.

'I don't think he knows too much about her. I'm absolutely certain that she's never told him the whole truth about herself, about her real father's hoodlum connections.'

'So you plan to show him the confidential report on her family?'

Lucia stiffened. 'I hope that will not prove necessary.' She paused. 'But if I have to show it to him, I'll show it to him.'

Shortly after midnight and the blowing-out of the birthday-cake candles, exactly as Lucia had predicted, Mark and Fran left the party in a mood of exhilaration. All parents relish seeing their children happy, and Rufus's happiness was so bright and so deep that it was almost tangible.

Towards three o'clock the party began to thin out. Alec, who had been given his instructions, waited until only eight guests were left. At precisely 3.30 he went up to Rufus to issue his summons.

'Excuse me for interrupting, Mr Rufus, but your grandparents would like to see you.'

'What, now?' asked Rufus incredulously.

'They are waiting for you in Mrs Cartwright's sitting-room. They asked me to tell you that were it not a matter of the utmost importance they would not be sending for you.'

'Gee, guys, I hate to leave you,' Rufus said, his arm about Gina's waist, 'but I guess the party's over.' He gave Gina one last squeeze, kissed her lightly on the lips and then whispered in her ear, 'See you later. Wait for me.'

Nothing in the world could have prepared Rufus for the scene that awaited him. As soon as he entered the sitting-room his grandfather got up and ostentatiously locked the door.

'We need to be private,' he said grimly.

'What's wrong?' Rufus asked, bewildered. Theodore's answer was prompt.

'Do you recognize that brooch?' he asked, gesturing towards the coffee-table.

231

'Of course.' He grinned. 'It's the Lalique dragonfly I was allowed to play with.'

'Your grandmother was going to wear it tonight, but when she looked for it this morning it was nowhere to be found.'

'I don't understand,' Rufus began.

'I hate to embarrass you, son, but do you recognize this vanity case?' Theodore continued relentlessly.

'Yes, sir, I do,' Rufus said slowly. 'It belongs to Gina.'

'We know that,' Theodore murmured.

'What are you getting at?'

'When your grandmother told me that she couldn't find her brooch, I did what I had to do.' He paused and shook his head. 'I ordered Jim Nilson to have every single guest-room searched.'

Rufus's gasp filled the room.

'I regret to have to tell you that to our great shock and horror the brooch was found in Gina's room, in the very vanity case you see before you now.'

'That's impossible,' Rufus exploded. 'She was with me all the time. Besides, Gina is not a thief!'

'No, Rufus, she was not with you all the time,' his grandfather said stonily. 'You and I had a brief meeting, remember. About the small matter of a substantial parcel of stock in Cartwright Pharmaceuticals.'

That stock had been an unexpected birthday present. 'She went to wash her hair,' Rufus said defensively, jumping out of his seat.

'She certainly is a very lovely young girl,' Theodore said. 'But unfortunately she is not honest.'

'Someone must have planted it,' Rufus protested violently. 'I *know* Gina. She could never have done such a thing.'

'You say you know her,' Theodore said briskly. 'But do you know that her real father, Alberto Rizzoli, was a two-bit hood?'

Rufus tugged at his tight curls and said nothing.

'He was dying. He begged to see her. She refused to see her own father. A closer blood relation to her than you are to me!'

Rufus sat down. 'How do you know all this?' he asked weakly.

'Her stepfather was a gardener. Did you know that?'

'No.'

'Her mother is a seamstress. D'you know that?'

'Yes.' He looked at him, his eyes stricken. 'But who could have told you all this?'

Now, for the first time, his grandmother entered the conversation. 'I received an anonymous letter about her.' Lucia sighed deeply. 'Your grandfather called in a private investigator to check it out.' Her eyes pained, she added sympathetically, 'I suppose she couldn't help it; Cartwright House and the Cartwright clan probably overwhelmed her.'

'Whatever the case,' Theodore said, 'we are not bringing any charges against her. Nor will we inform the police.'

Slumped in his chair, Rufus was speechless.

'I'll leave it to you to deal with it,' Theodore said softly. 'If you want Carter to drive her home, you have only to ask him. I'll let him know that you might need him.'

'Thanks,' Rufus said mechanically.

Taking off her ice-white dress, Gina placed it over the chintz armchair. It was about four o'clock in the morning and she felt vividly awake and tremendously excited. She wondered what Rufus would make of her gift to him – a vitrine lithograph of tennis players. She had not yet given it to him; it was to be a surprise. Hours and hours of thought had been devoted to deciding on an appropriate gift, and in the end it was Mirrie who had come up with this idea. She only hoped it would be as distinctive as Mirrie had said it would be. He had received countless pairs of Tiffany cuff-links, gold pens, leather-bound first editions, three identical Cartier key-rings and several matching Hermès ties.

It had been such a glorious night – the second best of her entire life. The very best night, of course, had been the night Rufus and she had first made love, the night of Kate's abortion. She still marvelled at the paradoxical way in which the greatest night of her life had been the worst night of Kate's life.

She released her hair from its chignon and went to the

bathroom to brush it out. The ingeniously mirrored walls of the bathroom meant that she saw herself reflected in an infinity of mirrors. Quite unashamedly, she liked what she saw; a tall, tanned girl standing in a lacy white bra and bikini panties brushing out a mane of shining shoulder-length hair.

She hoped Rufus would not be too long – he had said he would come to her when the party was over. Of course, she could not have gone to his room; it was far too close to his grandparents for that. Needing some body cream, she went to her vanity case. When it was not where she had left it on the table, she was unsurprised. She had already noted the fresh fluffy white towels and the crisp clean sheets on the bed, all of which meant that the maid must have done the room and put the case away somewhere. No matter, she would ask where it was in the morning.

Meanwhile she climbed between the crisp white sheets and waited for Rufus. A few minutes later she jumped out of bed to make sure that she had not locked the door. She returned to her high, white four-poster bed and fell asleep.

She overslept and, the next morning at eight o'clock, Carmelita, the Spanish maid, knocked on her door and opened the curtains. 'Mr Rufus wants to see you,' she said. 'He's waiting for you in the library.'

Bleary-eyed, Gina sat up to thank Carmelita. Placing a breakfast tray on her lap, Carmelita glided to the door. Suddenly Gina remembered her vanity case. 'I couldn't find my vanity case last night,' she called out. 'Did you by any chance put it away somewhere?'

'Sorry, Miss,' Carmelita said stiffly. 'I didn't see it or touch it.'

Chapter Thirty-Eight

Embarrassed that she had overslept, Gina took a bite of toast, gulped down a glass of orange juice and left the rest of the breakfast untouched. Looking for her shower cap, she searched once more for her vanity case. Then remembering that one of the drawers held a number of disposable shower caps, she put one on and stepped under the shower. Moments later she was drying herself and, about twelve minutes after Carmelita had left her room, she was ready in her tennis togs.

As soon as she entered the library, Alec left the room and closed the door. To make sure they would be entirely private, he would remain standing guard outside the door until he was sent for.

She had no sooner crossed the threshold than Rufus and Theodore rose to greet her.

'Sorry, I overslept,' she said with a light laugh. But even as she spoke she was uncomfortably aware that Rufus was not wearing his tennis clothes but a jacket and a tie.

There was no answering laughter or banter of the expected sort that follows on an apology over a minor lapse in manners.

'Won't you please sit down?' said Theodore coldly.

Responding to the hostile atmosphere, Gina said, 'Thank you, sir.' Suddenly she felt anxious; her mind seemed to drop into a hollow fright.

'I trust you are comfortable.' Theodore chuckled in a thin, mocking tone.

Now thoroughly alarmed, she said, 'Very comfortable, thank you.'

At that, Theodore ostentatiously directed his gaze towards the coffee-table. Involuntarily and understandably, Gina's eyes followed his. At that same moment, Theodore flung out his arm and pointed towards the vanity case. 'Do you recognize that?' he said, his voice heavy with sarcasm.

'I've been looking for it everywhere,' Gina exploded. 'How did it get here?'

'I merely asked you, Miss O'Connor, to state whether or not you recognized it,' Theodore said, his eyes glinting with malice.

Shocked, but nonetheless bold, she turned towards Rufus. 'What is this?' she asked him. 'An inquisition?'

She had hardly ended her sentence when, blocking off Rufus's chance to reply, Theodore snapped: '*You* recognize the vanity case, Miss O'Connor. *We* recognize *this!*' With that he jumped up and tapped the brooch with his pen.

'I recognize the brooch, too,' she said innocently. 'I've seen examples of Lalique's work in the Metropolitan Museum.'

This was too much for Theodore. The girl had the nerve to be arrogant. 'Don't add impertinence to your crime,' he snapped.

'Rufus?' she appealed questioningly. 'What crime? This is crazy!'

'Yesterday morning, Mrs Cartwright took the jewellery she was planning to wear from the safe and, as is her custom, placed it in a velvet box on her desk.' Twirling his pen between his long fingers, he paused dramatically.

'You're not implying—' Gina began.

'Allow me to finish. I would be grateful if you did not interrupt,' Theodore commanded. 'To return to what I was saying: Mrs Cartwright placed the brooch in the velvet box and, once she had completed dressing, she did what most women do, and went to put on her jewellery. It was then that she discovered the brooch was not there!'

Gina felt cold enough to shiver. Her mouth went dry, but her palms were wet and clammy. She tried to speak but no words could pass the huge lump in her throat. Despite feeling faint, she could no longer remain seated and she stood up, supporting herself by holding on to the chair.

'And so,' Theodore continued in that same accusing voice. 'And so – with the greatest reluctance – we were compelled to have our security people search the belongings of all our guests. The brooch was found in a pocket of your vanity case, wrapped in a scrap of crumpled tissue, beside your—' here he paused, then, in a voice laden with contempt, he went on, 'beside your contraception pills.'

'Rufus,' she begged, her voice trembling. 'Rufus, you can't possibly believe I took it? You can't believe I'm a thief!'

'None of this has been easy for Rufus,' Theodore said sternly. 'And the fact that he did not know that you are the daughter of Alberto Rizzoli did not make this any easier for him!'

She sat down abruptly and, grief-stricken, covered her face with her hands. Shocked and incurably hurt, she was beyond dignity, beyond pride, beyond everything except pain. She scarcely heard the harsh, ugly sounds that issued from her throat. How long she sobbed she did not know; she was scarcely conscious of anything except for the inexplicable injustice of it all.

However, Theodore's hard brays of laughter penetrated her heaving. 'Better give her a glass of water, Rufus, or our ears will burst!'

At that, the tears stopped.

There was a long, throbbing silence.

Finally Gina spoke. 'You've said nothing, Rufus. Nothing. Tell me to my face that you believe all this of me.' Her voice broke. 'Go on, tell me that in your eyes I am now a liar and a thief.'

Still Rufus said nothing.

Once more Gina repeated the challenge.

At last Rufus spoke. 'Carter will drive you home,' he said painfully. 'Your things are already in the car.'

Wordlessly, Gina left. As she reached the doorway she called out, 'Why don't you press charges against me, Mr Cartwright?' She took a few steps closer to him. 'I'd be perfectly happy to stand trial!' Then she walked right up to Rufus until her face was only inches from his, and said tonelessly, 'I feel sorry for you, Rufus. I feel sorry that you have a grandmother to stoop so low as to plant a brooch in my case.' Pressing her index finger into his lapel, she went on. 'And I feel sorry for you because you are too weak to talk to me yourself. Like all cowards, you let someone else do your dirty work for you!'

Half-way home she asked Carter to take her to Mirrie's. Whatever had happened to her, it was still Sunday morning and there was a good chance Mirrie would be home. She wanted to save her mother from witnessing her suffering. She toyed with the idea of asking Carter to stop and put her on a bus to New York, but she knew the limo would get to Mirrie's sooner.

Miriam sat her down in her cheerful kitchen and let her just talk and talk. She had a new kitten and placed it in Gina's lap, and as she talked she caressed it and grew calmer.

Encouraged by Miriam to tell her everything, she left nothing out. She told her about their love-making on the night of Kate's abortion, of how their time in bed reached greater and greater heights, of the wonderfully warm and friendly way in which the Cartwright family had asked her to join their receiving-line, of their secret time spent in a cabin in the Adirondacks, of his dismay at running into the Powells.

All of which took a long while. Only then, when Miriam knew all the wonder and glory of their love affair, did she tell Miriam of the inquisition that had taken place a few hours before.

'I thought he was so strong,' she sobbed. 'But he was so weak, so weak. He never gave me a chance.' Again and again she would say piteously, 'God, how I will miss him! I want to hate him, but I can't.'

Miriam knew enough to know that – too soon and too much – the hate would come. She also knew that Gina was only at the beginning of her withdrawal from her sexual addiction to Rufus. She, too, had suffered in this way and, as a pharmacist, she likened it to the physical and mental anguish of the process of withdrawal from drugs as lethal as heroin or cocaine. Sexual deprivation could be crueller than cruel.

Finally, by way of diverting her from this awareness of the

end of her physical relationship with Rufus, she said, 'We could, of course, sue them for slander.'

'Slander?'

'Well, the Cartwrights have done a grave and great injury to your reputation, haven't they?'

'There were no witnesses to what Theodore Cartwright said,' Gina scowled. 'Rufus was ready to believe the worst of me!'

'I've lost all respect for him,' Miriam said.

'It was easy for them to destroy me,' Gina said bitterly. 'A nothing and a nobody like me.'

'What do you mean, a nothing and a nobody like you? How dare you say that?' Miriam demanded.

Miriam knew that Gina hadn't heard her. She longed to take her in her arms and comfort her. But huddled up on the kitchen seat, lost in her own thoughts, her red-rimmed eyes desolate, and enclosed in a band of her acute pain, she seemed untouchable. The kitten stirred on her lap, but she ignored it. Miriam took the kitten from her. She sat for a while caressing the kitten as she would have wished to caress Gina. Presently she got up to brew some coffee. This ordinary everyday activity filled the silence like a welcome intruder.

When she returned to the table she found Gina sitting up straight. Her narrowed, red-rimmed eyes glittered with rage, and with a strange determination. Quietly Miriam set the steaming cup of coffee in front of her.

'Thank you, Mirrie,' Gina said, meaning it.

She's no longer unreachable, Miriam thought.

The silence continued.

Finally, when Gina did speak, it was with a steady, controlled anger. Now, deadly calm, her voice came out in a strong, prayerful whisper.

'His grandfather told me that the brooch had been found beside my pills!' she told Miriam.

Reminded of what had happened all those years ago to Gina's mother for using a diaphragm, Miriam shook her head from side to side. 'Bastard!' she spat out. 'What a bastard!'

239

'I felt like a prostitute when he said that. He made it all dirty. But it wasn't dirty, Mirrie. It wasn't. It was beautiful.'

Another storm of weeping overtook her. When it passed she asked Miriam for a cigarette. She had never smoked before. Then, in tones of extreme determination, she said, 'I've got my whole life ahead of me. And from now on, everything I do will be geared to make those Cartwrights know that I am *not* a nothing and *not* a nobody!'

'That's a healthy approach, Gina,' Miriam said fervently.

'Those Cartwrights put me in a limousine as if I were a bunch of dirty, discarded clothes they were sending to the poor,' Gina continued bitterly. 'They've probably forgotten all about me by now. I guess I'm not even a memory for Rufus!'

She picked up the kitten and held it to her cheek. Her eyes ablaze with determination, she said, 'But I, Gina O'Connor, will *not* be forgotten. I don't know how I will do it, I know only that I'll get even with them!'

Ah, thought Miriam, she's so young. Time will heal and she'll forget all about it . . . Out loud she said, 'Sure, Gina.'

'You're not taking me seriously,' Gina said reproachfully. 'Not only will they not forget me, but, more than a memory, I'll be a daily regret!'

She sounds a lot better already, thought Miriam. She'll get over this.

'Their security man wasn't pulling a fast one,' Gina said in a tense monotone. 'He really *did* find the brooch.' She paused and, clasping and unclasping her hands, continued, 'And I'll bet that it was planted there by Lucia Cartwright!'

Which horrendous fact had been obvious to Miriam from the outset. Once again she thought, Gina's young. She'll recover from this.

But Miriam was wrong.

Because Gina was never to get over what had happened to her that morning.

Chapter Thirty-Nine

Shortly before her eighteenth birthday, Gina's freshman year at Radcliffe began. Like her mother before her, she too looked older than her years. However, unlike her mother, it was neither physical hardship nor fear for her life that had refined her into something of a youthful yet mature beauty, but disappointment. Her fellow students acknowledged her as a rare beauty, and although she was friendly and outgoing, there was a strong sensation that she had been carved out of ice, frozen, never to be thawed.

Perhaps it was because, despite her ready laughter, or her sympathetic smile, or the seemingly limitless lengths to which she was ready to go to help – and often to coach – others, she gave nothing of herself away.

The young men were attracted to her and at the same time afraid of her; by the time her second semester came along she was seen as a challenge. Her reputation as an ice maiden made her more and not less of a prize. People speculated endlessly on her virginity – was she or wasn't she? Bets were laid down, but no one currently at Harvard or at Yale was destined ever to know for sure. It *was* known that she had dated Rufus Cartwright, who was now in Geneva, but unsurprisingly that was thought to be a brief relationship. It should not be forgotten that, until shortly before his twenty-first, their romance had been kept pretty secret . . .

Leonard Wilkes, Franklyn Phipps and Christopher Madden were all young men she had dated during her freshman year, apportioning them equal time, allowing each to believe that, when she was ready for a seriously committed relationship, he – and only he – would be the man of her choice.

Cecilia knew nothing of how her friendship with Rufus Cartwright had come to an end. 'There could be no constructive reason for telling her,' Miriam had decreed, and Gina had only been too happy to go along with her ruling.

One day, of course, Gina would inform her mother of every single detail. But by that time it wouldn't matter so much, for by then she would have all but destroyed the Cartwrights.

All too often the ambition or obsession for revenge is the motor force of ambition. Gina had not lacked ambition to start with, but it had never been focused. Once her ambition had a focus its dynamism was unstoppable. It turned her into a student of unbeatable excellence.

Everyone, including Rufus, had taken it for granted that, after the long summer vacation that followed on his graduation, he would fulfil his destiny: his career at Cartwright Pharmaceuticals would begin. Needless to say, he would be based at their headquarters in New York for a year or so, gaining administrative and financial experience, after which he was expected to move to Switzerland, where he would be given the opportunity to expand and develop their fledgeling company in Geneva.

'You'll test your wings in Geneva, son,' his grandfather had told him. 'It will be a heavy responsibility. You'll be our man in Geneva, a CFO. Nothing less than Chief Financial Officer for my grandson!'

Now, however, the plans were changed. Always a man of quick and final decisions, Theodore Cartwright had judged it both expedient and sensible to put an ocean between his grandson and Gina.

His French nanny had told Rufus often enough that, although Geneva was dull and humourless, it was *en route* to everywhere. The airport was less than a ten-minute drive out of town; travel was made so easy that some people went as far as to call Geneva a large transit camp. A keen skier, Rufus looked forward to weekends at Zermatt or Gstaad. Once in Geneva, he quickly acquired an apartment on the Quai du Mont Blanc that overlooked the lake and Mont Blanc, which guarded its snow even in the height of summer. Two weeks after his arrival he bought a motor boat. Now that he had the right address and the right accessories, Geneva would be anything but boring.

Though he was aware that he owed his precipitate presence in Geneva to his former connection with Gina, he welcomed the thought of an ocean between them. In spite of her having stolen the brooch and let him down, he still found himself aching for her. But, since it had not for one moment occurred to him to doubt Gina's guilt, less than a month after the event of the brooch he had stopped asking himself whether or not they would still have been writing letters to each other if Gina's dishonesty had not been uncovered. Fortunately, Gina had chosen to steal from the Cartwright household; any other family would have laid charges against her. Since his grandfather had made that very clear, he could only hope that she would not succumb again . . .

Pretty soon he and Fabrice became lovers. As the daughter and only child of the Count and Countess de Payot, one of the five great family bankers of Switzerland, it was perhaps inevitable that they would meet – Cartwright Pharmaceuticals (Switzerland) was one of the Banque de Payot's important clients. Now, if the Swiss had a reputation for being stolid, unimaginative citizens whose menfolk were ordered to carry a needle and thread in their army packs (military service was compulsory), Fabrice certainly gave the lie to that. In 1963, forty-three years after female suffrage in the US, Swiss women still did not have the vote. They were expected to be as docile as the cows who supplied the milk for their legendary Swiss chocolate.

Certainly, Fabrice did not conform to this or any other stereotype. Even as a rebel she was atypical, for her aristocratic status added a measure of nobility to her rebellion. Tall, and with a regal, graceful carriage, her looks were of the crowd-turning variety. Her expression, a paradoxical mixture of innocence and sophistication, had led more than one man to fall hopelessly in love with her.

In the late fifties, when de Gaulle gave Brigitte Bardot one of France's highest honours because she, along with Peugeot, was France's biggest export item, Fabrice's attitude towards the Establishment turned from mild disenchantment to fervent disgust. Fancying herself as a member of the Beat generation, she left the University of Geneva and went off to Berkeley to 'do her own thing'. There she exercised her licence to sexual freedom with the utmost abandon.

Unlike many of her greasy-fringed contemporaries, she refused to allow her long, copper hair, which fell to her waist like a luxurious curtain, to be anything but perfectly clean. Here, in a novel way, this relic of her Swiss upbringing turned her into a rebel among the rebels. Although her mania for generosity led her to dispense her sexual favours as indiscriminately as possible, she was more sought after than most of her sisters. She was, she believed, the very definition of sexual liberation.

Suddenly, she left the world of promiscuity and went to live with Leroy Collins, a musician and an ardent member of the drug culture. To prove the extent and the strength of his love for her, Leroy abandoned Marge, his wife of fifteen years. Fabrice had not yet run out of cash: there was enough to support them both for at least a year.

Four months after they had been together, he died of an overdose. Since his wife had had the grace to invite her to the wake, she had not had the guts to refuse. As she stood beside the open coffin, his suddenly fatherless daughter tugged her long hair and, in the assertive, unforgiving tones of a thirteen-year-old, announced, 'He looks beautiful, doesn't he, Fabrice? My mother says he died because of you . . .'

Dressed in black, along with the other mourners, Fabrice forced herself to look into the open coffin. It was at that moment that Leroy's mother shrieked, 'Get this woman who killed my son out of here, or, by Christ, you'll have another dead body on your hands!'

Somehow Fabrice got out of there. Too weary even to attempt to fool herself that she was Leroy's grief-stricken mistress,

Fabrice consoled herself that she had not as much as hinted that she was planning on leaving him anyway. Since she had kept silent in this way, she felt no responsibility whatsoever for Leroy's death.

She had exactly ninety dollars and thirty cents to her name. Enough to take her to the Four Seasons Hotel where, if she paid in advance, she could check in for a night. She took a long, luxurious bath and then, at precisely six o'clock, seated in the sparkling white fluffy bathrobe that went with the room, she placed a collect call to her parents in Geneva.

At precisely two o'clock in the morning, at the Château Beau Ciel, the telephone rang. It was her mother's sixtieth birthday, which was why her parents were hoping against hope that she would call. Neither of them had even attempted to go to sleep. Even as they waited, they could not help dreading the shrill, ominous ring.

'This is the United States calling—'

'Yes, yes. We will accept the call,' her father, the Count, snapped before the operator could finish her sentence.

Unable to stop herself from crowing out loud, the Countess said, 'I told you she would never forget her mother's birthday.'

Meanwhile her husband was saying, '*Chérie, chérie,* but your mother was sure, absolutely sure. I mean she had no doubt that you would call on her sixtieth birthday!'

At that point the Countess snatched the phone from her husband. 'Fabrice, Fabrice, just to hear your voice is the best present in the world.'

'*Félicitations, Maman,*' Fabrice responded clearly and unhesitatingly. She had, of course, entirely forgotten the date of her mother's birthday. 'And may the good Lord ensure many, many more birthdays!'

Her father had left the bedroom to pick up the extension telephone in his study. Chiming into the conversation, his voice breaking with emotion, he asked, 'Tell us, *chérie,* where you are.'

'San Francisco.'

'That explains it, then,' her father said triumphantly. 'You forgot that there was an *eight*-hour time difference between Geneva and San Francisco. Your mother thought it was only five hours, as it is from New York. That is why you are calling us at two o'clock in the morning.'

Whereupon both he and his wife gave delighted shouts of laughter.

'*Papa, Maman*, you are always right,' she said, her voice suddenly going tearful. 'I have missed you – both of you.'

'Are you short of money?' enquired the banker.

'When are you coming home?' enquired the mother.

There was a silence. To her utter astonishment, Fabrice found that she was flooded with warm tears.

'I'll instruct our New York office to forward the money to San Francisco and get it delivered to you. That way you will not need to go to a bank and fetch it,' her father ordered in his quickest staccato tones.

'You could get the first available flight,' her mother put in. 'We'll have the ticket sent to you. It will be easier for you.'

Fighting successfully for control, Fabrice said, 'A small second, please. I cannot hear myself think while you two talk at the same time.'

'*Tant mieux!*' exclaimed her mother happily. '*Tant mieux!*'

Although nothing specific was said about how much money was needed or how much would be sent, it was enough for her to mention that some very good friends of hers had suffered a grievous tragedy. The loss of the father would also mean a serious loss of income. But they did have the specific name of her hotel as well as her agreement to fly home to Geneva.

The following day, with Swiss precision, a one-way ticket was delivered to her hotel. An hour later, she signed for two envelopes, each of which contained 5000 dollars. She kept 2000 dollars for herself and then, armed with the envelope that now contained 8000 dollars, went to call on the recently widowed Mrs Collins. She stayed not a second longer than the time it took to put the envelope into Marge Collins's empty hands.

After leaving the Collins household she went to an exclusive boutique called Flamingo, where she bought herself one of those tailored but feminine little Emmanuelle Kahn suits that were being copied everywhere. From there she went to the hairdresser, where her long hair was lovingly put into a classic chignon.

When her plane landed early on Wednesday morning her parents – thanks to their privileged position in society – were waiting on the tarmac to meet her. Demure but remarkably chic, Fabrice attracted admiring glances wherever she went. As one hostess was heard to remark, she was indeed a classic example of youthful, all-round perfection.

Three months later, early in September, Rufus Cartwright arrived in Geneva. Naturally enough the Count and the Countess de Payot saw him as the answer to their prayers. Fabrice still seemed strangely drawn to America and to Americans. Needless to say, they would have wished that if their daughter could not marry *un haut Genevois*, then she would at the very least find *un vrai Genevois*. Still, things could have been worse, much worse, for although Rufus was an American, he was not without the right European connections. He was, after all, the grandson of the daughter of the Marchese and Marchesa di Cica . . .

Chapter Forty

Despite the fact that she won every award possible during the first semester of her freshman year at Radcliffe, Gina'a inner bitterness still raged. But it was a private bitterness, so well disguised, so well directed, that it presented itself in the bright light of a powerful, nerveless energy. She whirled through her essays, was in the tennis team, on the editorial board of the school newspaper. In short, as her math professor was heard to murmur, 'Gina O'Connor is that rare sort of once-in-a-generation student whom it is both a privilege – and a challenge – to teach.'

And in all the world it was Miriam Stern – and only Miriam Stern – who knew that the lust for vengeance was the true inspiration for Gina's excellence.

When Fabrice returned from San Francisco her parents could not reasonably expect her to stay with them in their family home, the Château Beau Ciel. Accordingly they bought her an apartment in the enchanting and highly exclusive *vieille ville*, the old town of Geneva. With its curving cobbled streets, old drinking troughs for horses, and restaurants such as Les Armures, from which the pungent, mouth-watering whiff of Gruyère cheese for *raclette* emanated, the old town was as romantic as it was dignified. Fabrice's apartment overlooked the famous ancient wall that, more than several hundred years ago, housewives had made famous. They had defeated those who had tried to conquer their city merely by hurling cauldrons of scalding soup over the wall and on to the hapless soldiers.

'It can't be true,' Rufus said when Fabrice told him the story. 'It's one of those legends.'

'Legend or not, we women take it very seriously,' Fabrice said solemnly.

'We women' was a favourite phrase of hers. An ardent feminist who saw the passage of the Equal Pay Act of 1963 as a victory for 'us women' in America, she made fierce attempts at campaigning for Swiss women to be given the vote. As a devoted follower of Simone de Beauvoir, she believed that 'we women' had a duty to espouse the Left. 'We women,' she would pronounce, as if she had hit on a new and vital truth, 'we women are political animals.'

It was, without doubt, the animal side of 'us women' that Rufus was interested in. And so he humoured her, for though she was three years older than him, he was nevertheless convinced that it was a phase she would grow out of.

She was a swirl of energy to him, a creature of tight, fathomless mystery. Again and again, his body fusing with his soul, he would feel himself possessed by what he had come to think of as her genius for lingering sexual excitement.

She had a genuine flair for titillation and she gave it full rein. Sensing that her time in San Francisco held a powerful and twisted fascination for him, she would speak of the orgies in which she had participated – multi-racial, multi-sexual, she said. Slanting upwards, her long, gentle eyes would turn reflective and she would explain that, although she was definitely not a lesbian, she had been to bed with lesbians.

'How often?' he would ask, excited.

'More often than I can remember,' she would reply, drawing her full lips inward in a long sigh.

Which would turn him on. Imagining her in the arms of another woman, he would make frantic, competitive love to her. He would drive them both to wilder and wilder heights, forcing her to lose herself in his strong male arms, just as he lost himself in her long, tangled hair. If she was a good teacher, he was an even better pupil. Afterwards she would lie beside him, innocent and peaceful, basking in their combined halo of tenderness. After a while, his eyes still shut, he would feel her short, sharp beginning kisses, like quickly falling raindrops, and then the sudden big single kiss that would draw him into her, leading them both to that shared whiff of eternity.

He would wonder, sometimes, how he ever got to work, for no matter how wildly unconventional her behaviour in bed, she would insist that he return to his own apartment, even if he only arrived there at 6 a.m. Behind his apartment house in the bustling Quartier Paquis he would stop at the *boulangerie* and consume several newly baked croissants, still hot from the oven.

She called herself a journalist – an American travel magazine had accepted one of her pieces. She was currently engaged in writing a long article for *Sport* on the golf courses of Switzerland. But the truth was that though work did not interrupt her days, she was not idle. She was a dedicated volunteer worker at a home for convalescent pensioners. On more than one weekend she had asked Rufus to drive a lonely, neglected parent to see his heartless family.

As his grandfather had predicted, Rufus's French became more and more fluent. However, he still tuned in to the *Voice of America*, which was how, exactly two months after he had arrived in Geneva, he learned that President Kennedy had been assassinated. That Friday night, feeling lonely and isolated, he cancelled his usual date with Fabrice and had too much to drink. Therefore it was with Dutch courage that he put a transatlantic call through to Radcliffe.

It is not uncommon for a shared grief both to obliterate the past and to grant forgiveness. It is not for nothing that it is said that at a funeral all is forgiven. They talked to one another for an hour (night in Geneva, day in Boston) and wept together and tried to comprehend that the unthinkable had happened.

Across the Atlantic he listened to her strike a match. Then he heard her inhale. 'I didn't know you smoked,' he said, surprised. Something in his tone suggested that he felt he ought to have known.

'I've been through nearly a whole pack since I got the news—'

She eventually said calmly. 'I didn't take that brooch, you know.'

'I've only just realized that,' he answered slowly, thoughtfully. 'I don't expect you to believe me, but it's true.'

'I do believe you,' she replied unexpectedly, her voice high and cold. 'At least I think I do.'

'I can't offer you any excuse of any kind,' he said, gritting his teeth. 'But would an apology be an insult?'

'I can't answer that,' she said reasonably. 'Not yet.'

'I'll be back home for Christmas.'

'Oh?'

'Is there any chance of seeing you?'

'I don't know.' She frowned. 'I'm not sure. We'll have to wait and see. Right now someone needs to use the phone!'

The next moment she had hung up. As he heard the phone click off he resolved to call her back. Perhaps she had merely wanted to cut the conversation and so had lied that someone needed the phone . . .

No sooner had he replaced the receiver, however, than the phone rang.

'I'm worried about you, *chéri*,' Fabrice said anxiously.

'Try to understand, I don't feel like talking. My president is dead. Shot. Assassinated.'

'But your line has been busy, chéri,' she pouted.

'Sure it was busy. I was speaking to an American.'

'Your ex-girl-friend?'

'However did you guess?' he asked sarcastically.

'We women know these things.' Her voice was heavy with reproach.

'Aw, give me a break, Fabrice—'

'I'm worried about you,' she persisted. 'I'll be with you in ten minutes flat.'

Shrugging, he lit the fire in the grate.

She was shivering when he let her in. Her high leather boots and mink coat did not appear to offer her any warmth. Her teeth chattered. She tightened the fur collar about her neck and moved towards the fireplace.

'A cognac, perhaps?' she suggested.

He said nothing, but crossed to the drinks trolley and picked up two crystal brandy-snifters and the bottle of Napoleon cognac and brought them to her. He poured the amber liquid into each glass. She took a long sip and then, in a single fluid movement, seated herself on the floor close to the fire. Her long copper hair gleamed – everything about her softened in the firelight – and she looked heartbreakingly vulnerable.

She sipped the cognac slowly. Other than the lamp on his desk and the glow from the fire, there was no light in the room. The crackle and hiss from the fire was the only sound.

She began to unbutton her coat. 'I'm warm enough now,' she said, when all the buttons were undone. 'I don't need my coat.'

The next moment her coat was off and he saw the firelight flickering over her wondrously unexpected nakedness and her knee-high leather boots. He moaned. Something that sounded close to a roar escaped from his throat and, in his clumsy rush to get to her, his glass of cognac went spinning to the floor.

'Fabrice!' he cried. 'Fabrice!'

'Wait,' she whispered. 'One small second and *voilà!*' As she spoke, in a single fluid movement, she turned her coat around so that they would have a blanket of fur. She took him to her breast and, with her thighs and knee-high boots, clasped him to her, and he was quickly inside her, calling her name in a thickened voice that she had never heard before.

Early the next morning, while she was still asleep, he left her to fetch the freshly baked croissants from the *boulangerie*.

'See,' he said when he returned. 'I don't turn you out of my bed for the sake of respectability.'

She laughed and, between mouthfuls of croissant told him she would have to leave him. '*Maman* always calls me at eight o'clock.'

He let her go and instantly calculated what time it was in Boston.

It was about two o'clock in the morning.

252

Too late to call her.

Dammit, he had promised himself he would call her again . . .

Over the next three weeks he called her several times. Even though she was always non-committal, friendly, there was no doubt in his mind that she would see him again when he returned to Boston for Christmas.

And then he and Fabrice and a group of friends went up to St Moritz for a skiing weekend and he broke his leg badly and stayed in Switzerland. He was not even skiing when the accident happened – he merely slipped on some ice. However, much to his surprise, disgust and embarrassment, it obviously made no difference *how* he broke his leg; he was put into an ambulance and taken to the hospital. The last thing he thought before he drifted off into his anaesthetized sleep was that such a stupid little accident could not possibly result in surgery. He ran a fever and they kept him in hospital for almost a week, and the whole thing was incomprehensible to him.

When he was discharged they put him in an ambulance and took him and his heavy cast back to the chalet. He would have to spend at least six weeks in his plaster cast . . . High up in the Swiss Alps, lying immobilized on the sun-deck, he felt as if he had no control over his destiny. Furious about his accident, and locked in an inner rage, he did not bother to call Gina.

Meanwhile, Fabrice would be his nurse.

Now that the friends had gone, he and Fabrice were alone in the chalet. The first night of his convalescence, his huge and cumbersome cast seemed to inspire Fabrice to ever more daring feats of sexual unpredictability.

But out on the sun-deck, at noon the next day, both were shocked to discover that it was not his plaster cast that was to be an impediment to their love-making, but the arrival of Fabrice's mother. As she watched her mother getting out of her neat Austin Healey, she exclaimed, '*Merde!* The Comte and Comtesse must have figured that nothing could possibly happen on the day of your return from hospital!'

253

Watching her race down to welcome her mother, and listening to the sounds of their excited feminine chatter, he felt a sense of alarm. But then, listening to the Countess saying that to tempt the appetite of the invalid she had brought all manner of delicacies, champagne, caviare, pâté de foie gras, he knew that he was doomed.

He was not wrong: his destiny had – at least for the next few years – been taken out of his hands.

For weeks Gina had been trying to convince herself that she had not really expected to hear from Rufus. He had been caught by the tragic drama of the moment, that was all, and because he'd been lonely and isolated in Switzerland he had called her. That was all.

But she wished he had never called. She had only just been beginning to try to get over him, and then his call had come and it had been a setback to her recovery.

There was no sane reason for her even to think of him, but the mysterious pain of him was buried deep in her. Night after sleepless night she would attempt if not to place it under an imaginary microscope for analysis, then at least to exhume it. But as constant as her own breathing, the wound of him would not heal. Nor would it be understood. She knew only that her soul belonged to him.

Aware that she had become known as the 'ice maiden', she tried hard not to be so unyielding, so unapproachable. But no sooner would one of her dates be courageous enough to press his lips against hers, than her lips would taste of iron filings, and he would feel her every muscle tighten against him; and her punishingly cool, contemptuous eyes would be no less effective than a switch-blade.

In this new era of the pill, she did not want to be a one-man woman, but the very notion of a physical relationship with anyone else was revolting to her; she could not become an accomplice in her own ruin. Why give up the security of possessing nothing in the world of love?

It was around this time that the new magazine *Elegance* was launched. The first issue contained photographs of the ten most beautiful women in America, one of whom was none other than Gina O'Connor. It was a great *coup*, but because he would not see it it was spoilt for her.

She was not to know that the magazine would be sent to him. But he was not to see it for several months. By then the de Payots' negotiations, in which he and his fate were to feature so prominently, would have been successfully concluded.

Chapter Forty-One

In the end, after many meetings and much consultation among the three de Payots it was decided – as they all had always known it would be – that the negotiations with Rufus should be initiated and conducted by Fabrice's father. After all, had he not had negotiating experience with presidents of multinational corporations, of other banks and even of countries? As he descended to his cellar from which he would select a bottle of wine from its numbered bin, he already knew that a dry, businesslike tone would serve him well. He allowed the wine to breathe for the appropriate time, and then went to the sun-deck to invite Rufus to join him for a drink in his study.

The transaction was to be conducted in English. Diplomacy decreed that the use of Rufus's mother-tongue would testify to the great respect in which he was held. It would also signal the seriousness of their tête-à-tête.

Once Rufus was seated on the leather cabriolet fireside chair, and his crutches neatly arranged, Count de Payot took up the seat opposite him and opened his negotiations. 'We Swiss are well known for our practical approach to life,' he said ponderously. 'That is why we believe the only sensible attitude towards the wine we produce is to drink it ourselves!'

Aware that this was the Count's idea of an amusing joke, Rufus summoned a laugh.

'But I have decided that in honour of this very special occasion, we would split a bottle of claret – a Bordeaux of *premier cru* – Château Lafite-Rothschild, 1951.'

He busied himself pouring the drink. Rufus glanced nervously at the fire. '*Santé!*' the Count said.

'*Santé!*'

'I suppose it could be said that at seventy-two, I am too old to be the father of a daughter as young and as beautiful as Fabrice—'

'I wouldn't say that exactly, sir—'

'You are too kind, and too polite—' said the Count in the businesslike tone he had elected to use. 'I was forty-eight when she was born.' Now, in spite of himself, his voice became charged with emotion. 'The moment I held her in my arms for the first time—' He paused and sighed with the enormity of his memory. 'Ah well, it was the greatest moment of my life. No deal – I repeat, no deal – not my monumentally successful underwriting and flotation of Zellerhof Chemicals which netted me profit that went into the millions – was anything like the day I first held my daughter.' Taking a reflective sip, he added, 'Millions, I tell you. Millions.'

'The Zellerhof deal made history—'

'The time has come for plain talk,' interrupted the older man, noting with satisfaction the sudden high colour in Rufus's cheeks.

'Plain talk?' Rufus repeated questioningly.

'Plain talk,' the Count echoed. 'A matter as delicate as the one I wish to broach with you is best served by plain, straight talk.' He looked at Rufus's glass. 'Allow me,' he said graciously, busying himself once again with pouring the wine. Pointing his glass towards the window and the snow-capped, majestic Alps, he said, 'Come! There is a car parked in front of our chalet. I believe you can see it from here. I also believe that she is a machine of such remarkably elegant power that she will be a joy to your eyes.' So saying, he handed Rufus his crutches.

'Thank you, sir,' Rufus said, rising awkwardly.

Count de Payot joined him at the window. 'Just in case the sun sets before I had a chance to show it to you, I had the driver leave the lights on.'

Rufus looked out and gasped out loud. For there, parked in front of the chalet as if it could belong nowhere else, was a gleaming jet-black Ferrari.

'What a beauty! Is that a 330 GT Ferrari?' Rufus exclaimed,

257

leaning further out of the window. He whistled between his teeth.

'It's yours,' the Count said in a matter-of-fact tone.

'Mine?'

'You heard me.'

'I don't understand—'

'Come, sit yourself down and I will explain.' He waited until Rufus was seated and then poured more wine. 'She is already registered in your name,' he went on conversationally.

'My name? I don't understand, sir.'

'The *comtesse* and myself have the greatest pleasure in presenting it to you as a gift.'

His voice high with incredulity, Rufus repeated, 'A gift?'

'You might call it an engagement gift,' the Count said smoothly. 'We have chosen something quite different for your fiancée – a jewel that has been in my family for many generations.'

Though he knew the answer with a terrible clarity, Rufus asked, 'Has Fabrice been told about this?'

'Yes, and a very happy young woman she is, too.' Despite an overwhelming impulse to get up and beat the American with his own crutches, the Count remained in his seat. 'The engagement will, of necessity, be short—'

Snatching up his crutches, Rufus stood up. 'Of necessity?' he demanded. 'How do you mean, of necessity?'

'I mean exactly what I say, and exactly what you think I mean,' the Count declared firmly. 'I think, perhaps, you had better sit down again.'

Dazed, Rufus could do nothing but obey.

'Yes, we have had our fears confirmed,' the Count said with a long sigh. 'Doctor Portierre was most reassuring. We have taken the view, the *comtesse* and I, that your worst fears can turn into your greatest hopes!'

Rufus thought for a long moment, and then asked simply, 'Why didn't she tell me herself?'

'Because she was too shy – and too ashamed!' Here the businesslike tone fled from his voice. 'She was – how shall I say? –

258

anxious as to how you would take it. But I knew I could safely tell her you would do the honourable thing. I told her that if I am any judge of character at all – and judging character has always been my strong point – you would not let her down.'

For want of something to do, and at the same time to give Rufus a chance to collect his thoughts, he got up and placed another log on the fire. It caught at once, and the fire flared upward. Its pleasant roar filled the otherwise silent room. Unable to think, still less speak, Rufus shifted uncomfortably in his chair.

The silence lengthened. At last the Count was forced to demand, 'Well?'

'When is the wedding to be?' Rufus asked tonelessly.

'We will decide that together – *all four of us*.' The Count's authoritative voice could not be defied.

A *Ferrari*! Rufus thought. *What a way to get a Ferrari*! The irony of it was too much for him and he laughed bitterly.

Whatever else it was, it *was* a laugh; enough, certainly, for his future father-in-law to make the most of. Hastily jumping up, he kissed Rufus on both cheeks and then, affecting his practised pretence of great merriment, called out to the maid to fetch his daughter.

Instantly, champagne and caviare and Fabrice and her mother entered the study.

Sufficiently dazed to be detached, Rufus watched the scene unfolding before him as if he were a member of an audience watching a second-rate farce.

Thus it was that he learned that in August 1964 he was to become a father. He also learned that he was to be married in Geneva on Wednesday, January 22nd. It was only when it emerged *en passant* that the de Payots were Catholics that he thought of his grandparents. Even in the midst of the so-called spontaneous celebration he thought that, like his grandfather Theodore, he was marrying a foreigner. However, unlike his grandfather, who had married at thirty, he was just twenty-one. He was about to write off nine years of his life.

Throughout all the jollity, no one mentioned the Ferrari. His

parents and grandparents were telephoned. Wedding arrangements – the church and the reception at the Château Beau Ciel
– were mentioned. From across the Atlantic, the congratulations
poured in as they always do after a successfully concluded
business deal, Rufus thought joylessly. Was there to be no
escape? Helped by champagne, his mind shut off.

The jewel that the Count had spoken of turned out to be an
'engagement' ring – a cabochon emerald. It was given to Rufus
to put on her finger. A small ceremony was made of this, and
more champagne appeared. He drank quickly, as if he had a
great unslakeable thirst. Soon, again with much hilarity, they
decided to help him into bed. He was tipsy, they said.

Early that morning, at about five o'clock, she came to his
room and they made love. In the dark she pressed her engagement ring to his lips. Her leave-taking was as soundless as their
love-making had been. No mention was made of her pregnancy.

His last thought as he drifted off to sleep was that he was
going to go in for a new sport – motor-racing.

An hour later he was awake, wondering how different everything would have been if Gina had come from the right sort of
family. She had told him she had not stolen that brooch and for
a while – about four days or so – he had almost believed her.
And then he returned to his senses. After all, the brooch had
been found in her bag, and it could not possibly have walked
there. Because who on earth could have planted it? A servant?
But then what would the servant have gained? Answer: nothing.
Gina had stolen it and, in stealing it, she had killed something
. . . It looked very much as if Gina had been attracted to his
position, to the wealth of his socially prominent family.

Unlike Gina, Fabrice had no need of his credentials. She had
her own.

Uncharacteristically, he slept until 10 a.m. It was only when
he awoke that he remembered that he was to become a father.
Overcome with a mixture of elation and despair, he thumped
his plaster cast with his fists. 'I can't wait to get out of this
fucking thing,' he groaned out loud. 'I can't wait to get out of
this fucking thing!'

Underneath the cast his skin itched furiously. It suddenly seemed as if his whole future life was imprisoned in the cast. But even as his fists beat against the plaster, the rest of his skin was alive with her, with the mystery of her and the scent of her, with his uncontrollable desire for her. He had always known that love and sex were for two completely different kinds of women. Yet here he was, rolling in one fell swoop into the trap of both marriage *and* fatherhood. Swearing silently, he felt as if he had suddenly been transformed into his most dreaded form of human life – a commuter . . .

It is said that *la bise*, the Alpine wind from the north, not only chills bones but breaks hearts, for when it blows the high suicide rate in Geneva climbs higher still. Understandably, therefore, there were many who took the raging wind on their wedding-day to be a bad omen. Yet everything went swimmingly. The groom's leg had healed perfectly and the bride was beautiful, and as spectacularly radiant as she was chic: her lustrous, sexy hair was in an elegant chignon. What gave the party an extra sparkle was that, unusually in that rather dour part of the world, the sexual charge between the couple was obvious enough to excite whispered comment between married couples. Speculation on the date of the arrival of the first-born turned the wedding from being stolid and serious into a light-hearted, genuinely convivial celebration.

But unlike his grandparents, Rufus's own parents, Fran and Mark, found no cause for celebration. On the contrary, the grim set to their son's jaw appeared to have pulled all the humour from his eyes. Though he smiled charmingly, it was through tight lips and with stony eyes. Fran's attempt to embrace him succeeded only in sending an iron chill to her very marrow.

Watching her stunningly beautiful new daughter-in-law (who, she knew, was three years older than her son) move with imperious grace among her guests, Fran felt anything but sanguine. Why, only last summer her son's heart had been

261

involved in what appeared to be a perfect teenage romance. How or why had that ended? What had become of Gina O'Connor she had never been told. The wedding party now in full swing, Fran shook her head as if to empty it of the ugly thought that far from being able to wish the young couple happiness, she could only hope that their inevitably savage marriage would not end in an even more savage divorce.

She sighed deeply. Who would have thought that at the marriage of her only son, the certainty of his future divorce would be uppermost in her mind?

Although the interior of the Château Beau Ciel had never been exposed to the public, still less photographed, the Count and Countess allowed *L'Splendide*, the exclusive French fashion magazine that had only recently begun to acquire an international following, to feature their daughter's wedding. When the magazine came out the senior Cartwrights, Theodore and Lucia, could find no fault with the article – after all, the brief paragraph that went into the details of Lucia's illustrious, noble family was highly satisfying. As far as the de Payot family were concerned, one short sentence ruined everything: the revelation that the Ferrari in which the young couple sped away had been the Count and Countess's engagement gift to their future son-in-law was the kind of vulgarity from which they could never expect to recover.

At the Montreux finishing-school a subscription to *L'Splendide* was especially significant; it was the ambition of almost every girl to appear in it. Early in March, Kate Hills, a student at the school, read that Rufus Cartwright was now a married man. She squealed with delight – it was the first time she actually knew someone in the magazine.

Because Kate's SATs had not been up to Ivy League standard, she had elected to go to L'Académie in Montreux. She now not only spoke perfect French but had acquired a real affinity with European culture.

'Why, this is Rufus Cartwright!' she exclaimed to her friend Monique. 'He and my best friend, Gina, were going together—'
Her voice trailed off and she handed the magazine to Monique.

Raising her supple brows, Monique said, astonished, 'But the bride is Fabrice de Payot.'

'You know her?'

'She's one of my sister's friends.'

'What's she like?'

'Pregnant with twins.' Monique giggled. 'They say her parents gave him a Ferrari. A 330 GT. It must have been the only way they could get him to marry her.'

Since leaving Talbot Hall, Kate and Gina had rather lost touch. Kate was about to cut the article out but changed her mind. She would append a note to the cover and send the whole magazine. *I'm told it was a shotgun wedding*, she wrote. *My friend Monique's sister, who knows Fabrice, says that she must have seduced him. After all, she is very much older. As Monique put it, what twenty-four-year-old woman would even go out with a twenty-one-year-old boy, let alone marry him? She's been wildly promiscuous – everyone in Geneva knows about her. She's a real tart, they say. The authentic thing. Everyone predicts divorce.*

Back at Radcliffe, Gina read the letter and studied the photographs in the magazine and then hurried to her class in cognitive psychology. Although she tried to concentrate, she heard little of what was going on, and when her own name was called it took her a while to respond. Forcing herself to get through the day like any ordinary day, she went ahead with her date with Brett Darrow that evening. By that time she was numb with shock and her lifeless eyes and wooden responses effectively stopped Brett from making any attempt to get closer to her.

Later, when she reflected on that day and that night, she came to understand that – though she had not quite died inside – something in her had been stilled.

As always, she turned to Miriam. After reading and rereading Kate's letter, Miriam studied the magazine photographs long and hard. Looking for the right words, she took her time about making any sort of comment. At last she said, 'You've had a lucky escape!'

Gina's laugh was as brief as it was bitter.

Ignoring that, Miriam repeated, 'Yes, Gina, you *have* had a very lucky escape! Never before have I seen anyone's character so completely exposed by a photograph.' As she clasped and unclasped her hands, her bangles clicked. 'Just look at his cruel eyes and his grim jaw!'

Gina merely shrugged.

Miriam continued in the same vein for a while longer, but she knew she had not found the right words. Perhaps, she thought sadly, perhaps there are no right words at a time like this.

'Of course we broke up months ago,' Gina said tonelessly. 'But to think that he's married and about to become the father of twins!'

Her voice broke, and a wave of sobbing overtook her. Perturbed, Miriam leaned over and took her in her arms. She knew now that she had been wrong to believe with such unequivocal certainty that because Gina was young it was inevitable that she would get over this. But she now learned that youth is not a magic wand, and that a woman's broken heart stretches back to eternity, and is therefore neither young nor old.

She also knew with a terrible certainty that, far from getting over him, Rufus would dominate Gina's life for ever.

PART FIVE

Chapter Forty-Two

After a summer spent working at Hammer's, the advertising agency in New York, life at Radcliffe was something of a let-down for Gina. Things were too tame (though she felt like a heathen for thinking it) and too pretentious about life in an ivory tower. While Radcliffe lived up to its reputation as a competitive school, the competition on Madison Avenue had the advantage of being open and honest. At Radcliffe the law of the jungle was disguised, uncontaminated by the reality of the market-place. The pursuit of academic excellence was therefore free to be noble and pure and sanctified.

But it was at the market-place, with its heady atmosphere of permanent emergency and constant challenge, where she felt most alive. For she had sensed that in her life competition was an emotion stronger than love and more powerful than hate. The stimulation – and the risk – of competition was all the emotion she would ever need.

Once, when she knew the President of Hammer's was away, she had asked his secretary, Marge Benson, to show her his office.

'I'm not sure I can do that.' Marge had hesitated. 'Why do you want to see it?'

'Because it's my ambition to be like you. A secretary to the president of a large corporation.' The lie had come swiftly to her lips.

'But you're a college kid!'

'Sure, I know I'm at college. I'm there only because it gives me a better chance to be a really important secretary.'

'Okay. Take a look,' Marge said, opening the door.

Gina instantly recognized the paintings of Dufy, Cézanne and

Monet on the walls of the huge office. The desk was the size of a small room. Oriental rugs covered the hardwood floor.

'It's almost as big as the White House Oval Office,' Marge said proudly.

'Your office is lovely, too,' Gina said.

'With your kind of ambition, you'll be sure to make it,' Marge said, her voice warm with encouragement. 'I've been with Mr Hammer for eighteen years, and you're the first girl who has asked to see his office!'

'Thank you for showing it to me,' Gina said humbly.

Later, looking back, Gina would believe that it was at that moment that a new – and totally unexpected – vision had come into her mind. She saw herself working in just such an office – not as a secretary, but as president of the company.

She left the President's office and returned to her cubicle. Perhaps her future lay in the field of advertising? Could she ever dream up as effective an ad as the famous *I only have one life and I'm going to live it as a blonde*?

Kate Hills returned to America bringing with her a brand-new husband. Gina was the first person to be introduced to him. 'I guess it's because you're the only human being in my life who has really cared about me,' she exclaimed over lunch.

Jean-Pierre had been a ski instructor. Now, other than the fact that he was Kate's husband, he had no idea who he was or what he would do.

'Why don't you do something related to sport?' Gina suggested casually.

'Ski-equipment, you mean?' Kate asked.

'Sports clothes – sportswear, that sort of thing. Healthy profits in fashion. And sportswear is not so easy to find, you know,' Gina continued speculatively. 'There's probably a gap in the market.'

'Hey, I didn't know you were so clued-up on business,' Kate said, sounding surprised.

'I've started to read the *Wall Street Journal*,' Gina confessed,

268

embarrassed. 'But, Jean-Pierre, you probably know much more about it than I do. If tourism is becoming a major industry, then ski clothes must be big business.'

In his halting English Jean-Pierre said, 'Many tourists, they spend more on the ski clothes than on the air ticket. It is – how do we say it? – it is *dégoûtant*.'

'I see nothing disgraceful in big sales,' Gina laughed. 'Anyway, if you do decide to go in for sports clothes, I'll write the copy for your first ad.'

Gina's grin may have been broad, but her resentment was limitless. It was all very well for the Kate Hillses of this world. They had the cash, the money, the venture capital to go into business on their own. They could afford to be entrepreneurs. But where in hell was she, Gina O'Connor, going to find the money to open her own business?

'I just realized that I don't know your name,' Gina said.

'It is Gachet,' Kate said quickly. 'But in Switzerland I can be known as Gachet-Hills. Women are allowed to keep their surname.'

'Congratulations,' Gina replied absently. 'Well, I hate to be rude, but if I don't leave this instant I'll be late for class.' Gathering up her books, she added, 'Don't forget to give the idea of women's sportswear serious thought. We must limit the clothing to *one* line: *women's* sportswear! This is the age of the specialist. We could go in for some great celebrity advertising, too.'

Chapter Forty-Three

In the summer of 'sixty-five Cecilia and Gina moved from their Monk's Bay cottage to a New York apartment. A fanatically keen golfer, recently a widower, who wanted to be close to the Monk's Bay Country Club of which he was a new member, made Cecilia an offer she could not refuse.

Because she had been used to leading a suburban rather than a city life, Cecilia was determined that their new Manhattan apartment should be overwhelmingly comfortable, deeply peaceful and as solid and warm as if it had been there for ever. So her two big, beige cushiony sofas, strewn with a profusion of her riotously coloured needle-point cushions, were the kind people could easily sink into. Gina's room, with its small four-poster bed hung with soft pink linen edged with white lace, conformed to Cecilia's definition of femininity. But the kitchen, warmed by wooden cabinets and floors, was the heart of the apartment.

Although Gina's second year at Radcliffe had been hectic, the idea of a conventional vacation was out of the question. She had returned to Hammer's Advertising Agency, who had been only too pleased to give her a summer job. She now spent many nights writing the copy for Kate and Jean-Pierre's new business. Her spontaneous suggestion – to go in for women's sportswear – had now become a reality, and she was writing their advertising. One night, over a fondue dinner, Gina had joked, 'I christen the company "High Season".'

Jean-Pierre had seized on it: 'High Season, *Haute Saison*. An excellent name!'

Marshall Leete, Kate's trustee, delighted to find that this

strange Swiss ski instructor was serious about going into business, offered to lend him 10,000 dollars. Putting his experience as a ski instructor to work, Jean-Pierre chose to open High Season the Specialty Store in Portland, Oregon, because that was where his most diligent students on the ski-slopes came from. At first, everyone thought that Kate would refuse to live in Portland, but when she did go, her sister could not decide whether it was to shock everyone or to follow Jean-Pierre.

They had only the tiniest budget to devote to advertising and were therefore relying on Gina to come up with a slogan. 'Something catchy,' Jean-Pierre said. 'Something like "as American as Apple Pie"!' In the end, after much fun and many three-way long-distance calls, Gina came up with a slogan: *Sporting Chic Is Always in Season.*

'You see,' she said seriously, 'you can't only sell your product. You have to sell more than your product—'

'But without a product there would be nothing to sell,' Jean-Pierre laughed edgily.

'That is why you need something more than product.'

'Ah, I see. We must sell tennis—'

'*That* goes without saying,' Gina said, 'but High Season will *sell* hope. High Season will *promise* love. High Season will *give* excitement.'

'That's too much to expect,' Jean-Pierre snapped.

'But don't you see, that's what advertising is,' Gina explained enthusiastically. 'Salesmanship in print – whether you buy Campbell's soup or Arpège perfume, your purchase is your reward. In other words, every purchase you make will somehow improve your life.'

'I'll buy that,' Kate said, giggling over the wires.

Gina's copy went a long way towards creating the right sort of individuality for High Season. More importantly, she acquired an intimate gut-understanding of the persuasive strength of advertising. And, as the Cartwrights were to learn so painfully, it would be put to excellent – if not always scrupulous – use.

*

271

The President of Hammer's Agency sent for her. Once again – this time by official invitation – in the office that was said to be larger than the Oval Office at the White House, Gina promised herself that she would preside over just such an office. 'I'm offering you a career opportunity with Hammer's when you leave Radcliffe,' the President said pompously. 'And you'll be paid no less than if you were a *summa cum laude* graduate.'

'That is extremely generous of you, sir. And, I confess, most unexpected.' Then she added daringly, 'Unlike your offer, however, the *summa cum laude* is *not* unexpected.'

'I'm glad to hear that,' Mr Hammer said irritably. She was too gutsy for a girl.

'I'd like to think about it, if I may?'

She's got balls instead of ovaries, he thought. Grim-voiced, he said, 'Take as long as you want.'

Not surprisingly, therefore, Gina began the next semester with serious doubts about the validity of what she was doing at Radcliffe. The relevance of college life to her was growing more and more remote. Still, she was not and never would be a quitter. She would see it through.

The endlessly earnest literary criticism was especially mean-ingless. Why couldn't one read for pure pleasure, instead of being forced to extract obscure meanings from a masterly teller of tales and the life of, say, Nathaniel Hawthorne? Yet it would be indirectly thanks to Nathaniel Hawthorne that her life would change . . .

It happened like this.

It was while she was visiting the Old Manse, the house in which Nathaniel Hawthorne had lived for two years and where he had spent his wedding-night, that the puppy, a golden spaniel with liquid amber eyes, attached himself to her. He simply followed her around as if he belonged to her. She was reading Hawthorne's message scratched on the window of his study, *Man's accidents are God's purpose*, when the curator approached her. 'Sorry, miss, but we don't allow them inside the museum.'

272

'Excuse me?' Gina said, abstracted.

'If you must have your dog in here, he should be on a leash!'

The puppy brushed against her legs and she looked down. Breaking into a huge smile which made her dimples dance, she laughed. 'Too bad he's not mine.'

'He's not your dog?' the curator repeated.

'I've never seen him before in my life.'

'But he followed you as you came in.' The curator was suspicious. 'I saw him follow you with my own eyes.'

'He *is* a lovely animal, isn't he?' she said, bending down to stroke his fur. 'He's still a puppy.'

'It looks like he's about three months old,' the curator agreed.

'But he's not mine,' she insisted. 'I think he must be lost or something.' She stood up. 'I'm leaving, anyway. If he follows me, I'll probably take him home with me and try to find his owner.'

'How will you do that?'

'I don't know,' she said frankly. 'I guess I'll put an ad in the classifieds for starters.'

The puppy following close on her heels, she left the museum. Hoping the dog would be seen by his owner, she slowed her pace. Suddenly the puppy bolted. Good, she thought, delighted. He's scented his owner. The next instant she heard the shriek of brakes, saw the puppy thrown into the air, saw him land on the street, saw the car speed away.

As she ran towards him, a scream tore from her throat. He lay on the tarmac, his eyes closed, whining gently. She picked him up and, cradling him in her arms, wept into his fur. It happened so horribly quickly.

A small crowd gathered but she was unaware of it.

Her face buried in the puppy's fur, she neither saw nor heard the man who said, 'May I help? Can I take you to the vet?'

When she made no response, the man gently tapped her back and again asked if he could help. She looked up, and – her face streaming with tears – nodded briefly, and then continued sobbing into the puppy's golden fur. She had not cried since

273

Rufus Cartwright's birthday party, but now that she'd begun, she was both unwilling and unable to stop.

Taking her arm he guided her to his car, and before long they were driving to the vet's office.

In an unmistakably educated voice, the man said, 'I'm taking you to Dr Garland. I've been told he's great in an emergency. He saved my cousin's cat . . .'

Once they were with Dr Garland, he took the puppy from her arms and laid him on his examining table. Moments later he was shaking his head. 'There's no hope for your puppy, I'm afraid,' he said sadly to Gina. 'The kindest and most humane thing I can do for him is to put him to sleep.'

'He's not mine,' Gina murmured.

'Forgive me,' Dr Garland said, turning toward the man who had brought Gina. 'He must be yours.'

'Actually, he's not mine either,' said the man with a wry smile. 'I thought he was the young lady's puppy. She and I have never been formally introduced. My name is Morgan Gibson, and I'll be happy to take care of all expenses.'

Gina stopped crying, 'I'm Gina O'Connor,' she said shakily.

'Well, now that you two have met, I guess I'll just have to go ahead and do what I have to do,' Dr Garland commented. 'There will be no charge.'

Walking towards his car, she said, 'Thank you for all you've done.'

'Would you care to join me for a cup of coffee?' Morgan asked carefully.

'I'd love to,' she said simply.

At mid-morning the small coffee-shop was a busy buzz of relaxation. The air of benign equilibrium with which he ordered their coffee and muffins had a soothing effect. She felt strangely comfortable with this slightly balding man in his mid-thirties. Indeed, she felt comfortable enough to relax her guard, something she had not done with any man for a very long time. It

274

may have been because he was an older man that, instead of her usual aggression, she felt a sense of peace. Accordingly she was neither brittle nor waspish, but soft and smiling.

Though his face was cerebral, lean and planed, and his neck too short, with his light green eyes so full of warmth his appearance was handsome. A Harvard graduate, he was now the sales director of a small pharmaceutical company, Keene Inc. Perhaps it was because he was more mature that he was not like any of the men she had known. Passionate about music and devoted to Bach, he was a deeply serious man – serious almost to the point of humourlessness. Some considered him dull.

Morgan lived and worked in New York, and if Benson's Drug Store, one of his major customers in southern New England, had not insisted on a meeting with him, he would not have been in Concord, and he and Gina would have been strangers to one another for all eternity.

Their shared distress over the puppy meant that they did not behave as if they were strangers, as if this were the first time they had ever met. All of which was responsible for the instant intimacy between them. They talked easily, as if they were old friends who had been parted for a long while and were now taking up their friendship from where it had left off.

She told him about her summers spent working at Hammer's Advertising Agency and to her utter surprise found herself asking his advice about whether she should quit Radcliffe for a particularly well-paid job at Hammer's.

'May I ask an indiscreet question?' he said with his serious smile.

'Feel free,' she grinned. 'I wouldn't have asked you if I hadn't really wanted your opinion.'

'Is the tuition a burden to your parents?'

'My father died,' she said quietly. 'However, ever since I went to Talbot Hall, a family friend has been taking care of my education.' She stopped short. Up until this moment, she had never confided in anyone. (Except, of course, Miriam, whom

275

she looked upon as a close member of her family.) To her amazement, she continued, 'The tuition is no sweat to Constance Courtney.'

'In that case, then, there's no real reason why you should even consider giving up on Radcliffe.'

'Oh, God,' she said, her eyes bright with sudden tears. 'I feel so sorry for the owners of that puppy. If only we could have told them what happened.'

He toyed with the idea of telling her that he strongly suspected the puppy had been abandoned. Recently, there had been several such cases. He decided against it. She was hurt enough already; why should he add to her pain?

'I had a dog once. A collie called Hercules.'

'After the son of Zeus, no doubt.' She smiled.

'He was given to me on my tenth birthday. I wanted him to be strong and courageous.'

'And was he?'

'He certainly was.' His voice dipped. 'Unfortunately I developed asthma and we had to send him away. It was proved that I was allergic to dogs . . .'

So it was that Morgan Gibson and Gina O'Connor, the unlikeliest two to form a couple, began dating. At Radcliffe it was the cause of much comment, some of it mocking, and some downright astounded. After all, there wasn't a guy within miles who wouldn't have given his right arm for her. Her fellow students wondered what it was that she could possibly see in a mild-mannered, balding and considerably older man of thirty-four, who only had a fairly good job.

'She's happier than she's ever been,' said Miriam to Cecilia, who was no less astonished than everyone else. 'She feels secure with him.'

'That's exactly why I can't understand why she is going with him,' Cecilia replied with some asperity. 'Gina needs a challenge. She is not the kind of girl who would choose to live behind a picket fence covered with pink roses!'

276

'Morgan Gibson is a fine young man,' Miriam said indignantly. 'He's good husband material, too.'

'If by "fine" you mean "ordinary", I'm ready to go along with you!'

Miriam could not help remembering the lost young Italian immigrant that Cecilia had once been. She made no comment about this, however, but gave her a long stare which ended in a shrug. 'Morgan Gibson is a good man, and don't you forget it! I'm grateful she isn't going out with one of those fashionable long-haired hippies, that's all I can say.'

'I suppose you wonder what I see in him,' Gina said to Miriam over lunch.

'It's perfectly clear to me what you see in him,' Miriam retorted. 'He's a good man, and you're smart enough to recognize him for what he is. Like all smart girls, you know a good man is hard to find.'

'It's true, he *is* a good man,' Gina said. Drawing deeply on her cigarette, she added, 'But that's because he is so civilized.'

'You mean, he's not going all out to get you to jump into bed with him—'

'That, and much more besides,' said Gina passionately. 'He's like a walking encyclopaedia, yet he's modest enough to say that his head is filled with masses of useless information.'

'And I suppose he smokes a pipe and cooks divinely.'

'He is a good cook. He calls himself one of Julia Child's disciples.'

'And are you in love with him?'

'I think I must be,' Gina said, frowning. 'He's in my mind all the time, and he really really cares about me. He's genuinely interested in everything about me.'

'In other words, *he* loves *you*. Isn't that what you're saying?'

'And what if it is?' Gina countered. 'It is certainly better than the other way round.'

'For God's sake, Gina, don't base your life on the crass, infantile stupidity of an inexperienced fool!'

'You forget, Miriam,' Gina said coldly, 'I loved Rufus. I gave myself to him and he threw me back, as if the unlovely gift I'd made of myself was a sour smell on his hands that he had to get rid of.' Stabbing her cigarette into Miriam's perpetually overflowing ashtray, she added, slowly and bitterly, and leaving a gap of pain between each word, 'And . . . I . . . loved . . . him.'

'A bitter taste on the tongue makes the poorest judge of the finest wine,' Miriam said calmly.

'What are you getting at?'

'You are allowing yourself to be devoured by your own bitterness, Gina.' She stared moodily at her wine before continuing, 'You are predicating your entire future on an event that is irrelevant to that future.'

'Oh, I know that Rufus Cartwright has forgotten all about me. There's no need to remind me of *that*!' Gina exploded. 'That's the whole point, don't you see? I simply refuse to be forgotten like a disconnected phone number. I'll make him remember me. I'll make *all* the Cartwrights remember me!'

Chapter Forty-Four

Two months later, on the last Saturday in January 1965, Gina and Morgan were married. Gina had only just turned twenty. The marriage took place at St-Jean-Baptiste on Lexington Avenue – the choice of which no one could disapprove. Everyone disapproved of her decision to quit Radcliffe.

There were, however, two notable voices of approval. The first was from Morgan, who backed Gina's decision on the grounds that since she was going to live with him in his New York apartment, as was only natural, she could not very well live in Boston at the same time.

Needless to say, John Hammer, President of Hammer's Ad Agency, not only applauded her decision, but supported it with an increase of the starting salary he had at first proposed. Gina was now one of the highest-paid copy-writers in his organization.

The wedding was small, intimate and as understated as Gina's bridal gown. A flagrantly successful copy of a dress they had seen at Saks Fifth Avenue, Cecilia had put all her skill and all her love into its creation. Made of simple organza and superbly cut, with a pale pink velvet sash pulling in Gina's already tiny waist, it showed off her magnificent curves. Yet, with its gently flared skirt and fastened by a row of more than forty minute buttons, it managed to be modest and sexy at the same time. Instead of a veil, she wore an incredibly flattering white, wide-brimmed straw hat. Her finely sculpted features, curving forehead and intelligent velvet-brown eyes meant that she had what is known as a 'hat face'. Aware, from then on, that hats did so much to set off her looks, she decided that when the time came they would become her trade mark. Kate and her husband, Jean-Pierre, were there. Kate was matron of honour.

279

Morgan's former room-mate at Harvard, George Vitali, was best man. If George was more than a little surprised by Morgan's invitation to be best man, he had the wit not to mention it. He and Morgan had lost touch; Morgan was inclined to be a loner.

The reception at the Pierre was Constance Courtney's wedding gift. Formidably elegant, as always, Constance continually referred to Gina as her protégée and did not try to hide her disappointment that the bride had joined the ranks of college drop-outs. Her husband, now ailing, was unable to be present. No one was surprised to see that Miss Armstrong, Gina's former headmistress at Talbot Hall, was there. She usually attended the weddings of her girls. What was surprising, however, was that Molly Lewis, the sharp-eyed, sharp-tongued cook at Talbot Hall, now in a wheelchair, was included among the guests. It quickly emerged that Gina had come upon her at a supermarket, discovered she was infirm, and now ran errands for her.

Morgan had invited the president of the company of which he was sales manager as well as two cousins. So it was not until she looked around at the small congregation that it occurred to Gina that her new husband might be unsociable.

It goes without saying that her mother and Miriam were there. Miriam wept openly.

In addition to reserving the bridal suite for them, Constance Courtney had gone to the lengths of arranging caviare and champagne. 'It was a spectacularly kind thing to do,' Morgan declared when they were alone. 'I've never even been close to caviare before.'

Gina merely smiled and said nothing. Once again her mind had jerked back to the past. Against her will she found herself remembering the story Fran Cartwright had told her about the caviare and champagne that had been sent to their room in Rome. 'We'd gone all the way to Italy, to keep a date Mark had made in Rome after the war,' she had laughed. 'Only to find that Mark's fellow officer had flown out of Rome on the very day we'd arrived.' Yes, she *had* liked Fran Cartwright . . . And, what was more, she had had the strangest, strongest feeling that neither Fran nor Mark had ever known anything about that Lalique brooch.

But what on earth was she doing thinking about the Cartwrights on her wedding-night?

How she hated them for being so constantly in her mind – like a worm that had burrowed under her skin.

Handing his bride a glass of champagne, Morgan said gently, 'Penny for your thoughts, my lovely.'

Pulling her mind to the present, she answered dreamily, 'I was thinking how exquisitely the choir sang.'

'Did I tell you how exquisite you look?' he asked, drawing her close. He began to kiss her but stopped abruptly. He turned his attention to the long row of baby pearl buttons with which her dress was fastened. While his fingers fumbled his whole body seemed to tremble. She could have helped him, of course, but some primitive instinct told her that his struggle would both heighten and intensify the moment that had so long been delayed. For of course she had elected to make him wait. If she had learned nothing else from her experience with Rufus Cartwright, she had learned the value of making a man wait.

He had been all too ready to accept that though she was no longer devout, her Catholic background demanded that she keep herself for her husband. She had no doubt that, though he had not been celibate, he was naïve enough and probably inexperienced enough to take her virginity for granted. Had he not told her, many times, that she was the only woman he had ever loved? And had he not also confessed that she was his first real relationship with a woman?

Eyes closed, she stood very still until the last of the diminutive pearl buttons was undone. After parting the dress wide enough, he slowly lowered it downward so that with a single, deft movement she could step out of it. Finally he could look upon her in her pure white lacy bra, lacy panties, and, miracle of miracles, saw her wearing a frothy white suspender belt, real stockings instead of tights, and high-heeled, classic shoes. How

281

long, how hard, and how often he had studied those magazine shots of her frolicking on the beach as she modelled swimwear. Other than in those photographs, he had never seen her in anything approaching undress.

'Oh, my lovely,' he said, his voice hoarse and thick. 'My bride, my beautiful, beautiful bride.' Now his fingers no longer fumbling, nor even trembling, he unlatched her bra as skilfully as if he had been doing it for years, and rapidly removed the rest of her underwear.

Now she was wearing nothing but her satin bridal shoes. Leaving these on, he swooped her into his arms and carried her to what he thought of as their marriage bed. He laid her down gently and then tore off his own clothes.

Not a word passed her lips.

Not an emotion crossed her mind.

An overwhelming sense of detachment had seized her body. It was neither icy nor cold, this detachment: it was merely absolute. But then, in spite of herself, her iciness gave way to the comfortable feeling of being loved.

He entered her, and she submitted. Then, exactly as planned, she cried out as if in pain. Before long it was over and, spent and grateful, he lay beside her, smiling into her eyes, and though she smiled back, the grip of inner detachment tightened and she felt nothing, nothing at all.

The next morning they flew to that part of Florida where winter never comes – Palm Beach. However, although it is not burningly and unbearably hot in summer, Palm Beach is, in fact, the winter counterpart of northern summer resorts of the likes of Newport, Southampton and Bar Harbour. There in The Breakers, the opulent hotel modelled after a French *château*, the rest of the honeymoon was to be spent.

Though the inner numbness never left her, she succeeded in keeping it entirely secret from her new husband. In other words – like countless wives and women, through countless centuries before her – she faked it. Meanwhile, her own libido had been deadened. Perhaps the anaesthetic would wear off and it would spring back to life. Perhaps not. The best thing of all was that the present stillness of her skin meant that she no longer hankered after Rufus.

She was not unhappy.

Morgan was ecstatic.

For the meanwhile at least.

It may have been because she was without real passion that she was so fulfilled by the hectic life of combining a full day's work at the ad agency, with transforming Morgan's ascetic bachelor apartment into a real home where real meals were cooked.

Though it was deep and quiet and passionless, there was no doubt in her mind that she felt love for her husband. She felt safe with him. She wished she could have a marriage of physical passion, and could only hope that Morgan had not seen far enough into her to have got the full measure of her passionlessness. Of course Morgan did not deserve to be hurt by anyone, and by his wife least of all.

She was in on the beginning phases of comparative advertising. She was tremendously excited by the success of Avis Rent-a-Car Systems which, having come up with the simple statement 'We try harder', was now a strong competitor of Hertz Corp. Accordingly, working on copy for Swope's baby shampoo, with her entire life seemingly given up to variations on the theme of 'We care the most', getting Morgan's meals ready on time was unexpectedly challenging.

Since she was a perfectionist, there was no alternative to becoming an excellent cook. With her mother as her instructor, how could she fail? Saturdays were frequently spent in the kitchen. Since Morgan worked on Saturdays, the two women welcomed their time together.

Early in March, one Saturday morning, she took her time about answering her mother's ring on the doorbell. After repeated ringing, the door was at last opened.

'Sorry, Mama,' Gina said. 'I was in the bathroom.'

'That's okay, *cara*,' Cecilia answered at once. 'You look pale. Is everything all right?'

She had no sooner spoken than Gina left her to return to the bathroom.

'I must have eaten something,' she said when she returned.

Cecilia held her tongue.

Moments later, Gina was again racing to the bathroom.

Quickly, Cecilia turned down her daughter's bed. 'I think you should lie down,' she said.

'I guess I had – ' Gina replied shakily, 'I feel *so* sick, Mama!'

After helping her into a night-gown, Cecilia left her to make a cold compress. However, before she could even lay it on her daughter's forehead, there was yet another race to the bathroom.

Back in bed once more, with the cold compress firmly in place, Gina said weakly, 'I feel better now.'

'That's good, *cara*.' Cecilia stroked her daughter's head. It was wet with perspiration.

'You are so good to me, Mama.'

Cecilia's sigh engulfed her entire body. Taking Gina's hand in both hers, she heard herself asking the very question which, only a few minutes earlier, she had vowed she would not ask.

'When did you have your last period?'

The quick movement of Gina's eyes told her that Gina was thinking fast. Suddenly Gina's eyes widened and without answering, she gave a short, wild laugh.

'When?' Cecilia persisted.

'I'm on the pill,' said Gina edgily.

'I know that,' Cecilia replied calmly. 'Even so, when did you have your last period?' She hesitated briefly, and then, forcing herself to continue, said, 'Before or since the wedding?'

Gina's shoulders twitched. 'Before,' she rasped. 'But if you're thinking I'm pregnant you're wrong,' she exclaimed with great heat. 'I'm on the pill! It's impossible. Out of the question.' But her mouth had gone dry. 'It's ridiculous of you even to suggest it!'

Once more Cecilia held her tongue. This time it was she who made the calculations.

'It's impossible,' Gina said again.

'If life has taught me anything,' Cecilia said, her eyes glinting with experience, 'it has taught me to expect the impossible.'

'This is not the time for philosophy,' Gina said rudely.

With an air of finality, Cecilia said, 'November.'

'What are you talking about?'

'Your baby will be born in November.'

'But the pill is the most reliable form of protection—'

'Reliable means reliable,' Cecilia said stubbornly. 'Reliable is one thing. Guarantee is another thing. And the difference between the two means you can't even sue.'

But Gina could not make herself smile. 'I'm not ready,' she wailed. 'I don't want to be ready.'

'I wasn't ready, either,' Cecilia murmured. 'I, too, was young. Very young.' Tears both of pain and of joy suddenly blinded her. 'Yes, Gina. I was even younger than you are now,' she went on. 'But I can honestly say to you that you are now and always will be the best thing that has ever happened to me!'

Gina rolled over on to her stomach, and buried her face in the pillow.

Suddenly, in ringing tones, Cecilia announced, 'Of course I *do* expect, one day, to have something or someone in my life who will be just as important, and whom I shall love just as much if not more than you.'

Watching Gina turn over on to her back, the better to listen, Cecilia thought: I knew she'd do that. She's still my curious little girl, wanting to know everything.

Aloud, she said, 'Your children, of course. I expect to love them, you know. It is not for nothing that people say that the children of your children are twice your children.'

So saying she felt a warning shiver slice through her body. For no reason that she could begin to decipher, an ugly fact that she had learned during a recent television documentary darted into her mind. 'Sometimes,' the bland voice of the presenter had announced, 'mother cats devour their young.'

285

Chapter Forty-Five

In the last month of her pregnancy, Gina quipped to Miriam, 'Even if I had not dropped out of Radcliffe to go to work full-time at Hammer's, this bulge in my belly would have forced me to drop out.'

As soon as her obstetrician, Dr Rodgers, pronounced that she was over the punishing and dangerous morning sickness that had lasted all day and all night, she had settled into her pregnancy, bringing to it the quality of serenity that is uniquely female. Aglow with the warm evidence of growing a new life, her inner numbness melted and vanished. She began to believe that if she had not fully recovered from Rufus, he was – at least for the moment – obsolete. More important, however, was that as the baby's first flutters grew strong enough to be felt as powerful little kicks, she came to understand that, simply because Morgan was the father of her child, he would always occupy a central region in her life.

She enjoyed 'playing the housewife', as she called it. Morgan came home to a delicious hot meal every night, and was delighted if he could persuade Cecilia to join them. He often went to the lengths of calling her specifically to invite her to dine with them. It was at this time that Gina discovered that she came into her own in the kitchen. She took to making her own pasta at home, and now no longer dreamed of buying factory-made spaghetti.

Miriam was not left out, either. Not a good cook, she was attempting, rather unsuccessfully, to knit for the baby. One night she brought her knitting. What with her needles clicking, and her bracelets jangling, they implored her not to knit them anything.

It was a happy time for all three of them. Gina acquired a red and white checked gingham table-cloth, and with lighted candles in two Chianti bottles, much layered with wax, every dinner was a romantic occasion. (An inspired cook, even while she still lived in the hated tenement with Al and Tina, Cecilia had gone without real necessities so that she could buy the best imported Italian olive-oil, and the finest Italian cheese.) As the days grew colder and there was a chill in the air, a thick minestrone soup simmered all day on the stove. Cecilia taught her daughter to make *osso buco*, because the marrow in the bone was good for the baby, and *vitello tonnato*, a different kind of veal dish, where lightly poached meat was baked in a rich tunafish and anchovy sauce. This last dish was forbidden to Gina – it was, her mother decreed, too rich for her. Magically tender rice – *risotto alla milanese* which, despite its rich beef marrow, was, like the *osso buco*, declared perfectly safe.

The many different kinds of pasta turned Morgan into something of a spaghetti connoisseur. Spaghetti neapolitan, spaghetti bolognese, spaghetti sicilienne, spaghetti vongole – Morgan never could decide which one was his favourite. All this good and tender loving care appeared to have helped his asthma. His attacks were less frequent.

Since Gina was going to have the baby by natural childbirth he went to the classes which included husbands.

'I dreamed it was a boy,' she said one morning. 'Only two weeks to go, and I'm now absolutely certain it is a boy.'

'Boy or girl – I couldn't be happier.'

'We'll call him John.'

'Why John?' Morgan asked. Throughout her pregnancy he had made it a rule not to contradict her. He was superstitious about naming a child before it was born.

'We are going to call him John because of Jack Fitzgerald Kennedy,' she declared triumphantly.

In the event, however, the natural childbirth classes proved useless, and the baby, a girl, was born by Caesarian section.

The surgery seemed to have done something to Gina, something not immediately definable. She had been counting on seeing her baby born, and sitting up during the delivery and watching his head being crowned, like the other mothers in her class had done. But the cord had twice wrapped itself around the baby's neck and, but for a Caesarian, the child would most certainly not have survived. The upshot of it all was that all her plans for breast-feeding went out of the window.

'She's making them give her tablets to dry up her breasts,' Cecilia wept to Miriam. 'My granddaughter deserves to have her own mother's milk. And she's got so much of it, too.'

'I know,' Miriam nodded sympathetically. 'I know.'

'She's got her breasts all tied up to squeeze the milk out. Bound up tightly, you know, like the little Chinese girls have their feet bound so they won't grow.'

'It's all because she feels a failure,' Miriam said angrily. 'That's the downside of natural childbirth. If a girl can't have her baby the natural way, with her husband massaging her back and participating in the birth, the girl has a terrible sense of failure.'

'I hadn't thought of that,' said Cecilia meditatively. 'She's never failed at anything before. She's never been anything but a straight A student.'

A deep scowl cut into Miriam's forehead. She knew that Gina believed her one and only failure in life was Rufus Cartwright. She was also aware that Gina could not handle failure – it made her vengeful. She could only hope that Gina would not make her new baby pay for her mistaken conviction that – because her baby had not been born naturally, but by Caesarian section – she had failed. Miriam had heard of this sort of thing happening to several mothers for whom the relaxation technique of natural childbirth had not worked. These dark thoughts darkened her eyes.

Reading her mind correctly, Cecilia asked simply, 'What's wrong, Miriam? I can tell something is worrying you.'

Miriam changed the subject. 'Have they decided on a name yet?'

'It just goes to show how worried I am about the milk,' Cecilia exclaimed. 'They are calling the baby Scarlett, in my honour.'

'Scarlett?'

'You're wondering how the name Scarlett could possibly honour a poor, wartime Italian immigrant like me, Cecilia Tortelli.'

'Quite frankly, I am,' Miriam laughed.

'*Gone with the Wind* was the first American movie I ever saw,' Cecilia explained. 'I saw it on the hospital ship. Gina remembered that, you see. So in my honour the baby is called Scarlett.'

'That's just a darling name,' said Miriam. Once again her eyes darkened, this time with a new anxiety. What if Gina subconsciously put the blame for the Caesarian on the baby? She had heard of such cases. All old wives' tales, she told herself angrily. But since Dr Rodgers, her old friend and Gina's obstetrician had told her so himself, it could not so readily be dismissed as an old wives' tale.

For the present, however, Cecilia and Miriam's misgivings about how Gina would take to motherhood were unfounded. It turned out that she had had her breasts dried up because she did not want them to lose their shape – to droop like faded flowers – and not because she did not want to suckle her baby.

'Same difference,' said Cecilia to Miriam.

'Not quite,' Miriam began. 'If she had not wanted to feed Scarlett, that would have been an act of active aggression.' She paused and, thinking deeply, blew a cloud of blue smoke towards Cecilia. 'There is nothing hostile about a woman wanting to keep her breasts beautiful.'

Not for the first time, in the long and harmonious relationship that had developed the strength and depth of trust between two loving sisters, Cecilia held herself from saying what was on her mind. Some silly illogicality made her believe that if she did not say it out loud, it might not be true. Therefore she did not tell

Cecilia that if Gina was not hostile, she was certainly selfish. Her hands merely rose and fell, and she said nothing.

It turned out that Gina was an avid mother, and watching her bottle-feed her contented baby, Cecilia began to believe that she had been old-fashioned. Why, some babies were even allergic to their mother's milk and had to be fed on a soy-bean concoction. Sometimes Morgan would feed the baby and then Cecilia would observe Gina growing restless; her hunger for the baby was so great that before long she would take the infant from her father's arms to feed her herself. Cecilia understood this; Gina's maternal instinct had taken over . . .

While the nurturing hormone poured into her blood during those early, radiant months, Gina's inner coldness lessened just enough for her to need her husband and his body. For the first time since she and Rufus had parted, she allowed herself to glory in her own body. Nude, in front of the bathroom mirror, staring at the very body that had brought forth life, she was aware that she was again a sexual being.

Cecilia fell into the habit of visiting Gina every day. She did the marketing for her, helped with the ironing and generally indulged herself in her daughter's domestic bliss. And why not? Remembering how Tina and Al had made her suffer when she had been a new mother, she felt she was entitled to this, the greatest joy in her life, her daughter's maternity.

Chapter Forty-Six

Even in Switzerland, the home of chocolate, the chocolate train birthday-cake was sensational. Count de Payot had himself commissioned an exact replica of a toy electric train for his grandson's second birthday. He had himself gone to the Chocolaterie du Rhône to give the order. No self-respecting Genevois could have been accused of conspicuous consumption, but as far as his grandson was concerned the notion of extravagance did not exist.

And why should he not have indulged himself?

Giving birth to premature twins had all but cost his daughter her life. He and his wife had stood helplessly outside the door of the delivery room, had heard her shriek and curse and shout. Again and again she had cried out for Rufus. Irrationally, the Count had hated his son-in-law for having flown to New York to attend a board meeting. And yet he had gone for only two days, and it was still at least five weeks before the babies were expected. Even as she cried out, Rufus was in an aircraft flying home to his wife. What more could he do? By the time he arrived at the clinic, the baby boys were four hours old. They were each in an incubator so he could not touch them, but with tears streaming down his cheeks, he watched them struggle for life. When, after fifteen hours on this earth, the younger of the two gave up, the reluctant father's grief had been terrible to behold.

But somehow they had got through those early, terrible days. Gradually, but only when it was safe, they had come to rejoice in baby Thomas. Finally, Fabrice and Rufus brought him home and for some weeks both parents appeared to be living in a state of endless bliss. Fabrice's beautiful breasts were blessed with flowing milk – so much so that she was compelled to have her excess milk pumped into large sterile bottles. This milk was then fed to other newly born babies in the clinic whose mothers could not feed them.

Too soon, however, they settled into parenthood, and when their highly trained Swiss nanny declared that mother's milk was no longer either necessary or good for baby Thomas, they were only too happy to hand him over to her. Still, in August 1966, they had made the effort to fly back from Monte Carlo to Geneva for their son's second birthday party,

'The best way to bring up children is to have doting grandparents,' said Fabrice to her father when she saw the cake.

The party was being held at the Château Beau Ciel because Fabrice and Rufus were waiting for their new house to be built. It was almost ready.

'Let me show you something,' her father answered. He led her through the cool, gracious rooms, and up three flights of their winding staircase to the top floor. Throwing open the door of what had once been his billiard-room, he asked, 'Like it?'

Fabrice gasped.

The billiard-table had been extended and now housed an array of toy electric trains, miniature stations, garages, cars and people. A second large table was home to a miniature racing-track. An assortment of teddy bears, some huge, some tiny, covered the leather button-set sofa which, like the tiny leather chairs and table, had been scaled down to fit children.

'It's a toyshop!' Fabrice exclaimed.

'I think Rufus will enjoy it, too,' her father chuckled.

'Of course he will,' Fabrice smiled to hide her anxiety. These days Rufus seemed to enjoy nothing. Endlessly bored, endlessly restless, and endlessly on the move, it was not easy to live with him.

Already she had uncovered a little affair – a harmless dalliance, he had called it. Correctly sensing that, for Rufus, women were to be conquered, and not loved, she had believed him. Besides, their time in bed together was more wildly wonderful than ever.

However much the Count disapproved of Rufus as a son-in-law, he could not but admire him as a businessman. Since he was on the Swiss board of Bernheim–Cartwright, he had a particularly good vantage-point from which to assess Rufus. Apart from the fact that sales had markedly increased in the two and a half years since Rufus had been there, Bernheim–Cartwright had, under his direction, extended their research and development programme. He had established a research unit and, using both his parents' names, had very simply called it the Fran–Mark Research Institute. Here, as the Count and everyone else in his family had concluded, Rufus had, for the first time, been influenced by his father, Mark. Canny though he was, not for the life of him had the Count been able to determine precisely why it was his grandfather, Theodore, and not his father, Mark, who had been the major motivating force in Rufus's life. Although he had not been present at the watershed conversation between father and son, Rufus had recounted it to him practically word for word. He had done so because he had needed his father-in-law's support in the hefty inducements he had been about to propose to Dr Joseph Bradley, the chief chemist at Solenia, the great British pharmaceutical company.

'Allow your researcher to follow his creative ways,' Mark had told his son, 'and you and he will go far, believe me.'

Making no effort to hide the boredom in his voice, Rufus had replied, 'I'm not following you, Dad.' Rufus had not. 'Are you saying that I should inhibit my researchers?'

'First of all, Rufus, never speak of a scientist of the first rank as one of your researchers. Never even let him *think* that you think he belongs to you!' his father had retorted. 'Any true creative thinker would, quite rightly, interpret that as an impertinence.'

'Well, if you're done with the lesson in manners—'

Ignoring his son's blatant disrespect, Mark went on, 'Scientists are extremely sensitive; many, if not most of them, have disproportionately fragile egos.' He leaned forward. 'Everyone knows of artistic taste; few know of scientific taste. A great scientist can feel about science the way a Chopin feels about his music, or a Monet feels about his painting.'

'Hey!' said Rufus. 'Now *that* I can understand.' His tone abruptly changed from thinly veiled contempt to one of respect. 'Go on, Dad.'

Warming to the subject that had long been sitting in his mind, Mark continued, 'You've heard of Inderal, the beta-blocker developed by ICI?'

'Who hasn't?'

'The FDA have not yet passed it in the States,' Mark said with some disgust. 'The beta-blocker is used in the treatment of heart disease. Put quite simply, it is one of those incredibly rare and revolutionary scientific breakthroughs that will, with all its ramifications, change the course of the disease process itself.'

'Change the disease process itself? ' Rufus interrupted. 'That's a long shot, isn't it?'

'Let me make my point, will you?'

'Sorry,' said Rufus, unusually contrite.

'As I understand it, there are some scientists who, rather than attempting to *find* anything, believe it is possible to create something unique – a compound that could, perhaps, change the very chemistry of specific cells.'

Already, one or two fairly major new hypotheses had resulted. The Fran–Mark Institute now had some of the greatest creative thinkers on its staff.

All of which, as only a Swiss banker could begin to calculate, could result in major profits. Had he not himself made in excess of 5 million francs merely by following – or, more accurately, copying – one of his client's portfolio investments in Syntex, the company that invented the pill?

Ah, yes, it was possible to predict a great financial future for Rufus Cartwright. On the other hand, unfortunately, his marital future was distinctly precarious.

Chapter Forty-Seven

It was around this time – in August 1966 – that a restlessness, similar in some ways to the one that was afflicting Rufus, began to infect Gina. Years later, her mother would attribute the enmity between her daughter and her granddaughter to the fact that Gina had refused to suckle her baby. Bored with motherhood, but at the same time weighed down by it, her husband's position at Keene Inc. was a source of discontent that was as vicious as it was profound.

'What is the use of being a sales director if you've got no stake in the company?' she demanded fretfully one night.

'It's a good job, with a good pay check, and I like to work.'

'There's no real pension to speak of,' she scoffed.

'Listen, I've got a certain authority in the company. It makes me feel good!'

'Authority? What sort of authority?'

'The kind that brings me respect. That's the best kind.'

'I'd like to know more about the kind of job that's long on respect and short on money, but still makes a Harvard graduate feel good!'

Night after night, over several weeks, Gina carried on in this vein. Then she began agitating for him to demand an interest in the company. She even took to calling him at work. If he was not there she would leave messages, sometimes as many as three a day, asking him to call her.

Finally he begged her to stop calling him. 'Mr Keene wants to know how come you call me so often—'

'How does he know how often I call you?' she asked suspiciously. 'He doesn't answer the phone.'

'The secretary writes down all my messages.'

'Everybody's messages get mixed up?'

'No. Each of us has a small message book of our own. As you know, we share the same secretary.'

'And Mr Keene reads everyone's messages. Even private ones like a wife calling her husband—'

'That's right.'

'It's not as if you were just a clerk,' she protested. 'You're the sales director.'

'He's done that since day one.'

She shrugged and said nothing.

In the early hours of the following morning, she snapped on her bedside lamp and woke him up. 'I've got an idea,' she said excitedly.

'What *is* this?' he grumbled. 'Switch that light off! It's 4.30 in the morning, for Christ's sake!'

'I know what time it is,' she said softly. 'But I've been awake all night waiting to tell you my idea.'

'Well, it will just have to wait till tonight—'

'I'm so excited about this, Morgan. I've never done this to you before, have I? Can't you guess how important it is if I wake you up to tell you about it?'

Realizing that she would not let up until she had had her way, he said wearily, 'Okay, so tell me about it.'

'That other company, the one that gets up Mr Keene's nose, because it makes a lot of the same stuff as you do.'

'David Minton? So what's David Minton got to do with us at this unholy hour?'

'How would Mr Keene feel if he thought you were going to work for Mr David Minton?'

'I wouldn't think of doing such a thing. Not in my wildest dreams!'

'I'm not saying you would leave Keene to go to David Minton. I'm not that crazy.' She got up and hastily lit a cigarette.

'So, what *are* you saying?'

'I'm saying that Mr Keene will think, a) that Mr David Minton is trying to hire you and b) that you might be considering taking up his offer.' Blowing a stream of blue smoke in his

296

direction she went on quickly, her voice tense with excitement. 'Always, and without fail, he reads your messages, right?'

'Without fail; he always reads through my messages. It's become a habit.'

'So how would he react if he were to read one or two messages from Mr David Minton inviting you to lunch? And what would he think of a message informing you that Mr Agnell is happy to confirm a meeting at his office during, say, the time you are supposed to be working for Keene?'

'He'd fire me, I guess.'

'He'd be that ready to lose you? You can't possibly mean that you think you are that easy to replace. Unless, of course, there's someone in the company who sells as much as you do—'

'No one comes close to me!'

'Good. That's exactly what I figured.' She giggled suddenly. 'If Mr Keene insists on reading your private messages, he will have to find out that Mr David Minton is wooing you.'

'It sounds risky.' Morgan's voice went oddly high. 'But go on. It also sounds interesting.'

'Within two weeks, Mr Keene will offer you a raise,' she said calmly.

Morgan laughed.

'Yes, he will offer you a raise and you will tell him that you will have to think about it.' She put out her cigarette and instantly lit another. 'And when he hears you say you have to think about accepting a raise, he will get your message.' In her excitement, she prodded him in the ribs. 'And your message will scare the shit out of him, because he'll jump to the conclusion that Mr David Minton has offered you even more—'

'I'm beginning to like the sound of this—'

'So he'll offer you still more, and again you will tell him that you have to give it a great deal of thought. You will murmur something about the difference between a raise and a stake in the company. And then it will be you – and not he – who will terminate the interview.'

'Right. I bring the interview to a close. And then what?'

'Two, maybe three days later, he will offer you a 5 per cent interest in the company. And if you dare accept, I'll leave you!' Suddenly she broke into a laugh that shook her whole body.

'I don't see what's so funny about that,' he said seriously.

'What's funny is that you'll tell him that you want 10 per cent of the company or you'll have to consider other possibilities.' She laughed.

'You're one smart lady, Gina.'

By now it was daylight. 'I'll make you scrambled eggs on toast for breakfast.' She smiled. 'Is it a deal?'

'It's a deal.'

'One more thing,' she added. 'No matter what happens, no matter how well we do, we'll never never tell anyone about our strategy.'

Two weeks later, entirely as Gina had predicted, Mr Keene offered him 10 per cent of the company. There was, however, one problem – Mr Keene wanted to be paid a considerable amount of dollars, calculated on 10 per cent of the profits over five years.

'What did you say when he told you that?' she wanted to know at once.

'I told him I'd have to think about it,' he answered with one of his rare smiles. 'I thought that was what you would want me to do.'

'You're damn right, that's exactly what I would have done.'

'It's at least a hundred times more than we have,' he said dolefully.

'You have access to his balance sheet?'

'Yes.'

'Good.' She swallowed deeply. What if, having got so far, Morgan would refuse to go along with the rest of her scheme? All but trembling with anxiety, she handed him a photocopy of what at first glance appeared to be a legal document. There was only one page, and at the bottom of that page he saw the empty space that awaited the signature of Arnold J. Keene.

'You sign this, take it to the James Barret Bank – the small

298

branch, you know the one where we have a checking account, and they'll lend you the money.'

'But that's fraud! We haven't even seen a lawyer! You typed your document yourself!' he exclaimed.

'True,' she agreed. 'It would be an outright case of fraud if there was anything in that agreement that differed in any way from the deal you made.'

'This goes against the grain,' he said pompously.

'Spare your self-righteous indignation for Mr Keene!' she said in disgust. 'You will be giving the bank the official balance sheet of Keene Inc. The agreement is unsigned. If they ask for the signature – and they will – you'll get it. By then the loan will have already been arranged and *their* money will be in *your* bank.'

He shook his head, and went along with her.

The ruse worked.

But even then, she was not satisfied.

'Tell Mr Keene that you want your *own* secretary.'

'He'll never agree.'

'Want the best?' she laughed. 'I know someone – admittedly, not a college graduate – who's prepared to work for you for much much less than the going rate.'

'What's the catch?' he asked suspiciously.

'It's me,' she said simply. 'I'm the catch. I'm the girl who dropped out of college, remember.' Now her tone became brittle. 'There's only one route for me to get into that business, and I'm taking it!'

'But Scarlett?'

'Mama will be only too happy to take care of her all day,' she said confidently. Suddenly her expression changed. 'Of course, without my mother I couldn't think of working full-time. It's bad enough leaving my darling baby as it is – even though I know she'll be well and truly loved . . .'

Thus, while Rufus could get away with giving only minimal attention to his work, and maximum attention to his preferred career, that of a prominent playboy of the French Riviera, Gina gave her whole heart and her whole soul to making the most of her opportunity. Mr Keene was sixty-four: with both his daughters married to successful surgeons, she reasoned, he could afford to have the Gibsons take over the running of the company. And, if things were to go according to plan, why should they not take over the entire company? It was small enough – just the right size to take off and grow.

Later, when journalists, competitors – as well as her staff – would come to analyse and to try to penetrate the secret of her enormous success, it would be universally agreed that her formidable energy was the major ingredient. Gina, of course, would scoff at this; it's what you do with the energy that counts, she would think privately. In any case, what about enthusiasm, passionate curiosity and drive, and confidence and loving a challenge, and drive, drive, drive? She was driven, she always would be driven, and the quality she respected most in herself and in others was staying-power. It was this tenacity that elevated her from being a secretary to a powerhouse.

She was also blessed with a flair for constructive criticism. Although she had moved heaven and earth to become a secretary at Keene Inc., it was only when she arrived to take up her position that she saw the inside of the building in which the company was housed. Since Mr and Mrs Keene had made it a strict rule never to socialize with the staff, they had never met them. Needless to say, Gina wanted Morgan to tell her all he knew about her future boss.

'You've told me that he's got a quick temper, that he's a nervous man who dresses well, but I know very little about him,' she said to Morgan over a candle-lit dinner in their kitchen.

'What is he interested in?'

'Boxing and baseball,' he said with distaste. 'He's got a framed, signed photograph of Joe DiMaggio hanging on his wall.'

Gina wrinkled her nose in agreement. Their contempt for boxing and baseball was one of the few things they had in common. There is nothing quite like a shared dislike to bring people closer. 'Boxing *and* baseball,' she said. 'Ugh! Don't tell me he's got a photograph of Joe Louis as well!'

'*Un*signed,' he sniggered.

'Mr Keene is obviously the suspicious type.'

'Suspicious?' he asked. 'Why? What makes you say that?'

'Easy. If he had trusted you, would he read your messages? No.' She gave a brittle, brief laugh. 'One thing is for sure. He's not a fool.' She leaned forward.

Making the most of her housewife's eye, it was possible for her to combine the highest efficiency with the highest femininity. The unhygienic, chipped coffee-cups were changed the next day. Before long, the grimy offices and grimier factory had been spruced up with a coat of white paint.

'A clean atmosphere makes everyone feel better. Don't you feel better after a hot shower?' she asked Mr Keene.

'Sure I do.' He grinned. 'First thing I do, when I get home from here, is to take a scaldingly hot shower.'

The point made, there was no need for Gina to comment.

It was more of a packaging and bottling plant than a factory. Machines and moulds put the corticosteroid creams into tubes, jars, or bottles. There were mixtures for nose drops, for cough drops, for tonic drops. Most – if not all – of these found a ready outlet among the drugstores whose custom Morgan had so assiduously cultivated. Although it was quickly apparent to her that single-handedly among the sales staff, Morgan had built up the business, she said nothing. How he had not demanded an interest in the company years and years ago was quite beyond her. With great difficulty she forced herself to bide her time. But during her short experience in the advertising world, Mr Hammer had taught her that 'timing is all, timing is everything'. Her philosophy was simple; if you don't learn from your experience you're a fool.

Gina relayed her recommendations or innovations through Morgan. She was horrified by the slack stock control. Now that computers were not only manageable in terms of space but designed to fit customers' needs, effective stock control was

301

possible. (Here, Gina foresaw the time when the supplier would also have the relevant details of the customer's stock situation.)

Meanwhile, Morgan persuaded Mr Keene to hire the services of a computer relevant to the needs of Keene Inc.

Within six weeks, Mr Keene invited Gina to call him by his first name – Arnold.

'I've too much respect for you to do that,' she demurred.

His face fell.

'May I call you Mr K?' she asked.

With growing incomprehension, Gina watched Christmas of 1966 come and go as if it were entirely irrelevant to Keene Inc. To Gina, the loss of such an important sales and marketing opportunity was nothing less than sinful. Still, she said nothing.

Because Cecilia's kitchen experiments were proving amazingly interesting. Though Keene's hand and foot creams were effective – or efficacious, as the medical profession would have said – there was something lacking.

She asked her mother to diagnose what it was.

'The foot cream soothes and the hand cream smooths, yet something is missing,' Cecilia said.

'You make it sound as if you want to taste it, but you're not sure what you should add to it, Mama,' Gina laughed.

Her mother laughed with her. It was so good to see how much happier Gina was these days. Yes, her daughter was the kind who could not live without a challenge. 'But I have tasted *both* creams, *cara.*' Then Cecilia did something Gina had never seen her do before. She winked. 'Don't worry, *cara.* It will come to me. It will come to me.'

'But hurry,' Gina joked. 'Both Helena Rubinstein and Elizabeth Arden are dead. There's a gap in the industry.'

It was because the product had become as tired and as old-fashioned as it looked that its sales had fallen so drastically. Indeed, Keene only kept it going because several customers regularly ordered it.

302

'We sell pharmaceuticals, not beauty products,' said Morgan when she drew this to his attention.

'There's much greater profit in hand cream than in steroidal cream, isn't there?'

'Yes.'

Meanwhile, Cecilia had found the solution to what was missing. She merely added the almond essence she used in her almond-orange cake to Keene foot cream, and liquefied cucumber to the hand cream.

By six months later, in August 1967, Gina's and Morgan's secret strategy and her ultimatum had been refined and formulated. To her astonished delight, she and Morgan had developed into a great team.

Morgan dictated the proposal to her. When it was typed, he read it quickly. It was sensible and gutsy, he concluded. He would leave the negotiating to her.

The very next morning Gina opened their negotiations.

'Mr K,' she said with a commanding ring, 'we must have a meeting.'

'I've always got time for you, my dear,' he replied courteously. 'And there's no time like the present.'

'It's quite a heavy agenda.' She opened her diary. 'Would next Monday do?' she suggested.

'It's Wednesday today. Can't you make it sooner?'

'Sorry, things are too hectic.'

Watching him swallow deeply – his Adam's apple more prominent than usual – she exulted. She had won the first round. She was euphoric; he would capitulate, she knew. Thanks to arthritis, his health was not what it had been. If his will to fight had weakened, waiting six days for the meeting would weaken it still further.

Her terms could neither have been more simple nor more harsh. Either he could sell them the remaining 90 per cent of his company for 50 per cent of its value, or they would sell their

303

10 per cent to David Minton, his major competitor, and set up their own new company, which had already been registered, and walk out. 'Of course, as I need hardly tell you, Morgan's established client base would follow us.'

'My wife didn't trust you,' Mr Keene said sadly. 'She warned me you'd steal the business from me.'

'If that's how you see it, don't sell!'

'I should have listened to my wife.'

'Then, Mr K, you accept our terms.'

He nodded.

'Our lawyer will draw up the contract and submit it to your lawyer.'

Gina found that she was not entirely ruthless.

She forbore from telling him that the contract was already in her briefcase.

Chapter Forty-Eight

Rufus had followed his father's advice and Dr Joseph Bradley, formerly chief biochemist at Solenia Pharmaceuticals, now headed the Fran–Mark Institute. With hundreds of scientific papers and seminal discoveries to his credit, Dr Bradley was indeed the man of scientific taste whom his father had suggested.

Dr Bradley's ambition was to create new, healthy cellular processes rather than to uncover the pathways of disease.

Already his results were promising, very promising.

By August 1967, Rufus and Fabrice had been married for three and a half years, during which time she had grown even more beautiful. Her obsession with Rufus had also grown. At dinners, parties, on yachts, in casinos, chalets, and on the ski-slopes, she would stop and stare at him as if she had never seen him before. She made no effort to hide her obsession – any attempt would have been doomed to failure.

A talented leader, Rufus's easy gift for finding and keeping the best meant that he could delegate without fear. He was interested in concepts, not in details. Since he was a 'natural', there was an effortlessness about it all, an effortlessness which eradicated any and all sense of achievement. Which led, inevitably, to an endless search for escape. Sometimes he would think of Gina and fantasize that if she had been at his side it would all have been different. He had become, he felt, a member of the idle rich with time to kill.

'No gambler is ever bored. Winning is exciting, losing is thrilling,' Rufus confessed to Fabrice.

'I've caught the bug, too,' she replied. Which, though it was not altogether true, was certainly wiser than admitting that it was one way of keeping him within her range of vision.

Eventually, however, roulette, blackjack and finally even *chemin de fer* began to pall. Here he was betting against chance, and he was dependent on luck. It was hardly a contest of skill and nerves of the likes of poker when the combinations of the opponents are unknown.

It was one of Dr Joseph Bradley's British colleagues, Dr Paul Kincaid-Smith, who took him to the plush, five-star Fountains Hotel in London. This time he refused to allow Fabrice to accompany him. He won £20,000 the first night, and on the second night he lost a cool £40,000. Overtaken by a moment of black rage, he was rash enough to say, 'It was a rigged game.'

'Would you care to repeat that?' demanded the biggest winner.

'Sure,' Rufus said coldly. 'It was a rigged game.'

The winner's plummy voice continued, 'Do my ears deceive me?'

'No, sir,' Rufus said, his voice grim. 'Your ears deceive neither you nor me.'

The neck supporting the shiny silver hair whirled to the left and was the second-last thing that Rufus saw. The next moment he both felt and saw the two heavies who came to get him. Then he saw nothing at all. He was beaten unconscious. When he awoke two days later in the London Clinic, Fabrice told him that he'd been mugged. Two strange American men had saved his life. It seemed they'd found him, bundled him into a car, dropped him off at the London Clinic, and then sped off into the dark night . . .

PART SIX

PART SIX

Chapter Forty-Nine

In May 1970, a little more than two years later, Theodore Cartwright lay dying. Summoned from Geneva to Cartwright House, Rufus and Fabrice quickly perceived that though they had to struggle hard to hear the old man's voice, which was as frail as he was, his concern for his country was undiminished. But America had let him down, and he railed against the society that tolerated Black Power yet opposed the patriotic duty to fight in Vietnam to save their country and the world from Communism. For all his patriotism he predicted – accurately, as it was to turn out – that the deaths of the four anti-war student protesters among the stone-throwing crowd at Kent State University would have dire consequences for the Cartwright family.

Much as Theodore Cartwright abhorred the mass burning of draft cards in the anti-draft demonstrations, in his most secret heart of hearts he was grateful to the accident in London that had rendered his grandson unfit for military service . . .

Patriotic or not, thought Fabrice, the ochre-shaded bedroom in which he lay more properly belonged to a European than to an American. The great four-poster bed with a fabric styled after Napoleon III, oriental carpets, and the fabric of the sofa cushions were immediately recognized by Fabrice as belonging to the Second Empire. The room was endowed with an air of hallowed, solid dignity. Of course, she had been in other homes where the decorator had gone all out for the French look, or the Italian look, but none of them had succeeded in capturing the tone of authenticity that came so naturally to Lucia Cartwright. After all, much of the furniture had been in her family for generations.

309

Physically weak though he was, Theodore's dry white lips still conveyed that aggressive proud leadership, that stubborn, prideful determination that had made him a legend.

Having dispensed with the ills of Women's Lib, the sexual revolution, the rock, the drug and the 'drop-out' cultures, he said, 'And now, my dear Fabrice, I must ask you to leave us alone. We have a few small business matters to settle.'

She rose at once and, dropping a kiss on his parched forehead, teasingly said, 'Your great-grandson will be ready to see you at the end of the afternoon. Will that be convenient to you?'

'I'll be waiting for him.' He smiled.

Suddenly, Rufus found himself praying for the strength not to show his emotions. Involuntarily, he clasped his hands. Not yet, he prayed silently. Not yet.

Even *in extremis*, his grandfather's shrewd, all-seeing eyes missed nothing.

In a voice as calm as if it were coming from the confessional box, his grandfather said, 'You are a man's man, my son.' He sighed briefly and continued, slowly. 'All my life my greatest strength has been my gift for leadership. You have inherited it.'

'I only wish I had—'

'Real leadership is inherited and not learned.' He spoke with a schoolteacher's patience. 'Unfortunately, all the learning in the world proved useless in your father's case. The pity is that instead of *leading* his conscience, your father *followed* his conscience.'

A silence fell. Sensing that his grandfather was marshalling his thoughts, Rufus straightened his back and held his tongue.

'An overdeveloped social conscience proved his undoing. He is more concerned with prestige than with profit.' He raised his hand. 'Don't get me wrong. My son – your father – has no great fondness for losses, either.' His weak but still sarcastic laugh was as mocking as ever.

But the laugh had taken more out of him than he could spare. His eyes directed Rufus to a pitcher of water. Rufus poured him a glass. He knew enough not to help his grandfather, and so placed it in his hands. After a few birdlike sips he signalled Rufus to take the glass away.

'Your father has been too virtuous to be a man's man, you know. I don't believe he has ever looked sideways at another woman.'

Rufus's tongue suddenly felt too thick and too large for his mouth.

'You, of course, cannot claim such virtue, can you? Too much virtue can be most unfortunate!'

Realizing that his grandfather had made a joke, Rufus managed a low chuckle.

'As the head of the family, I have had to acquaint myself with both the strengths and the weaknesses of its members. Womanizing can never do irreparable harm to Cartwright Pharmaceuticals.' Sinking his voice to a meaningful whisper, he added, 'Only gambling has the power to do that.'

'I know—'

'You know? Is that *all* you can say?'

'I know *and* I agree, sir,' Rufus said, his voice oddly high.

'I am relieved but not surprised to hear that, my son.'

He proffered his hand and Rufus grasped it, and held on to it as if he would never let it go. After a long while, his grandfather made a light movement, and Rufus understood and lessened his hold.

'One last repetition of the secret of our success at Cartwright Pharmaceuticals.' His grandfather's voice had become fainter. 'The trick is to spot those areas that might lead to breakthroughs. And we could only do that because we had the edge on the scientific side – biology and chemistry. But even that would have got us nowhere if we had not been able to recognize the medical importance of what we were discovering.'

Lucia had made sure that things would go on as usual. Accordingly, the summer lunch was served as if it were a

311

luncheon party for a group of guests. Since Dr Fairbairn had warned them to be close at hand, Fran and Mark had left New York and were now living in the home Theodore had given Mark all those years ago when he had returned with his Silver Star and Purple Heart from the war. Although little Thomas's presence at the table succeeded in lightening the atmosphere, Rufus soon made his excuses and left.

He needed to be alone.

He took himself off to the stillness of their private lake. There, seated on a rock beside the rushing waterfall, he was suddenly reminded of the pure well-water he and Gina had tasted together, high up in the log cabin overlooking the rough range of mountains rearing out of the forest. Seven long restless years had passed since those glorious days at the Adirondacks, when he and she had believed themselves to be as invincible as they were immortal. Realizing that that was probably the last time he had let his emotions spill into tears, he rested his aching head in his hands and allowed himself the luxury of uninhibited weeping. He cried for his dying grandfather, for his squandered youth, for his fear of the future and for the unlimited void that Gina had left.

He made the most of those precious few hours alone.

Later, at the end of the afternoon, he joined his wife and son in his grandfather's bedroom.

Looking at his small great-grandson with his head of tight chestnut curls that was so like his grandson's, the dying man murmured, 'You should have called him Theodore.'

'But we will, grandfather. We will!' Rufus cried out urgently. 'It's not too late. From now on your great-grandson will only be known as Theodore. I'll get Charles Briggs to make it absolutely legal.'

'Briggs?' his grandfather repeated, his mind beginning to fail at last. 'Do I know him?'

Charles Briggs had been the family lawyer for the past forty years.

'We must leave him now,' said Lucia firmly. 'It's time for Nurse Holloway to give him his injection.'

312

It was the last injection Theodore Cartwright was ever to receive.

Thus, at the age of seven, Thomas Gaston Cartwright officially became Theodore Gaston Cartwright. For Rufus there would always be something comforting about having fulfilled his grandfather's dying wish. However, as happened immediately, the boy, with his clear honest eyes, demanded to be known as Theo.

Two months later, when summer was at its height and the peonies and roses were at their most lush, Mark Cartwright announced that he was going to resign his executive position at Cartwright Pharmaceuticals.

Contrary to all expectations, he *had* inherited his father's sense of patriotism. As he saw it, his country's war in South East Asia was as immoral as it was futile. 'To win the Vietnam war,' said Benjamin Spock, 'we will have to exterminate a nation.' George McGovern, the senator from South Dakota, was a leading advocate for putting an end to the war in Vietnam. Leaving that aside, however, the Senator was committed to a broad programme of social and political reform. Accordingly, since George McGovern suited both his conscience and his patriotism, it was only reasonable that he should go and work for him.

Besides, it was rumoured that McGovern was going to be the next Democratic presidential candidate.

'Grandfather said you had an overdeveloped social conscience,' Rufus exploded in a burst of fury. 'You would never have had the guts to do this while he was still alive.' Beside himself, he added, 'No, you had to wait for him to die! You used his death to buy your freedom!

'I'm too young,' he wanted to scream. 'I'm not ready. It's too soon – too soon!'

But solace was in sight; his inner hysteria would be stilled without too much difficulty. It was easy enough to roll a joint.

Which was how, at the age of twenty-nine, Rufus became the President of Cartwright Pharmaceuticals.

Chapter Fifty

Reading the *Wall Street Journal* with her usual avidity, Gina came upon the brief report announcing Rufus's appointment as President of Cartwright Pharmaceuticals. How would he react, she wondered, if he knew she was president of her own company, Gibson–Keene Inc.? Annoyed with herself for even considering his reaction, she flung the paper into the bin and laughed scornfully. At this moment in time Gibson–Keene Inc. was beneath his contempt but it was early days yet, she told herself, early days.

She was at her kitchen table, hard at work writing the copy for her newest advertisement for her newest product – Morning Crisp, the daytime tonic for the executive woman. The announcement about Rufus's appointment as President of Cartwright Pharmaceuticals had so unsettled her that she no longer found her cool cucumber kitchen satisfying. It was now shortly before midnight. Though she had told Morgan she would come to bed earlier than usual, she was already thirty minutes later than she had promised. Rubbing her aching eyes did nothing to alleviate the image she had of Morgan waiting for her. Because of his hiatus hernia, he would be propped up on pillows, ramrod straight and stiff with longing for her.

If only Morgan were Rufus! Her very skin remembered and cried out for him. But Morgan was not and never would be Rufus, nor anything like him. He was what he was – dull, boring, dependable and without a shred of sex appeal. She trusted him as much as she trusted her own mother. He may have had no sex appeal for her, and yet he gave off an aura of strength. The thought of his being unfaithful to her was as abhorrent as it was frightening. Even so, she imagined him again, tense and hard with his desire, and her whole body twisted in one long frown of acute distaste.

Gina drew in her lips with irritation.

There *were* times when she could not escape what had become her wifely duty, and this was one of those times.

She corrected herself. Sex with Morgan had not *become* a wifely duty; it had started like that.

Morning Crisp or Morning Promise? She could not decide. Both were good.

Her own range of skin-care products – Gina Gibson Skin Health – was not yet four years old, and although her company could well have afforded an advertising agency by now, it was an article of faith with her to keep the costs down and the profits up. Accordingly, making good use of her experience at the Hammer Agency, she wrote her own copy and devised her own brand-names. There were five products so far: a deep cleanser, a quick cleanser, a nurturer, a purifier and a lubricator. Now that she was about to market her multi-purpose cream, she was looking either for a new word – or a new combination of words. Morning Promise or Early Morning Promise?

The name was at least as important as the product.

She picked up her pencil to test the look of the words on paper.

She was, by now, forty minutes late for Morgan, which meant that it was, technically, early morning . . . Should it be Early Morning Promise?

Tomorrow she would test her ideas on her proven sounding-board, her mother. A sudden smile of victory lit up her face. What a long way she had come since her mother had added liquefied cucumber to her hand cream!

She neatened her papers and went to Morgan.

She brushed her teeth, slipped off her clothes, and slipped into bed beside him.

His gratitude chastened her. She wished she could honestly have been turned on by him.

Thankful that he was at last safely and soundly asleep, she could give her entire attention to Gina Gibson. The beauty behind her beauty products was that they were only sold in

315

drugstores. She had made the most of Keene Inc.'s customers. From the very beginning she had had a ready-made tri-state pool of clients, and she had made Morgan introduce her to every single one of them.

Since drugstores were her only outlet it was only logical that her packaging should have the simple and clinical look of their medicinal products. After all, the skin-care products were all herbal-based and dermatologically tested. The look was right and the price was right. Though economical, there was nothing shoddy about the packaging. Cucumber green on white was easy to read, easy on the eye, and with the built-in advantage of the surgical *feel* of professional competence.

Gina understood the concept, the meaning and the mystique of 'feel'. Her customers were women and since time immemorial women have relied on, and been well-served by, feel.

Feel – that vital sixth sense given to women, so sadly lacking in men . . .

'Do you think men have a sixth sense?' Gina asked Kate the next morning.

These days Gina and Kate saw one another less than they used to but the telephone kept them in almost daily contact and they were as close as they had ever been.

'A sixth sense? Men?' Kate scoffed. 'They don't begin to understand what intuition means.'

Gina smiled. She and Kate had spent many hours discussing the weaknesses of men and, as though they were staunch feminists, had humorously concluded that men were a necessary evil.

Replacing the receiver, Gina stopped for a moment to reflect on her long-standing friendship with Kate. She felt fortunate to have a woman like Kate in her life, a woman generous enough to understand that she had little leisure time for lunches and the like. High Season had become a star company, and Gina was delighted.

*

316

Now almost five years old, little Scarlett Gibson was closer to her grandmother than to her own mother. Although Scarlett was the light of her life, Cecilia believed that she needed to see more of her own mother, her own father. Wonderful though it was to have Scarlett stay with her during the week, Cecilia decided that she would buy an apartment closer to Gina. Perhaps even in the same apartment house.

As always, Cecilia clarified her thoughts with Miriam.

'Of course the child needs her mother, kiddo,' Miriam agreed. 'But you're wrong about being too old for Scarlett. Women still give birth at forty-seven.'

'I can't make up my mind if I should talk it over with Gina first and then buy it, or buy the place and tell her afterwards.'

'D'you think she'd mind having you so close, kiddo?' Miriam asked bluntly.

'I don't know,' Cecilia responded bleakly. 'I simply can't tell.'

Back and forth the debate went, exploring first Gina's and then Morgan's reactions, and finally their marriage. It was this last which troubled Cecilia most. 'You see, Miriam, the business comes first. I swear she's in love with it! She loves fighting as much as she loves scheming—'

Suddenly seeking attention, Scarlett deliberately picked up one of Miriam's collection of colourful toby jugs and crashed it to the floor.

'Oh, Miriam, I'm so sorry,' Cecilia apologized. 'I'll do everything I can to replace it. I can't think what's got into Scarlett to do a thing like that.'

'You can't blame the child for being bored! We must amuse her. Children ought to be entertained.' So saying, Miriam's eyes darted hither and thither about the place, looking for something for Scarlett to do. Her eyes alighted on her upright piano. Instantly she snatched Scarlett up, took her on her lap, opened the piano, and guiding her index finger began to tap out the melody of the first children's song that she could remember: 'Twinkle, twinkle little star'.

She did that a few times, singing as she played. Then, thinking

317

she had lost Scarlett's interest, she played a few scales, and finally sounded every note through treble to bass.

'My turn,' Scarlett insisted.

Since she was still three months shy of her fifth birthday, Miriam took her little index finger in her hand and began once more to guide her over the keys.

'*No!*' Scarlett exploded with the impatient force of a five-year-old. 'My turn, I said. I'll do it by myself.'

'She always wants to be independent,' Cecilia explained lovingly. The next moment, Cecilia and Miriam exchanged a glance and fell silent.

Effortlessly, and as naturally as if she were rolling a ball, Scarlett picked out the notes of 'Twinkle, twinkle little star'. Having done that, she moved on to 'Rock-a-bye-baby', hummed the tune and found the right notes to go with it.

'The child's a natural,' Miriam proclaimed. 'She's got to have lessons! Hey, isn't that amazing?'

'Do you think so?' said Cecilia doubtfully. 'Where would we find a music teacher?'

'We'll need advice,' Miriam rattled on excitedly. 'Finding her the right teacher's important. Hey, kiddo, you could have a child prodigy on your hands.'

'A prodigy?' Cecilia repeated, questioningly.

'Why not?' In her excitement Miriam poked her friend in the ribs. 'Yehudi Menuhin made his concert début when he was only seven years old.'

Thus was Scarlett's fate decided. Her lifelong, life-consuming dedication to music had already begun.

Chapter Fifty-One

Some love affairs begin after a long and carefully orchestrated campaign of chase and conquest. But when there is no campaign, no chase and no conquest, love affairs begin innocently, as if by chance. 'It just happened,' the lovers will tell one another. If the affair progresses from absolute to relative secrecy, the lovers will tell a few, selected friends how this experience – so unique to them – 'just happened'. Sometimes, both by way of excuse and explanation, again to themselves and to others the lovers will cry: 'But we were thrown together.'

The love affair between Gina's husband Morgan and her best friend Kate 'just happened' because they were 'thrown together'.

To be more specific, Kate and Morgan were thrown together when Gina decided at the last moment not to join them at the theatre. She needed to hone the advertising copy for Heaven and Earth – the name she had finally hit on for her multipurpose cream.

Jean-Pierre was in Switzerland visiting his ailing mother and Kate was, as she liked to put it, minding the store. High Season had proved surprisingly successful. Gina had been right about the gap in the market, and they already had three stores and three more on the planning-boards.

The play, *Susan's Sister*, was one of those heavy, slow set pieces destined to close within ten days.

'The playwright may have written the lines, but he didn't hear them,' Kate said to Morgan during the intermission.

'You're absolutely right. That's what the trouble is. You've hit the nail on the head,' Morgan replied. He laughed suddenly, a great gust of rare, uninhibited laughter.

'I didn't think of it,' Kate said gravely. 'I stole it from something a conductor once said about a musicologist.'

'What was that?' Morgan asked.

'He said that musicologists read music but don't hear it.'

Emboldened by his laughter, Morgan said, 'I have to say I don't much feel like seeing or hearing the next act.'

'I'm glad,' Kate said quietly. 'I was hoping you might say that. Nor do I.'

Morgan touched her lightly on the arm. 'Would it be very wicked of us, do you think,' he asked, 'to go and have our dinner now?'

She made no answer, but smiled at him and walked with him to the exit.

Just before he raised his hand to hail a cab, he said, 'La Caravelle?' She nodded, and moments later they were on their way. The Caravelle was an elegant French restaurant whose murals of Provence were set off by the three-dimensional framing devices of real awnings and shutters.

Once in the cab he took out his Ventolin broncho-dilator and rapidly sprayed his mouth.

'Do you still have asthma attacks?' Kate asked sympathetically.

'Only sometimes,' he said, smiling awkwardly. 'It's your scent in an enclosed space. Do you mind if I open a window?'

'Of course not!' Kate replied. 'I'm so sorry.'

'No problem,' he said, embarrassed. 'It's okay now.'

'D'you always carry that magic spray with you?'

'When I go out, yes,' he said shortly. 'I've got them in every room in the apartment.'

Seated on a banquette in the softly lit restaurant, she observed how different he was from the slim, shy man she had first met nearly seven years ago. His face had filled out and his impercep-tibly crooked nose gave him a look that was sometimes sensitive, sometimes tough. She had not begun to fathom what it was that Gina had seen in him. But now, as she listened to him give their orders, she thought it must have been his benign professorial air

320

of quiet reliability that Gina had found appealing enough to make her marry him.

Morgan, for his part, found that her clear, bold eyes with their long upward-curving lashes held a touch of sadness, and also a hint of mystery.

Over coffee he said unexpectedly, 'Tell me about your mother. I heard she remarried recently.'

'It's her fifth marriage and her fifth husband,' Kate responded. 'She's always lived in the fast lane and on the gossip pages, yet I guess there's nothing I wouldn't do for her.'

'You're a generous spirit.'

'Not really. She's my mother, and I love her.'

He remembered Gina saying something about the girls at Talbot wanting to expel her from their club-within-a-club because of her mother's flagrant disregard for convention. Hadn't she stripped naked and jumped into a pool at Monte Carlo? Tactfully steering the conversation away, he asked her about her son, Matthew.

Within seconds her expression was lightened by the most tender smile he had ever seen.

'Max Sonford took some shots of him the other day. Would you like to see one?' she asked, whipping it out of her purse without waiting for a reply.

'How did you get Max Sonford?'

A leading society photographer, Sonford was not only wildly expensive but tremendously selective about who and what he photographed. 'I didn't know he did kids—'

'You're right, he doesn't usually. My mother asked him to do her favourite grandson, so he did.'

Taking the photograph from her, he immediately exchanged his glasses for reading-glasses, and, although nothing bored him more than looking at the photographs of his friend's children he gave it all his attention.

Suddenly he let out a long, low whistle.

'He's the living image of Jean-Pierre!'

'Yes,' she said quietly, 'he sure is.' She took the photograph

321

from him and studied it intently. 'Even before we were married, we decided to adopt. We always knew I'd never be able to have children. You have to have a womb to do that—'

'I know,' he said simply. 'You had a bum rap.'

That phrase – 'bum rap' – was so distinctly at odds with a man of his dignity that it set up an instant cosmic charge of intimacy between them.

Kate smiled. 'You're right, of course,' she said. 'Matthew *is* Jean-Pierre's son.'

'If you'd like to talk about it, please do,' Morgan said in a kindly manner. 'If not, I'll understand.'

So she told him the truth of how Matthew had come into her life.

'Matthew's mother Claudine and Jean-Pierre had been childhood sweethearts in the town of Vevey in which they lived. Everyone expected them to marry. And then he met me.' Pausing to recollect, a half-smile hovered about her lips. 'It was, at least on my part, a matter of instant, powerful attraction. Skiing can be so exhilarating – so fatally glamorous. And I lost no time making my feelings for him known to him. I didn't know about Claudine, then. But even if I had—' Her hands rose and fell, and she did not complete the thought. 'I've often asked myself what I would have done,' she continued. 'And I can't honestly decide the answer.

'The whole thing is academic, really. Because he stopped seeing her the day before our wedding-day. He and Claudine spent the whole day together – it was a Friday – and the whole night together, too. His parents were beside themselves. He didn't return home until two hours before the wedding. Imagine how they felt! They were at their wits' end. It was quite a while before he told me that his parents knew where he was . . .

'But I'm getting ahead of myself.

'We'd only been married for about four months when I found the letter. I think, now, that he meant me to find Claudine's letter. According to the postmark, it must have arrived three weeks earlier. In it, she said that she was pregnant, and

Catholic, and didn't want to upset him – she was crazy about the guy, crazy! But so was I.

'Luckily something told me not to tell him that I'd read it. My mother was in Europe, in Rome actually, so I called her to ask her to say that she had sent for me to discuss a problem with her. She didn't ask me what the problem was, but co-operated at once. She sent a cable begging me to join her. I told Jean-Pierre I'd go for two to three days, but only if he agreed.

'Of course I had no plan to see my mother. I went to Vevey and not to Rome. A little earlier tonight you told me that I was generous. But you can see, now, why I'd do anything for my mother. She came through for me when I needed her.

'Claudine worked for the Banque de Vevey. I knew that because she had written to him on their notepaper. I didn't even call her from the States. I flew straight to Geneva and went directly by taxi to Vevey. I called her and begged her to see me, and eventually she agreed. But in Vevey she said she couldn't risk being seen with me. So back to Geneva I went, and the next day she met me at the Intercontinental Hotel, where no one of her acquaintance could possibly be.

'We talked very openly. I told her about my hysterectomy. I said that what had happened was the best possible thing for Jean-Pierre and for me. Putting all my cards on the table, I confessed that Jean-Pierre did not know I'd seen the letter. I assured her that I'd give him up, that she could decide . . .

'That was when she showed me *his* letter. He would do his best by her, he wrote. But never never would he divorce me or give up the good life to marry her.

'So I did a financial deal with her.

'And then I did an emotional deal with Jean-Pierre.

'I gave her 50,000 dollars and she gave me her baby. How my lawyers got my trustees to part with an extra 50,000, I'll never know. So we adopted Matthew. The whole thing was legal, as clean as the clinic in which he was born. Everyone thought it would be best for all of us if the baby were born by Caesarian. That way, it was easier to give the baby into my arms. He was only a few minutes old when I held him.

'Claudine broke our agreement only once, and that was to tell me that she had had another baby, a boy. I thanked her for telling me. I was very happy for her.

'Nobody knows Matthew is Jean-Pierre's natural child,' she concluded, exhausted. 'Everyone thinks he's adopted.'

Throughout the long tale, he had held both her hands firmly under his. Now, applying a subtle pressure, he asked, 'Will you tell Matthew?'

'Ah,' she said sadly, 'that's the 64,000-dollar question. We don't yet know what we'll do.'

At last he moved his hands away. 'Excuse me,' he said in his old-fashioned way. 'But I must leave you for two or three minutes. Don't go away, I'll be back.'

Stripped of her secret, she felt suddenly naked. She also felt lighter, as if a great burden had been lifted. She felt suddenly as if she had come in after a long and dark silence. She knew why. It was the first time since her marriage that she had been able to speak with absolute candour to anyone, including Jean-Pierre. She sensed that the same sort of thing was true for Morgan, that in stepping out of his role as Gina's husband – or appendage – he too had emerged from the wilderness of feeling through which he had been blundering. Together, they might just have the healing touch. She was only aware that every fibre of her being had been straining for his return when he slipped into his seat opposite her.

Taking her hands once again, he said, 'Do you know the Commodore, in Prestyn?'

'I've heard of it,' she answered. 'I've never been there. You can never get in.'

'I've just reserved the guest-house there for tomorrow. If you like, you could meet me. I'll be there from about 10.30—'

'Morgan, I can't believe what I'm hearing.'

'Believe it, Kate,' he said. 'It will give you time to think. If you do come I will be a very happy man. If you decide against it, we'll pretend I never asked you. Okay?'

'I'd like a cigarette,' she said nervously.

'I'll be there, waiting for you until four o'clock.'

He called for the bill.

Ruled by an inner flurry of conflicting emotions, she flashed a smile at him and said merely, 'Thanks, Morgan. It's been a grand evening.'

Later, she would tell herself – as they would tell one another – that though she had tossed and turned and debated with herself it had not really been possible to deceive herself that the longing in her was too great to admit of any argument. It was not until dawn that she realized that not once had either of them made any attempt to analyse – either to themselves or to one another – the state of their marriages.

Towards noon she arrived at the Commodore. She had stopped at Balducci's, where she'd bought smoked salmon, Brie, ice-cold champagne, plump pink peaches and fresh French bread packed into a wicker picnic basket. Not a woman who enjoyed shopping, she had allowed herself to fantasize what a joyful experience it would be to shop for him. Then she climbed into her car, a Mercedes sports, placed the picnic basket on the back seat, caught a glimpse of herself in the rear-view mirror and was assailed by the feeling that she had made a terrible mistake.

Surely, surely she should have gone to the hairdresser to get her long and newly streaked blonde hair attended to? After all, which woman going to meet a brand-new lover would give food-shopping priority over her hair?

But – and again this was a truth she would only face later – so wholly had she concentrated on the prospect of a new love that it had not once crossed her consciousness that she was about to be unfaithful to her husband. Much later still would it come to her that just as a victim denies an illness so, too, did she deny what she was about to do to her husband.

Meanwhile, she imagined his fingers on her skin. And then, almost before she knew it, she was at the guest-house, and he was taking the picnic basket from her, and taking her clothes off her and tearing the clothes off himself and soon – but at last it was skin against skin and his fingers were everywhere, everywhere and she was grateful and proud, and finally, finally in harmony with herself.

Over the following two years they met regularly, at least twice a week, but never at night. She took a lease on a loft in Canal Street, and furnished it as she might have done her home.

Often, in an affair, one or other lover feels the need to confide their precious secret to at least one outsider. Whether it's to court some kind of minor publicity among their circle, or to give their delicious secret an additional and more dangerous flavour (what if their secret is betrayed?) the telling subtracts from the totality of their union. But in Kate and Morgan's case their union was as precious – and as sacred – as their marriages.

They were simply too honest with one another to claim that they were unhappily married. If it was true that Gina and Jean-Pierre were obsessed by their growing corporations it was also true that the world of business was a fascinating world. Morgan was not the centre of his wife's life, and Kate was not the centre of her husband's life, but this did *not* mean that they were sufficiently unhappy to break up their families.

The plain and simple truth was recognized by both: their affairs made their marriages perfect.

Chapter Fifty-Two

And then, after two years and four months of their combined extra-conjugal bliss, a single imprudent caring gesture of Kate's gave the whole thing away.

As they had done for years, the Gachets and the Gibsons continued to meet once or twice a month. It was an irresistible opportunity to see one another; and it was also best to carry on as if they were not carrying on.

At dinner one evening after the theatre Morgan developed one of his asthma attacks. He took up his broncho-dilator and sprayed it. He did this, as usual, with the least amount of fuss. He was always so casual about it, that he could well have been taken to be lighting a cigarette. This evening, however, his dilator was empty.

'Damn!' he said, more to himself than to anyone else. 'It's empty.' Again, he might have been talking about a cigarette-lighter that had run out of gas.

The next moment Kate opened her purse and slid a new one to him.

He took it, used it, passed it back to Kate, and the moment passed. The whole thing took no more than a minute, during which time the conversation about the opening of Jean-Pierre's thirtieth High Season store had not stopped.

But it was long enough for Gina.

Things whose significance she had not understood now fell into place.

For one thing, Morgan's interest in sex seemed to have waned. Since they had been married for nearly nine years, she had accepted it as if it were only to be expected and with a large measure of gratitude. Suddenly she understood why his eye flickered over Sagittarius whenever he read the astrological chart – Kate's birthday was on December 16th.

Seething all through dinner, she managed to hold her tongue. On the way home she decided that she would neither do nor say anything until she was good and ready.

Very, very unusually she took a Macron, a sleeping-tablet made by Gibson–Keene Pharmaceuticals.

The next morning she hired a firm of private investigators. She was always to remember that bleak day and her even bleaker ride downtown to engage a 'private eye'. She felt as if she were in one of those B movies she sometimes watched when she was too wound-up to sleep.

It was expensive, but she decided that Morgan was to be followed for a full four weeks.

'But not at night,' she said emphatically. 'My husband is never out on his own at night.'

'If he is cheating on you and he's at home every night, then it's with a married woman,' Sam Harvey, the private investigator, answered equally emphatically.

Gina said nothing, but her chin jutted forward enough for Sam Harvey's professionally trained eye to notice.

He said, 'Look, Mrs Gibson, if you have any inkling who the lady in question is, you should tell me.'

Gina hesitated.

'You're thinking your expenses would double,' Sam suggested smoothly.

'Three weeks,' she replied tonelessly. 'Watch them both for three weeks.' Opening her address book, she gave him Kate's address.

'Kate Gachet and I have been close for fourteen years,' she said sadly. 'We were room-mates at school. She's my best friend.'

'That figures,' Sam Harvey said cynically. 'A best friend makes it all that much safer.'

'Safer?' she queried sharply.

'Sure, it's safer when you're workin' on familiar territory.' He sounded bored.

328

Glancing at her watch, she swiftly rose and hurried back to her own office.

'This could not have come at a worse time,' she fumed inwardly.

She was in the midst of a delicate negotiation to take over Farnsworth's, a formidable competitor of theirs. It was a deal to end all deals, not least because her mother had come up with a good deal of the finance. It was unbelievable, but true; her mother had become a shrewd dealer in stocks. This time, Cecilia would receive an interest in the newly formed company. Farnsworth's had a particularly effective brand of hair colouring. Gina had already come up with a marketing strategy.

'Shit,' she said out loud. 'Shit!'

Because if her suspicions were justified she had no idea what she would do. Loyalty, for her, was a cardinal quality of life. Loyalty was her watchword. She was loyal to her staff and, in turn, they were loyal to her.

For all that she was known to be a tough, astute business-woman, she was ill-equipped to handle emotional treachery.

She could only hope that if she had, in fact, been betrayed both by her husband and her best friend, she would not give way to the murderous impulse which even now began to rise in her . . .

Chapter Fifty-Three

Rufus Cartwright surveyed his newly decorated office and for once experienced a moment of pride. The hand of a professional decorator was nowhere to be seen; he had done it all himself. The couches were beige chamois leather and the walls were covered with ancient Thai wall-hangings. The curved glass desk, made by the sculptor Eduardo Ribetti, was a masterpiece. Since he had no need for drawers, his desk somehow conveyed both the shape and the sensation of a test-tube. A similar glass coffee-table made by the British master craftsman Frank Bentridge held a collection of early microscopes. A lamp, cunningly designed from an authentic scale used by one of the first apothecaries in America, was further testimony to the culture of science that he wished to celebrate.

Although the dark wall-panelling he had inherited from his grandfather appeared to have gone without a trace, it was in fact hidden behind the Thai wall-coverings. A plain beige carpet protected the wooden floors. Jewel-bright antique silk oriental rugs from Keshan decorated the carpet.

Rumour had it that he had an appetite for opium. Certainly his predilection for things oriental was well known.

The rumour, however, had no foundation in fact. Rufus would take 'uppers' to get through the day and the night into the early hours, when he would take 'downers' to let him sleep until dawn. This way his continual transatlantic flying was not an inhibiting factor in his life. And of course he had experimented with and enjoyed the occasional trip, the occasional joint. It was the kind of orgiastic celebration both hippies and high livers had in common.

A year had passed since Dr Bradley and his team of brilliant research chemists and biologists had been transferred from Geneva to their new state-of-the-art laboratories in Cartwright Pharmaceuticals' recently completed New York building. Dr Bradley's new wonder-drug for hypertension, Laroc, had been passed by the FDA and was now on the market.

Laroc, of course, was available only on prescription. And it seemed that, for the moment at any rate, market forces had dictated that most of the advertising budget should be given over to the promotion of the safer drugs – tranquillizers and anti-depressants. Women were the primary targets for the expanded use of tranquillizers. To be sure, his own wife was a prime example of the success of this campaign.

Which was why an effective and unconventional method of advertising was needed.

Thus it was that Rufus hit on the idea of working out a deal with Domestic Air. Since Domestic Air was anxious to launch their frequent-flier programme, it was agreed that for every patient or doctor started on Laroc, he or she would receive one thousand miles' credit. Small wonder, then, that Laroc became one of the most commonly prescribed blood-pressure-lowering drugs whose annual sales were expected to reach a billion dollars by 1976.

Constantly featured in the gossip columns of the western world, Rufus was now a leading member of international high society. Always on the go, on land, at sea or in the air – whichever was necessary to follow the season or the sun or both – his energy was as unremitting as his restless search for excitement.

Some said that his flamboyant life-style was owed to the saying of the famous Sheikh Aoud. 'My father took a gold sovereign and tossed it on the carpeted floor. It made no sound. Then he took the same gold sovereign and flung it on the marble floor. It made a sound loud enough to attract the attention of every servant in the house. You can spend your money as quietly as a wasp or as flamboyantly as I do. People know me. I don't look for business; it looks for me.'

Certainly successful deals were constantly brought to Rufus; it was so boring, it had become like betting on a certainty.

Uncertainty was what he craved.

Private casinos and public casinos became his natural habitat. It was in a private casino on a Boston yacht that he saw a 250,000-dollar bet placed on a single card.

So great was Fabrice's obsession for Rufus that she had succeeded in convincing herself that she was totally free from sexual jealousy. Here, desperate for reassurance, and without the consolation of her parents, who were both now dead, she had been helped by an Egyptian psychic, who had told her that Islam has never restricted sexual pleasure for men. It is only when it leads to adultery in women that it is condemned. 'You see,' the psychic Soraya went on to explain, 'sexual intercourse is seen to be no different from any other bodily function.'

'But what has Islam to do with Rufus?' Fabrice had demanded.

'Everything and nothing,' Soraya replied enigmatically. 'Except to teach you that more than a thousand years ago, the great Mohammed himself knew of the immense differences between men and women. He had ten wives and at least three concubines.'

'Come on,' Fabrice exploded impatiently. 'Next thing you'll tell me that the Koran approves of slavery!'

Soraya's serenity was unruffled. 'Give me your palm again,' she said calmly. 'Ah, I see you are doomed to succeed. Your husband will never fall in love with another woman. Never.' What Fabrice would never know was that she was not in fact that woman.

Gratefully, Fabrice had stared at the psychic, Soraya. She had taken in her sharp sad all-seeing eyes, and like countless women before her been comforted by them.

Nor was she ashamed of consulting a psychic. Indeed, she was proud of her courage to do so. She was only following in the tracks of her mother.

'You are thinking you are brave to come to me,' said Soraya suddenly.

'How did you know?'

'But I myself do not know how I know,' Soraya had answered in her low, musical voice. 'I ask you only to understand one thing. Because if you understand this thing your life will be less painful.'

'Tell me,' Fabrice cried out emotionally. 'Please tell me.'

'Human beings have human instincts, and instincts are neither oriental nor occidental. Instincts are universal.'

'But why do you tell me this?' What is the point?'

'There you go with your western logic. What is logical about maternal instinct?' A sudden wince cut across Soraya's angular face. 'What is logical about love?'

'I wish I knew,' Fabrice muttered.

'But the answer is obvious,' Soraya countered. 'Love and logic? There is nothing logical about love. I sometimes think hate is more logical than love,' she added contemptuously.

Fabrice smiled a sad smile of recognition.

'The western mind insists on logic. The western mind is naïve enough to believe that values evolve from logic. Have you ever stopped to ask yourself whether the Freudian theory of the conscious and unconscious mind would be applicable in the Arab world?'

'I confess not,' replied Fabrice, bemused. 'Harems were unfashionable in Austria in Freud's time.'

But Soraya insisted, 'No harem woman ever thought of making a scene over sexual jealousy,' said Soraya with an intelligent smile. 'The more wives the husband added to his harem, the more he was respected.'

'I don't want to hate Rufus, and I don't want to love him,' Fabrice burst out. 'I would give my soul to be indifferent to him!'

Chapter Fifty-Four

Very exceptionally, Gina left her office in the middle of the afternoon to go home. Too enraged even to attempt to drive, she hailed a taxi. Lurching about in the back seat, she felt her furious heart buzz in her ears. Sam Harvey's report nestled in her briefcase as if it were just an ordinary document among other ordinary documents.

Sam Harvey had delivered it, as he said, 'in person'. And she had paid him 'in person'. He had asked for cash – and he had been paid in cash. It suited Gina. She preferred not to have the name of a private investigator recorded in her checking account. And, according to his report, Morgan and Kate were still in bed with one another. Yes, even now, even as she and the cab were stuck in a traffic jam.

Her husband in bed with Kate, her friend – her very best friend. It was too much.

As the cab neared Central Park she said, 'Let me out.'

Perhaps if she walked in the park she would feel less dizzy, less unhinged.

An interior monologue began as she strode unseeing through the park. 'But you don't really care for him,' she argued. 'While he loves you.'

'True, but does that mean you want him? Or does it mean that although you don't want him, you don't want anyone else to have him either?'

'Me? A dog in a manger? Definitely *not*. Besides, he's cheated on me with my best friend.'

'But if you had not known the woman, he still would have been cheating on you.'

'That would have been bad enough. But this is worse – infinitely worse.'

'Why?'

'Because Kate's always, always wanted what is mine.'

'But if you had loved him, he would not have strayed.'

'Stop this!' she said out loud. 'For God's sake stop—'

She stared about her wildly and all but ran home.

In the apartment she went at once to their bedroom. Again, this was unusual – she was not the sort of woman who used her bedroom for anything other than sleep. Now, seated at the dressing-table, she examined herself in the mirror in a way she had not done for years. She had, of course, routinely inspected her admittedly remarkably clear complexion. It was, after all, her stock-in-trade – living proof as to the excellence of her skin-care products. Unable to face the hurt, shocked look in her own eyes any longer, she turned away.

Her mind leapt again to the last time she and Kate had lunched together. Kate had looked wondrously alive; an emerald-green scarf worn at her throat had made her green eyes startlingly bright. What she lacked in looks she made up for in elegance. Ever since she had married Jean-Pierre, Kate had used elegance and style to compensate for her lack of good looks. Gina now recalled that she had noticed, over the past few months, an air of strong but subtle confidence that had been added to that elegance. Even Kate's laugh had sounded a new note of assurance.

The cause of the confidence was now damningly obvious.

What a fool she, Gina, was to have been so easily deceived! How they must have laughed at her.

Burning with the agonizing blow to her ego, she turned her mind to what she must do.

Even as she sat in front of the mirror, they were making love. *Ugh!* She groaned out loud, and the sharp sound of her own voice brought tears to her eyes.

She would not cry. Tears were not for her. Tears would bring her no relief. Revenge, however, was quite another matter.

Revenge could – and would – bring loving relief.

Although undecided whether to confront him or not, Gina picked up the telephone and dialled her mother's number.

'Mama!' she said when the phone was answered.

Her voice must have sounded urgent, for her mother immediately asked, 'What's wrong?'

Swallowing hard, she replied, 'Nothing's wrong. I only wanted to ask you if Scarlett could spend the night with you.'

'Why not? All her clothes are here. Everything. Her Chopin was wonderful today. Wonderful—'

'Good,' she interrupted. 'I'll call you tomorrow, okay?'

Unable to trust herself to speak, she hung up.

She still did not know what she was going to do. However, just in case she would throw him out of their apartment and out of her life, their seven-year-old daughter would not be there to stop her.

Were they still making love?

Or, having reached the showering stage, were they now taking a shower together?

Perhaps, right now, at this very minute, they were gorging themselves on smoked salmon and bagels. The private investigator's report had told her that, before every assignation over these past four weeks, Kate had stopped at Balducci's to buy all manner of delicacies: wild strawberries out of season, mangoes, Swiss Toblerone chocolate, Alpine dried beef and caviare were some of the more exotic foods she had chosen.

According to the report, their love-nest on Canal Street was paid for by Kate and not by Morgan.

Still deciding what sort of action she might take, Gina looked around their bedroom. The rich subdued colours of the sage-green and burgundy Scotch plaid on the bedroom walls gave the room a distinctive kind of warmth. The sage-green and gold

Tiffany lamps she had bought when an older house had been demolished for a freeway had been a source of intense satisfaction to her, not least because they were worth six times more than she had paid. It was a room that would have sat well on the pages of *House and Garden*. What was more, it could have been photographed at any time. No advance warning would have been necessary – nothing need have been changed. Except, perhaps, Morgan's Ventolin spray-inhaler in its small pressurized can.

It ruined the look of the room. Why couldn't he keep it in the drawer? But of course she knew why. It was because he liked to have it instantly available. No fumbling in a drawer to hold him up, to delay getting that spray into his mouth to prevent a major attack of asthma from developing. Looking at it now with acute distrust, she picked it up and took it to the bathroom. It ought to be kept in the bathroom. She opened the closet door and was about to put it with his reserve supply, when she decided none of his things should be in the bathroom that had suddenly become her bathroom.

Moments later she had removed all his toiletries to Scarlett's bathroom. Next she returned to the bedroom to take his reading-glasses from his bedside table. Opening the drawer to get them, she found a new, unused Ventolin spray.

Hell, no! she thought, he was not going to sleep in *this* bedroom ever again. With that firmly in mind, she tipped the contents of his drawer into a plastic bag, and marched into the guest-room and left it there.

The rage in her began to gather still more momentum. Her very throat was burning. To do this to me, Kate, after all I have done for you . . . A huge howl of rage shook her body.

She would have to decide what to do.

Something would have to be done.

Thinking that their bedroom was now *her* bedroom, she did something she had never done before. She lit a cigarette. She thought she would break the crucial ban against smoking in the bedroom that Morgan's asthma had imposed on her.

But the smell of cigarette-smoke in the bedroom would immediately alert him to the fact that something was seriously wrong.

Furious with herself over her uncharacteristic indecisiveness, she knew only one thing was certain – she would have to take him by surprise.

It was then that she heard his key in the lock.

'Scarlett, darling,' he called out. 'Come see what Daddy has for his favourite little girl.'

Toblerone chocolate, of course. So that was where the Toblerone had come from . . . Great though her rage had been, up until this moment it had been no more than a flicker. Now, as her fury threatened to go on the rampage, she yelled, 'Scarlett's with Mama!'

'Oh,' he said, and in her present state of heightened awareness she fancied she could hear his face fall. 'Why?'

'Come here and I'll tell you.'

'You're in the bedroom?' A creature of absolute routine, she knew that he was hanging his coat and his jacket in the hall. Seconds later he was at the doorway. 'Are you okay, Gina?' he asked gently in his concerned way.

Whipping round from her dressing-table seat, she said accusingly, 'You brought Scarlett some Toblerone, didn't you?'

'Sure I did,' he replied quietly. 'But I was asking you—'

'You kept some chocolate for Scarlett,' she cut in, her voice dangerously calm. 'But the smoked salmon, the bagels, the wild strawberries and the Pouilly-Fumé – that flinty, pungent white wine of the Loire—' She stopped to throw her hands in the air. 'Those delicacies you did not keep for our daughter.'

She watched his pallor become luminous. 'A good enough menu,' she continued. 'But I would not have chosen the bagels. I would have gone for rye—'

'How long have you known?' he asked, his voice dry.

'What's that to you?' she replied sharply. 'More to the point is what Jean-Pierre will say when I tell him.'

338

'You wouldn't do that, Gina,' he said in a half-plea, half-whine. 'You can't do that—'

'Why not?'

'Think what it would do to him.'

'I don't know what it would do to him and I couldn't care less.'

'Oh, my God,' he said, covering his face with his fists. 'Jean-Pierre will take his kid away. She'll lose Matthew,' moaned Morgan. 'She'll lose Matthew.'

'So Matthew *is* his kid,' she said, shocked. 'So that's how the adoption deal was done.' Her eyes narrowed. 'A custody case with a difference – one of those freaky stories the *National Enquirer* loves: "Custody to natural father or to adoptive mother?"'

Keeping time with her rising temper, her fevered, staccato voice lost control. Part shriek and part roar, it drowned all sound save its own. Lost in the sensations of her own wildly growing rage, she gave herself up to her anger as if it were a great grief. Shaken by fierce sobs and blinded by a storm of tears, she neither saw nor heard his ominous wheezing.

It was her first experience of hysteria, and she did not even want to try to bring it to an end. Instead, she dropped to the carpeted floor, where she rolled about like a child in a tantrum.

It was only when at last she fell silent that she heard his wheezing.

'An asthma attack,' she whispered contemptuously. 'How convenient.' Rousing herself from the fluffy cream carpet, she said in a high, clear voice, 'It must have been the Pouilly-Fumé that brought on this attack. A new allergy to go with a new wine. Yet maybe the wine is not new—'

'Gina,' he gasped. 'Ventolin ... please ...' Fighting for breath, he implored, 'I ... beg ... you ...'

Let him suffer, she thought coldly and quickly. *Let the fucker suffer. He's brought it on himself. Now that he knows I know, he's stressed out in case I'll tell my best friend's husband about my husband and my best friend.* Rage split and disfigured the right side of her face. *Let him wait. He'll get the Ventolin when I'm good and ready to give it to him.*

Her eye fell on the small, exquisitely designed Tiffany alarm clock on his night-table. He had said that he had bought it as a birthday present for himself. *Liar! Scumbag! Liar.* But the clock reminded her of a TV commercial she needed to see, so she went to the kitchen to watch it. She was too late, damn it!

She went back to their bedroom.

A sudden and unmistakable change in the sound of his struggle for breath forced her to rush to his side. She saw that he had propped himself against the Scotch plaid headboard and that his tie was undone. She saw the light had gone out of his face.

The inhaler . . .

Where was it?

She remembered.

Praying out loud . . . Dear God . . . Rushing to Scarlett's bathroom . . . The Ventolin in her hand . . . Flying back to the bedroom . . .

Forcing the inhaler into his mouth . . . Frantically depressing the minute pump . . . Don't die . . . Stay alive . . . I won't tell Jean-Pierre . . . The sound, the obscene sound of a dying breath . . .

Then the futile, too-late dash to the telephone . . .

With trembling fingers she dialled the numbers of the ambulance, the doctor, the doorman and Miriam.

It was Miriam who ordered Dr Benson to give Gina a powerful injection to calm her hysteria. Once again, exactly as she had done ten years earlier when poor Mike O'Connor had died so young, it was left to Miriam to take over the arrangements.

But after that first injection, Gina refused all other sedatives. Numbed with shock and grief, she got through the next few days like an automaton. She said little, and more or less did as she was told.

Friends and business associates poured in to offer their condolences. Kate and Jean-Pierre Gachet were, of course, the first of Gina's friends to be informed of Morgan's death.

Jean-Pierre came at once, but without Kate. 'She's all broken up,' he explained regretfully. 'She says she'll be of no use to anyone right now.' Clasping and unclasping his hands, he added, 'She feels so guilty about letting you down, Gina—'

'I understand,' Gina said softly. 'Please tell her not to be sorry.'

Kate, needless to say, was the last person Gina wanted to see now or ever. But she would have to see her and, what was more, she would have to pretend that all was well between them. What choice did she have? Kate had to believe that Morgan had taken their secret with him. Otherwise she might stumble on the truth . . .

Oh God, God, God, why had she taunted him like that? Why?

Moments later her mother arrived carrying Scarlett in her arms. She had suggested that her mother should not be told till the morning, but after phoning Jean-Pierre and a few others, Miriam had overruled her. 'Cecilia would never forgive me,' she had pronounced. 'And I wouldn't blame her.'

Now, seeing her fatherless daughter, the limitless weight of Scarlett's loss closed in on her. Then the bile of guilt and grief and rage rose and compelled her to go to the bathroom.

When she returned, it was to lie on the long chcolate-brown velvet couch. She could not go into the bedroom. Morgan's body was there . . .

About two hours after that Kate burst in. 'I had to come,' she cried brokenly. 'I had to come to be with you.'

Gina managed a silent nod.

'She's taken it hard,' Miriam whispered to Kate.

'Look how white she is,' said Cecilia.

Fanning her fingers over her lips, Gina said, 'I need the bathroom.'

At once her mother brought her the bowl that she had in readiness. She held her daughter's head, helping her over the episode as only a mother can. An infinitesimal jerk of her head was enough to convey to Miriam the message that Gina would rather be alone.

Cecilia's entire being strained to help her daughter.

341

Chapter Fifty-Five

Later, Gina was to say that but for her mother she never would have made it through those first ten awful, guilt-ridden days.

Again and again her mother urged her: 'Let your strength be equal to your courage.' But without her mother she would have had neither the strength nor the courage to go on. She got through the funeral, and then quite literally submitted to her mother's nursing. Her mother forgave her silence and let her be. If her maternal instinct sensed some deeper, fathomless reason for her daughter's wholly uncharacteristic humility, she bit her lips and held her tongue.

For Gina's silent, listless exterior was the barrier behind which her mind was free to roam along endless paths of uncertainty and endless circles of doubt. What is homicide? The killing of one person by another. True, she had not shot him or poisoned him but she had definitely been the cause of his death. She had deliberately withheld the cure for an attack.

She was, whichever way she looked at it, a murderess. So what if she had not intended to kill him? Perhaps at some deep subconscious level she *had* intended to kill him. If only she had not removed his inhaler from its usual place. He had begged her for his Ventolin, and she had forced him to wait. And the terrible irony of the autopsy findings – that he had died from *too much* broncho-dilation – only served to deepen her guilt.

On the eighth day after his death, she took refuge in the thought of suicide. Today was worse than yesterday and tomorrow will be worse than today, she concluded. But the next day could be a void – a guiltless, painless peace. The comforting haven of suicide endured for two more days.

Towards dawn, on the tenth day, she was ready. She left the guest-room she now occupied and went to take one last look at Scarlett. Her method would be both foolproof and instant. A quick jump off her thirtieth-floor balcony and she would be gone before she even hit the ground.

Wet-cheeked, she bent down to kiss her daughter. One last, light, fleeting embrace. Perhaps she meant to wake Scarlett, perhaps not; at any rate, Scarlett awoke. As if in a dream, she murmured, 'Don't die, Mommy.'

Gina was never to be sure whether or not she had hoped her light touch would wake her child and save her own life. She knew only that if Scarlett's voice and words, 'Don't die, Mommy,' had not echoed in her ears, she would have made her final exit.

As it was she crept out of Scarlett's room and went to the bathroom to wash her hair. It was the first positive action she had taken since that terrible night. Perfectly groomed by six o'clock in the morning, she was ready to read the pile of urgent mail that Monica Martins, her devoted secretary, had brought to the apartment.

Her new range of herbal care products was ready to roll. All that was missing was the name. A chemist and a herbalist had worked together and the formulae for specialized shampoos, conditioning creams, styling lotions and a lacquer and even a hair colourant had been perfected. Suddenly, almost unbidden, the perfect name came to her. She would call the range, Raison d'Être – Reason to Be . . .

The possibilities were endless.

Hair with reason to be glamorous, sophisticated, sensuous, shining, silky, glorious, lustrous *and* romantic.

The hair colourant certainly had a romantic touch. An infusion of mature privet leaves would bring a touch of chestnut to the hair. It was said that the Venetian beauties painted by Titian had used this ancient method. Mix the infusion of privet leaves with quince juice, and the result would be golden.

Raison d'Être.

343

Reason to Be.

Unquestionably, Scarlett had given her a reason to be. Even in her sleep, she had said, 'Don't die, Mommy.'

Scarlett was her reason to be.

Unquestionably, Raison d'Être would have a great future.

When her mother and her daughter came into the green kitchen for breakfast, they found Gina seated at the table surrounded by papers.

'Mommy's better,' Scarlett said simply.

'Yes, darling.' Gina rumpled her daughter's hair. Across the table her eyes sought and found her mother's. The crisis had passed. She set about gathering her papers.

'Yes, darling,' she repeated in a firmer voice. 'Mommy's better.'

Soon Cecilia's delicious waffles and maple syrup were ready.

'Mommy came to see me, when I was sleeping,' Scarlett said to Cecilia. 'Mommy was crying.'

Once more Gina and her mother's eyes met and locked in understanding. Yes, there had indeed been a crisis, but it had passed.

Together, in absolute unison, Gina and her mother said, 'Mommy's better now.'

Breakfast over, the two women set about putting the kitchen in order. It was the first time Gina had done anything in the kitchen since Morgan died. Throughout those terrible days Cecilia had anticipated her every need, and she had not so much as opened the fridge door. About to resume the running of her own home, Gina inspected the freezer. A high, plump chocolate cake was the first thing she saw.

'Kate's cake,' she muttered.

'She's been dropping by every day.' Cecilia smiled. 'Cookies, cakes – she didn't know what to do for you.'

'And smoked salmon and bagels?' Gina asked drily.

'No,' Cecilia replied, shaking her head. 'She didn't bring any bagels. I guess she left that to Miriam—'

'Thank God for small mercies.'

'What's the matter, don't you like bagels?' Cecilia asked puzzled. 'I'll go call Kate now. I promised I'd call her as soon as you were okay.'

'Not yet, Mama,' Gina said painfully. 'Not just yet.'

Much as she hated Kate, however, she would have to see her. She could not possibly take the risk of giving Kate the smallest leeway, for surely Kate must have had some instinctive suspicion, however minute. After all, only two hours before his death he and Kate had been in bed.

Chapter Fifty-Six

Although Gina was not wrong about Kate, she had underestimated both the extent and the strength of her suspicions. As the days dragged into weeks, and the weeks into months, Kate's doubts grew even stronger. The strain of keeping up the appearance of a concerned close friend to Gina and of an adoring wife to Jean-Pierre, whilst at the same time concealing her own raging grief, had taken a huge toll.

At the very outset of their affair she and Morgan had mutually – and whole-heartedly – reached an understanding not to break up their families. Divorce was out of the question. Even the fantasy of divorce was forbidden.

But they had allowed their fantasy of a place of their own to become a reality. Which was why she had taken that loft in Canal Street. She was, after all, the daughter of the Ogden Hills banking family and financial considerations were not a problem. There, in that secret loft, she felt that she had at last come home. There she had come into her own. She had not only been free to express herself, but she had wanted to.

So she had refused to allow Morgan's death to take this – their dream place of their own – away from her, too.

In that loft, his presence was almost palpable. She was there now, lying on their large bed that was framed by bookshelves. She came there whenever the mood took her, which was often.

'You know, Kate,' he had said dreamily one afternoon, 'you and I are not having an affair.'

Wide-eyed with alarm, she had replied instantly, 'This isn't an affair?'

'It is a *love* affair, and a love affair and a mere affair have nothing in common.' He stopped to give her a long, loving kiss. 'So we will have to measure our time together in terms of intensity—'

'I know what you mean,' she had said quietly. 'A day like today will be with me for all the days of my life . . .'

And it had turned out to be all too true. Now that he was gone, she found herself living off those days they had had together.

For about the thousandth time, she picked up Morgan's Ventolin inhalant. It was small enough to fit into the palm of her hand. Once again, she caressed its smooth, sculptured lines. And again the same, recurring monstrous question: how was it possible that Morgan could have sprayed too much of the medication into his mouth? Because he knew it could be lethal, he had always been ultra-careful.

And again, the unchanging, equally monstrous answer: it was impossible for him to have over-medicated himself unless the Ventolin spray had not been to hand. In other words, it was only if the inhalant was not immediately accessible to him that his attack would have run violently out of control, forcing him to exceed the safe dose. And if the spray was not where he expected it to be, where was it? And who had removed it from its usual place beside his bed or in the bathroom?

Her knowledge – both of his attitude to the Ventolin and the way in which he handled it – was no less intimate than that of a loving wife. For example, he had told her that although he had thought his spray was empty that night the four of them had gone out together, he had been wrong. The smallest adjustment and the spray would have worked. Had she not given him the emergency extra spray she kept in her purse for him, he would very quickly have got his own spray to work.

She shut her eyes and clasped her hands in prayer. But it did no good. She could not stop herself from imagining his desperate, frantic search.

And the worst thing of all. Oh, worse than worse. Had Gina found out about their affair, confronted him, and so provoked

347

an attack? Stress and asthma, as everyone knows, go hand in hand. Had she then deliberately withheld the Ventolin to punish him?

Did Gina hate her, or was it her own guilty conscience that made her think so? That she had let down her best friend was one of those unforgivable facts of life. But the awful reality was that, in many ways, the betrayal had made their affair extra spicy. And yet, though she had always thought of Gina as her best friend, she knew that she had long known that theirs was an unequal friendship, if only because Gina had been the only person in her life on whom she could depend. Gina, of course, had her mother and Miriam . . .

She crossed the room to switch on one of their favourite tapes, Martha Argerich playing Mozart's E flat concerto, the one they called his 'little' concerto. Just like little Scarlett, Martha Argerich was born with perfect pitch.

Even before Morgan died, she had collected in an album the secret photographs they had taken of one another in their loft. But she had included other photographs, of family outings. She was particularly drawn to the photograph taken on a visit to the zoo, with the two children, Scarlett and Matthew. Morgan and Jean-Pierre joined them – Gina, as usual, had been too busy. She looked now with hungry eyes at a grinning, ecstatic Morgan carrying Scarlett on his shoulders. She had loved his looks, loved his sensuous, smiling lips that she had only felt when they were alone together. Oh, God, how drab, how empty and how boring was life without him!

The Mozart tape came to an end, and she flicked the switch so she could listen to it again. She remembered him explaining the difference between listening to a recorded concert and a live one. 'The perfection achieved in a recording studio is fake perfection – a single note, if necessary, recorded and re-recorded. It's like the difference between an original painting and a reproduction of it.' Even as he spoke she had been tracing the outline of his lips. 'Always choose a live recording of a live concert.'

348

'Like you,' she had replied, feeling her desire rise to her very eyes. 'You are a live concert.'

Exquisitely attuned to her body, he had made love to her at once.

She lay quietly now, letting the tears roll slowly down her cheeks. She could do whatever she chose in their loft, she thought. She could even cry as long as she liked.

Only last night, Jean-Pierre had told her that Morgan had been extravagantly well insured. Much as she did not want to recall what Jean-Pierre had said, their entire conversation came unbidden to her mind. 'Let's face it,' Jean-Pierre had confided, dropping his voice. 'Morgan's death is the best thing that ever happened to her.'

'That's unkind,' Kate replied, flushing deeply.

'I knew you'd say that,' he continued impatiently. 'You always stick up for her. You can't be objective, can you?'

'That's unfair,' she said, scowling.

'But yes, if you were capable of being dispassionate about her, you would *see* what a cold-hearted bitch she is. And you would *feel* the ice in her veins!'

Trying to change the subject, to put an end to this distinctly uncomfortable conversation, she said, 'I must check on—'

'She's gone blonde,' Jean-Pierre interrupted. '*Une bombe blonde.* She's changed her hair-style. Cut it short, like a twenties' girl. A flapper, I think you say.'

'Blonde? Gina, blonde?'

'She's changing her "persona", she says.' He laughed briefly with disgust. 'She asked me to call on her at her flashy office. She wanted me to include a sample of Raison d'Être foot balm with my tennis shoes.'

'And will you go along with her? she asked mechanically.

'But yes, it makes sound business sense.' He gave a Gallic shrug. 'The funny thing is that she has changed her looks. Certainly she was always a classically beautiful woman, a woman of elegance and charm, of *je ne sais quoi*. And now—' At a loss for words, he stopped to shake his head.

349

'And now?' she prodded.

'And now she has the glamour of a movie star. The aura of power, and the magnetism of the unattainable.' Warming to his subject, he added, 'She is the sort of woman who does not like sex. A great switch-on, that—'

'Turn-on,' she said, automatically correcting him.

'Turn-on,' he amended. 'Some poor slobs are vain enough and foolish enough to think they can teach her to love lust. For them, the conquest of a Gina Gibson is as dangerous as it is futile.' Raising his eyebrows speculatively, he concluded, 'She will go to bed, occasionally, and as elusive as gossamer she will be an eternally free spirit, never to be possessed by any man.'

Wrenching her mind back to the present, she got up suddenly and began tearing open the large poster-sized package she had gift-wrapped so carefully. Yet another long and furious interior debate had preceded the choosing of this gift. She had had the photograph of Morgan and Scarlett blown up into a poster. It was beautiful enough to be sold as one of those romantic father–daughter ads that sometimes become posters in their own right.

The gift was for Gina, and there was no telling how she would react to it.

In no doubt at last about giving it to Gina, half sighing and half smiling she fetched a new roll of wrapping-paper and made yet another parcel. Gina had taken advantage of the fall in real-estate values and now owned a penthouse on Park Avenue, no less.

Yes, she would give the poster to Gina. It would be the perfect gift for the extravagant party that Gina would not fail to give. She would wait. She had all the time in the world.

Madame Rosenstein, her music teacher, had had a mild stroke and could no longer teach Scarlett. The search for another teacher was on, and Gina, Cecilia and Miriam had decided that they would settle for no less than the great Monsieur Marceau himself. At his height, he had been ranked with such magical concert pianists as Vladimir Horowitz, Wilhelm Backhaus,

350

Arthur Rubinstein and Wilhelm Kempff. He had only one other pupil, Jeremy Goodman, aged twelve, who had recently given his first concert with an orchestra at Carnegie Hall.

Miriam had arranged for the audition. It was to take place at Monsieur Marceau's apartment. Not surprisingly, one of Gina's particularly crucial business meetings prevented her from taking Scarlett to her audition.

'It's probably just as well,' Miriam said to Cecilia. 'I hate to say this about your daughter, but I get the feeling that Gina makes Scarlett nervous.'

Cecilia had the same feeling. 'Why do you say that?' she asked carefully.

'Do you want me to be frank, kiddo?'

'What a thing to ask!' Cecilia protested.

'Brutally frank?' Miriam persisted.

'Sure.'

'Gina is kind of irritable when she's with Scarlett. Sort of jerky, as if the very sight of her makes her want to itch. As if she's allergic to Scarlett.'

'She *is* jumpy when she's with Scarlett,' Cecilia agreed painfully. 'But why? *Why?*' A low moan escaped. 'And Scarlett adores her.'

'Of course, Scarlett is the living image of Morgan. Same sea-green eyes, upturned, slightly crooked nose, generous lips. Why, she's even inherited his shy smile.'

'So?'

'So she's a living reminder of him. Can't you see that?'

But Cecilia could not bear to answer.

'Gina has done everything she can to get Morgan out of her life.'

'But he's dead,' said Cecilia, her voice flat. 'Morgan is dead.'

'I mean, to get the *memory* of Morgan out of her life,' Miriam corrected herself. 'That's one of the reasons why she moved out of their apartment. She told me so herself. That's why everything – from their furniture to a teaspoon – was sold. She said she didn't want anything around to remind her of him. She told me she asked you to keep the photographs and the home movies.'

351

'That's right. I've put them away. The photographs hurt her. Who can blame her for that?'

'That's the whole point, kiddo,' Miriam said with a nod. 'If a photograph is too much for her, then how much worse it must be for her that she's got a real live, walking, talking image of him around the place.'

Again Cecilia made no answer. The same thought had occurred to her, but she had brushed it aside. Not too successfully, however, for she had never forgotten how Scarlett had been deprived of her own mother's milk.

'I'm sorry to have to say that I agree with you, Mirrie,' she said, in a faintly bitter tone. 'Scarlett *will* be more confident without her mother.'

Over the years, scores of young supplicant would-be musicians had come to Monsieur Marceau's apartment in the Village for an audition. And almost always they were attended by nervous, proud parents. 'But never,' he was to repeat in tones of wonder, 'never before did I receive a child pianist who brought along her grandmother and the friend of her grandmother!'

A trembling Cecilia introduced Miriam before she presented Scarlett to him.

Taking Scarlett's wide hands in his, he said, 'Yes, you have the right instruments for the work.'

Next, he asked her what she would like to play.

'Chopin's Grande Polonaise,' Scarlett replied.

'Ah, a festival of tears,' pronounced Monsieur Marceau.

Scarlett began. Miriam watched the maestro, mesmerized by the way in which his entire body appeared to be concentrated in his ear.

You cannot play Chopin unless you have been in love, thought Monsieur Marceau. And yet this child plays more luminously, more fluently and more tragically than most. Strange, very strange. Yet not so strange. The child's painfully sad eyes, her grandmother and her grandmother's friend . . . Could this poor creature be an orphan? A child, a mere child, putting sorrow

352

into every sob. It would be a privilege – and a pain – to teach such a child.

And so it was that in the summer of 1975, a few months short of her tenth birthday, Scarlett Gibson became a pupil of maestro Monsieur Serge Marceau.

Her first lesson began at once. 'What a pity,' the maestro announced, 'that you have been taught to play with a low wrist! We will change that directly.'

That evening Scarlett, Cecilia and Miriam waited for Gina to come home. 'We'll tell her face to face,' Cecilia said excitedly.

'I don't give a damn whether Gina will mind my being here to share it with you or not, I'm staying!'

'She has to go home to change for the opera,' Cecilia said joyously.

Not much later, Gina was with them. Looking at her chic and enormously successful daughter, Cecilia's heart filled with pride and she almost forgave her coldness to Scarlett.

'But of course Maestro Marceau accepted Scarlett,' she said in a cool, brittle tone. 'How much does he charge for a lesson?'

'We didn't ask,' Miriam said, disgusted.

'We'll find out soon enough,' Gina said dismissively. 'Is he married? Does he have a wife?'

'We met Madame Marceau briefly,' Miriam replied. Gina's become a bitch, she thought angrily, a heartless bitch. 'Why do you want to know whether he has a wife?' Her voice sounded harsh even in her own ears.

'Scarlett can give her my complete Raison d'Être range,' Gina added sarcastically. 'I take it that meets with your approval, Miriam?'

Don't make waves, Miriam begged herself. Don't make waves. It's Scarlett's day. Don't spoil it. 'Why, Madame Marceau will be delighted, Gina. Great idea.'

'Anyway, darlings, I too have some good news to give you.' Gina smiled. 'I got a wonderful present for my mama,' she said proudly. 'I've bought poor Mr Kaiser's apartment, for the best mother in the world!' Turning to Miriam, she explained, 'Poor Mr Kaiser had the apartment below ours on the twentieth floor.'

353

'Why "poor" Mr Kaiser?' asked Miriam, with her usual bluntness.

'His mortgage was foreclosed,' Gina said shortly. 'Just to prove to you that I had no doubts whatsoever that Maestro Marceau would accept you, Scarlett, I made enquiries about a Steinway piano.'

'A Steinway!' Scarlett squealed.

'I called Constance Courtney this morning. I remembered that she had one.'

'You called Constance?' Cecilia said, clearly delighted. 'How is she? I tried to reach her but she was in London.'

'That's where I called her,' Gina said patiently. 'She said she'd be happy to sell it to me. I have the strangest feeling that things have not gone too well for the Courtneys. Their house is being taken over by a school. I heard they sold it for a song.'

'I can't believe it,' said Cecilia, distressed. 'How awful! Mrs Courtney was always so kind to me. And to you, Gina.'

'I have never forgotten, and I will never forget, that she paid for me to go to Talbot,' Gina replied smoothly.

'Constance Courtney did more than just pay for you to go to Talbot,' Miriam said heatedly. Her bracelets jarred. 'She arranged the interview with Miss Armstrong.'

'Sure, Constance Courtney was Lady Bountiful,' Gina sneered. 'I always believed she thought she was living in the last century, dispensing cakes to the poor!'

'*Gina!*' her mother said, aghast. 'Is gratitude so painful to you?'

'Constance Courtney is only too pleased to have her Steinway taken out of store,' Gina plunged on. 'She made a joke of it – thanked me for taking it out of quarantine.'

Her eyes flickered distastefully over Scarlett. 'Stand up straight, Scarlett,' she ordered. 'Up! Up! How many times do I have to tell you not to slouch like your father? You're beginning to remind me of the Hunchback of Notre-Dame.' So saying, she swept out of the room, leaving Cecilia and Miriam staring after her in undisguised horror.

She hates Scarlett, Cecilia thought sadly. She hates her own daughter. The anxieties she had felt over Gina's aptitude for motherhood had never quite died down. Recently it had even occurred to her that Gina *might* have reacted differently if Scarlett had been a boy. She would have fared better as a mother to a son than to a daughter.

Sighing, she hugged herself with her suddenly weary arms and pulled her mother's shawl tighter. Gina was only thirty-one. Much time had passed since she had become a widow, and there was still no sign of a man in her life. A beautiful young woman like Gina – could it be possible that she neither wanted nor needed a man? And yet, far from being unhappy with the way things were, Gina appeared to be on a positive high, like a woman in love. Which was true, Cecilia thought grimly. She was in love – with her business.

Once Gina had laughingly told her, 'Mama, there isn't a man alive who could compete with Raison d'Être! Believe me, Morgan is not missed!'

'But, Gina,' she had protested, 'a woman needs a man.'

'Not this one,' Gina snapped. 'I don't need a man to provide for me or for my daughter. I provide for all of us. I don't need a man to father a child, I already have a child. I don't need a man for excitement. I have Gibson–Keene Inc.!'

'What about—' Cecilia began hesitantly. 'What about – bed?'

'Bed!' Gina repeated, her voice crackling. 'Thank goodness I don't have to do my duty any more.' Seeing her mother's crushed expression she went on in a softer tone, 'Morgan and I, well, we got the chemistry wrong. It didn't work too well for us.'

'Are you saying you didn't live as man and wife?'

'Oh, I'm not saying that, Mama.'

'Do you think he had someone else?' Cecilia asked shrewdly.

'I don't know.' Gina shrugged.

'Anyone I know?'

'How would I know?' Gina lied.

'Did you *never* love Morgan?' Cecilia asked sadly. 'Did you feel nothing for him?'

'You make it sound as if I've *never* been in love,' Gina said roughly. Then, almost as if she wished to hurt her mother in the

355

way that daughters sometimes do, she added sharply, 'Once was enough for me.'

'You fool!' Cecilia retorted angrily. 'You think you're a one-man woman, is that it?'

'Maybe.' Gina frowned. 'Anyway, in many, many ways I'm happier than I've ever been.' Fiddling with her double row of pearls, her most recent acquisition from Cartier, she murmured. 'I suffered once over a man. I made up my mind I would never, never let that happen to me again. Not ever.'

'But, Gina, you're only thirty-one.'

'True,' Gina agreed. 'But right now I don't need a man to complete my life any more than you need one to complete yours.'

As usual, she had got to the heart of the matter.

'But, *tesoro mio*, I am a grandmother!'

'Yes, Mama, and I am one hell of a businesswoman.'

Gina had laughed then, and her laughter had been as serene as the sound of flowing water.

Meanwhile, as Cecilia consoled herself now, there was no shortage of escorts in Gina's life. She was seen at all the right places, with all the right men. Of course, the man had to be a high achiever. Apart from success, her only other criterion was that the man should be unmarried. She was as comfortable with straight men as she was with gays.

Strange, the way Gina had said she did not miss Morgan at all.

But Cecilia missed him. She had loved him. He had been good to her; she had always considered him to be the best son-in-law in the world. Besides, he was half of the most important and most wonderful person in the world. He had fathered her treasure, her darling Scarlett. He had made her a grandmother.

Chapter Fifty-Seven

The very day that Kate returned from her private loft sanctuary with the firm decision to give Gina the poster of Morgan and Scarlett, she found an urgent message to call her mother in Paris. Urgent messages from her mother were unfailingly exaggerated. Often enough, after frantic calls, she had located her mother in a restaurant or at the hairdresser. Her mother was only in Paris to attend a party. For all that, she called the George V at once and was immediately put through to the concierge, who told her that her mother had had an accident, that she now had *une maladie grave* and was in the American Hospital.

That same night she and Matthew left for Paris. As so often happens, the most neglected daughter turns into the most dedicated daughter. Kate stayed on in Paris, where she nursed her mother with exemplary devotion. Since her elder sister, Evelyn, came and went as the mood took her, it was left to Kate to remain stalwartly at her mother's side. Jean-Pierre could not have been more co-operative. He flew to Paris whenever he could but, when the end came, she was alone.

Of all the possessions her mother bequeathed to her, there were only two that she did not either sell outright or send to Sotheby's.

She kept the delicate carving of a grape arbour of the Qing dynasty. Sotheby's told her it could have fetched at least a million dollars. Throughout her childhood and early teens she had been strangely drawn to its luminous colours; she had believed it to be magical. It was said to be the link between earth and heaven, the bridge from life to immortality.

By the time she returned to New York, a long time had

357

elapsed since Morgan's death. Nonetheless, she would go ahead with her decision to present Gina with the poster.

So she called Gina and, though the note of impatient reluctance was obvious, they made a date to meet. Thus it was that on a cold February Saturday in the winter of 1976, Kate presented Gina with the poster of her smiling, dead husband and his laughing daughter.

Recently, Gina had taken to giving a typical English tea on a Saturday afternoon, and already invitations were highly prized.

Once she had invited Kate and Matthew, she reasoned that she might as well include her mother and Scarlett and Miriam. Accordingly, scones and strawberry jam and thick cream arranged on a silver salver, and finely cut cucumber sandwiches and the famous almond–orange cake, which she still baked, made up a sumptuous tea. Surveying the table, with its sparkling white damask cloth and its gleaming silver tea-kettle kept hot over a tiny flame, Gina could not help feeling a satisfying sense of victory over Kate. After all, she had not forgotten how greatly awed she had been when she had visited Severn Woods in Connecticut.

If it seemed strange that Gina *invited* her ten-year-old daughter, there was a good reason for this. Scarlett and her Steinway had now moved with Cecilia into the apartment below Gina's penthouse, the one that had been bought from poor Mr Kaiser.

Scarlett had promised to entertain them with a forty-minute concert after tea. Gina had acquired a new Steinway for her penthouse and Scarlett was to test it out.

Moments before Gina rose to announce that Scarlett was to play a Chopin nocturne, Kate fetched the large gift-wrapped package from the hall and presented it to her.

'Why, thank you,' Gina said. She took the parcel and propped it up against the wall, thereby indicating that she did not plan to open it until her guests had gone.

Having predicted that Gina would do just that, Kate now

said brightly, 'That package is for both you and Scarlett.' She moved to take a cucumber sandwich. 'I'm dying to see whether you like it or not,' she went on. 'By the way, Gina, this sandwich is perfect.'

'Okay, Scarlett,' Gina half sighed and half smiled. 'Go ahead and open it!'

Moments later the brilliantly coloured gift-wrap, styled after a Mondrian painting, lay in a few jagged scraps on Gina's floor.

But two layers of tissue paper formed a veil, and so the poster was not yet exposed. It was then that Gina lost her patience, lunged forward and, in a single, vicious movement, ripped the tissue.

'It's Daddy!' Scarlett exclaimed. 'It's Daddy and me!'

Unable to control herself, Gina snatched up the poster and turned its face to the wall. 'But, Kate, you *know* I don't want any pictures or even snapshots of Morgan. You *know* how I feel about that.' She felt her temper rise but, forcing it back under control, she clenched her fists and said in a ragged whisper, 'Why have you done this to me?'

Kate, who knew her former room-mate very well, saw those tell-tale clenched fists and at once concluded that Gina was struggling to control her rage. And in that instant, just as surely as if Gina had told her so herself, she knew that Gina knew about her affair with Morgan. The two of them were – or had been – best friends. She had betrayed that friendship in the worst way. Kate had long searched her mind for the truth of why Gina had failed to confront her with her treachery.

At long last her search was over – *Gina's silence could only be connected to the way Morgan had died . . .*

Clearly, Gina had found out about Morgan's affair with her. Not the person readily to forgive any wrong done to her, she had hit upon a simple and, as it turned out, lethal form of punishment.

In all the world nothing could have been easier or more effective than hiding and then withholding Morgan's medication.

The look of recognition that passed between the two women locked them into a strange alliance of permanent enmity. Neither one of them would ever be free of the other.

Kate knew that if she were to expose Gina she would in turn also expose her affair with Morgan. Jean-Pierre had always warned her that if she ever dared to have an affair she would run the grave risk of losing custody of Matthew to him. After all, Jean-Pierre was his biological father, and Kate was only his adoptive mother . . .

Gina knew that if she were to expose Kate she would run the risk of a deeper investigation into the cause of Morgan's death. And even if there were no official investigation, it was highly likely a vengeful Kate would run a whispering campaign.

A hush had fallen over the small group. Even Miriam's bangles were still.

Kate was the one to break the silence. 'If the photograph of Morgan is so distressing to you – and I can well understand why it would be – why don't you give it to Scarlett?'

'I'd keep it in my own room, Mom,' Scarlett said nervously. 'It would look real nice in my room.'

'Of course you can have it, Scarlett,' Gina said coldly. 'Why don't you all go down to your room and hang it up right now?' Drumming her fingers impatiently on the arm of her chair, she turned to Scarlett. 'You can't hang pictures and give a concert, can you?'

Another stunned silence fell.

Smiling a difficult smile, Kate picked up the poster. 'I'll be happy to help you hang it,' she said.

Yet another look of enduring hostility was exchanged between Kate and Gina.

It was picked up by Miriam.

There's bad blood between those two, she thought. It will end badly.

If Gina had not been engaged in two genuinely earth-shattering events, she would definitely not have missed Scarlett's school concert. Gina herself could not decide which of the two was the more crucial. Was it her new lover, Clarence Fowler of *the* famed Fowler Gallery, or was it the damning reports on Cartwright Pharmaceuticals' hair colourant? Both were exciting, both were challenging, but, as always honest with herself, she knew that if she were asked which one had priority, it would be Cartwright's hair colourant.

ANAPHYLACTIC SHOCK CAUSED BY CARTWRIGHT HAIR COLOURANT

Never, not even in her wildest dreams, could she have hoped for such a stroke of luck. And to think that she had actually been at Guy-Jacques, *the* famous hairdresser in New York, when it had happened to Fabrice Cartwright! She had seen Fabrice's face rapidly turn crimson. Within seconds her neck was covered in a bright red rash, and then, almost at once, Fabrice had experienced difficulty in breathing. Instinctively, and in a state of high agitation, Fabrice had ordered the assistant to wash the tint off.

Even as Lewis rinsed the tint out of her hair, he saw that her neck had turned into a series of scarlet blotches.

'My ears,' she murmured faintly. 'Throbbing in my ears . . .' Her voice trailed off.

'You can sit up, Mrs Cartwright. I've got all the tint out,' Lewis said anxiously.

But Fabrice gave no sign of having heard. She remained where she was, her eyes closed. Because it was not uncommon for the clients to close their eyes while their hair was being washed, Lewis repeated loudly, 'You can sit up now, Mrs Cartwright.'

Seated beside Fabrice, Fiona Blake, one of the customers in the row of recumbent women having their hair shampooed, sat up abruptly. 'Mrs Cartwright has fainted,' she announced briskly. 'I don't like the sound of her breathing.' She stood up. 'Call an ambulance,' she ordered. 'It looks like she's allergic—'

Within seconds there was a flurry of activity. The manageress called the ambulance. Guy-Jacques and Lewis covered the carpet with the salon's good crested navy-blue towels, carried her away from the sink and made a bed of sorts for her. Guy-Jacques tried to take her pulse but it was so rapid that he quickly lost count.

Minutes after the SOS call, two paramedics and a stretcher were in the beauty shop.

'She said her ears were throbbing,' Lewis told them.

'Palpitations do that,' the paramedic said curtly as he pumped up the sphygmomanometer cuff around her arm. 'BP's fallen,' he said urgently to his colleague. 'Eighty over fifty.'

'She's not going to die, is she?' Guy-Jacques asked, biting his nails.

'She's had an acute allergic reaction,' the paramedic said gruffly. 'Looks like anaphylactic shock to me.'

The paramedics went into their skilled routine, administering oxygen and setting up an intravenous line. Her pulse was rapid and out of rhythm, and it was clear that she was deteriorating. Working frantically, the paramedics had no alternative but to risk giving her an intramuscular shot of adrenalin. But she was still in respiratory distress. Concerned about the swelling of her larynx they rapidly set up suction, opened a clean oxygen suction pump and prepared the intubation instruments. Moments later they had inserted a tube down her nose into her lungs to help her breathing.

A tearful Guy-Jacques watched the paramedics as they hastily wheeled her out of the salon and into the waiting ambulance. 'Someone should call the husband,' he wept.

'I've already called him,' said the manageress.

'She's going to die!' Guy-Jacques moaned.

As he watched Fabrice leave for the Franklyn Hospital, Guy-Jacques began to sob. 'Oh, my God, she's going to die! And it will be my fault!' He blew his nose into a silk handkerchief. 'It's Blonder-Briter – a brand-new product.' Beating his hands against his head, he repeated, 'She's going to die and it will be my fault.'

Gina's heart lurched. *Blonder-Briter*! The new product that her chemists had been running around in circles to reproduce in

Gibson's laboratories. Blonder-Briter halved the time needed to get the tint to work. And in all the general confusion, no one noticed her remove the rollers from her hair and leave the salon while her hair was still wet.

She jumped into a taxi, gave the address of Melanie Wilson, her public-relations consultant, and lit a cigarette. Her hands trembled. Thoughts whirled about her brain. Guy-Jacques was the most famous hairdresser in New York. His salon – tastefully decorated in English chintzes – occupied four floors and was the last word in discreet luxury. At Guy-Jacques, an ordinary visit to the hairdresser was turned into a pleasurable event. If she had been on the third floor having her hair styled, instead of tinted, she might have missed everything.

'You'll catch your death of cold, lady,' the cab-driver said, 'with wet hair in the middle of winter.'

She stormed into Melanie's office and quickly gave her the whole story. After sending for a towel to dry Gina's hair, Melanie listened.

Her stern face was transformed by a wicked smile. 'It's all so simple,' she pronounced. 'It seems too good to be true.'

By the time Rufus reached the intensive care unit, Fabrice was already on a ventilator, the machine that breathed for her. Sedated to the point of paralysis so that she would be unable to attempt to disconnect the mass of tubing connected to her body, she was scarcely conscious. Although her blood-pressure had not yet been stabilized, the doctors were, as they put it, cautiously optimistic. The sight of her white face on its nest of pillows made him catch his breath. A ventilator tube had been fed into her mouth, but the area around the closed eyes was stamped with its familiar expression of sad patience.

Dr Hawley, tall with kindly, knowing eyes, explained that some chemical in the new hair colourant that had been used had caused her to go into anaphylactic shock. 'It's rare,' he said carefully. 'Extremely rare. She probably had a dry, itchy scalp, which she must have scratched. Even a superficial pin-prick of

363

a lesion would be enough to allow the substance to be absorbed into the bloodstream.'

'She has beautiful hair,' Rufus said. 'Thick, lustrous—'

'Then she probably didn't even know she had a slight inflammation,' Dr Hawley surmised swiftly. 'I've seen this sort of reaction in one or two people who unexpectedly developed an allergic reaction to the starch in their shirt collar. A slight shaving-cut resulted in a life-threatening respiratory collapse.' He shook his head. 'Some patients go into anaphylactic shock after a bee-sting.'

'She's not going to die, is she, doctor?' Rufus asked painfully. 'A hair colourant couldn't kill her?'

'The cause of her shock is not relevant,' Dr Hawley replied carefully. 'We have to look at her current state. We are hoping her blood-pressure will improve—'

'I want to be allowed to stay right beside her,' Rufus said softly. 'Please.'

It was against all the rules, but the doctor relented. There was a small chance that Rufus's mere presence might have a positive effect on his wife. Dr Hawley had long since concluded that loving promotes healing . . . So Rufus was at her side, talking to her, telling her how much he loved her, begging forgiveness for his past selfishness, promising a happier future. 'If you will only just stay alive,' he said, over and over again. 'If you will only just stay alive.'

Doctors say that following a crisis, day two is the day of hope, and so it was in Fabrice's case. She was more responsive and alert, her cardio-vascular signs improved, she began to breathe on her own and her heart drugs were slowly tapered down. The ventilator prevented her from speaking, but she could write.

Shaping her thumbs and forefinger into a writing posture, she signalled that she would like to write. Nurse Edmunds handed her a pencil and paper. Still very weak, her handwriting was spidery but legible. 'Love you,' she wrote and, reading it, Rufus laid his head on the edge of her bed and wept.

But on day three, at four o'clock in the morning, her temperature rose, climbing rapidly from 102 degrees to 103 and then

364

remaining stationary at 104. Instantly the ventilator was restarted. A huge fan blew overhead and her body was swabbed so that her skin, under the fan, would grow colder and cool down. Frozen packs of saline were placed under her armpits and between her legs. Blood cultures were taken and analysed, and a non-specific fungal infection was found. Once more her blood-pressure dropped alarmingly. Owing to her state of shock she was highly susceptible to infection; intubation at the hairdresser, or even the ventilator itself, could cause it.

Inflammation of the heart muscle – myocarditis – was diagnosed. Suddenly the cardiac monitor showed her heart dancing wildly out of rhythm, dancing with a crazy pulsating energy. Moments later the monitor showed a straight line: cardiac arrest! The next second Nurse Edmunds slammed her fist into the middle of Fabrice's chest. Rufus had moved out of the way of the nurses and, though he was several paces away from her bed, he heard the sound of her ribs cracking. Meanwhile, several nurses answering the coded emergency alarm raced into the ward and began ripping open the drawers of the crash-cart, preparing the defibrillator paddles by smearing them with blue gelatin, which would act as a conductive medium and shock her heart into action.

Four 100-watt seconds of electricity jolted her body a few inches off the bed. Her arms flailed wildly, like a rag doll being tossed about by a child in a tantrum, but her heart had started again. Still out of rhythm, her heart fibrillated for at least an hour and then it stopped again. Once more Rufus listened to the terrible sound of the electric shock to the human body. He heard the hollow click, the noise of a car door being wrenched out of the car, a sound that reminded Rufus of a hundred steel fists beating in unison against an open wound.

She had been given inotropic drugs to stimulate the contraction of the heart. Ironically, one of the inotropic drugs, Intol, had been invented at Cartwright Pharmaceuticals. Despite these powerful drugs, however, her heart muscle had been affected to such a degree that it could no longer pump.

*

Rufus had not slept since Fabrice had been admitted to the ICU, but his mind had never been more alert. After the first day his own sense of shock had worn off, which meant that his sense of reality was as acute as it was painful.

She had always been too good for him. He had always known that, but had refused to recognize it until now. He had not deserved her, so she had been taken from him. Her death was his punishment. He was to believe that until the day he died.

Too late, Rufus fell hopelessly in love with his dead wife. Alas, he was not the first man to do so.

Chapter Fifty-Eight

Born in America, educated in England at Eton, and later back in his own country at Yale, Clarence Fowler, grandson of the founder of the Fifth-Avenue Fowler Gallery, was undoubtedly the most eligible bachelor in New York. Now thirty-six years old, Clarence had had affairs with a glittering array of famous women, ranging from movie stars through to designers, fashion editors and lastly, a ballerina. His liaison with Clara Tarrejan had been much chronicled in the gossip columns, where it was said that the spectacular emerald engagement-ring he had given her had once belonged to the Grand Duchess of Essen.

Gina had met him at a press–celebrity party aboard the *Renwick*, an elegant ship that sailed Manhattan's East River. Given to launch Versailles, a new French perfume, the usual caviare and champagne had been augmented by mountains of lobster. The scent of thousands of white frangipani flown in from Hawaii was so overpowering that, much as Gina wanted to stay to see and be seen, she began to think of leaving early.

It was now about eight months since she had made it her policy to have a high profile. These days she regularly attended the opera on the smart nights, was a frequent guest of the much-chronicled great hostesses of New York and, having acquired among other paintings an early Datnow of the school of von Luben, was already becoming known as a patron of the arts.

Still, since she could not abide that scent, she had no alternative but to leave at once.

Making her way out through the crush, she recognized Clarence Fowler.

'Excuse me,' she said politely. 'I know I'm being rude, but I simply have to leave or I'm going to faint.'

'The frangipani?' he said sympathetically.

'Right first time,' she replied.

'You look stunning,' he said unexpectedly. 'Are you free? Could I take you to dinner?'

'On one condition.'

'You have a condition?'

'Yes,' she nodded, smiling. 'I'd like to be told who you are.' She was lying, of course. Everyone who was anyone knew who Clarence Fowler was.

'Forgive me, Gina,' he said with a slight playful bow. 'My name is Clarence Fowler.'

She looked puzzled.

'I asked who *you* were,' he explained.

At the elegant La Grenouille, a restaurant in one of the last brownstones on East 56th Street, he said, 'Your dress is as stunning as you are.'

She was very quickly to learn that stunning was one of his favourite adjectives. That remark, coming from him, was not in the least affected. Style, after all, was his business. She was wearing a simple but sensual cream silk shirt with an appliqué of leaves and a matching skirt, a perfect exemplar of the art of understatement.

Conversation flowed easily between them. Since she had immersed herself in the world of contemporary art these past eight months, this was hardly surprising. What was surprising, however, was the skilful way she manoeuvred the talk towards Clara Tarrejan, the ballerina, the current woman in his life. Yes, he was still seeing her. 'Clara is in New Orleans for the night,' he told her.

'My goodness,' she said demurely. 'I wish I'd known that. I wish you'd told me.' She paused and lapsed into silence.

'Why?' he asked, jumping into the silence. 'Why do you wish I had told you?'

'Your whole attitude seemed to me to be so footloose and fancy-free that I took it for granted that you were not involved.' She shook her head sadly and continued, 'You see, I don't do that sort of thing.'

368

'What sort of thing?'

'I do not go to dinner with an unmarried man who has someone important in his life,' she said coldly. 'And other than my own husband, I have never been out with a married man in my life.'

'But Clara and I are all washed up,' he protested. 'It's all over. She'll be collecting her things when she gets back from New Orleans.'

Which was not entirely true. But it was because he found Gina so refreshingly forthright and – in his distinctly unprincipled world – so remarkably principled, that he took the decision to break with his thoroughly devious Clara.

Chapter Fifty-Nine

At the back of his stretch limo, after a long, boozy lunch with his lawyer, Rufus read the daily sales figures and the attached magazine clipping and angrily screwed the pages into a tight ball and flung it out of the window. The numbers for the entire range of Cartwright Hair Care had fallen drastically. He swore softly. It was eight months since Fabrice had died, and the media were still at it. His decision to keep the range going owed more to emotional than to business considerations. All is fair in love and war, he told himself, and the same principle holds good for business. And, like all business warriors, he too had ambushed his rivals in a price-slashing trap.

Even so, to capitalize – as clearly the competition was capitalizing – on his wife's death was, in his view, going beyond the bounds of human decency. Surely, even in business there was a code of conduct, a sort of Geneva Convention? There was no point in even trying to sue. Legally they were outsmarted, defeated by nothing other than the truth.

If it had not been his wife, there would have been no story. As it was, it had turned into a media event. Whoever or whichever company was behind the orchestration of the media had not been content to settle for having succeeded in forcing him to recall all their Cartwright Hair Care colourants. Instead, it seemed, their strategy was to eliminate Cartwright Hair Care from the market-place.

There could be no doubt about it – the whole thing smacked of a personal vendetta.

But by whom?

And why?

Because whoever it was seemed to have endless funds and

endless time to devote to this vendetta. Why, all his clients – every single drugstore who stocked Cartwright's Hair Care – had received a copy of the newest unfavourable publicity almost as soon as it had appeared.

He fervently hoped that their newest firm of corporate intelligence consultants (whom his lawyer had engaged) would come up with something good. They certainly charged enough.

By the time he reached his glass sculpture of a desk, he found that he was trembling. He pressed a button in the wall and the door to his concealed bar slid open. He poured a large gin into a sparkling crystal glass and quickly gulped it down. The shaking stopped. He went to the window and, looking down at the human ants below on the street, he breathed more easily.

He flicked a switch. 'Send him in,' he ordered curtly, not even bothering to mention the name of the corporate private eye.

'Mr Kendall will be with you right away,' said Jane Singleton, his personal assistant, smoothly informing him of the name of the man who had come to see him. Gaunt-cheeked, the fat purses under her eyes enlarged by the thick lenses of her large, horn-rimmed glasses, Jane Singleton was the very definition of a devoted, adoring personal secretary. Now in her mid-fifties, she had worked for Rufus's grandfather Theodore. Her long and intimate association with the Cartwright family led her to protect Rufus no less fiercely than a devoted mother. For good or ill, her heart-break over his constant drinking made her still more protective.

'Any success, Mr Kendall?' he asked crisply.

'We've narrowed the field to about twelve,' Mr Kendall replied nervously.

'I did not ask for statistics,' Rufus snapped. 'A simple answer to a simple question.'

'It might be constructive at this time, Mr Cartwright, sir,' said Mr Kendall, who was at least fifteen years Rufus's senior, 'if you could think again about who your enemies might be. The consensus among my colleagues is that you are right, there *is* a vendetta.'

371

'I've already told you,' Rufus snarled sarcastically. 'Joe Finlayson of Pax Inc. is the only enemy I might have made.'

'Pax have been steadily losing their market share,' Mr Kendall said earnestly. 'They've been excluded.'

'I guess it's time for a drink,' Rufus replied. 'Care to join me in a gin and tonic?'

'Thanks,' Mr Kendall answered, snapping open his briefcase. 'I could do with one.'

For a second Mr Kendall had the sneaking suspicion that Rufus Cartwright was drunk. But then Rufus's mood lifted and he offered him a cigar, and the moment passed.

Taking a bulging file from his briefcase, Mr Kendall said, 'This is a file we've compiled of top executives, CEOs and even a few key sales managers. It is possible, Mr Cartwright, that one of these may have had a fairly intimate relationship with you. He – or she – might even have worked for you. Executives who are redundant turn into desperate men and women.'

'Sure,' Rufus said pleasantly. 'We all know about that.'

'If you'd care to take a look at these photographs, sir?' Without waiting for a reply Mr Kendall began laying them out on the glass desk, separating the men from the women.

First, Rufus flicked through the photographs of the men. He shook his head. 'There's nothing here,' he said abruptly. He stopped to pour himself another gin, and then took his time going through the photographs of the women.

'Who's this sexy blonde bombshell with the cigarette-holder?' he demanded aggressively. 'Reminds me of someone, some movie star I saw when I was a kid.' Gina had been colouring her hair blonde for so long that it now seemed to be entirely natural. But Rufus, of course, was not to know that.

'Gina Gibson, President of Gibson–Keene.'

'I knew a Gina once,' Rufus said. 'A curtain of jet-black hair, she had. My grandmother told me that she married a bricklayer and went to live in Dayton, Ohio. I guess I should have married her and she wouldn't have gone to Dayton, Ohio.'

Mr Kendall shook his head. 'Gibson–Keene also have a range of hair-care products called Raison d'Être,' he explained painfully. 'We couldn't see why they would want a vendetta with you.' He began gathering up the photographs. 'Our motto is to leave no stone unturned, you know. I guess that's why my partner, Steve Jackson, and I agreed that there was no harm in trying.'

'Try harder then,' Rufus said irascibly. 'Try harder.'

You win some, you lose some, thought Mr Kendall wearily.

The interview terminated.

Chapter Sixty

It has been said that in love – as Clarence Fowler had cause to remember – one partner proffers the cheek and the other kisses it. In other words the less the love, the greater the control. Crazy as he was about Gina, Clarence sometimes had the vague sensation that she was using him. And then he would try to reason with himself that if she didn't want him, she could so easily walk away. Hell, they didn't even live together. They'd been going together for two years, goddamn it, and not once in all that time had she ever allowed him to stay the night. Indeed, he was beginning to suspect that she did not trust herself. He took it as a hopeful sign that she was afraid of losing her heart to him.

He had just made love to her and, as usual, she had not so much responded as co-operated. He looked at her now, smoking, a slim, amber cigarette-holder in her right hand, silken sheets drawn up to her chin, eyes closed, lost in thought. Hatching yet another successful marketing plot no doubt, he thought.

If only she would let herself go and lose herself in him. He longed to hear her moan or gasp or cry out with the sound of her soul. Instead it was his frantic heart that was lost in her draughty house.

He did not yet know this, of course, but Jean-Pierre's diagnosis of Gina as the unattainable woman had been all too accurate.

Against his will he asked her, yet again, to marry him.

She turned her nose – perfectly sculpted, but absolutely natural – towards him. 'Thank you, but no,' she said politely. 'Why spoil things?'

'Scarlett is twelve now. She was only ten when we began.' He

374

thought he sounded like a pleading woman and he hated himself for it.

'But what has that got to do with us?' she asked, puzzled.

'Two years is not two months, you know.'

Ostentatiously she focused her eyes on her Cartier bedside clock. 'Speaking of time, darling Clarence,' she said in a low, sleepy voice, 'it's gone midnight and I've got a slew of early morning meetings.'

As soon as he had left, she went to her onyx bathroom and took off her make-up. She could not help admiring the friendly, distinctive logo – navy-blue on white – of Raison d'Être. She could easily have married Clarence Fowler, for he could not have been more suitable. But until the nightmares stopped she could never marry Clarence – or anyone else.

Screaming nightmares of ragged shadows of Morgan would wake her from the soundest sleep. 'I didn't mean it,' she would hear herself shriek or sob. 'I didn't mean him to die.'

She dared not take the risk of falling asleep beside Clarence. They had gone away for the odd weekend, but even when it had been for a night in Rome or in Paris, as on two occasions it had been, she had insisted on separate bedrooms in their shared suite.

She had come to believe that she had forfeited the right to relax for ever.

It was this same fear of exposure that kept her chained to Kate. Kate had always coveted what was hers. Kate had always been jealous of her academic and sporting distinction – she had wanted to go to Radcliffe but had instead ended up at a Swiss finishing-school. Convinced that the only possible attraction that Morgan could have had for Kate was that he belonged to her best friend, Gina had spent many futile, sleepless nights dreaming of a way to get even.

Ironically enough, Kate had even succeeded in keeping her out of her own daughter's bedroom. From the moment Kate had helped her hang that heart-breaking photograph of Morgan and Scarlett in Scarlett's bedroom, she had vowed never to enter

375

it. Ah yes, she knew Kate well enough to know that the gift of the photograph had been nothing other than an act of the purest spite.

And now Kate had jumped in and insisted on giving Scarlett a concert party in her new home off Gracie Square, with that incredibly seductive view of the East River and its clumsy tugboats. Fitting a cigarette into a different holder – this one made of ivory – she lit it and inhaled deeply. Hateful thoughts of Kate churned in her mind.

The first she knew of this party for Scarlett – her own daughter, for Christ's sake – was when an invitation in the shape of a grand piano arrived in the mail. Dessert and champagne, the invitation stated. Three months ahead of time, too. *Mama mia*, but this was too much for any mother to take. She would simply have to call Kate in the morning and give her a piece of her mind – or, to be more precise – a tongue-lashing. She killed the cigarette and hastily lit another.

The party was to show off Scarlett's pianistic talents and introduce her to the circuit. If she was to go to the Juilliard, it certainly wouldn't hurt to have musical patrons at this early stage.

What had made Kate think that she was not planning on throwing a party for her own daughter herself? A storm of black rage blew over her, and she felt as if she were being swept away by a torrent of falling stones. The first time she had been blown away by such a gale of rage had been on the day she had read the magazine that Kate had sent her from Switzerland with the account of Rufus's marriage to Fabrice.

Don't get mad, get even. Jack Kennedy's words, written, it now seemed, just for her. How far away – and how dead – was that young idealistic girl who had campaigned for Jack Kennedy? Raging against Kate was as useless as it was wasteful. Would Kate stop at nothing? Not content to have had an affair with her best friend's husband, Kate now wanted to take over her best friend's daughter.

Towards dawn she was resigned to the fact that she would

376

have to call Kate. She had no choice but to check on the guest list, to make sure, for example, that Mort Greenaway of Greenaway Drugs – more than a thousand stores in twenty-five states – had been included. And besides two or three other major clients, there were, of course, several notable socialite luminaries without whom any New York society party would be doomed.

Gina had trained herself to need less sleep than most. Still sleepless at 5.30, she found it easy enough to go into her small but well-equipped gymnasium. There, seating herself astride the stationary indoor bicycle, she began her exercise routine. She felt wide awake and very alive, and the physical activity took over and dismissed Kate from her mind.

At another neighbourhood in the city, in a loft in a spacious industrial building on Canal Street, Kate stared into space, listening to Wilhelm Kempff playing a Mozart concerto.

Jean-Pierre and Matthew were away on their first shooting weekend together, so she had seized the opportunity to spend the night in the loft in which she and Morgan had spent their too few sanctified hours together.

Beside her on the bed lay one of the three cashmere sweaters Morgan had kept there. It still had his scent, and she buried her nose in it, breathing deeply. It calmed her, and as she felt the knotted cords of her taut nerves begin to unravel, she wondered what Gina would have made of her invitation to attend Scarlett's party.

Though she was in every sense a mother to Matthew, her wombless maternal instinct reached out and embraced the fatherless Scarlett. She knew that by now Gina would have received her invitation to Scarlett's party.

Visualizing Gina's fury, she almost smiled. Perhaps now, at last, Gina would be angry enough to have it out with her. Because finally Kate was convinced that only a terrible secret could have forced Gina to hold her tongue and keep the peace.

Even so, she had not been able to resist flaunting the mutual, unspoken secret that neither could confide to the other and which bound them together in a knot of blood tightened by time.

It was 10.30 in the morning in London, and Rufus had been without sleep for forty-eight consecutive hours.

Lorraine, the girl whom the New York escort agency had arranged to spend the night with him, was in the shower. Researching for her doctoral dissertation on an obscure English poet, Lorraine was spending her spring vacation in London. As always, he had asked for a brunette – if possible from one of the Ivy League colleges, preferably Radcliffe. But although Lorraine fitted that description, the night had been as rough as it was unsuccessful.

As soon as she emerged from the bathroom, wearing a crisp, businesslike linen suit, he stood up. Wordlessly, he handed her the briefcase that went with her carefully contrived executive image. He had agreed to accompany her as she left. That way she would appear to be like an ordinary working woman instead of a lady of the night.

A heavy schedule of meetings awaited him, and already his head throbbed. Glancing at the empty bottle of Dom Pérignon on the coffee-table, he wondered why his head ached. Then he remembered that, when Lorraine had told him she was allergic to champagne, he had drunk the whole bottle himself.

She took the briefcase and sat down, which surprised him. Usually girls like Lorraine would escape at once.

'Can you give me five minutes?' she asked in her elegant and educated voice.

'I'm running late as it is,' he said politely. 'I guess I can be five minutes later.'

'You're a good guy, Rufus,' she began hesitantly. 'I like you.'

'Thank you.'

'I like you enough to be frank with you.'

'Meaning?'

For a moment she made no reply, but looked him boldly in

the eye. She really was a classy girl, he thought. Nothing at all like a high-class call girl, either.

'Why don't you see a therapist about your drinking?' she asked in a low, brave tone. 'Why don't you stop trying to self-destruct?'

Chapter Sixty-One

Once Monsieur Marceau had said that Scarlett was ready for a concert party, it was Cecilia who had gone to Kate and asked if she would give it. Kate had most willingly obliged.

The piano had been moved to her large dining-room and most of the furniture had been cleared. Chairs had been found and placed in rows.

When the guests began to arrive Scarlett was a little nervous, but she soon calmed down. And when they were all sitting down, and an expectant hush had fallen on the room, all she could think about was the music. She walked swiftly to the piano-stool, sat down, and Mozart took over. First she played the Sonata in B flat – she didn't hear the applause which followed – and then the Sonata in D. When she came to it was all over, and she was standing by the piano in a daze, as the clapping washed over her.

If the party after the concert was more for Kate than it was for Scarlett, it was spectacular none the less.

To begin with, the glittering array of celebrities and other luminaries felt as if they had stumbled into a country house in the middle of New York instead of a large apartment on two floors.

Monsieur Pachoud, the celebrated French *chef de pâtisserie*, was responsible for the truly amazing array of desserts, all of which had been uniquely designed on a musical motif. Delicate meringues shaped as musical notes danced on mountains of crème Chantilly. The theme of the party was Mozart, which was why the waiters were dressed as eighteenth-century Austrian courtiers. Strains of Mozart string quartets filtered through the sound-systems.

Furious that the party had been given by Kate and not by herself, exactly ninety long minutes after the party had begun, Gina insisted that Scarlett be taken home.

'But, Gina,' her mother said, mistakenly hoping that she was teasing, 'of course you're not asking me to take *tesoro mio* home?'

'Right first time,' Gina snapped at her mother. 'I'm not asking you, I'm telling you.'

'Remember, Gina, that you speak to your mother.'

'And who, might I ask, is the mother of *tesoro mio*?' Gina mocked. 'She's *my* child, and if you won't take her home, *I* will. She's had quite enough excitement for one day.'

'This is not the moment to make a scene, Gina,' her mother said sadly. 'I'll take Scarlett home.'

'Did I hear you right, kiddo?' asked Miriam. 'Surely you can't be taking Scarlett home?' She sounded incredulous.

'Her mother wants her to go home to bed.' Cecilia winced. 'It is late, I guess.'

Understanding at once, Miriam said, 'In that case, I'll go home with you.' She shot a withering glance at Gina and turned on her heel.

All of which only served to swell Gina's rage to the point of bursting. Fighting for control, detaching herself from the guests, she went on a solitary inspection tour of Kate's newly decorated apartment. It was months since she had been in Kate's home, she realized. She mounted the gracefully curved staircase and went up to the private sitting-room where she and Kate used to spend time together.

Suddenly, she understood that she had missed her time with Kate. If it was no longer a friendship, it was still a lifelong association of close on twenty years. Why, they had known one another since they were fourteen years old.

A sudden sense of unexpected loss came over her.

But when she saw how Kate's sitting-room had been changed, she felt even angrier. Gone were the warm, cosy chintzes. The room was now as white as a shroud. In magazine parlance it was white on white, or a symphony in white. A glitteringly white marble floor, as cold and as sterile as a surgeon's scalpel. White linen couches, stiff as hospital sheets. And on the walls, impressionistic art – gashes of colour, wounds of every primary hue.

Photographs in standard silver frames provided the only other source of colour. Matthew was everywhere, his resemblance to his father strikingly obvious. Once again, and for about the thousandth time, she heard Morgan telling her on that fatal night, '*Jean-Pierre is his natural father. If ever he finds out about our affair, she'd lose custody of Matthew to him.*' Clasping her hands over her ears, she turned her attention to the other photographs.

A series of about six photographs seemed to chart the friendship of the two couples, right up until the time of Morgan's death. After that, there was nothing. Quivering with rage, she lifted up the enlargement that had captured her staring into space, plainly bored, while Morgan looked into the camera, his full, sensuous lips curved into a smile of confidence. She put it down carefully and turned to leave the room.

It was then that she caught sight of the exquisitely delicate apple-green, mottled lavender and white jadeite carving. She had first seen it at Kate's country home, and even though she had known nothing of its antiquity she had found it awesomely beautiful. It was, she knew, Kate's proudest possession – apart from the photographs of Morgan, of course. She left the room to go in search of Kate.

She felt herself encased in a capsule of hate.

'Kate,' she called out brightly when she saw her, 'this apartment is a triumph.'

'Thank you,' Kate said, pleased.

'Actually, I wanted to ask you to tell me about some of the paintings in your sitting-room.'

'Of course,' Kate replied. After excusing herself from her guests she said, 'I haven't been able to make up my mind whether that room really works.'

Oh, it does, thought Gina. The room works too well, as a matter of fact.

When they reached the sitting-room, Gina pointed at once to

the delicate jadeite carving. 'How old is that, do you think?' she asked. 'The grapes look fresh enough to eat.'

'A thousand years – even, perhaps, thirteen hundred years,' said Kate, reverently.

Moving closer, Gina began to stroke the carving lovingly, as if the very leaves were alive.

'Jean-Pierre and I call this arbour "the romance of many moons".'

'It must be very valuable,' Gina commented drily.

'Yes.'

'I suppose it is insured?'

'Of course. Why do you ask?'

'Against theft?' asked Gina, raising her supple brows.

'Naturally.'

Now Gina gently lifted the carving from its Plexiglass stand. 'It's not insured against breakage, I take it?' Arms outstretched, she raised it slowly until it was at right angles to her head. She focused on Kate with her fullest intensity and their eyes met. Without as much as a blink, her eyes still locked on to Kate's, she merely relaxed her grip on the carving. Throughout the long, slow-motion seconds it took for the ancient, priceless sculpture to crash and crack against the marble, her unwavering eyes bored ever deeper into Kate.

Though not a word passed between them, they had said everything.

PART SEVEN

PART SEVEN

Chapter Sixty-Two

The boardroom tea-party, as Gina's famous board meetings came to be known, was really the brainchild of Clarence Fowler. Needless to say, the boardroom tea-party was not to be confused with her Saturday afternoon tea-parties at her Park Avenue penthouse, where the atmosphere was at least meant to be friendly. Despite the elegance of its specially woven earth-toned carpet, the burnished mahogany of its wide and gracious Georgian dining-table and the brilliance of Kline and de Kooning on the walls, the boardroom was, if not a killing-field, then a war zone.

For those executives who were not winning, the clink of the delicate Royal Albert teacups sounded horribly like an active machine-gun.

Not surprisingly, victory was the primary objective. Victory as defined by a greater and greater market share. 'We must win,' proclaimed Gina, 'merely to stay in place.'

And, by the spring of 1980, Gina Gibson was winning. Raison d'Être had cornered the hair-mousse market.

Apart from the boardroom tea-party, Clarence Fowler had dreamed up the idea of a music competition. 'You could call it the "Raison d'Être Prize",' he had suggested one night. 'Or the "Raison d'Être Competition for the Piano".'

They had been on a quick Paris weekend together. Gina was there to have meetings with the publicly owned French company, Archot, who hoped to acquire Gibson–Keene. Clarence was in Paris to advise on the way in which the art treasures of an eccentric collector should be disposed of. Hoping to keep her in bed with him for a little bit longer, he went on: 'Imagine the kind of publicity it would attract.'

'Not the piano,' Gina murmured thoughtfully. 'That would exclude Scarlett. She couldn't possibly enter her mother's competition.'

'Just think of the publicity,' Clarence repeated shrewdly. 'Think of the mileage you'd get out of it.'

Her nose seemed to quiver with excitement. 'The "Raison d'Être Competition for Violin",' she pronounced. 'How does that grab you?'

'It will do,' he said, grinning victoriously. He opened his arms and she went into them at once. 'Marketing turns you on, doesn't it?' he asked rhetorically, his voice thick with desire.

'Marketing is the key to power.'

'You're quite blatant about it, aren't you?'

'About power?'

'Yes,' he sighed. 'I mean power.'

She giggled. 'That's because power is the ultimate aphrodisiac.' In a voluptuous whisper she went on, 'Aphrodisiac was called after Aphrodite, the goddess of love, who was created out of sea-foam.'

Letting himself move off into oblivion, he kissed her hungrily.

But certain events were to banish the whole idea from Gina's mind.

When she returned to New York she found the usual accumulation of matters needing her personal attention awaiting her. Although she no longer wrote her own copy herself, she checked every single word of every advertisement. She had been known to call Ed Fielding, her marketing director, at all hours of the night, sometimes to register a new name she had dreamed up, and sometimes to criticize the existing copy. For example, one of her coups had been to change Night Time Purifiant to Overnight Purifier.

It was now 10 p.m. in New York and 3 a.m. in Paris, but Gina was still at her desk. Although jet lag had never been a problem for her, she had hit upon what she thought was a brilliant idea for a new product during the three and a half hours it took to fly on the Concorde from Paris to New York. She had already made the arrangements to have Fligh-High, the new name, registered. She made a few projections, did a bit of number-crunching, and took one of those quick, sure-fire decisions for which she had become justly famous. Fligh-High was to turn out to be one of her own ideas that she would have no difficulty in discarding.

She looked at her simple, new Cartier watch – a gift from Clarence, bought on impulse only that morning in Paris. Only now, with the time-change, it was yesterday morning. Idly wondering how many wrist-watches she now owned, she decided she would spend no more than thirty minutes at her desk and then go home. One last chore: to go through the pile of press clippings that had been collected for her during her absence.

'Nothing vitally interesting,' she said out loud.

And then she came to the obituary in the *New York Times*.

Fran Cartwright – died on March 20th, 1980 . . .Her eye fled to the end of the notice. *Survived by her son, Rufus* . . .

For a second or two her thoughts flashed to her personal assistant, Monica Martins, and she made a quick mental note to congratulate her on her efficiency in assembling information on the competition.

Rereading the obituary notice, she saw that Fran Cartwright had died at the age of sixty. Fran had been nothing but kind to her; it was Lucia Cartwright who had been such a witch. She experienced a moment of great bitterness. Lucia Cartwright was, of course, alive and well. Thriving beside her cauldron, no doubt.

With a shock she realized that when she and Rufus had been going together, Fran Cartwright had only been about four or five years older than she was now. And it occurred to her again that Fran Cartwright had probably not been told about that terrible experience with Lucia's Lalique brooch . . .

When she finally left the office, she took the obituary notice with her.

*

Seated behind his glass desk, Rufus read the mail that his PA, Jane Singleton, had marked 'Personal'. Sadly he picked them up and began reading. More condolence letters. His mother had been much loved, and he was only just beginning to get some idea of how many people she had helped. *Your mother gave of her purse and she gave of her time*, he read. Impatiently he thrust the letter aside. Was *he* now expected to give of his purse?

Then he came on a short letter which compelled several readings. After the third or fourth reading, he picked up the ancient brass scale beside his telephones and smashed it against his heavy glass desk. He listened to the sound of the glass crackle as it shattered into still more pieces. He bent down to retrieve the fallen letter, and cut his finger on the sharp edge of a jagged shard. He wrapped his handkerchief around the finger and reread the letter yet again.

Dear Rufus [he read],
   I was very much saddened to read of the recent death of your mother.
   Although I did not know her for very long, and it is many years since last I saw her, I count it as a privilege to have known her at all.
   I shall always remember her as a woman of outstanding compassion.
              Yours,
                 Gina

From the desk of Gina Gibson, President, Gibson–Keene.

Of course, he recognized her handwriting.

And of course he knew at once who it was who had been behind that deadly media coverage.

Gina Gibson . . . Mr Kendall, his very own private eye, had shown him a photograph of Gina Gibson. An elegant, synthetic blonde with a certain calm, intelligent beauty, he remembered now. But not a trace of Gina's long, lustrous raven hair and absolutely no sign of that warm, feather-soft girl with the rippling laugh. No wonder that photograph had reminded him of a movie star when he was a kid. Christ, he and Gina had been kids together. But the flawless, glacial beauty of the woman with the cigarette-holder was light years away from Gina O'Connor.

He reached out to buzz for his stalwart PA, Jane Singleton, but all his electronic equipment lay tangled in the glass. Behind his colossal, heavy oak doors his office was sound-proof. Wrapping his handkerchief still tighter round his index finger, he strode out into Jane's office.

'My goodness, Mr Rufus,' she said, 'what have you done to your finger?'

'The desk just shattered into tiny pieces.'

'Quick! Let me look at it,' she answered, busying herself with Band-aid and Cartwright disinfectant. When she had done, she said, 'At least you don't need stitches.'

'Have the Porsche come and get me,' he said curtly. 'I'm going to Cartwright House.'

'Are you driving yourself, Mr Rufus, or do I get Collins?'

'I'll be driving myself, and I haven't touched a drop.'

'Of course, I know that, Mr Rufus,' she said. 'You'll live.' She smiled. 'You don't need stitches,' she said again.

Driving a fast car hard, Rufus decided, was the best way to burn his unwelcome nerves. If the cops stopped him they could breathalyse him as much as they liked, and he would be absolutely innocent. Well, there had to be something good about being on the wagon . . .

A pity about the desk, he thought. A prize-winning artefact, too. Burnished wood, he thought. He would replace it with a wood that reflects like a mirror.

His grandmother would be expecting him. Jane Singleton would have warned her of his impending visit. She would have been told that he was stone cold sober. She would be waiting for him in the library, the very room in which Gina had pressed her face close to his and told him, 'I feel sorry for you, Rufus. I feel

391

sorry you have a grandmother to stoop so low as to plant a valuable brooch in my case.' Then she had jabbed her index finger into his lapel and continued, 'And I feel sorry for you, Rufus, because you are too weak to talk to me yourself. Like all cowards, you let someone else do your dirty work for you!'

Her words had been branded into his heart. Often, for no reason that he could uncover, those very words would return to him, and he would hear not only the words, but the brave bewildered tone of her incurable wound would ring in his ears.

His grandmother was waiting for him in the library.

'Why, Rufus, what a splendid surprise,' she said, rising to greet him. 'You'll have coffee, won't you, dear?' she asked.

Rufus made no reply but went up to the mantelpiece to look at the portrait of his grandfather, Theodore. The uncompromising angle of his jaw and the fearless intelligence of his eyes had been captured by Albert Byrne, the portraitist whose work now hung in the Museum of Modern Art.

'Aren't you going to kiss your grandmother, dear?' Lucia demanded.

Reminded of his manners, Rufus approached her and kissed her on both cheeks. 'We're in the very room in which Gina O'Connor was at once unjustly accused and condemned for having stolen the brooch you had planted in her vanity case.'

'You received a condolence letter as well, I see,' Lucia replied, unfazed. 'And, as I recall it, the name was not O'Connor but Rizzoli.'

'As *I* recall, Grandmother, you told me that she had married a bricklayer called Dick Walters and gone to live in Dayton, Ohio.'

'Dick Walters? You can't seriously expect me to remember the man's name after all these years. How long ago was it, anyway?'

'Sixteen years. What's the difference?' he replied bitterly. '*Why did you lie to me?*'

392

'I only repeated what I had heard, and I had heard that she got married.'

'You lied then, and you are lying now.' He made no attempt to conceal his disgust. 'How could you possibly have known who the letter was from if it was signed Gina Gibson and not Gina Walters?'

'Have you no respect for your elders, Rufus?'

'The long and the short answer to that is an unequivocal *no*!'

'I'm almost glad your poor mother didn't live to see this,' she said piteously. 'Have you no mercy?'

'Have *you*?' He flung his arms in the air. 'Where was your mercy when you threw her out of this house and out of my life as if she were a common criminal?'

'Rufus! Please!' she said, clutching at her heart.

'You haven't got a heart!' Rufus exploded, beside himself. 'You thought you'd got the better of her, didn't you? All these years you believed you'd got rid of her as if she were as meaningless and as disposable as an empty milk carton. Well, I've got news for you! Gina got the better of *you*, of *us*, of *Cartwright Pharmaceuticals*.' The level of his voice stopped just short of a shriek.

'What are you talking about?'

'It's because of her we had to recall our hair colourant. It's thanks to her that we lost our image of integrity!' He thumped the table, making the coffee-cups tremble. 'And what's the bottom line, Grandmother?'

She shook her head.

'The bottom line is we've given up on all our hair-care products.'

'But that means millions of dollars.'

'You're damn right, Grandmother,' he said mockingly. 'Many more millions than you could even begin to imagine.'

'Why do you think she wrote to both of us?' Lucia asked timidly. 'Is she trying to tell us something?'

'What do you think?'

Lucia had hoped he would ask her that. He needed to be

warned. 'She wants you to know that she will not rest until she destroys you.' Her old but still bright eyes had lost nothing of their shrewd shine. 'But she's making a grave error of judgement. Giving you advance warning of her intentions is a big, big mistake.'

He listened carefully, nodding his head.

'Your grandfather always said that if he had listened to me he would have avoided all his worst mistakes.'

Rufus knew that. The whole family knew it, too. It was as much a part of his grandmother as the noble ancestry of which she was so proud.

'I'll destroy *her*,' Rufus said. 'If I do nothing else with my life, I'll do that. I *will* destroy her!'

'Be careful,' warned his grandmother. 'Revenge. What is it? A pinch of madness, a dash of malice, a handful of hatred and a smattering of stupidity,' Lucia said, frowning. 'I don't know what the recipe is. I only know that the quest for vengeance destroys judgement.'

In spite of himself, and out of habit, he sought his grandmother's wisdom. 'Does vengeance lead to forgiveness?' he asked.

'Alas, no,' she answered at once. 'There is nothing quite like the emptiness that follows revenge.' She stopped. A sound very much like a cough colliding with a moan escaped. 'I now know why she wrote to us,' she said slowly. 'It was in itself a stroke of revenge and an act of spite.'

At long last Rufus's life was charged with meaning. He had found a cause to which he could devote his very soul. All those years ago, when he and Gina had been together, they had both vowed to follow President Kennedy's dictum: 'Don't get mad, get even.'

And he was going to get even with Gina.

Chapter Sixty-Three

And so it was that, early in April 1980, unbeknown to her, Gina's life was put under the microscope. Rufus began by sending for George Kendall, the specialist in corporate intelligence he had hired previously. He would have to eat humble pie – George Kendall had earlier suggested that Gina Gibson might be the power behind the endlessly harmful media attention that had finally defeated Cartwright Hair Care.

Never one to mince his words, he said abruptly, 'You were right and I was wrong.' It was years since he had come close to apologizing to anyone.

'We don't hear that too often from a client, sir,' replied Mr Kendall with a weak laugh. Looking around Rufus's large and sumptuous office, he said: 'Something is different.' He stroked his moustache slowly, as if he were adjusting an antenna. He nodded. 'It's your desk.'

'My desk?'

'Your glass desk, sir. It's gone.'

'I broke it.'

'You *broke* it?'

'I broke it the day I discovered that you were right and I was wrong.'

'I don't get it.'

'The gallery of photographs you brought here. You called them mug shots, and you spread them all over the desk.' Rufus sighed deeply. 'The sexy blonde bombshell with the cigarette-holder you picked out. Gina Gibson. Remember her?'

'Sure,' said Kendall.

'Well,' Rufus said grimly, 'I want you to put Mrs Gina Gibson under a microscope.' He selected a cigar and took some

395

time over lighting it. 'I want you to tell me who her friends are, where she goes, when she takes a shower or a shit. I want to know what she eats for breakfast.'

'No problem.'

'She was smart enough to make us pull back on our hair products.' Rufus sucked in his lips. 'A promising growth product-range, and we had to withdraw.'

'Mrs Gibson won the battle?'

'We couldn't even fight. When my wife went into shock and died because of one of our own products, and she found out about it, she tied our arms behind our backs.' He smiled a crooked smile. 'We went together when we were kids. Hell, man, she was not even eighteen. She was a lovely, soft brunette then, he said, his voice softening in nostalgia. 'She was beautiful – a *natural* beauty. She had a great body, too. She modelled swim-suits.' He tapped his pen against his teeth. 'And after all those years, she's still out to destroy me? I don't understand it.'

'Would I be wrong in assuming you jilted her?'

'It was the worst mistake of my entire life.'

'She didn't need any hair-dye when you and she were going together, I guess.'

'She certainly did not,' agreed Rufus. 'She was the best-looking girl I've ever seen.'

'How come you broke up?'

'Let's just say I had family pressure.'

'Did she know that?'

'My grandparents gave her the walking orders.'

'That is not something a young girl would forgive or forget, if you don't mind my saying so, sir,' said Mr Kendall, stroking his moustache again. 'Are you sure you want to go ahead with the – ah – investigation?'

'I sent for you, didn't I?'

'You want to know everything from day one?'

'That's right. From the day she first drew breath. Everything.'

'If you knew her all that long ago, you'd know who her childhood friends were.' He stopped to stroke his moustache. 'Men make buddies. Girls make best friends.'

'Same difference.'

'Not exactly,' Mr Kendall said with a slight wince. 'Best friends can turn into powerful enemies.' Warming to his subject, he went on: 'Take it from one who knows, Mr Cartwright. There is no female enemy quite as resourceful, or anything like as vengeful, as one who has been betrayed by her best friend.'

Rufus stirred restlessly. 'Are you speaking from professional or private experience?' he asked.

'Both,' Mr Kendall replied with a deep sigh.

'I thought as much,' said Rufus with a half-laugh. 'But it should be up to you to get the names of all her friends. You'll just follow her around, won't you?'

'It's not exactly that simple,' Mr Kendall said, wincing again.

'Well, if you want somewhere to start,' Rufus said drily, 'when she was at school she was pretty close to Kate Hills.'

'Hills? The bank?'

'Right.'

'Which school are we talking about?'

'Talbot Hall.'

'In Connecticut?'

'You have a pretty broad database, Mr Kendall.'

'I guess that's why you hired a specialist in corporate intelligence, Mr Cartwright.'

In due course Gina received two formal handwritten notes thanking her for her message of sympathy. The notes from Lucia and Rufus arrived on the same day. Shrugging her shoulders, she put them in the waste-paper bin. She thought that was the end of the matter.

George Kendall saw this assignment as a pleasant change from the usual financial and personal investigations that went with buy-outs, mergers or hostile take-overs. Since his brief was to take his time and do a thorough job, he decided to do just that. He would do the work himself – it would be more in the nature of entertainment than a job.

Mr Kendall had come to the conclusion that in his line of

work the starting-point that looked too obvious to be the possible was the intelligent and indeed the only logical place to begin.

Accordingly, his first line of attack was Kate Hills.

He bypassed Talbot Hall and went directly to one of Kate's trustees. She would not have to resort to bureaucrats to find out whom Miss Kate Hills had married. If she had never married, the secretary would tell him so soon enough. The simple explanation that he was throwing a surprise party for his daughter's thirty-fifth birthday, and second marriage, and was looking for the addresses of a few of her fellow students of the class of 'sixty-two at Talbot was enough to get him immediately connected to Mr Hills's personal assistant, Penny Marcher.

'I couldn't dream of having a party for my Marylou without Kate Hills,' lied Mr Kendall effectively, pretending to sound like an anxious doting father.

'She's Kate Gachet now,' said the secretary, sounding amused. 'Has been for about sixteen years—'

'Oh, I know that of course,' protested Mr Kendall. 'But she'll always be Kate Hills to me. It's her address I need—'

And so Kate Hills-Gachet came under surveillance. Within three weeks, Mr Kendall had jimmied her lock and let himself into her private loft one evening. By then he had established that she never visited the place at night or on weekends. The place had an eerie atmosphere, like a doctor's empty waiting-room. At the same time he knew at once that it was not an office. A huge blown-up photograph of a remarkably ordinary, balding man with kind, intelligent eyes took up one entire wall. Opening one of the two clothes closets he found that it, too, had the same feeling of emptiness – a few shirts, two sweaters, one tie and two pairs of socks. The second one belonged to Kate and, other than some sexy lacy lingerie and one sweater, there was nothing.

He wondered whether she changed into one of those black lace bits when she visited . . .

On the counter of the open-plan kitchen he found a note from the cleaning lady. 'Dear Mrs Hills,' he read; 'Call plumber for toilet.' It was dated yesterday's date, he noted. Inside the fridge he found a few cans of carrot juice and some cottage cheese. A health nut, he thought wth some disgust. Seconds later his eye fell on the two bottles of champagne lying at the back of the fridge. Dom Pérignon, no less . . . He began to feel some sympathy for Kate. To the left of the fridge was a drawer of Tiffany cutlery – two of everything. The same thing went for the china: two cups, two mugs, two soup-bowls and two plates.

The bed was covered with an antique quilt. He lay down on top of it and stared again at the huge poster on the opposite wall. There was a serenity about the man, he decided, an air of quiet authority and an aura of civilized compassion. It was weird. He was in a kind of bizarre shrine, he realized. Amused, he half expected to find some incense. Instead, his eye hit on the Ventolin spray at the side of the bed. He knew what that was and why it was there. He had done his homework. Opening the drawer of the lacquered Chinese bedside table he found yet another spray, this one still in its box. Both sprays were useless; the expiry date read October 1977, and it was now November 1980.

Still lying on the bed, he picked up an average-sized photograph in a silver frame. It was taken in this very apartment – he recognized the ink-blue wall and the bed-cover. Kate and the man in the photograph laughed into the camera, one of those you could set to take a photograph of yourself. Their heads thrown back, the laugh had been frozen in time. It must have been a great shout of a laugh, he thought. He studied it for so long that he believed he could almost hear the laugh.

It may have been because this experience was so far removed from his usual line of corporate investigation that he found himself reacting emotionally to that photograph. In some ways he felt as if he had stumbled on two people making love, and in other ways he felt as if he had stepped into a graveyard.

Pushing superstition to the furthermost reaches of his brain, he pulled himself together and returned to the world of reality. That *frisson* of superstition had activated his memory.

399

He had really lucked out this time, and it gave him a good feeling. Because he had already seen a photograph of that poster of Morgan Gibson in Scarlett's bedroom.

His contact at Melanie Wilson, Gina's public-relations consultants, had served him well. Everything that had ever been written about Gina Gibson – all the considerable publicity that she had received – had been conveniently and efficiently collected into several fact-files. If you could believe what you read in the papers then he already knew Gina Gibson. Only he did not exactly trust the press.

But right now his jaundiced view of the press turned to gratitude. For it was in the *Architectural Review, House and Garden* and *Town and Country* that Gina's penthouse apartment had been featured. *Home Vistas*, however, had devoted several very glossy pages to what they had billed as the 'apartment of a prodigy'. When he had read it, he had resented it, for it seemed to him that *Home Vistas* had gone out of their way to represent Cecilia O'Connor's apartment as if it belonged to her twelve-year-old granddaughter, Scarlett, and not to her.

Hastily opening his briefcase, he pulled out the relevant glossy clipping and quickly read it again:

Except for the larger-than-life poster of Scarlett and her father, who died six years ago, the bedroom is otherwise so authentically Victorian that it might very well have belonged to a Victorian teenager in Bloomsbury, England. A budding pianist, and therefore no ordinary fourteen-year-old, daughter to Gina Gibson (that self-styled genius in skin care), Scarlett felt she needed and deserved her own space. And – *voilà* – she and her grandmother live together in her own Fifth-Avenue apartment on the very floor below her mother's legendary penthouse (see *Home Vistas*, July 1978).

'Along with my Steinway piano, the poster of my father and me is my most treasured possession.' Scarlett told this interviewer. 'It is the only picture of him that we have.'

'Why is that?' I asked this rather ingenuous prodigy, who already shows signs of developing the shape – if not the persona – of a prima donna.

'My mother's friend gave it to me as a present. I guess photographs of my dad make my ma too sad.'

Mr Kendall was in no doubt about who that friend was.

It might not be a bad idea for him to meet Kate Hills-Gachet. And where better than in this very loft?

Drawn to the collection of classical music cassettes, he went over to the bookcases and took down Mahler's Titan Symphony. Suddenly he was impelled to play it. Soon the startling harmonic and orchestral effects soared. It was almost midnight. He had been in the loft for far longer than he had intended. But he would not leave until the magic of Mahler had ended.

He was thirsty.

He declined to take her carrot juice, but permitted himself a glass of water. He drank the water and went back to lie on the antique quilt. He closed his eyes, passed his hands over the squares that had been so lovingly stitched together, and settled back to listen to Mahler. Suddenly his hand came upon a hard object, like a book. It seemed to fill an entire square. Even as he searched for it and found the opening in the square, he was reminding himself that although he was a corporate intelligence consultant and not a private eye, he had no right to have any qualms about reading it. But the triumphal music of Mahler and the general vibes of the place interfered with his professionalism.

He stroked his moustache nervously.

He had already invaded Kate's sanctuary and if he violated her further by reading the book – probably a diary – whose pages he now turned, he felt he would be inviting a terrible curse to descend on him. Reading greedily, like a man starving, he was forced to conclude that his fascination exceeded his professionalism.

Yes, it was a diary and, incredibly, the very first line that Kate had written was:

A curse will be visited upon me, for I was never the owner, but only the custodian, of a jade carving of the fruit of the vine.

He quickly shut the diary and told himself not to continue. After all, was this discussion of a curse not a warning? He reproached himself for being primitive, and continued:

It fell to me to be the guardian of an exquisitely rare and ancient carving of the Qing dynasty, hundreds of years old, the alluring vanished world of creativity, mystery and beauty.

Delicately wrought, the carving had survived time. But Gina raised it above her head and, staring me full in the eye, flung it to the marble floor as if she hoped that by destroying it she would destroy me, too.

A flash of rage, and a million dollars was cut in two, just like that . . . The only object of my childhood that held any meaning for me, and the only possession I inherited from my mother. In breaking the jadeite statuette, Gina broke the symbolic link between earth and Heaven, the bridge from life to immortality. Therefore I am no longer the custodian of a piece of pure perfection. Rather, I am at once the prisoner and the custodian of a fatal secret. Gina's secret.

There, the diary entry ended.

Chapter Sixty-Four

The new high-protein diet that everyone swore by had not worked for Scarlett. On the contrary, she had *gained* four pounds.

Beside herself with rage and frustration, Gina turned her fury on her mother. 'I suppose you thought you'd make her a little tagliatelle. A small helping, you know, like a huge soup-plate.'

'Gina,' her mother said helplessly.

'Grandmama did nothing of the kind!' Scarlett interrupted angrily. 'I was hungry, so I had a few cookies.'

'Another binge,' Gina replied bitterly. 'No wonder you're getting the reputation for looking like a prima donna!'

'One shitty article in a shittier magazine, two years ago, and you go on and on and on about it.'

'I've told you to watch your language with me.'

'With you?' Scarlett rounded mockingly on her mother. 'I'm hardly ever with you, so I guess I'm out of practice speaking to you—'

'We were talking about your diet,' said Gina wearily. 'You binged on chocolates, too! Your newest crop of pimples tells everyone when you've stuffed yourself with chocolates.' Clicking her tongue angrily, she threw her hands in the air. 'I'm in the skin-care business, and my daughter gives herself acne!' She brought her hands down and slapped her thighs. 'Can you beat it?'

'I hate you, Mother,' Scarlett said coldly. 'I've been thinking about you long and hard, and I despise you.'

'*Scarlett!*' Cecilia exploded, aghast.

'Leave me alone,' Scarlett yelled, walking from the room as quickly as her large bulk permitted.

'Let her be,' Cecilia pleaded. 'Let her be.'

But Gina ignored her. She had, she believed, tried everything in the book to help Scarlett control her weight. Doctors, from psychiatrists to psychologists to endocrinologists, had been consulted. The psychiatrist held that she had an eating disorder that was closely akin to anorexia. The psychologist was convinced that the strain of her musical career put an intolerable burden on her life that isolated her from her peers. The endocrinologist diagnosed hormonal changes caused by the onset of menstruation.

Seating herself on the yellow checked chair, Gina announced, 'Dr Sontag has agreed to take you on.'

Scarlett made no response.

'Dr Sontag has an eighty per cent success rate,' she persisted. Her cigarette was coming to an end and she looked around for something approaching an ashtray. Her eyes lit on a little porcelain box and she opened the lid and put the cigarette out in it.

'Your cigarette stinks,' Scarlett said coldly. 'Smoking is a disgusting habit.'

'Have you ever tried it?'

'No,' Scarlett replied. 'I don't want to.'

'It would help keep your weight down,' Gina said evenly. 'It might not be such a bad idea, you know.'

'I knew you'd say that!' Scarlett exploded. 'Everyone knows it's dangerous and gives cancer, and you, my own mother, you *want* me to smoke! I can't believe that even you would say that!'

'Only because you're obese!' Gina yelled. 'If you would only try to stop doing this to yourself—'

'You couldn't care less about me or what I'm doing to myself,' Scarlett said with all the defiance of any average fifteen-year-old daughter. 'You're more worried about what other people think of *you* than of me.' Her voice trembled and she stopped for a moment. Regaining control, she stared at the wall opposite her bed, the wall on which the outsize photograph of her father hung, the wall which Gina had studiously avoided. 'If only Dad were alive,' she said brokenly, 'everything would have been different.'

404

A huge sigh of irritation shook Gina's entire body.

'You never talk about him,' Scarlett wailed.

'Why should I talk about him?' Gina replied, her voice ragged. 'He's gone. He's dead. He can't help me and he certainly can't help you.'

'Sometimes I think you're pleased he's dead,' Scarlett whispered.

'Get off that bed,' Gina commanded. 'Get off that bed at once and repeat what you just said to me.'

Because it was years since Scarlett had heard her mother speak in that authoritative tone which compelled obedience, she did as she was told. 'I think you're pleased he's dead,' she said again.

Altogether out of control now, Gina lashed out at her daughter, striking her full in the face. Observing her mother with wide, staring eyes, Scarlett was too stunned to react.

As she wheeled round to leave, Gina hissed, 'For what you've just thrown in my face, I should have broken every bone in your hands. Then you'd never play the piano again.'

If she had been trying to get a wildly hysterical response from her daughter she had certainly succeeded. The high, wrenching, sobbing screams that tore from Scarlett's throat brought Cecilia rushing into the room. As if frozen in the horror of her own words, Gina stood motionless.

Cecilia took in the entire scene at a glance. 'Leave Scarlett alone,' she ordered. 'Get out of here this instant!'

Gina must have realized she had gone too far, for she stalked out of the room at once.

Later, when Scarlett was calm enough to speak, she told her grandmother: 'She said she should have broken every bone in my hands so that I'd never play the piano again—'

'She didn't mean it, *tesoro mio*,' Cecilia said over and over again.

But even as she spoke, an old saying came roaring into her mind. '*It is not unknown for a mother cat to devour her young.*'

*

405

After a close friendship that had endured and, like a good wine, matured over thirty-five years, it was hardly surprising that Cecilia and Miriam had developed their own shorthand. Not only that; each could now read the small print behind the other's words.

Which was how Cecilia knew that Miriam must have had some disturbing news. Clearly she was not yet ready to talk about it. Eventually she would, of course, but this was not the moment to pry. Meanwhile, as so often these days, they talked about Gina and Scarlett.

'I feel so torn, Mirrie,' Cecilia said, hugging her shawl about her. 'Gina is my daughter, and Scarlett is my granddaughter, and I love them both.' She paused and shook her head in disbelief. 'And though I don't want to take sides and go against my own daughter, I have to protect Scarlett from her.'

'It *is* one hell of a problem, kiddo,' Miriam said sympathetically. 'As long as Gina nags and criticizes her the way she does, she'll eat more.' She rose to empty her overflowing ashtray.

'You smoke too much,' Cecilia said automatically. 'Believe it or not, Mirrie, but Gina is actually encouraging Scarlett to smoke. She says it's a good way to control her appetite.'

'She must not do that,' replied Miriam, stricken.

"You're the pharmacist, Mirrie. Tell me, do cigarettes cut down the appetite?'

'Nicotine speeds up the metabolism. As for me, coffee and a cigarette can feel like a whole meal.' She waved her wrist in a gesture of disappointment and her bangles clicked. 'But I am surprised that Gina, who is into fitness in such a big way, would encourage anyone to smoke.'

'But she smokes herself.'

'That's exactly why she should know better!' Miriam snapped.

'You know, Mirrie, I am going to tell you something I've only just discovered.' She closed her eyes and rested her chin on her hands. 'I should have seen it before, of course, but I guess I couldn't face it.'

A comfortable silence fell. Miriam laid her head against the high wing chair and waited for her friend to continue. She had long admired Cecilia's living-room. The strong yellow theme – sunshine yellow, Cecilia called it – added a background of warmth and light. The coffee-table was upholstered in bright yellow velvet, and Miriam thought it a triumph. Photographs of Gina and Scarlett were everywhere, and there were two photographs of herself. She was disproportionately pleased, she thought, to find herself included in this collection of family photographs.

Following Miriam's gaze, Cecilia said: 'It's been a year since Scarlett has allowed us to take a single publicity shot.'

'That's very understandable. She has got broader,' said Miriam with her usual candour. 'She looks a lot like her father – she has the same eyes.'

'And Gina is beginning to look more and more like *her* father,' Cecilia said, her voice ragged. 'Of course she's always had his dimples, but just lately it seems as if she has inherited his expression, too. If she doesn't like something, she half screws up her eyes and she gets that same mean look. I used to freeze when I saw it on her father—'

At that moment the phone rang. It was Gina. When the conversation with her daughter was over, Cecilia said, 'She's got hold of a Dr Osrin, *the* diet doctor. She's going to have him start Scarlett on a new course of weight-reduction medication.'

'We know how we feel about that,' Miriam murmured.

'Mirrie, why don't you tell me what's wrong?' Cecilia heard herself asking unexpectedly.

'What makes you think there is something wrong?'

'I don't know,' replied Cecilia uncertainly. 'I guess I just feel it.'

Miriam examined her cigarette, inhaled, then took her time about putting it out. 'I've just smoked my last cigarette, kiddo,' she said in a low voice. 'I didn't want to tell you this, but I've been seeing a cardiologist. He tells me I have to have open-heart surgery – this thing they call the bypass.'

'When?'

'In five days' time. Wednesday, November 10th.'

'Good,' Cecilia said lightly. 'That's good news.'

'Why?' Miriam asked. 'I can't say I agree with you.'

'They only operate on hearts that are strong enough to take it,' Cecilia said reasonably. 'There are certain patients that doctors will not operate on because they are too much of a risk.' Hoping to encourage Miriam still further, she added, 'So you can't be much of a risk, can you?'

Miriam smiled weakly. 'Okay, kiddo, have it your way.'

But Cecilia saw that her friend had been relieved and comforted by what she had said.

Chapter Sixty-Five

On the very day that Miriam submitted to the surgeon's knife, Rufus received Mr Kendall's detailed report. It ran into hundreds of pages. Nothing of Gina's life, it seemed, was too trivial for inclusion. Everything was there – from how much time she spent in the bathroom in the early morning to what she wore when she went to sleep. There was so much information that Mr Kendall had resorted to underlining the most salient points with a marker pen.

Comprehensive lists of friends, acquaintances and business associates had been compiled.

Reading about Kate, Rufus's eyes widened with astonishment. At least fifty typed pages had been devoted to her, and he devoured them all. Christ, Kate paid the rent on a secret loft, a kind of sanctuary, an altar to her dead lover. *Twice a week Kate visits this temple of love where some of her dead lover's belongings (clothes, medications, music and books) have been preserved as if they were graven images.*

But what intrigued and excited him most of all was the name of Kate's lover. To think that he had been none other than Gina's husband! A small photograph of the large poster of Morgan had been included in the report. How the hell could she have married such a weak, effeminate wimp who was nothing to look at? Clearly, Morgan was in every respect Mr Average.

Kate had written a little memo to herself, and this too had been copied and included.

Autopsy report wrong.
As a pharmacist, Morgan knew too much about
Ventolin to have exceeded the dose. But if he could not get

hold of it in time, if it had been removed from wherever it was his practice to keep it, then, in desperation, he could have overdosed.

Question a) Who removed it and why?

Answer a) Gina; b) because she found out about Morgan and me.

But I am powerless, powerless.

He laid the report down and let his mind fly back to the first time he had heard of Kate Hills all those many years ago. A quick calculation told him that at least eighteen summers had passed since he and Gina had made love in the cool, clear air of the Adirondacks. Transported back in time, he was suddenly acutely aware of the pure young girl who had been Gina, and the confident young man he himself had been. Ironically – and as things turned out, perhaps prophetically – it was Kate's abortion that had given birth to their union. But, as Rufus had come to learn, paradoxes are the staff of life.

Although, to this very day, he and Kate had neither met nor as much as seen one another, there could be no doubt that, if only because of their close connection with Gina, they already had a sense of knowing one another very well, if not intimately. Yet another of life's many paradoxes, he reflected with satisfaction.

A further and infinitely more dangerous paradox was imminent.

He and Kate would have to be introduced. It would be one of those wonderful meetings where the flow of conversation would be as forceful as the circumstances which brought them together.

But where would they meet?

And how could it be engineered?

Then he discovered that Kate was in Switzerland, and not expected to return much before the end of January. Of course, he could very easily have flown to St Moritz and found someone over there to effect an introduction, but he believed it would be more productive for them to meet in New York.

Suddenly a new idea made him leap from his chair. He and

Kate would meet sooner or later. Meanwhile, what was stopping him from renewing his acquaintance with Gina? He picked up his private telephone and swiftly punched out Mr Kendall's number. 'You've done a great job,' he said when he was put through. 'I'm calling to thank you for a truly magnificent piece of work.'

'Thank *you*, Mr Cartwright. We—'

'I couldn't have done better myself,' Rufus quipped. 'Listen, I'd like to discuss this with you at much greater length, but right now I urgently need to have some additional information.'

'Be glad to help,' said Mr Kendall, sounding positively cheerful. 'It's been an interesting assignment.'

'I want a list of *all* Gina's future social engagements,' Rufus said. 'I particularly need to have details of her forthcoming parties. Especially those parties she'll be giving in her own home.'

Ten minutes before her first guests were expected, Gina swept through the principal rooms of her apartment, making a final inspection of the floral arrangements. She knew the flowers were perfect. The real reason for doing this was to take in the grandeur of the European salon atmosphere that she had created. Although it was a New York apartment it had the look and the feel of a large country house. Interestingly enough, Gina had only recently become consciously aware that her inspiration for the decoration of her apartment had come from the weekend she had spent at Cartwright House.

Meanwhile she waited in the hall, admiring her two sets of tall Régence doors – so elaborately carved that one could almost say embroidered – which added to the grandeur of the place. Lighted candles in her collection of large bronze candelabra imparted a warm, romantic glow to rooms whose opulence might otherwise have been coldly forbidding.

If it is true that society in the United States is based on nothing but money then Gina's parties certainly did not qualify. While her guest list could well have been an international *Who's*

411

Who of the business world, they could equally have been a *Who's Who* of the political world. Because she never failed to invite the chemists who worked at Gibson–Keene, she was considered to be more than a little eccentric. Even so, she would not have dreamed of giving a party without including Monica Martins, her personal assistant. Both her mother and Miriam Stern had been frequently included. She had a distinct talent for mixing her guests. Somehow her apartment exuded a warm welcome and the most unlikely combinations resulted in excellent conversation. Tonight she was hosting what she called a simple drinks party for fifty or so.

To this end banks of waist-high red roses filled the rooms. Since the ceilings were fourteen feet high, tall candelabra with four-foot candles provided all the light that was necessary. Electric light was outlawed.

It was the sort of drinks party that was also a light meal. Generous platters of pâté de foie gras flown in from Paris that morning, quantities of caviare, smoked salmon and delicate choux pastry filled with still more caviare as well as spinach and mushrooms tempted almost everyone to break their diet. For those social X-rays who resisted, silver trays of carrots, cucumber and celery sticks served with a low-calorie yoghurt dressing were constantly on offer. Vintage champagne as well as freshly squeezed orange juice were in endless supply.

That night her guest book would include a retired associate justice of the Supreme Court, several captains of industry and not a few media celebrities, including her very own Gina Gibson model, the alarmingly beautiful Angie Baynes with the most exquisite cheek-bones in the business.

Once all the guests had gone and Niza and Augusto, the Portuguese couple who took care of her, were safely in their beds, Gina walked slowly through her empty apartment. A long-standing habit of hers, it was the time when she most enjoyed her home, when she could truly feel the private embrace of all the splendour she had created.

412

She lit a cigarette and put it into the gold, diamond-encrusted cigarette-holder that had once belonged to a great actress, took a long, luxurious puff, picked up her half-full glass of champagne and slowly crossed to the mahogany-and-gilt-framed mirror. Staring at herself intently, she could not but reflect that the image which stared back at her was one of her creations. Gina Gibson products had now captured a major share of the market. Her companies were now a huge force to be reckoned with, and hundreds of employees and their families now depended on her. And she had built it all by herself. The *Wall Street Journal* had called her a 'powerhouse of an entrepreneur'. All well and good, but living up to her reputation was just as difficult as building it up had been.

Smiling into the mirror now, she congratulated herself on her achievements. Her smile broadened and her dimples flashed. Thinking of Scarlett, and the way her dimples had been lost in layers of fat, the smile was wiped from her face. What had she done to deserve such a daughter? As always, there was no answer to that one.

So absorbed in her own reflection was she that she was altogether unaware that anyone else had entered the room.

But she was not alone.

Her reverie was rudely interrupted. Beyond her range of vision, a male voice said: 'A lady as lovely as Gina O'Connor should never drink alone!'

Gina's glass fell to the floor. She screamed.

The voice drew closer. 'I see I've frightened you.'

Instinctively, Gina turned and ran. Almost at once her wrist was in an iron grip. 'I'm only here to renew an old friendship.'

'*You!*' Gina gasped.

'Allow me,' said Rufus, gently disengaging her fingers from her cigarette-holder.

Stupefied, Gina watched him remove her cigarette-butt, light another one, insert it in the holder and hand it to her.

'What do you want, Rufus Cartwright?'

'To get even.'

'*You* want to get even?'

413

'You exploited my wife's death and wiped out part of my business.'

'But that was years ago,' she gasped.

'I didn't know then that it was you,' he snapped. 'I only knew it was you when you sent me a condolence letter when my mother died.' He jerked her arm violently. 'You use death, don't you?'

'You're hurting my arm—'

'So the death-user hurts, does she?' he said, mockingly. 'I've read about people like you. People who walk over dead bodies.'

'Let go of my arm!'

'Like I said,' he continued pleasantly, 'I want to get even.' He released a low, ugly laugh. 'I want you and I'm going to fuck you out of sight!'

'Me?'

'Yes, you,' Rufus replied. 'But not yet.' Taking the cigarette-holder from her hand, he said: 'It's gone out.'

'How did you get in?'

'With the greatest of ease,' he answered mockingly. 'But you and I are hardly in the mood to speak of boring matters such as security.' So saying, he took her hand and led her to the white antique brocade sofa. His grip on her wrist did not lessen.

'I want you to get out of here, Rufus,' she said, her voice purposefully neutral.

'Don't be rude,' he retaliated. Gesturing towards the two portraits of her painted by the famous Rhys Grange, he said, 'You sure think you are one hell of a woman.'

'I *am* one hell of a woman, Rufus,' she retorted. 'You've seen my portraits and that should be enough for you. Now get the fuck out!'

'Naughty, naughty Gina.' He wagged his finger.

'I'm going to have to call the police.'

'Go right ahead,' he agreed politely, further tightening his hold on her wrist, 'call them.' Almost purring with pleasure, he added, 'Don't be a fool, like your friend Kate Gachet, and wait until it's too late to call the homicide squad.'

She gasped but made no reply. She turned her eyes away

414

from his. Too shocked to speak, she could do nothing about the silence, which grew steadily more oppressive. This suited him, and he wielded it like a weapon – the longer it endured, the better for him.

At last she broke the silence. 'What has Kate got to do with all this?'

'You tell me,' he shrugged. 'I don't believe I even know her.' He allowed a low laugh. 'Of course your husband, the late lamented asthmatic Morgan Gibson, knew her much better, didn't he?'

'So what?'

'So your best friend and your husband had a torrid affair, and you found out about it and decided to punish him.' Pushing his face right up against hers, now openly full of menace, he added, 'Only you didn't expect him to croak, did you?'

Unwilling or unable to draw her face away from his she moaned, 'What do I have to do to get you out of here?'

His lips almost touching hers, he said: 'You want me to leave you like this?'

She swallowed deeply and again made no reply.

He rammed his lips up against hers and kissed her deeply. Then, to the everlasting astonishment of both of them, she made no attempt to push him away, but opened her mouth to welcome him. Once again, but too late, they breathed one another's breath. Once again, but not too late, though for the second time that evening, there was a silence between them. This time, however, their silence was crowded with passion.

With a degree of urgency neither of them had ever before experienced, he helping her and she helping him, they were quickly naked. Far from slipping away, the eighteen years of their separation intensified their love-making.

'I need you,' he groaned. 'I've always needed you.'

She said nothing, but allowed her body to speak for her. Each time more thirsty than the last, they took one another three more times that night. He told her that he had always needed her, and she told him that she had never recovered from him. Other than that, however, little else was said. Their energies

415

and their minds were concentrated in their bodies. Exhausted and sated – incredibly, as each thought later – they fell asleep on the carpet.

She awoke first. The dawn came and, with it, reality. Very soon her Portuguese butler and housekeeper, Niza and Augusto, would be opening the curtains. He must leave at once, this very minute. If it was unthinkable to be found with a man in her own bedroom, what would it look like if the help came in and found her with Rufus in her living-room? Besides, there was no way she was going to turn into a clinging woman of the morning-after variety. Usually it was the men who pulled up their trousers and walked away. Well, she would ring the changes, she would be the one who walked away. That way, when he wanted her again, he would have to pursue her again . . .

'You've got to go right now,' she said firmly. 'The help will be in here in two minutes flat.'

'Hold your horses, Gina,' he said angrily. 'I'm going to take a shower.'

'No, you're not!' she said, stamping her foot furiously.

Silently she watched as, grim-lipped, he dressed quickly. When he had done, he turned to her and, all but spitting, said: 'Only a whore refuses to let a man take a shower after a fuck!'

'Rufus!' she cried out, reaching for his hand. *'Please!'*

But he thrust her hand away. 'You are in my way, Gina,' he said pleasantly.

After Rufus had left, Gina hastily picked up her underclothes and took them to her bedroom. Then, to her everlasting astonishment, she climbed into her four-poster bed because she was under a strange compulsion to lie naked between her silken sheets. The last thing she wanted was a shower or a bath. His scent was still on her skin, and she wanted to keep it there as long as possible. Stretching voluptuously, she lay back and recalled the night before. She had treated him like a gigolo and he had called her a whore, and for some inexplicable reason this

416

had not made her angry. It seemed her body – so well loved, so perfectly understood, so deeply penetrated – had gained ascendancy over her mind. Even now, hours later, her remembering nerves were rejoicing still. Trailing her fingertips over her alert skin, she felt once again feather-light, feather-soft. He had made her so.

Because her whole world had turned upside-down, she decided to pamper herself. She would have a real breakfast in bed instead of the standard cup of coffee at her desk in the library. She telephoned the kitchen and very soon Niza carried in her breakfast – grapefruit, buttered toast, strawberry jam and coffee – on a perfectly appointed wicker tray. Delighted, for once, to be unproductive, she ate slowly and did not as much as glance at the *New York Times*.

Breakfast over, she reached for the telephone and pressed the button that would immediately connect her to Monica Martins, her secretary.

Noting with satisfaction that her phone was answered almost at once, she said, 'Guess what, Monica – I'm taking the day off.'

'Are you okay?' Monica asked nervously.

'I'm doing great,' Gina replied. 'Why?'

'Well, there's the meeting with the Madison board—'

'I know about that.'

'Lunch with Stephen Montagu of the Montagu Bank, then a three o'clock interview with Zandra Masters of *Exquisite* magazine—'

'Tell them all I've gone to Paris for the day, and fix a new schedule for everyone. Okay?'

'Okay,' Monica said weakly. 'Zandra Masters will freak.'

'The magazines need me far more than I need them,' Gina said coldly. 'They need my advertising—'

'They most certainly do.'

'Monica – no calls to be put through to my apartment. Of course, if you need me urgently, you can call—'

'I'll take care of that. No calls.'

'Monica?'

'Yes, Mrs Gibson?'

'If Rufus Cartwright should call, you can have him call me here, okay?'

'Certainly, Mrs Gibson.' So that was what it was all about, thought Monica. The ice-cold, steel-hard Gina Gibson had finally succumbed. And, what was more, to none other than Rufus Cartwright of Cartwright Pharmaceuticals. Not a very smart thing to do, Monica concluded. If anything, it was downright dangerous.

So far had Gina departed from her customary routine that she lay back on the pillows and fell into a dreamless sleep. When she awoke two hours later, she returned to her senses.

Rufus Cartwright knew altogether too much about her. How in the hell did he know about Kate and Morgan? And why had he even mentioned the homicide squad?

She leapt out of bed, put on a robe and paced the room like a caged tiger. At last it came to her – he had done exactly what she would have done in his place: he had hired private detectives. He had been right about one thing, though – it *was* too late for the homicide squad.

Could Kate have told him? Did he even know her?

Well, when next they met – tonight, of course – she would ask him to tell her everything he knew about Kate. She went into her marble bathroom but, still determined to keep his scent, she did not use her jacuzzi. Instead, she removed her make-up and then applied her newest confection – extra-rich, extra-sparkling Roman Spring moisturizer. It soothed her face, thus satisfying her primary requirement – every skin-care product had to feel like a balm.

Then she returned to her silken sheets, now unusually rumpled, and lay back to wait for his call and to fantasize about the kind of love they would make that night.

High up in his fiftieth-floor office, Rufus reached for the telephone, lifted the receiver and then replaced it. He seemed to be doing that every ten minutes, like some sort of reflex. What an effort of will it was not to call her, not to hear her voice. Making love last night, the tone of her voice had changed and once again it had been feather-soft and rippling. But he would not call her.

His need to call her, to have her and to be with her was at least as strong as his need for vengeance. But the success of last night's mission depended on his *not* calling her. His mind flipped and somersaulted. Together, last night, they had achieved perfection. Even now he felt a stirring in his loins. And yet he had made up his mind to follow his grandfather's simple but deadly philosophy. *Fuck 'em and leave 'em.*

Last night he had thought of leaving a few hundred dollars, but had decided against it. He had too much respect for call-girls to do that. Besides, there was no conquest with a call-girl. But he had conquered Gina, and he wanted her to know that. He also wanted her to know – and to suffer – the humiliation of being a one-night stand. It might take her a while to believe it, but in the end she would have no choice.

Then his leading research chemist, Dr Bradley, was on the line, effectively banishing Gina from his mind. So far, the clinical trials of his blood-pressure drug, Cartsyn, were excellent. It looked as if it could be launched in the market-place very soon. The next few hours were taken up with all sorts of complicated marketing strategies and calculations. He broke off for lunch with his family lawyer, Clinton Baker. When he returned to his office he had a meeting with his newly recruited researcher, Dr Ben Moore. It was while this meeting was in progress that his secretary buzzed to announce that a personal call was on the line waiting for him.

He had been waiting for that call and, though he had no doubt who it was, he asked: 'Who is it, Jane?'

'Mrs Gina Gibson.'

'I see,' he replied thoughtfully. After a long pause he said, 'Ask her to hold a minute . . .' He needed time to think. But in a flash he had decided what to do. 'Tell Mrs Gibson,' he ordered, 'that I have asked you to tell her that I said don't call me, I'll call her. Got it?'

'I am to say this to Mrs Gibson.' Speaking very quickly, Jane

419

said. '"Mr Cartwright has asked me to give you the following message – don't call me, I'll call you."' She gave a half-chuckle. 'Have I got it right, Mr Rufus?' she asked.

'You sure have,' he growled teasingly. 'You always get it, don't you, genius?'

It was easy enough to imagine her rage. Allowing his mind's eye to dwell briefly on it, he saw her puffing furiously on one of those cigarette-holders. He gave a sardonic self-satisfied smile and turned his entire attention to the new research programme that Dr Ben Moore had been presenting to him.

Lying on her four-poster bed in her bedroom decorated in every shade of white, Gina slammed down the telephone. Trembling with rage, exactly as Rufus had imagined, she lit another cigarette. Looking down, she saw that an unfinished, lighted cigarette lay in the ashtray. God! She was now reduced to smoking two cigarettes at once.

Her mind raced. How dared he send such an insulting message to her via a secretary? She should *never* have called him. She had not wanted to call him, but had been unable to stop herself. She burned. Raging against herself for her lack of self-discipline, she itched with hate for him. So he wanted to get even and a one-night stand was his way of going about it! And *such* a one-night stand. Her body still tingled with him. Her heart raced, too. Oh, the humiliation! He had had fun with her, but he had played with her. How he must have laughed at her, how he must be laughing even now! Feeling herself encased in layers of rage alternating with layers of remorse, she rolled about the bed like a dog trying to shake off fleas.

Of course she had made the most of his wife's anaphylactic shock! He would have done the same. Business was war and business people were warriors. But not only had he got even, he had conquered her. But then, of course, her conquest was his revenge. At this last thought, her body racked with ugly sobs. Whereupon she hated herself as much as she hated him. He had made her lose control last night, and he was making her lose it now. If she allowed herself to carry on like this, she would be utterly destroyed.

'Stop this!' she said aloud, through clenched teeth. 'Stop this at once and get on with your life!'

Then she stepped under an ice-cold shower and washed every trace of him off her skin.

Only he was under her skin . . .

Even so, if he wanted war, he would have war. She would call her broker; perhaps she should increase her stock in Cartwright Pharmaceuticals . . .

When she returned from her shower to her bedroom her phone was ringing. So Rufus had thought again, she exulted. It could only be Rufus, of course. No one else knew she was at home. In no doubt at all that it was Rufus, she picked up her phone and, in her sexiest voice, said: 'Mr Cartwright, I presume—'

'What?' said her mother. 'Is that you, Gina?'

'Who told you I was at home?'

'Monica.' Cecilia sighed loudly. 'Monica happens to think I am your mother.' Her voice broke.

'Sorry, Mama,' Gina said. 'What's wrong?'

'Miriam's dead.'

'Dead? But that's not possible. How? Why?'

'She needed a pacemaker after her bypass operation. Something went wrong. It stopped. The funeral is tomorrow. I thought there was a chance that you might like to attend.'

'Of course I'll be there. Where are you?'

'Where I live.'

'What? I don't get you.'

'You asked me where I was and I told you that I am where I live. In my own apartment, in the same building as your penthouse—'

'I'll be right down, Mama. I'll be with you in less than three minutes.'

Chapter Sixty-Six

That same afternoon, lying on her antique quilt in her secret loft, Kate felt frightened. She was now convinced that her private sanctuary had been invaded. Camel cigarette-butts were in her ashtray again. The first time she had found only one cigarette. She had asked her cleaning lady about it and she had believed her when she said she did not smoke.

There was very little of Morgan left now. She was honest enough to admit to herself that she had stopped grieving, that the loft was no longer Morgan's shrine. Rather, it was a secret place that was entirely hers. A magical place where she could have both her own space and her own identity. There she could be Kate – just Kate. Not Kate Hills or Kate Gachet or the mother of Matthew and the wife of Jean-Pierre.

There, where she could belong to herself, she could be wholly herself.

But the cigarettes had taken the secrecy out of the place. Suddenly she was afraid of its former magic. She wondered whether this mysterious invader could have had anything to do with Gina. Ever since Gina had smashed her precious carving, she had felt she was out to destroy her. And yet, refusing to be either cowed or blackmailed, she had continued to see Scarlett. Sometimes they met at Monsieur Marceau's studio after an exacting music lesson, and sometimes at Kate's home in Gracie Square. They both knew this irritated Gina, but so what?

Far from allowing Gina to come between them, they had even worked on school projects together. Right now, at her suggestion, Scarlett was busy with a project on the history of jade. She had promised to take her to an exhibition, but so far had done nothing about it.

Her eye fell on a collection of short stories she had read recently. She shivered a little, for she remembered that she had felt as if the one and only tragic story in the collection had been about herself. In the story the woman, who was about her age, thirty-five, had taken a private room in an hotel. The mother of four and the wife of a successful lawyer, she had felt that the great edifice of the family and household she and her husband had constructed was too much for her, and so she had rented a cheap room in a cheap hotel where she could be herself. Neglecting her family, she had gone there every day. But when she knew that her husband had her watched by a private detective, and so learned where her secret haven was, she had gassed herself.

Meanwhile, her secret loft had been violated and she now had no choice but to give it up. She had expected to feel resentful, but instead she felt liberated.

It occurred to her that her time in the loft was harmful to her, to Matthew and even to Jean-Pierre. Matthew was sixteen – she could not now lose him to Jean-Pierre.

Now, with the benefit of hindsight, she could look back on the night she and Morgan had fallen so in love and understand why and how it had happened. She and Jean-Pierre had been going through a bad patch and, with the distance lent by time, it now seemed highly unlikely that Jean-Pierre had found himself involved in an affair. But whatever the circumstances may have been, she and Jean-Pierre had now arrived at a new stage of their lives together, and she was no longer so dreadfully insecure with him.

At any rate, she had taken the decision to let go of the loft, and of Morgan.

Why, she might even tell him about the way Gina had smashed her jade carving.

Christie's had a very special exhibition of Tang antique jade, and she had promised to take Scarlett. They could meet at Monsieur Marceau's studio and go on to the exhibition from there.

She picked up the phone and called Scarlett. To her amazement Gina – who was never at the apartment – answered.

'Hi, Scarlett,' she said when the phone was answered.

'This is not Scarlett,' said Gina, who had answered the phone. 'Who is this?'

'Kate Gachet.'

After a long silence Gina repeated, 'Kate Gachet.'

'That's right,' replied Kate, who now recognized Gina's voice.

'Scarlett is not at home,' Gina said coldly. 'I'll tell her you called.'

'Is anything wrong?' continued Kate, undaunted. 'You're usually in your office at this time.'

'We've just heard that Miriam died.'

'Miriam Stern? Scarlett will be heart-broken.'

'I'll tell Scarlett you called,' Gina said again.

The phone clicked off.

Scarlett returned from school and, shocked to find her mother at home, was told the news about Miriam, rushed into her room and fell into a storm of weeping. After a while she had cried herself to sleep.

Not since Mike O'Connor had died had Gina seen her mother so distraught. Though she had been only nine years old when Mike had died, somehow she had known how to comfort Cecilia. Now, in the days following Miriam's funeral, her mother – always so robust, so efficient and so elegant – appeared to shrink before her eyes. At fifty-three, Cecilia drew her dead mother's shawl about her and seemed to revert to her peasant origins in the slums of Rome. Again and again she described how Miriam had saved her life by taking her to hide in the cloisters of a Jewish orphanage.

Up until this time Gina had known nothing of the terrible beatings her father and his sister, Tina, had inflicted on her mother. But it seemed as if, in losing Miriam, Cecilia had lost not only a dear friend but also a lifetime of support, encouragement and approval. In an effort to make Gina understand the depth of her loss, she spared her nothing – even the details of

424

what had happened to her when Tina and Al had found her diaphragm under the floorboards were laid bare.

'No one will ever call me kiddo again,' she whimpered. 'Mirrie was like a mother to me.'

'Mama – what can I say?' Gina responded helplessly. 'What can I do?'

She wanted to say, 'Quit nagging Scarlett about her weight.' But she said, 'Nothing, Gina, *cara*. Nothing.'

Overnight, it seemed, Cecilia had turned into a frail and elderly woman. She would wear nothing but black. Shoes, stockings, dress and – something new that she had adopted – a black kerchief: all were black. Without a trace of make-up she looked older than her age and, to Gina's shocked, bewildered eyes, frighteningly mortal.

The timing of Miriam's death, coinciding as it did with Rufus's cruel revenge, could not have been more unfortunate for Gina. The sight of her weak and weakened mother unravelled her already ragged nerves. During this heart-breaking time she saw both her mother and daughter every day.

Just as her mother seemed to turn into more and more of a primitive peasant who muttered to herself, so Scarlett appeared to grow fatter and fatter. Towards the end of the third week after Miriam's death, she called in on her mother and daughter and found Scarlett seated at the kitchen table calmly finishing off an entire blueberry pie. If she had not seen the whole pie only half an hour earlier, she never would have guessed that Scarlett had actually devoured the whole thing.

But she did see it, and her nerve snapped.

'You've eaten the whole pie!' she shouted, snatching the plate away. 'I saw that pie; it was untouched a few minutes ago!' She flung the plate into the trash can. '*Why* did you have to eat the whole pie? Why, Scarlett, *why?*'

Scarlett made no answer.

'I'll tell you why,' Gina yelled. 'You ate it to get at me. You've always hated me!'

'Mother!' Scarlett said, sounding bored.

425

'Don't you Mother me, you fat slob!' Enraged, Gina rushed over to Scarlett and tried to shake her massive shoulders. But she made no impact. 'Oh God,' she yelled. 'What did I do to deserve a daughter like this?' Whipping her own thighs, she went on to answer her own question. 'You do it to spite me, don't you? You hate me, don't you? You do it because you are plain and I am glamorous. You do it because I'm in the beauty business.'

'You got one thing right, Mother,' replied Scarlett, with all the insouciance of a fifteen-year-old adolescent. 'I do hate you.'

That was too much for Gina. Lunging towards Scarlett, but in a single graceful movement, she slapped her full on the face with the flat of her hand. Once she had done that she lost control, and again and again she hit her daughter's face.

At last Scarlett yelled. 'Stop it, you bitch! Stop it!'

That was when Cecilia came in.

Scarlett's face was already flushed and swollen. Saying nothing, Cecilia opened the freezer and removed two packs of frozen peas. She wrapped them in a kitchen towel and, as if speaking to herself, murmured, 'These make a very good cold poultice. Miriam told me so.'

'Look at you, Mama,' Gina snapped. 'Look what you look like in your widow's weeds.' Beside herself now, she slapped the kitchen table. 'Now I've got a fat slob of an obese daughter and an uneducated primitive peasant of a mother.'

'Leave this room, Gina.'

'You're telling me to leave!' Gina yelled. 'This is my apartment. I bought it for you!'

'You negotiated the purchase, Gina,' her mother corrected her. 'It seems I have to remind you that I paid for it.' Cecilia reached for a wooden spoon and tapped it hard against the kitchen table. 'You get out of here,' she said, her voice laden with anguish, 'and don't come back until you've learned some manners.'

'I'm sorry, Mama,' Gina said, contrite. 'I should not have spoken to you like that.' Then she went to Scarlett and tenderly

426

stroked her flushed and swollen cheeks. 'I'm sorry, *tesoro mio*,' she murmured over and over. 'Forgive me, *cara*, please, please forgive me.'

She's not really bad, Cecilia thought with relief. She has got a heart . . . All the same, it was time she stopped wearing black and pulled herself together for Scarlett's sake.

'What do you want, Scarlett?' Gina begged. 'If you take off only ten pounds I'll buy you anything in the world that you choose. Anything.'

'I don't want you to *buy* me anything, Mother,' Scarlett said in a low voice. 'I only want you to leave me alone.'

A month after Miriam's death, which was also a month after her strange and humiliating interlude with Rufus, Gina arrived home one evening and found her apartment filled with dozens of crystal vases of hundreds of red roses. Each vase held a card, and the message on each card was the same. *You are irresistible. I can't live without you a moment longer. Forgive me, R.* Squealing with delight, she rushed from vase to vase, ripping open the small white envelope that contained the card: *You are irresistible. I can't live without you a moment longer. Forgive me, R.*

The telephone rang. Usually she did not answer the telephone herself, but flushed and flustered with joy and excitement she picked it up.

'Gina? Is that you, Gina?' Her name sounded like a song.

'This is me,' she began. 'I mean, this is Gina.'

'Will you?'

'Will I what?'

'Forgive me?'

'Don't call me, I'll call you' – his unforgivably insulting message had been loud and clear. But she was far too proud to let him know how close he had come to destroying her. 'What is there to forgive?' she asked lightly. Why let him know how he had hurt her? 'What for?' she asked.

'I behaved like an arrogant adolescent.'

427

'Oh, that.'

'Yes, that.' She could hear him swallowing. 'Listen, are you free tonight?'

'No.'

'Are you free later tonight?'

Say no, she told herself; say no. But she said, 'Later? What does "later" mean?'

'It means whatever you want it to mean. Towards midnight, past midnight, 3 a.m., 6 a.m. . . . We could watch the sunrise – anything you say.'

She could visualize him tugging his tight curls and she could see his rugged, sensitive face take on a quizzical, anxious expression. Say no, she told herself fiercely. Say no! She longed for him. Her very skin ached for him.

'Gina?' he said into the silence. 'Gina, are you still there?'

'Yes. I'm still here.'

'Do you remember the Powells?'

'The Powells?'

'Senator Powell and his wife. We had coffee with them, remember? We met them when we were at the Adirondack cabin.' He didn't wait for a reply but rushed on. 'I ran into them the other day and they asked after you. They wanted to know if you were still so pretty. I said you were *not* pretty. How do you like that?'

'That's okay,' she replied, affronted.

'I told them you were never pretty because you were always beautiful. It's hard to believe you could have grown even more beautiful now than you were when you were a kid, but you have.' He paused and repeated, feelingly, 'You have. You have.'

'Thank you,' she said. Oh God, she thought, if only he had not mentioned the Powells.

'The stroke of midnight?'

'Yes, Rufus. I'll see you at midnight.'

I'm weak, she thought distastefully, after they had hung up.

She did not want to want him. She felt that insistent wriggle in her loins again. Why him? There were other men in the world besides Rufus Cartwright, so why in God's name did it have to

428

be him? So what, if he had been her first man? Every woman and every girl in the world had a first man in her life. It was a commonplace, a profoundly ordinary commonplace. Except that it seemed her skin found nothing profoundly ordinary about his skin. Because every nerve of her body danced to the rhythm of his touch. She knew he had used her body – satisfied by his celestial skills – to master her and to humiliate her.

She could cancel the night that lay ahead. She need not be there when he came. But even as her mind formulated these ideas, her fingers reached out to dial the number of the hostess who expected her at her dinner-party. Since she was so meticulous about keeping dates, her mumbled excuse about an infected throat was readily believed.

Instead of being out at a dinner-party given in honour of two ambassadors, she was luxuriating in her jacuzzi. She wanted to stop herself from preparing for the night ahead, but her mind appeared to be powered by her skin. Sexual attraction, sexual chemistry: surely she was more than the sum of the molecules?

And then, at last, it was midnight and he and she were in her canopied bed dressed in pristine lace, and their bodies soared to invisible peaks where molecules were irrelevant. It was a wordless time, a time of bodies cramming seventeen lost years into a single night. Sleep was the last thing they wanted, but ruled as they were by their bodies they had little say in the matter.

Towards dawn, his butterfly fingers brought her awake.

'I have to be in Geneva today,' he said gently, 'but I want to make a date with you.'

'A date?'

'I want everyone to know that we're seeing each other,' he said. 'I want you to be my date at the small black-tie dinner-party the Ripleys are hosting for Lord and Lady Blackwell.'

'You certainly move in the right circles,' she said drily.

'So do you.' He grinned. 'Will you accept?'

She laughed softly. 'When is it? I'll have to consult my diary.'

'It's on March 6th,' he said, tracing the outline of her lips. 'Exactly one month from now.' He removed his fingers from her

429

lips and tugged distractedly at his curls. 'I'll be in Europe for all of that time, but I'll be back in New York on the morning of March 6th. Okay?'

'I shall be delighted to accompany you,' she said solemnly.

'I won't call you,' he said gravely. 'I hate to phone, but I'll communicate with you every day except Sunday. Okay?'

'Don't call me, I'll call you,' she quipped.

They both broke into laughter and rolled about the bed, clutching one another, and before long their demanding bodies took over and blew them away.

There was only one person in the world whom she could have told about last night, and that was Miriam Stern. She had not yet altogether believed that Miriam was dead, but now that she needed her so badly the terrible frailty was borne in upon her. Outwardly she appeared unchanged. She went about her business as enthusiastically and as ruthlessly as ever, and her board of directors now included a former secretary of state as well as a former Harvard professor of economics. Since she had been a major contributor to President Reagan's campaign, she had been to several intimate White House dinners.

Inwardly, however, she was a churning mass of nervous questioning. What had he meant by saying he wanted everyone to know they were 'seeing' one another? Did this mean that they were now an item? His wife was dead. What if he had marriage in mind? Their heads knew that they were ruthless competitors, bitter rivals and enduring enemies, but their hearts, it seemed, were indifferent to all that. Or was she now, at thirty-six years old, confusing her body with her heart? All because making love again with a long-ago lover had taught her that her soul resided in her skin . . .

But for one detail, her routine did not vary. That detail was Clarence Fowler. She contrived to have a huge row with him over a trumped-up disappointment, and broke the relationship. To be more accurate, though, she was smart enough to let Clarence think he had ended things.

She expended more energy and more thought on the dress she would wear than she had ever done before. Noted as well as feared for her decisiveness, she could not now make a firm choice. In the end, after considerable agonizing, she chose a long-sleeved, sophisticatedly simple sheath of black velvet, low cut; it offered a tantalizing but elegant back view, and a huge bow of the iridescent colours of the rising sun set off her tiny waist.

Throughout that endless month of waiting, every day two dozen long-stemmed red roses arrived, always with the same note: *Avec mes hommages, R.* When, thanks to some snarl-up at the florist, the roses did not arrive until late at night, she was utterly devastated. In fact she left the theatre at intermission.

To everyone's total astonishment she took off the entire day of March 6th. She had a facial, a waxing, a blow-dry, a Swedish massage, aromatherapy and reflexology. Arriving home in the middle of the afternoon she found that the apartment was once again filled with dozens of vases with hundreds of roses. There was also a message telling her that he was flying in on Sir Edward Thornton's Gulfstream and would meet her at the Ripleys.

Waiting for seven o'clock was impossibly difficult. She would have gone down to see her mother, but she could not face Scarlett's bulk. Scarlett would be at home by now. In the end she went into the small gym and did some exercise on the ballet rail.

Gina arrived at exactly five minutes after seven. She had never been to the Ripleys before, but she recognized Clark, their butler, who had once worked for the Greenaways.

'Good evening, Clark,' Gina smiled. She looked up at the vaulted, panelled ceiling she had so often seen reproduced in magazines.

'Good evening, Mrs Gibson,' Clark replied.

Did she imagine it or was Clark somewhat flustered? The very next moment Chester Russell, a former secretary of state, and his wife Jean arrived. Gina knew them, and they greeted one another warmly. While the maid took their wraps, they chatted for a few moments. Clark had disappeared for the moment and they all waited good-naturedly for him to return. When Cory and Cy Rinzler arrived they were still standing in the hall. Gina felt her hackles rise. Fierce competitors, currently engaged in a price war, Gina and the Rinzlers were definitely not on speaking terms. Since they did not as much as nod at one another, the atmosphere grew distinctly chilly.

Where the hell is Clark? Gina wondered irritably. How much longer would he leave them standing in the hall? She tapped her black velvet heel on the marble floor. At last Clark appeared, walking behind the host and hostess, Marcia and Reginald Ripley.

Marcia Ripley seemed to have some difficulty with the velvet train of her dress. It made her hobble, rather than walk. Perhaps, Gina speculated, she was not really meant to walk in that dress? She was a slight woman, with a chignon and darting eyes that were eager but secretive. She came to a halt beside Gina and swayed slightly. 'Mrs Gibson?' she said in a high, girlish voice. 'I'm Marcia Ripley and I'm delighted to meet you.'

Gina extended her hand. 'Glad to meet you, Mrs Ripley.'

Mrs Ripley took her hand abstractedly. 'This is very embarrassing,' she half twittered and half mumbled. 'An unfortunate mistake. I hardly know what to say.' Turning to her husband, she said: 'I don't believe I introduced you to Mr Ripley—'

'How do you do, Mr Ripley,' Gina said, nonplussed.

Taking her hand in his, Mr Ripley held it in his plump hand for rather longer than was necessary. 'Delighted to make your acquaintance.' He released her hand. 'A most regrettable – uh – oversight, I guess,' he mumured, his jowls shaking. 'But unfortunately, Mrs Gibson, we were not expecting you.'

Flushing deeply, she said, 'I'm supposed to meet Rufus Cartwright here.' Her voice artificially bright, she continued, 'I'm his date for the evening.'

'But Rufus sent his regrets way back last month,' Marcia

Ripley was aghast. "Course, I could be mistaken,' she said, sending beseeching glances towards both her husband and her butler.

'No, Mrs Ripley, ma'am, you are not mistaken,' Clark said gravely. 'I recall your disappointment when Mr Cartwright's refusal came.'

It took Gina all her strength to remain standing. Ashen-faced and in a cold sweat, she somehow managed to preserve her dignity. 'I must have got my wires crossed,' she said bravely. 'Please forgive me.'

She turned to leave, but had to suffer the further humiliation of having her sable coat handed to her. Suddenly everyone in the hall started talking animatedly. As she was leaving, Lord and Lady Blackwell arrived. She stopped to let them pass, said a polite good-evening, and then at last she was on the street, frantically hailing a taxi.

Instinctively she told the taxi-driver to take her to her office suite. The doormen would note her elaborate evening dress and could raise their eyebrows as high as they liked – she simply could not face going home to all those hundreds of waist-high red roses. When she reached her office suite the satisfaction she usually drew from its newly decorated emerald velvet walls and cobalt upholstery evaporated. Suddenly everything – the bare, gleaming wood floors with occasional silk oriental rugs, the windows lavished with yards of billowing cobalt taffeta, the Tiffany glass ceiling-lamps, the mosaic fountain – seemed to mock her. She marched through the boardroom, with its huge antique Georgian dining-table, through the informal sitting-room furnished as if it belonged to an English country house, through the massage-room with a rubbing table and a sun lamp, until she came to the bathroom with a marble-topped wash-basin and gold-plated fixtures. There she hastily changed into one of the fresh business suits she kept for emergencies so that she would always be nothing less than immaculate.

Demanding perfection from herself as well as from others, it was little wonder that she had become known as the woman who said, 'All I demand is perfection.' *Haute couture* or not, that

433

dramatic and magnificently crafted evening dress she had worn to the Ripleys would never be worn again. But what to do with it? The answer came at once – she would give it to the St Vincent de Paul Society, a Catholic charity who would make certain that it would go to the right person. The decision taken, she immediately set about packaging it herself.

Only then did she sit down at her desk. She would refuse to think about what had happened at the Ripleys. Making money, as Andy Warhol had said, is the greatest art. It is also the greatest therapy, thought Gina. Thank God Gibson–Keene Inc. was privately owned, and therefore safe from corporate raiders and hostile take-overs. Cartwright Pharmaceuticals, however, was a public company and therefore vulnerable. Though she already owned a substantial holding, she was not yet in a position to do any real damage. Now she badly needed to hurt Cartwright's. So she decided to put in another buying order from a different set of nominees, even though she knew this would be a decision based on emotion rather than on sound business principles. Well, she could afford it, couldn't she?

Right now, there were other pressing and far more vital decisions that needed her attention. Her range of male skin-care products was almost complete. She now needed to take two final decisions: the name – and the method – under which it would be marketed. Because research had shown that male homosexuals spent nine times more than the average on toiletries, she had been contemplating a low-budget campaign targeting the gay market like the French cigarette company Régie Française des Tabacs, manufacturers of Gitanes, whose 'statement about style' had resulted in a 30 per cent sales increase.

On the other hand, AIDS, first observed in the late 1970s, had only this year, 1981, been identified. And, since other research indicated that 70 per cent of male toiletries were bought by women, she had also been considering whether or not to advertise in women's magazines. Her original products had required no advertising, but that was way back in the mid-sixties, when things had been very different. She was living and marketing in the expanding eighties, and she planned to make the most of the boom.

Burning over what Rufus had done to her, a renewed attack of heartburn made her reach for her antacid. She felt so defeated, so impotent . . . She returned to her calculations as one turns to warmth in the cold. Only her business and its concomitant tough decisions could save her, could stem the hot, angry tears which even now threatened to overtake her. Breathing deeply, she concentrated on the breath in her nostrils, but to no avail. She gave way to a storm of weeping.

After some time she looked up and, without meaning to, caught her reflection in the panelled mirrors on the opposite walls. Her puffy, reddened eyes were as she expected them to be. It was the bitter, hard, ravaged expression that was so shocking and so painful. She looked beaten and defeated and as resigned as if she had been trained to expect grief. She looked like a woman who had abandoned hope . . .

She crossed to her bathroom, turned on her solid gold taps and rinsed her face in ice-cold water.

And then it came to her that even the most hopeless women could buy hope in a bottle. Why else would 70 per cent of men's toiletries – including skin-care products – be bought by women? Because she felt herself identifying with them, she decided to target women in her own age group, late thirties, and take it up to the late forties. She would run a campaign of father-and-son advertisements. The father would look like President Kennedy before he had been elected – a square, handsome face, untidy hair, with the tall, careless elegance of privilege. The son would be seen graduating from college, holding his certificate and receiving his father's gift – Ivy League Cologne. This way she would attract the yuppies, their fathers and their grandfathers. Because the mothers and the grandmothers would do the purchasing . . .

It would turn out to be a winning name and, very soon after its launch, its huge sales would exceed all expectations, but Gina was not to know that.

435

She knew of course that her humiliation would be compounded by the gossip columns. The Rinzlers would make sure of that. Let the Rinzlers have their fun. They would never be able to survive the kind of price-slashing she had in mind.

In the Gibson–Keene press office, two days after the Ripley fiasco, Monica Martins, as always, clipped whatever was relevant to Gibson–Keene. When she came upon the blistering comments on Gina Gibson her hand trembled, but she cut them out none the less. As she filed them she wondered if they should be sent to Mrs Gibson's office. At that moment the phone rang. When it turned out to be Mrs Gibson herself, she began to tremble again. Even her voice shook.

'Send all those clippings about the Ripley party to my office,' Gina said crisply, as if there was nothing out of the ordinary.

'Certainly, Mrs Gibson,' replied Monica shakily.

'Watch the press very carefully over the next few days and keep sending me whatever you find.'

'Of course, Mrs Gibson.'

'None of those articles or comments are to be kept in your office,' Gina continued. 'All of them must be sent to me.'

Gina read them all – they kept coming in.

She would get even with Rufus. So far no definite strategy had evolved, but something would come to her and, in the end, she would find the best way to destroy him.

She would take over Cartwright Pharmaceuticals.

Chapter Sixty-Seven

These past three years since Miriam had been gone there had been absolutely no one to whom Gina could turn to help her deal with the worst humiliation of her adult life, so she had no choice but to brazen it out. In an important sense, she came increasingly to look upon what she called 'the Ripley affair' as a major watershed. A high noon in her life, it provoked reappraisal and promoted change. From that moment on, her life-style changed dramatically.

Once Clarence Fowler was out of her life it had been easy enough to seduce other men into it, and she embarked on a series of affairs whose only meaning was that she had the required escort to go with her life-style, the way she had the perfect accessory, such as a handbag, to go with her designer clothes. Too young for a walker, she nevertheless wanted it to be known that she was a hot, full-blooded woman with an enviable appetite for sex, success and excitement.

And the truth was that she now had all three. For sex, she had a new and remarkably handsome lover called Humphrey Gray. Her success was both financial and social – her parties were as legendary as the growth of Gibson–Keene. Excitement was in keeping it all going, of owning a great country house in Connecticut and a home in Palm Beach.

And yet in one area of her life she was an abject failure.

Scarlett.

Obese, pimply Scarlett.

Scarlett who now, at the age of eighteen, refused to see a dermatologist or a dietician, or indeed anyone in the medical or paramedical professions. Sometimes Gina felt she would burst with rage. Dr Littlewood, the renowned dermatologist whom she had only recently lured to the board, had been certain that if only he could meet Scarlett she would agree to be treated by him. Instead, as soon as Scarlett had realized what he did, she had been downright insulting.

As for chocolate – well, it seemed Scarlett was an addict and, as she had been told again and again, neither love nor logic can cure an addiction. Except that love, teenage love, was different. Gina knew that because of Rufus. Indeed, the omnipotent force of that love was with her still. In fact she was still endlessly trying to replicate that love, and that time when she had been in love with a man who loved her. With the benefit of hindsight, it looked as if she had been in love with herself. Well, even if that were true, she reasoned, it was because she had felt good about herself.

It was six o'clock in the morning and she was in her jacuzzi, which, as she liked to joke, was the best place to think.

She recalled Dr Payson, the clinical psychologist's, comment: 'Your daughter has an eating disorder, the root of which is self-hatred . . . She has – among other severe problems – a reality problem. None of this is made any easier by the rigid, relentless discipline that her music imposes on her.' The doctor paused to glance at his notes and continued, 'We've done all we can, Mrs Gibson.'

'Correct me if I'm wrong, doctor,' she had answered curtly, 'but did I understand you to say that neither love nor logic can cure an addiction?'

'Sadly, that has been our unrewarding experience.'

'You say love,' Gina had queried. 'Do you mean parental love, or maternal love, or family love?' She stopped to light a cigarette. 'Or do you mean the love of a lover?'

'I mean—'

'No, no, wait,' she replied impatiently. She rose from her desk and stood beside the window, staring at the masses of people-ants below. 'I'm thinking, and you are my sounding board,' she said. 'I hope you don't mind?'

'I'm glad to help,' smiled Dr Littlewood.

'Scarlett needs to fall in love,' she said, her voice as high with

438

excitement as if she had only just stumbled on a new name for a new product. 'What do you think, Dr Littlewood? What sort of man would she fall for?'

'I think she's so afraid of falling in love that she's wrapped herself in cushions of fat.'

'I know that,' Gina responded restlessly. 'That's obvious.' She returned to her desk. 'Please answer my question, Dr Littlewood. What sort of man would she fall for?'

The doctor made no reply but gave a momentary shrug.

'I know what you're thinking, Dr Littlewood,' Gina said sharply. 'You are thinking that with her looks no man would possibly fall for her.' Again she did not wait for a reply, but went on, 'Would you like to take a bet with me? If she falls in love and has a love affair, the weight will melt away like snow in the sun.'

'I agree with you, Mrs Gibson, and I can't take that bet.' Dr Littlewood grinned. 'Scarlett *is* addicted to chocolate, but chocolate is not like heroin.'

'Good.' Gina stood up. 'I'm glad we see eye to eye.'

Now that she had gone through the whole conversation she stepped out of the jacuzzi and ran a loofah over her body to stimulate the circulation.

Her mind revved. As always, the faster her mind went the more she relaxed. Like a racing car, she found it uncomfortable to travel slowly. She decided to have a chat with Warren Masters, the male model in her hugely successful father-and-son ads for Ivy League. Warren, of course, was too old for Scarlett; he played the father. Warren had, as they say, been around. She had heard that he had done a stint in LA escorting older women. She would speak to him. He would know of a likely candidate for Scarlett . . .

PART EIGHT

PART EIGHT

Chapter Sixty-Eight

In the Alice Tulley Hall, on a bright afternoon in the spring of 1983, Scarlett's entire being was given over to Laura Schiffley playing the dramatically lyrical Rachmaninov Second Piano Concerto. Several unwrapped bars of chocolate lay on her lap and from time to time she silently popped one into her mouth. At intermission the young man who had the seat beside her said, 'Hey, man, I'm starving! Mind if I take one of those?'

'Go right ahead,' Scarlett replied, handing him one.

'Great,' he said, taking it. 'I'll buy you a coffee or a Coke after the concert, okay?' He settled into his seat and, chewing vigorously, gave all his attention to the programme notes.

Scarlett ate some more chocolate as she waited for the second half of the concert to begin. The bleak textures and tough harmonies of Sibelius's Fourth Symphony meant that this was not one of her favourite works. To her astonishment, the boy in the seat beside her removed one of her chocolates and popped it into his mouth. She thought she saw him wink, but couldn't be sure, and blushed in confusion.

The concert ended and, as she rose to leave, he joined her, and once again – like the wink she could not be sure she had seen – he guided her out of the hall, his brushing arm merely a presence at her elbow.

'I do *not* like Sibelius,' he said when they reached the foyer. 'Today was the last effort I am ever going to make to try to like him.'

'My grandmother doesn't like him either. She was going to come with me today,' Scarlett answered, 'but when my mother asked her to run an errand for her, she jumped at the excuse to miss Sibelius.'

'That was my luck, I guess.'

'What was your luck?'

'That your grandmother didn't make it.' Now she was aware of his hand closing round her arm. 'I got her ticket. You handed a ticket into the box office, didn't you?'

'I did.'

'So that was the ticket I bought.' He grinned. 'C'mon, I'm taking you to the Russian Tea Room. It's my way of paying you back for your Hershey bars.'

'Thanks,' she said quietly, 'but I can't.'

'You can't? Why?'

'I don't know you.'

'Allow me to introduce myself. I'm Carl Daley.'

She looked at him in his rumpled cords and brown tweed sports jacket. Like his spotted red tie, his blue shirt was immaculate. Because he was not especially handsome she did not feel too uncomfortable with him. Besides, she liked his humorous eyes. Somehow, in some unidentifiable way, he reminded her of someone . . .

'I'm Scarlett,' she said, in spite of herself.

'I know.' He nodded. 'You are Scarlett Gibson.'

She said nothing, but looked anxious.

'You'd like to know how I know your name?'

She nodded.

'I was at your recital—'

'Recital?'

'At the Weill Recital Hall. You played Chopin.'

'That's right. I played Chopin there last November.'

'You were good.'

Suddenly she realized that they were on their way to the Russian Tea Room. 'Are you in music?' she asked.

'I guess you could call me a groupie,' he said, sounding embarrassed. 'I go to concerts, I listen to records, I've got a great stereo – but I can't play a note.' He frowned for a moment. 'I guess I'm just like one of those boxing fans. They couldn't box to save their lives, and yet they know more about boxing than a boxer.'

She laughed.

'Hey,' he said, suddenly serious. 'You should do that more often. You look real pretty when you laugh.' Then, as if he had said nothing out of the ordinary, he went on: 'Are you gonna let me buy a coffee or what?'

'Thanks.' She smiled. 'I'd love a coffee.'

In the Russian Tea Room he ordered her coffee and a Coke and cheesecake for himself. 'Sure you won't have any cake?' he asked when the waiter brought their order.

'Sure,' she said. This was very unusual. She never refused cake. Very soon she would come to understand that that was when her dieting had begun.

For many months after that, she was to subsist only on proteins and ten glasses of water a day. Now that she had the motivation, the discipline came easily.

He told her that he was a freelance researcher, presently engaged in collecting information on riff-rock and late-night songs – American music – for a professor of musicology who lived in Germany. He also said that he was researching for a director working on a documentary on affordable housing in Harlem. During the following weeks he took her to the Blue Note, a famous jazz club on West 53rd Street.

'Jazz,' he told her, 'was the universal basis of American composition.' She loved the mood and the rhythm of the improvisation of jazz, and he seemed to love unfolding a new world of music to her. He understood that she had been steeped in the world of classical music.

What was so wonderful about it all for Scarlett was that it was so deliciously secret. Not even Grandmama knew who he really was. 'He works for a professor of musicology,' she told Cecilia. 'He does research.'

'That's nice, *tesoro mio*,' Cecilia said gently. 'What does he research?'

'The basis of American composition.'

'It sounds very important.'

'It is,' Scarlett said happily. 'But don't tell my mother about Carl, okay?'

'If you don't want me to, I won't, of course. But I would like to meet him one day.'

'You will,' Scarlett laughed. 'You will meet him.'

It was now six months since Scarlett and Carl had met. Scarlett had lost thirty pounds and the dimples that had been buried by fat were revealed. Cecilia missed Miriam, the only person who could have possibly told her how to handle things. Given her background, Cecilia was surprisingly modern. 'I like to be with it,' she would say, and she would mean it. Of course in Rome, in her day, Scarlett would never have been allowed to see a young man no one knew. But all that was light years away. For good or ill, Gina's success had taken all of them into another universe . . .

Meanwhile, the weight was dropping off Scarlett. Her complexion was clear and altogether devoid of pimples. She wore no make-up. Although her eyes were bright and her gaze confident, Cecilia was nevertheless certain that Scarlett was still a virgin. Her instinct told her that it would only be after Scarlett and Carl had become lovers that she would be asked to meet him. 'What's to complain?' she asked herself. Scarlett had gone down to a size twelve!

Monsieur Marceau broke all his rules and allowed himself to be complimentary. 'Her distinctive gift means that she will be a pianist of the first rank,' he said. 'She has passed through the stormy seas of adolescence. The partnership between us, between the student and teacher, is harmonious. After her début at the Alice Tulley Hall next spring, her gifts will be recognized!'

And yet, despite the rigorous discipline of practice, Scarlett did not seem nervous. She was to play Beethoven's Piano Concerto No. 1. 'Some of his phrases are pure poetry,' pronounced Monsieur Marceau. 'She is not disabled by nerves because she is too young,' he explained. 'Sadly, she will learn to be nervous as she gets older.'

Several times during those months Gina attempted to take Scarlett on a shopping spree. After Scarlett and Carl had known

446

one another for eight months, she tried again. 'You've taken off a bit of weight, Scarlett,' she said carefully. 'It suits you.' Weight had long been a taboo subject. Frankly, she was scared to mention it.

'I'm glad you approve.'

'I saw this lovely dress at Saks. I brought it home on appro, but I think it will be too big.'

'What size is it?'

'Twelve.'

'I'm a ten. It is too big.' But she did not laugh or even smile.

'I could change it for a ten,' Gina suggested quickly.

'Thanks, Mother, but no thanks.'

'But what about the concert?'

'It's all arranged. I have already told you that I'm wearing a cream silk shirt with an electric-blue velvet skirt.'

'I had something very different in mind. Something dramatic, something theatrical.'

'Thanks, but no thanks, Mother.'

It was almost Christmas, Gina reminded herself, and the concert was not until March. There was time enough for Scarlett to change her mind.

So far, in the ten months they had been dating, they had only met once or twice a week. Some weeks they did not meet at all. And when they did meet, it was to visit a museum or go to a concert or to see a foreign film. The Whitney Museum of American Art quickly became one of their favourite meeting-places. Scarlett and Carl loved sitting at one of the scattered tables at the little bar and thought the espresso was the best in New York. He never took her to expensive places; dinner at a small, square table in the intimate atmosphere at the Café des Artistes had been his greatest extravagance. They seemed to have arrived at a perfect financial understanding. They always split the bill and went Dutch and took advantage of going to free places such as the Whitney Museum.

That Christmas he went home to his family in Indiana and

she and her grandmother joined Gina at the house party she was giving at their new home in Connecticut. Excluding Cecilia's and Scarlett's rooms, the house had eight guest-suites, so that they were twenty in all. Since Gina's concert was less than three months away, Gina had acquired yet another Steinway so that Scarlett could practise.

Before they went, Scarlett and Carl exchanged gifts. He gave her a hundred-year-old original manuscript of an obscure composer called Vakoska, and she gave him a Chagall lithograph of a clown playing a violin.

Although Scarlett was pleased with herself for having lost so much weight, and liked herself more than she had done, she still did not know that she was beautiful. It had already been said by Monsieur Marceau that she was a young woman of classical beauty. But he had not wanted her to hear it; after her concert she could become as swollen-headed as she liked, but not before. Her dark, soulful eyes in her ivory-white, clear complexion compelled attention. When she smiled, which these days was more and more frequent, the three dimples to the left of her lips began their dance. From the very beginning, six years ago, Monsieur Marceau had taught her to carry herself as a concert pianist should. Consequently her back was straight, her walk graceful and her presence regal.

When Carl returned from Indiana he invited her to dinner at the loft he shared with his artist friend, Jamie Pearson, in Soho.

'Jamie's away,' he said somewhat defensively. 'I've cleaned it up a bit. It would be really neat if you could come.'

Because she understood that this was no ordinary invitation she hesitated.

'It would mean a lot to me if you would come,' he persisted, his voice low. 'We've got an infra-red griller and I could grill you a steak.'

Loving his crooked smile, she said: 'Thanks, I'd love to come.'

'Thursday?'

'On Thursday.'

'Hey, you don't even know where it is.' He laughed. She joined him, and they laughed long and loud, drawing the

448

attention of others in the little bar. The Whitney had become one of their favourite haunts. 'It's in SoHo,' he said.

Scarlett had never been in anything remotely like Carl's loft. For one thing, he had never told her that because his room-mate, Jamie, painted birds he felt he had to live with them. Orange and green dominated his work, so the loft had a brilliant orange and sea-green toucan, two green, glossy starlings and a pair of green-crested hornbills. Because they preferred to shower, the bath-tub in the orange bathroom was never used. Instead it was filled with goldfish.

He plunged his hand into the water and brought out a bottle of white wine. 'About time we drank something besides coffee and Coca-Cola.' He grinned.

He was obviously proud of the place, of the canopied iron-framed bed hung with fabrics from Afghanistan, especially. Tumultuously colourful paintings were everywhere.

Two tall Bristol-blue wineglasses stood beside the bed on a red lacquered Chinese night-table. He made a great ceremony of uncorking the wine. Then he poured it and swirled it around his glass. 'Very fruity,' he said, imitating an English accent.

'Very fruity,' she echoed.

Which was another cause for laughter. By now they were seated on the edge of the bed. The laughter took over and ripped out of them and then flung them back on to the bed. After a while the laughing stopped and their eyes met and held, until slowly he began to undress her. She shut her eyes then and said nothing but acquiesced. He took her gently, and her body was locked in fear. When it was over she was rid of fear and ready to respond.

The second time she felt the electricity shooting between them, back and forth and from head to toe. It was as if she were made of dance and song and speed, as if she had been translated into pure poetry.

She was slim and proud of it. She was no longer a virgin and was proud of that, too. The toucan cawed, and she knew she

449

was proud to know someone like Carl, someone who could live and share his space with a painter and his birds.

She felt as if she had been through a mystical experience and when, too soon, she was in her own bedroom she stared at herself in the mirror, convinced that her changed status must be as obvious to everyone as it was to her. Like millions of young girls before her, she found it strange, indeed incomprehensible, that though she was irrevocably different the most momentous transformation of her life was invisible.

It was two months before she invited him to meet her grandmother.

'You'll love Grandmama,' she said excitedly. 'She wants you to have dinner with us on Thursday night, and she'll make you her lasagne. You've never tasted anything like it.'

'I prefer the taste of you,' he said, taking her in his arms.

How good it felt to be thin, to like her body instead of hating it. And how miraculous it was not to loathe herself. Why, she was beginning to feel less angry with her mother. While it would be too much to say that she actually liked her, she did not dislike her with anything like her previous intensity.

She had an extra class that afternoon so she could not go to his place. They arranged to meet at the Museum of Modern Art before their dinner-date. There was a Rothko retrospective they planned to see. She was wearing jeans and a hot pink silk shirt. He loved bright, primary colours and she went out of her way to please him. Since she had known him, and since she had lost all that weight, she was often pleasantly aware of the appreciative glances from men.

'I don't like the way that guy is looking at you,' Carl said in a harsh whisper.

'Who?' Scarlett lied, pretending that she had not noticed.

'Him,' Carl said, pointing at a nondescript man.

'This is a great painting, Carl. It blows my mind.' Holding his hand, she stopped in front of one of Rothko's predominantly red paintings. 'Red fascinated Rothko more than any other colour as a carrier of emotion.'

450

'Your mother has one almost exactly like it in her boardroom,' he said casually.

For a long moment she was silent. It looked as if she was lost in contemplation of the canvas. At last she said, 'I don't remember having seen it.'

'It's opposite the Jackson Pollock,' he said. 'You must have—'

The force of her anguished expression stopped him.

She removed her hand. 'So you know my mother,' she said dully. 'You were in her office?'

'Yes,' he said miserably. Realizing he had given the game away, that she now knew that their meeting had not been accidental but had been set up by her mother, he felt sick. He had never wanted her to find out about it like this. In fact, as they had got to know one another better and better, he had hoped that she would never know anything of the way in which they had got together.

'Who took you to her office?'

'Warren Masters.'

She said nothing but began moving off. He followed. Suddenly she halted.

'When did Warren take you to meet my mother?'

'About a year ago,' he replied quickly. 'But it isn't the way you think it is, Scarlett. When you got thin, and I saw how beautiful you were, I fell for you.' He sounded desperate. 'I happen to be in love with you.'

'Coming from you,' she said acidly, 'the word love sounds as dirty as you are!'

He tried to take her hand, but she jerked it back. She whirled away from him and once again he grasped her hand. 'Let me explain, Scarlett,' he said brokenly. 'I love you.'

'Don't give me any of that shit!' she exploded. This was not her kind of language and it shocked him. 'Get out of my way!' she yelled, beginning to run.

He caught up with her and grabbed her arm. 'We must talk,' he said urgently.

451

'Take your hands off me or I'll scream,' she said coldly. 'I'll scream for the police.' And she ran off.

Powered by rage, she ran all the way to her mother's office suite. When she got there she pushed past the receptionist and raced into her mother's office. It was empty. Following the sound of clinking teacups, she burst into the boardroom. 'Mother!' she yelled. 'You're a pimp!'

'Scarlett!' Gina responded, shocked. 'We're in conference.'

'That's too bad,' Scarlett said coldly. 'Fuck your conference!'

Visibly frightened, Gina said, 'If you'll excuse us.'

No one said a word. The members of the board hastily gathered their papers and quite literally fled from the room.

'I was going to take Carl to Grandmama's tonight,' she rasped. 'Your mother has been cooking for your rent-boy.'

'I don't know what you're talking about,' her mother said coldly. 'You're a slim and lovely girl now. What's got into you?'

Scarlett seethed. In a flash, everything fell into place. Her mother had chosen, bought and paid for a lover to take off her weight. Carl, her lover, a weight-reduction machine of the human kind. Her voice a rasping whisper, she said, bluffing, 'Don't lie to me, Mother. Carl told me *everything*.'

Because this was not a business deal, Gina's nerve snapped. 'I'll grant you that Carl Daley is not the most handsome man in the world,' she said, her tone dangerously calm, 'but it worked, didn't it?'

Her head spinning with hurt, Scarlett backed away from her mother as if from a woman pointing a gun at her head. 'I hate you,' she sobbed. 'I hate you!'

To her astonishment, Gina found herself sobbing too. Even as Scarlett fled, she heard her mother's strange, wrenching sobs. However, she did not even turn around, but continued her wild race to get away.

Gina was bewildered. She had always given Scarlett everything of the best. It was only because she loved her so that she had been compelled to find a Carl Daley for her. Some mothers did not give a damn what their daughters looked like. Okay, so she had taken an original – and even dangerous – approach to obesity. But it had worked, hadn't it? After all, Scarlett was her only child. Which was why she was entitled to nothing but the best and would inherit the entire Gibson–Keene empire.

In time, Scarlett would understand that she had done this for her own good and would appreciate how generous she had been. If Scarlett was beautiful now it was because her mother had helped her to become beautiful.

Chapter Sixty-Nine

Cecilia found it all so hard to bear. For so long, Scarlett had weighed too much. Now she weighed too little. She ate almost nothing. Cecilia was certain that she could not weigh more than ninety pounds, which meant that she'd lost a total of at least eighty pounds since Carl had come into her life. Apart from that, it had taken her days and days of entreaties, assurances, threats and promises to get her to believe that she had not known anything of Carl's relationship with Gina.

In the end, even though it meant taking the most cruel and painful decision of her whole life, she had been compelled to accept Scarlett's terms. Unless she had nothing to do with Gina, Scarlett would have nothing to do with her. She had heard of this form of torture, of course, but could hardly credit that it was happening to her. A mother, forced to choose between her adored daughter and her worshipped granddaughter . . . And yet, given the circumstances, did she really have a choice? The answer was far less complex than the question – her granddaughter needed and depended on her, and her daughter did not.

In any case, when she decided to move from the apartment a floor below Gina's penthouse, Gina said she would never forgive her. But she did move, first to a rented furnished apartment and from there to a pleasantly beamed Tudor-styled house in Monk's Bay. Thus it was that in May 1984, thirty years after her beloved Mike's death, she returned to the little town of Monk's Bay in which she had been so happy.

It was here, in her rustic kitchen, that she told Scarlett an edited version of the events that had led up to the trust which she still mistakenly believed had come from Vincenzo. It was because she wanted Scarlett to know, and to accept, that she was not dependent on Gina for funds that she told Scarlett about the trust. And even then it was a last-ditch, desperate measure to try to persuade Scarlett not to cancel her début, not to leave the Juilliard School and Monsieur Marceau.

But she failed. She enlisted Kate's support, but without success. Whatever ambitions Scarlett may have had vanished as her weight had vanished.

Other than Kate, they saw no one they had known in New York. Every day Cecilia thought of Miriam; she not only grieved for her, but needed her. If Miriam had been alive, Scarlett would never have given up the piano. Though very different, and much younger than Miriam, Kate's role in their lives had gradually become more and more important. She had a shrewd suspicion why Kate and Gina had fallen out. It had a lot to do with Morgan, she was sure, but there was somethng else, something more. She knew nothing of Kate's million-dollar piece of jade that Gina had thrown to the floor.

Scarlett's and Kate's friendship had not altogether surprised her. After all, Kate did not have a daughter. For that matter, Scarlett did not have much of a mother. Not that this meant that she lacked for love – far from it, she had a doting grandmother. But as a grandmother she could not be a mother. For one thing she was too old and for another she was not American-born, as Gina was. With all the will in the world, she could not replace Scarlett's mother.

Nor, of course, could Kate.

It seemed that Kate's estrangement from Gina was the basis of Scarlett's acceptance of her. Put very simply, if Kate and Gina had not been enemies, Scarlett would not have been remotely interested in her.

The weeks stretched into months, and although Scarlett had two part-time jobs she saw no people of her own age. Still, it could have been worse; Scarlett could have turned to drugs instead of away from people.

455

'It is a severe depression,' the doctor told her, 'the sort that used to be called a nervous breakdown. Go easy, don't push her. She will heal, but it will take time.'

'But how long, doctor?' Cecilia had asked anxiously. 'How long?'

'The fact that she has two part-time jobs is encouraging,' Dr Payson had replied, evading an answer.

'Two part-time jobs,' Cecilia echoed mournfully. 'Accompanying a dance teacher for the under-tens, and a physiotherapist for the over-seventies.'

In the light of all this, Kate was a welcome diversion. When Jean-Pierre told her that he was leaving her for another woman, the first person Kate confided in was Scarlett. She was honest enough to admit that she was relieved. It had never been a good marriage, but it had given her Matthew.

'Matthew is Jean-Pierre's son,' she said.

'Sure he is,' Scarlett said with a half-smile. 'He's the spitting image of his father.'

'But he is not my son,' Kate continued unexpectedly.

'Hey,' Scarlett said. 'I don't get this.'

'Matthew was conceived the day before my wedding-day,' Kate began. 'I don't know why I'm telling you all this, but I feel I want to share it with you.' She clasped and unclasped her hands and went on, 'Only four people in the whole world know about this: Jean-Pierre and I, and Claudine, Matthew's mother, and one other.'

Scarlett gasped audibly.

'Jean-Pierre dropped Claudine when he met an American heiress on the ski-slopes of Zermatt,' Kate smiled sadly. 'I was the heiress, of course.'

'Oh, Kate,' Scarlett said, reaching out towards her. She laid her hand on Kate's arm. 'How terrible.'

'It was very bad when I found out he had been making love to her the night before our wedding,' Kate said, her voice flat. 'But the irony, or the miracle – you decide which, Scarlett – was that in the end it turned out to be the most beautiful thing that ever happened to me.'

Kate's eyebrows rose. 'Why?' she asked, stroking Kate's arm.

'Good question,' Kate replied, gratified that she had broken through Scarlett's numbness. 'You see, I could never have had a child of my own. I had an abortion, it went wrong and they took out my uterus. You can't have a baby without one.' She sighed deeply. 'Anyway, I was still at Talbot at the time, and your mother helped me through it.'

'How terrible for you, Kate,' Scarlett said again.

'If I had had a girl, I would have called her Claudine,' said Kate dreamily.

'Who was the fourth, Kate?' Scarlett asked softly.

'The fourth?'

'The fourth person who knew about Matthew.'

'The fourth person was the only man I ever loved. He was intelligent, he was gentle, he was educated, he was kind and he loved me.' The words tumbled out of her mouth. 'I never got over him, and I don't even want to.'

'What happened to him?'

'He died.'

'Was it long ago? Did you know him before you were married?'

'I wish I had known him before I was married,' she said moodily. 'He died twelve years ago,' she said wistfully.

'Twelve years ago? I was about seven. That was when my father died.'

'He *was* your father!' Kate said.

'So that's why you had that photograph of him!' Scarlett sparkled. Dropping her voice, she added, 'I'm glad he had you to love him.'

'So am I,' Kate said simply.

'Did my mother know?'

'I think so. I think she knew later.'

'Did she ever tell you that she knew?'

'Not in so many words,' Kate said with a conspiratorial smile. 'Not in so many words.'

'I'm so glad you told me,' Scarlett's face burned with pleasure. 'I feel better about things.'

457

Chapter Seventy

Over the following three years, despite the fact that Scarlett never went out on a date, Cecilia suffered from the sensation that time was galloping away. She never knew how Kate had managed to persuade Scarlett that it was unnatural to expect her grandmother to choose between her daughter and granddaughter. Thanks to Kate's intervention, she and Gina were now on speaking terms. But even though Gina had humbled herself to write several letters of abject apology, Scarlett would not – could not – forgive her mother, whom she called a professional con-artist.

In October 1987, on Scarlett's twenty-second birthday, Gina sent her a long letter and an all-but-priceless jade necklace and matching bracelet. Scarlett did not read the letter, but kept the jewellery. She took it to Spore's who specialized in jade jewellery, and sold it for 135,000 dollars. She gave the money to Bluebird House, the home for the elderly where she worked. Then she sent her mother a copy of the cheque from Spore's as well as the thirty letters of thanks she had received from the Bluebird residents.

The cold spring day that Gina received the letters from Scarlett was the very day on which Cartwright Pharmaceuticals capitulated to her hostile take-over. Thinking that the thick envelope marked 'Private' would be the long-awaited acceptance letter, Gina's personal assistant, Monica Martins, handed it to her unopened. Gina tore the envelope open, saw the cheque from Spore's and one of the thank-you letters. She handed them to her secretary and wearily asked her to put everything in Scarlett's file.

Cartwright Pharmaceuticals' stock had been plunging ever

458

since it had been revealed that they had rushed their blood-pressure drug, Cartsyn, to the market-place, even though they had already received reports of liver damage among users.

Cartwright's weakness was Gina's strength. However upset she was about Scarlett's most recent insult, she set off for her meeting with the Cartwright board. She had waited for this moment for too long to delay it.

But October 20th, 1985, was not the moment of triumph she had expected it to be. If anything, it was anticlimactic. She was told that Mrs Lucia Cartwright was indisposed and that Mr Rufus Cartwright was in France. Proxies had been appointed.

When Gina returned to her office she asked not to have any calls put through to her. Then she read every single thank-you letter and replied to each one in her own handwriting. After that, she did something she had not done for years. She allowed herself to give way to a lengthy fit of weeping. Everything was meaningless. Huge companies, and no daughter to leave them to. What was it all *for*? she asked herself. What was it all for?

So she controlled Cartwrights now.

So what? She could not help knowing it was a bitter victory and an unworthy conquest. She was forced to conclude that the quest for vengeance was infinitely more rewarding than its fulfilment.

Waiting for Maxine Sawyer, the physiotherapist who used dance therapy for stroke victims, Scarlett surprised herself by playing a Chopin nocturne for the sheer pleasur of using the new piano. She soon forgot that the piano had been her mother's gift to the Bluebird Home, and went on to play parts of the Mozart piano concerto she had been meant to perform at her début. Well, all that was behind her now. The Juilliard School, Monsieur Marceau, the hours of practice and the terror of not being good enough were part of her past. Believing herself to be no more than moderately gifted, she had been in a state of permanent nervousness.

Lost in her music she was altogether unaware that she had an audience of one. As her last note ended the sound of a solitary person clapping made her look up. A young man with curly chestnut hair and sea-green eyes and a springy walk came up to her and said, 'That was beautiful. You did justice to the piano.'

'You consider this upright a good piano?'

'I know a Steinway when I hear one,' he said seriously. 'You're Maxine's pianist, aren't you? She told me your talents were being wasted.'

'She's always going on about that,' Scarlett said shyly. 'What are you doing here, if you don't mind my asking?'

'My old nanny is here, Mary Peterson—'

'Then you must be Theodore.'

'Theo.' He smiled. 'How did you know?'

'She talked a lot about you.' Scarlett shook her head sadly. 'Before her last stroke, of course.'

'You're a very good pianist—'

'I seldom play the way I did today.'

'Why is that?'

'It's a long and boring story.'

'Will you tell it to me over dinner tonight?' he asked, tugging at one of his curls.

'No.'

'Does that mean you'll have dinner with me, but you won't tell me?'

She made no answer.

'Do you live here or in the city?'

'I live right here in Monk's Bay,' she replied. 'I live with my grandmother on River Street.'

'Good. I'll come and get you and we'll go to Thurber's and eat lobster.'

'I'll meet you there,' she said softly. 'There's no need for you to come and get me.'

'Eight o'clock then—'

And suddenly he was gone.

She sat quietly at the piano, thinking about him. But she had absolutely no intention of meeting him at Thurber's.

*

460

Cecilia and Scarlett had just finished dinner when they heard the doorbell chime. They raised their eyebrows at one another because they were not expecting anyone, and Scarlett went to answer the door.

A large bouquet of white tulips hid the caller.

'Scarlett Gibson?'

She recognized the voice. 'How did you find me? You didn't even know who I was,' she demanded.

He lowered the tulips and handed them to her. 'I asked who you were.'

'Why?'

'I wanted to see you again. Do you mind if I come in?' he persisted. 'I'll wait for you to get ready and then we'll go to Thurber's.'

'I've just had dinner with my grandmother.'

'So you'll come and have coffee with me at Thurber's.'

She let him in, introduced him to Cecilia and then went to fetch her purse. It was a fine spring evening and, because Thurber's was informal, she did not change out of her jeans and white silk shirt. Although slim, she was no longer skeletal. Her hair moved and bobbed as she walked, and she looked like a teenager.

At Thurber's they talked about his work. Newly qualified, he was an intern at the Albert Einstein Hospital. He was deeply troubled; his Catholic faith led him to believe that the premature babies whose lives had been saved would go on to a short life of pure purgatory. Had he done them a service by keeping them alive, by forcing them to live? Scarlett said little but listened intently. The subject changed to her music. Though he tried to get her to tell him about it she was unforthcoming, so they talked about the new, harrowing and controversial play, *Child by Child*, which both of them had enjoyed and which was to close next week. He offered to take her to see it again and she said she would love to, and this time she meant what she said.

'You don't know my name,' he said suddenly.

'I know your Christian name, not your last name.'

'It's Cartwright.'

461

'Any connection with Cartwright Pharmaceuticals?' she asked dully.

'You could say so.' He grinned. 'If you go back to the founder, my great-grandfather, that makes four generations of Cartwrights.'

'My mother just took over your family company in a hostile take-over.'

'I heard about that.' He whistled through his teeth. 'I don't see too much of my father. Anyway, I'm not in the business – that's one of the perks of being a doctor!'

'I don't see too much of my mother, either,' she said grimly. Then, although she could barely credit what she was doing, she began to tell him the whole story about her mother and Carl Daley. On and on she went, her words rushing out, not leaving anything out until he knew all about her weight problem too. She felt easier when she had done. The tense expression left her face.

He saw her as often as his work allowed. Within two weeks she had moved into his tiny New York apartment and was commuting daily to her work in Monk's Bay. Revelling in one another's emotions and minds, they had as much in common in bed as they had out of it. Their bodies, like their minds, were tuned into one another; their overall chemistry was perfect. They belonged to one another.

'I'm not letting you go,' he said. 'I'm taking you to meet my grandfather.' Suddenly serious, he added, 'We are quite close, my grandfather and I.'

'Why is that?' she asked.

'My father was far more into being a grandson to the great patriarch, Theodore Cartwright, than a father to me.'

'You've already met my grandmother.' She giggled. 'And she and I are definitely very close. Like you and your grandfather, I guess.'

The next weekend he drove her to the country home in Connecticut that had been given to his grandfather soon after he returned from the war as a hero. It was there that Scarlett was introduced to Mark Cartwright, the man whose indirect role in her own life had been incalculable. But for Mark Cartwright, her grandmother Cecilia would never have got on that hospital ship and emigrated to America in the first place . . .

Chapter Seventy-One

From the very moment that Scarlett entered Mark's library she reminded him of someone, but who it was he could not say. He liked her at once, but though the memory of the person she resembled did not surface, it grew more and more insistent.

They were having their second glass of champagne when, in his deep and rolling voice, he said, 'You remind me of someone; Scarlett.' He smiled ruefully. 'That's the penalty for having lived in so many countries, I guess.'

They were chatting about the growing number of AIDS cases Theo had had to see, when something jogged his memory. 'Forgive my rudeness, Scarlett, but what is your mother's name?'

'Gina Gibson,' Theo said, answering for her. 'You already know our connection with Scarlett's mother—'

'Of course,' Mark said. 'I think I need to know her grandmother's name. That way I might work out who it is that she reminds me of.' He gave a low chuckle. 'I'm asking you to humour an old man, Scarlett. Perhaps I knew your grandmother.'

'I very much doubt that, Mr Cartwright,' Gina smiled. 'My grandmother was born in Italy.'

His memory was begining to grow clearer. 'She probably came to this country before the war?' he asked guardedly.

'Strangely enough she was one of those lucky ones who got out in 1944.'

Suddenly the penny dropped and everything fell into place. 'Do you by any chance know what her name was before she married?'

'Cecilia Tortelli.' Her face glowed. 'Grandmama and I are very close,' she said proudly.

'How did she come here? By plane?'

'No, by ship.'

'A hospital ship?'

'What is this, Gramps? An inquisition?' Theo joked.

'If your grandmother is the same Cecilia Tortelli I met in Rome, then she would have got here as a nurse's aide on a hospital ship—'

'Called the *Harton*,' Scarlett interrupted.

Visibly shaken, Mark leapt from his chair. 'Good God, that's amazing! Cecilia, that beautiful girl? Of course, Scarlett, you have her lovely eyes! You know, this must have been pre-ordained.'

Typical of young men of his age, Theo was uncomfortable with this kind of talk. Hoping to lighten things, he said, 'Pre-ordained or not, I plan to marry this young lady just as soon as she gives me the go-ahead.'

'You really knew Grandmama?' said Scarlett. 'Holy cow!'

'If the two of you are being serious I have the feeling that my son Rufus won't be too pleased about this,' Mark began. 'He's still apoplectic about the Gibson–Keene take-over.'

'Your son Rufus is *my* father, and nothing pleases *him*. I stopped trying years ago – '

'Same with me and my mother,' Scarlett said, her voice brittle. 'We are not on speaking terms. You see, we're – uh – estranged.'

'I'm sorry to hear that,' Mark responded. 'Is there nothing to be done?'

'It's one of those things,' she replied gravely. 'I would not want her at my wedding.' She jumped up abruptly. 'Hey, you guys,' she said, 'I think I've just had a marriage proposal.'

She moved towards him and he went towards her, and then they were enfolded in one another's arms, swaying together and rocking together, as if they were two children oblivious to the world.

There was a silence.

Unexpectedly, Mark felt hot tears pricking against his eye-

465

balls. Fran should have been here, he thought – she should have shared this intimate moment with our grandson.

'But there is no law that can compel you to tell anyone about your marriage plans,' said Kate when Scarlett came to explain her dilemma. 'Get married and then announce it.'

'We want it to be simple,' Scarlett said thoughtfully, 'but we're nowhere near setting a date.'

'After you've told everyone you're a married lady, I'll give you lunch at the Four Seasons,' Kate said airily. 'You have all the time in the world to decide, and you can ask as many or as few as you like.'

'I'm going to tell Theo your idea,' Scarlett said. 'I'm sure he'll agree—' She broke off suddenly. 'I forgot to thank you for offering to give us lunch.'

For two days and two sleepless nights from the very moment that Scarlett told her who Theo was – in other words, that he was the grandson of Marco, the man who had literally saved her life in Rome all those years ago – Cecilia was in a turmoil over both the past and the future. Painful as it was to be confronted by her past and the terrible suffering she had endured at the hands of Maruccia, her stepmother, and Vincenzo, the American soldier, the future was far more disturbing and far more uncertain.

Should she warn Gina that her daughter might be marrying the son of her hated enemy, Rufus? Scarlett had said they were thinking about marriage, but Cecilia correctly interpreted this as a fixed decision. In any case, should she tell Gina all the facts about the young man with whom her daughter was living? So far she had managed to say no more than that he was a doctor, and a very good sort of person. Gina had been delighted to learn that Scarlett had a new and appropriate lover, not least because it allowed her to hope that she might be forgiven. She might even enlist the support of the young man, persuade him to make Scarlett see reason.

466

As for the past, what to do? Cecilia thought of inviting Marco to dinner, but was uncertain whether or not she should be the one to initiate the reunion. On the other hand, if she had had no association with the man who could easily become her grand-daughter's grandfather-in-law, she would most certainly have invited him to dinner.

By the time the third morning came, she was resolute. She would invite Marco and she would serve her *spécialités de la maison*. She would either start with *melanzane alla parmigiano*, baked aubergines with parmesan, or *carciofi al tegame alla romana*, baked stuffed artichokes. For the main course – *scaloppine al marsala*, sautéed escalopes of veal. Lastly dessert, her own home-made sorbet and *crostata di ricotta*, Roman cheesecake.

And she knew what she would wear, too. A black silk dress, cinching the waist under a bloused bodice, and moulded over the hips; elegant, flattering and not excessively youthful. She had copied it from a magazine photograph of one of Chanel's creations.

Only one decision remained: should she write or call? She would ask Kate. The thought gave her a pang of anguish – of guilt, even. Once she would unhesitatingly have asked Miriam, and in asking Kate she felt somewhat disloyal.

After their dinner it was impossible for Cecilia to recollect everything that had been said. She needed time to think; in a way it had been shocking to discover that ever since 1954 she had owed her trust fund to him and not to Vincenzo. For days, all manner of things fluttered about her brain, and she learned a great deal about herself.

Although she was more than grateful to him, she wished he had not told her the details of the trust. She felt at a disadvantage; she had suddenly discovered that she and Gina had an unrepayable debt. After all, it was with that money that she had been able to fund Morgan's purchase of Keene Inc.

They had not been altogether comfortable with one another. The past had come flooding back to them. She found that, even after all this time, these forty-three years, Marco's physical presence brought long-suppressed memories back to life. She felt again the same shame she had felt then. She could scarcely wait for the evening to end; she wanted to go upstairs, take a long bath and have a long drink to make her sleep. She felt vulnerable, and her self-confidence evaporated and conversation became awkward.

For his part, Cecilia's physical presence revived Mark's sense of guilt. He, too, found that suppressed memories came to the surface. He, too, remembered shame – the shame of the confession he had made to his uncle, General Byrne.

At the same time he was aware that, but for that confession, Cecilia would never have been able to board the hospital ship for New York. In which case they would not have been dining together . . .

Both were thinking that it would have been easier if the children had joined them. Since they would now have common grandchildren, they were bound to meet from time to time. But always with other people, never à deux, where the past could rear up and strike them with remembered pain.

But the best and the worst consequence of the whole affair, of Scarlett and Gina and Rufus and Theo and Marco, was her keen understanding that she was afraid of her own daughter. Until now, she had chosen to believe she was simply being sensitive to her daughter's needs. She realized that the truth had been too frightening and too distasteful; Gina's rages were too much for her.

Chapter Seventy-Two

Early in the new year of 1988, true to her word, Kate gave Scarlett and Theo a wedding lunch at the Four Seasons. It was a particularly cold and windy January that year – icy draughts cut through the skyscrapers and the winds were so high that several people were thrown off their feet.

Two days later, Gina came storming into her mother's kitchen. She had only recently given up smoking and could barely contain herself. 'Not only does my daughter marry the son of that bastard Rufus Cartwright,' she yelled, 'and that bitch Kate Hills gives her a party at the Four Seasons, but I have to hear about it from Clarence Fowler!'

Almost spitting with rage, she paused to catch her breath.

'And you, my own mother, you knew about *my* daughter all along, *and you didn't tell me!*'

She paused to stamp her foot. 'To crown it all, you even went to the wedding lunch Kate Hlls gave!'

'Gina, *please!*' Cecilia began.

'Gina, please,' said Gina, mocking her mother. 'If my own mother can't be loyal to me, who can?' Thumping her chest in anguish she went on, 'I'll never forgive you. Never!'

So saying, she whipped around and tore out of her mother's kitchen.

Over the following weeks the flames of Gina's rage turned to smouldering ashes. Work was her therapy, and she submerged herself in it. She had by now acquired a sizeable real-estate portfolio, and her collection of American Expressionists had grown formidably. Openings at the Museum of Modern Art, the

469

Guggenheim and the Whitney seemed incomplete without her. Photographs and articles about her appeared in *Town and Country* and *Vogue* magazines, and the *New York Times*. And she still had time to give to several prestigious charities, ranging from AIDS to the New York Symphony.

But she was not yet ready to see her mother. And she very much doubted whether she would ever be ready to see her daughter. Smouldering with hatred and resentment and bitterness was – as she well knew – not without physical consequences, but she was powerless to stop herself. And when, a year after Scarlett's marriage, she was finally compelled to consult her physician about the severe abdominal pain she was suffering, she was unable to confide in either her mother or her daughter. A tumour had been diagnosed, so she revised her will and left more to charity than she had previously, but still bequeathed the bulk of her estate to Scarlett.

When she went in for surgery it was her devoted personal assistant, Monica Martins, who was at her side. But when the hospital authorities asked her to name her next of kin she said she would have to think about it. In the end, of course, she gave them Scarlett's name.

It was therefore a bitter irony that, when Gina had a serious set-back and Monica Martins was compelled to send for Scarlett, she and Theo were not in New York but on a tragic mission in Los Angeles.

After Gina's take-over of Cartwright Pharmaceuticals, Rufus decided that he would leave the business world. After all, he would only be following the example his father had set years before, when he had done the same thing. There was, however, an important difference: his father had left for a life of altruism, whereas he left for a life of hedonism. He was still only forty-five, he reasoned, and was therefore young enough to acquire new skills and new interests.

So he learned to fly aeroplanes and to hang-glide. He became an expert deep-sea diver. As a challenge, he began to accept several professional commissions.

It was while he was off the California coast, diving too deep for coral, that some freakish fault in his oxygen cylinder led to an excess of carbon dioxide and nitrogen in his blood. Borne down by his own weight and the weight of his equipment, he drifted unconscious to the bottom of the sea-bed.

Which was why Cecilia, Scarlett and Theo were not in New York when Gina needed them, but in Los Angeles. They were there to arrange for Rufus's body to be cremated. He had left instructions that he was to be cremated wherever he happened to die.

Gina felt a moment of triumph. She was alive and he was dead. And his death had set her free. At last she was liberated and ready to do her own thing.

Fortunately Gina's tumour turned out to be benign, and she and her mother and daughter reached a diplomatic reconciliation, although there was a gaping, ever-increasing void in her life. She had not expected to recover from her surgery. She had believed she would die.

Awed, perhaps even humbled by her close encounter with death, she knew that it would take her more than time to heal *all* her wounds.

Rufus's death meant nothing to her.

Her business meant nothing to her.

Meaninglessness was everywhere, threatening to devour her.

She needed a change.

She needed distance.

She needed a different kind of meaninglessness in a different kind of place.

She decided to take a year's sabbatical in London.

471

Chapter Seventy-Three

In June 1989, London was at the start of one of its hottest summers for years. From the window of her taxi, driving in from Heathrow Airport, Gina saw the haze of heat that hung shimmering over the motorway. Perspiring drivers, open-necked and visibly angry, hooted as they passed in the outside lane. The capital was in the grip of a transport strike and the roads were heavy with traffic.

The taxi took two hours to reach the Ritz, where Gina checked in for one night only. The next day she moved to a less opulent hotel, the Executive in Belgravia, because it would be from there that she would look for a furnished apartment in which to live. She wanted to live an ordinary life, like an ordinary person. She wanted to do her own household shopping, cook her own meals, buy her own stamps, drive her own car (she planned to get a modest Ford Escort). She desperately wanted to cut through the numbness and the layers of ice that prevented her getting in touch with her feelings.

There had been a time, after her humiliation at the Ripleys, when she had prayed for this numbness. Anything and everything, she had thought, would be better than the grinding, searing emotional pain of Rufus's cruel rejection. It really was a case of be careful what you pray for lest your prayers be answered. For her prayers had been answered, and when she had taken over Cartwright Pharmaceuticals Rufus had been defeated. Some said that she had annihilated him; that, after her take-over of Cartwright Pharmaceuticals, he had lost the will to live. It was even said that his drowning was not an accident, but that he had taken his own life. Gina knew of these rumours and

472

felt neither grief nor guilt. Painfully she learned that numbness was accompanied by emptiness.

So she did not make use of Gibson–Keene's London office. Instead she looked for her flat through the ordinary channels: she registered with several estate agents and went on the rounds. There was something oddly comforting about walking through the kitchens and bedrooms of people she did not know. Everywhere was evidence of the ordinary lives ordinary families lived. The accoutrements of domesticity were what she was seeking.

In the end she found a small basement flat in Chelsea, just off the busy King's Road. Part of a large family house, the basement had been converted into a self-contained unit that opened out on to a handkerchief-sized garden. However small, though, it was a real rose garden. Her next door neighbour, Margot Hunt, talked to her, and before long she found herself learning the names of the roses. Other than with Margot, a retired schoolteacher with a passion for collecting antique porcelain dolls, the only other brief conversations she had were with the local newsagent.

In New York, no one – not even Monica Martins – knew her address. In the event of an emergency, however, she could be reached through her new lawyer, Andrew Walters.

Almost as a matter of course she stopped colouring her hair. She no longer even went to the hairdresser, but cut it short and took care of it herself. Strangely, this mundane task gave her a great sense of satisfaction. Stranger still, she took real pleasure in her achievement. Slowly she was getting to know herself. She could not remember when last she had experienced a sense of pleasure in anything. It was gradually borne in on her that the sense of triumph she had sought, and frequently experienced, was not nearly as rewarding as the calm sense of pleasure she now felt.

She understood that in confusing triumph with pleasure there had been no space for peace.

*

Perhaps it was because Mark and Rufus had never been close that Mark felt his loss so acutely. Rufus had always preferred to be with his grandfather. Pointless though it was to go over the past, Mark did just that and his days and nights were filled with regrets and self-recrimination. He withdrew from everyone and only occasionally agreed to see Theo and Scarlett.

In despair, Scarlett called Cecilia.

'Grandfather is losing weight and not eating,' she said anxiously. 'He's in a deep depression and will not allow Theo to give him a check-up.'

'I only wish I could help, *tesoro mio*,' Cecilia replied, distressed. 'I tell you what, he's mad about bridge. You should fix up a game for him.'

'Do you think we haven't tried?' she replied angrily.

'It's not so long since Rufus—'

'It's four months,' she exploded. 'Four months, not four days.'

'For an old person, four months seems more like four days.'

'Listen, Grandmama, we hit on an idea, Theo and I.'

'I'm listening.'

'Remember the night he came to you for that dinner?'

'Sure I remember,' Cecilia said. Her voice rising, she added, 'He had two helpings of my *melanzane alla parmigiano*, and then he finished every scrap of his veal *scaloppine al marsala* and he still had room for my Roman cheesecake.'

'I told Theo you'd remember,' she exclaimed. 'Well, the idea is that you are going to cook that same menu and the three of us, you, Theo and me, are going to ring his doorbell and he'll open it and we'll all march in and tell him we're all having dinner together.'

'I'll cook it and you can take it—'

'No, no. You come too, or it's no deal.'

What could she do? How could she refuse to help her grandchildren? She and Scarlett had always got along, but she and Theo seemed to have a unique affinity.

'You've got yourself a deal,' she promised.

*

474

Three evenings later they put their plan into operation. When Mark answered the doorbell he had no choice but to welcome them. It was easier being with him when they were with the children, Cecilia discovered. The talk centred on an offer Theo had had to work in a paediatric unit in South Africa.

There was good food and plenty of Chianti, and inevitably the talk drifted back to the liberation of Rome. Mark found himself telling them about the way he and Cecilia had met on that golden evening fifty years earlier, when all the bells of Rome had rung out; when he and Cecilia, along with countless thousands, had gone to St Peter's to give thanks before the Vicar of Christ.

'But for a bar of chocolate, we probably never would have met again,' Mark ended.

'But you didn't date her, did you, Gramps?' Theo asked.

'Hardly,' Mark said with an awkward smile. 'I was a married man—'

Sensing his discomfort, Cecilia said: 'Your grandfather had a friend called Vincenzo – he was my date. My friend and I could hardly believe that Americans could speak Italian.'

'Did Gramps speak good Italian?' Theo asked.

'His Italian was excellent, but his friend, Vincenzo, was different. He spoke badly, with an ugly accent,' Cecilia said.

'His American was excruciating too,' Mark said drily.

'Vincenzo's American was excruciating,' Theo repeated, mimicking Mark's tone.

'You sound *exactly* like your grandfather,' Scarlett said, laughing. 'Do some more.'

Laughingly, Theo complied. Scarlett laughed with him, and Mark and Cecilia joined in, and suddenly their past was no longer as painful or as threatening as it had first been when their memories had been unearthed and revived. Looking over the heads of the young, they found themselves sharing a long and wonderfully intimate glance. The strain between them lifted. They felt easier together, and the discomfort vanished.

*

475

It was so refreshing, Gina thought, to be able to have an acquaintance like her neighbour, Margot, who made no attempt to pry into her life. She knew that it was not indifference but a kind of respect for other people that stopped Margot from asking any questions about why she was living, alone and unemployed, in a basement flat in a foreign country in a foreign city.

There was something gloriously peaceful about living in the present, of living as if she were without a past, of talking about roses and listening to Margot, who was childless, telling her about her former star students. She had lived alone in New York, of course, but life had been much too demanding and too exciting and too affluent to go in for anything like as self-indulgent as straightforward enjoyment for its own sake. It seemed now that every single social activity in which she had engaged had some sort of ulterior business motive.

Margot's life had a routine and a pattern that Gina envied. Three times a day, whatever the weather, she walked her Scots terrier, Boomer. She would walk him before breakfast, and when she came home she would sit down at the perfectly laid breakfast table she had prepared before she left. Gina knew this because the kitchen door had been slightly ajar, and she had peeped in. Margot loved the serial on Radio Four, *The Archers*, and in the voluminous correspondence she carried on with several of her former students the goings-on of *The Archers* would be discussed. Their interest in *The Archers* was so contagious that Gina found herself tuning in.

So her peaceful days passed healingly.

In October, when Margot came down with a severe attack of flu, she came in her dressing-gown to ask Gina to walk Boomer. So Gina walked Boomer and soon found herself offering not only to do Margot's shopping but also to prepare her meals. Though childless, Margot was a distinctly mothering – albeit fiercely independent – type of woman. Even so, she submitted to Gina's nursing and the mothering role was reversed. This, too, was another new experience for Gina. Except for the early months of Scarlett's life, she had not really mothered her ... She had mothered her business.

476

It was time to make some changes. She had her lawyer fly over to London to take her instructions. Wearing a hat so that she would not look too different, she met with him at the office of her new lawyer, Andrew Walters. When she told her lawyer to make over 51 per cent of all her companies to Scarlett, he was shocked and showed it. She took that in her stride, and, with none of her former arrogance, asked him to go ahead as quickly as possible.

Chapter Seventy-Four

Once again Cecilia was cooking a surprise dinner for Mark. This time it was for his seventy-second birthday. The whole thing had been Scarlett and Theo's idea. Mark's sister Betty, and her son Taylor, who was at Columbia University, and Kate and her son Matthew, who was now the successful managing director of his father's legendary company, High Season, were included.

At the last minute Theo had thought of inviting his great-grandmother Lucia, but she had declined. He had also invited his great-uncle, General Byrne, and he had accepted.

The party was being given by Cecilia in her own home, and she was overjoyed. 'Black tie,' Theo had decreed, with a chuckle. 'Black tie in the kitchen.'

Truth to tell, Cecilia's kitchen was no ordinary kitchen. In fact, it was the kitchen that had seduced Cecilia into buying the house in the first place. Oak beams, an oak refectory table, a large old gas stove and an open hearth with a roaring log fire made it especially welcoming. And of course her inspired and talented cooking meant that any meal she prepared would be a memorable experience.

Although the room was large enough to take a table for twelve, they had decided to restrict the numbers to ten so that everyone could be comfortable.

Mark had been told that Cecilia had invited Scarlett, Theo and himself to have a drink with her before setting out for La Poissonnerie, the restaurant that was reputed to have made Monk's Bay famous.

Precisely as planned, Cecilia met him at the door, took his coat and led him into the living-room. He had no sooner seated

478

himself than, pretending to be flustered, she said, 'Forgive me, Marco, but I need your help.' She wrung her hands.

'Marco, the champagne cork is stuck in the bottle in the kitchen. Can you please open it for me?'

'Of course, Cecilia,' he said, standing up at once. 'Lead the way. I'll be right behind you.'

Leading him to the kitchen she was suddenly conscious of the way her black silk dress clung to her hips. Opening the door on the darkened kitchen she said, or rather wailed, 'This is not my day! The lights have failed.'

At that moment the lights went up and all nine guests sang 'Happy Birthday'. Flabbergasted, Mark said, 'I can't believe it. I had no idea. You took me totally by surprise.'

'In the military, we say surprise is of the first importance,' the General joked.

'A lot of military planning went into organizing all this.' Mark laughed.

It may have been because there were no waiters and no chefs, and that it was in a kitchen, that the party took off at once.

Introducing Kate to Mark, Scarlett said quietly, 'I particularly wanted you to meet Kate because she has been like a mother to me.'

'Delighted,' Mark responded politely. 'Is there any news from your own mother?' he asked.

'She sent some documents over for me to sign,' replied Scarlett dismissively. 'I met with the lawyers and signed them.'

Theo and his cousin, Taylor, attended to the champagne, which seemed to flow in a never-ending stream. 'We decided against wine,' Theo told Mark. 'Nothing but champagne is good enough for my grandfather!'

Everything except the dessert had been made by Cecilia. Neither Mark nor his sister Amy had ever been to a dinner party in a kitchen before.

Cecilia, flustered and anxious about her excellent *abbachio alla cacciatora*, braised lamb; the candles flickering in their Chianti bottles, the oak benches covered with red and white checked

479

gingham; the sound of laughter and of champagne corks pop-
ping; the glow of the fire in the large hearth – all these things
combined to make the evening into an occasion that was at
once relaxed and uplifting. And, of course, the flowing Dom
Pérignon.

Just before the dessert – a large, square, iced cake with a
replica of part of the front page of the *New York Times* on the day
Mark was born – his uncle rose unsteadily to his feet.

'Before I pay tribute to our superb hostess Cecilia, her
excellent assistant Scarlett, and her superlative food,' he began,
'I should like to salute my nephew Mark. As you all know – and
if you don't, you should – Mark and I served in the United
States forces in what we all hoped was the war to end all wars.
We were together in Italy, at Anzio, and in the liberation of
Rome.'

He paused to take a long sip of champagne. 'My nephew
fought well, and was decorated for his valour.' He put his empty
glass on the table. It was instantly refilled. 'I well remember the
day he came to see me about using my authority to arrange for
a beautiful young woman to flee the ravages of war. That young
woman, still beautiful, is with us tonight.'

Raising his brimming glass, he continued, 'I did not know
then, when I gave the appropriate order, that one day my
nephew's grandson would meet and fall in love with the
granddaughter of the beautiful young woman it has been my
privilege to meet for the very first time tonight. The granddaughter of that beautiful woman, Cecilia Tortelli, is now the
granddaughter-in-law of my nephew Mark.

'May I ask you all to rise and drink a toast to Cecilia and to
Mark.'

More champagne was downed and Scarlett kissed Cecilia and
Mark. Moments later, Mark rose from his seat and then he, too,
kissed Cecilia. This kind of gesture was wholly uncharacteristic
of him, but he could not help responding to the warm and loving
atmosphere in the kitchen. Besides, he had never consumed so
much champagne in a single evening. Unlike his father, Mark
had never had a great capacity for drink, which was why when

the evening ended and everyone rose to leave, he had passed out stone cold.

'He hasn't changed,' said his uncle, the General. 'He never did have hollow legs!'

'I wouldn't like to wake him up and take him out into the cold night,' said Theo, the doctor, sounding professional. 'I think he should stay here,' he added superfluously. 'You won't mind, Cecilia, will you?'

And so they carried Mark to the living-room and laid him on the couch. Twenty minutes later everyone had left.

Cecilia fetched a blanket and a pillow and did her best to make him comfortable. Then, because she did not want to clean up in her silk dress, she went upstairs to change into her nightgown. She lay down on her bed for a moment and, though she did not plan to, fell fast asleep.

Thanks to the champagne, she slept later and longer than usual. When she awoke, she thought she was still dreaming: the smell of coffee drifted upstairs. She put on her dressing-gown and went downstairs to the kitchen. The table had been cleared and, though the kitchen could hardly be said to have been returned to its normal state of order, a great deal of cleaning and tidying seemed to have gone on.

As if there were nothing out of the ordinary, Mark said, 'I was wondering when you would wake up.'

'What time is it?'

'Eight-thirty.'

'I never sleep so late.'

'And I never sleep in the home of my hostess.' He smiled. 'What happened?'

'You passed out and they carried you to the couch.'

'I thought as much,' he said apologetically. 'I'm sorry.'

'Don't be sorry,' she heard herself saying as she took a seat at the table. 'I'm glad to have you here.' Then, almost without thinking, she added, 'It's a long, long while since I had breakfast with a man in my own kitchen.'

481

Mark handed her a cup of coffee. 'I'm glad to be here,' he said gravely. 'It's a very good feeling.' Leaning over the table, he placed his hand over hers. 'It is a wonderful feeling,' he said, his voice hoarse. 'It was a great party last night. I should feel a fool for having passed out like that last night, but I don't. Instead, I feel—' he broke off.

'What do you feel?' she asked. Then it was she who leaned closer towards him over the table. Very deliberately, and equally significantly, she placed her hand over his.

Three hands were now clasped on the kitchen table.

There was a long silence; only the humming refrigerator was audible.

Across the oak table their faces were very close to one another. It seemed an eternity before he placed his hand over hers and when at last he did, it had all the meaning and all the solemnity and all the finality of an unspoken but binding agreement.

Only a hair's breadth separated their faces.

'You know,' he said tenderly, 'you are one hell of a beautiful woman, but you forgot to take off your make-up last night.'

Her heart pounding in her ears, she said, 'I guess my mascara is all smudged.'

'It is,' he said. 'It's beautiful, though.'

Detaching her hands from his, she flung her arms about his neck and there, separated by the refectory table, their lips and their mouths and their breath and their lives were joined.

Chapter Seventy-Five

Because Margot Hunt was not altogether recovered from the flu, Gina continued to do her shopping for her. She never deviated from Margot's shopping-list and she always gave Margot the cash-register slip, and accepted exact payment for it. But one chilly Tuesday, as autumn was slipping into winter, Gina could not resist buying herself and Margot a treat. Since she had moved into her basement flat she had fallen into the habit of eating like a vegetarian – pasta and vegetables made up her diet. Passing by the small delicatessen on her way to the supermarket, she had decided to go and get some bottled Italian artichokes. There she had seen a fresh side of salmon, and had suddenly given way to an impulse to make smoked-salmon sandwiches for herself and for Margot.

Waiting for the salmon to be sliced, she decided to make Margot an old-fashioned English tea, with cucumber and cress and egg sandwiches. Now in her tiny kitchenette – about a fifth of the size of her dressing-room in New York – she set about preparing a tray of sandwiches to take to Margot as a surprise. When the sandwiches were ready she took it to Margot's flat and let herself in with the key Margot had given her.

Because Gina heard the sound of a man's voice she very nearly turned back – she had no wish to make polite conversation with yet another of Margot's students.

But Margot heard her and called out, 'I'm so glad you're here, Gina. Come in and meet my nephew, who has just returned from a Venetian holiday.' Beaming, she turned to Gina. 'I say,' she said enthusiastically, 'doesn't a Venetian holiday sound grand?'

The flat consisted of a bedroom, a living-room, a kitchenette and a bathroom. The layout of these rooms was such that there was no way Gina could cross to the kitchenette and deposit her tray without first passing through the living-room. So she carried the tray in and laid it on the large oak coffee-table, constructed from an old church door that Margot had found.

'Oh my goodness,' she cried. 'You've brought in an English tea. And neither you nor I knew that my nephew would have decided to bring his old aunt a Venetian glass vase for her roses. Gina, meet Hugh Jenkins. Hugh, this is Gina.' Almost groaning with delight she added, 'How can I thank you, Gina?'

'By tucking into her sandwiches, I should say,' said Hugh. He had, of course, risen as soon as she entered the room. Now he went towards her and stretched out his hand. 'You must be Mrs Gibson. Aunt Margot has told me so much about you. Allow me to thank you for having been so helpful.'

'Gina has been mothering me,' Margot said.

'Now let's not exaggerate,' Gina said with a dry laugh. 'I barely mothered my own daughter,' she mumbled.

'What was that, dear?' Margot asked.

'Nothing, really,' Gina said politely. Turning to Hugh she said: 'Your aunt has often spoken about you and the work you do. You're just putting the final touches to a chapter you're doing for a book on multi-modal therapy.' She laughed. 'See what a proud aunt you have?'

'I do indeed,' replied Hugh. 'I am spoilt, you know.'

'I never had an aunt,' Gina said reflectively. 'I often wondered what it would have been like to have had an aunt.' Suddenly the memory of Tina, the mountainous aunt she had seen just the once, came flooding into her mind. 'I guess I—' she began. She seemed to think better of what she was about to say and rapidly changed the subject. 'Shall I put the kettle on?' she asked.

'Sit down and put your feet up,' Hugh said. 'I'll do it.'

Over tea he told them about Venice, about the famous Bridge of Sighs, which was formerly used by political prisoners on their way from the Ducal Palace to the austere building in which they were housed. The talk drifted to the bargain package tour he

484

had been on, and when he mentioned something about the rich philistines who saw nothing but the Cipriani Hotel she could only give an inner smile and whole-heartedly agree with his comment.

'I'm told you're becoming quite an authority on roses, Mrs Gibson.'

His voice was soft and musical; she had been in London long enough now to detect a public-school accent.

She liked him well enough to say, 'Please call me Gina.'

'Do you like the theatre? I suppose you chose Chelsea because of the Royal Court?'

'I think so,' she said. Why had she chosen Chelsea? She had never known why. Perhaps it was because of the vibes – part suburban and part city – and very peaceful, while at the same time only a few yards from the hub and the throb of the King's Road.

'A new play will be opening in a couple of weeks' time,' he said. 'If you two would like to accompany me, I'd be delighted to be your escort.'

'I don't think I should venture out at night just yet. A Saturday afternoon matinée, perhaps?' his aunt replied.

'I'll be working most Saturdays for the rest of the year,' he said. 'Perhaps you would like to come to the theatre with me, Gina?'

'I'd love to,' she said.

'Excellent!' he said in his musical voice. 'I'll get tickets for next Wednesday, then.'

Dressing for the theatre, Gina smiled at her very different self. Her hair had grown out and was no longer blonde. Untouched by hairdressers, it had turned out to be darker and frizzier than she had remembered. Considering that she had not managed her own hair for twenty-five years or so, she reckoned she was not doing too badly. She had been cutting it herself, and now wore it in a light bob. She wore very little make-up – mascara, but no lipstick whatsoever. Perplexed, she stared in wonderment

485

at her reflection in her tent-like Laura Ashley electric-blue velvet dress with its demure white lace collar and cuffs.

Was this – could this possibly be – Gina O'Connor Gibson? Or was it Gina Rizzoli O'Connor Gibson?

Although she wore no disguise at all, she doubted whether anyone in her world would recognize her. Perhaps even her own mother would pass her by. She turned on the tap, moistened a small wad of cotton and removed the mascara from her eyelashes. She wanted nothing contrived, unnatural or artificial about her appearance. Her disguise was her undisguise.

Was this new image with the softer voice merely a borrowed imitation or her real persona? She could not say. However, whatever else it was, it was peaceful and she was not unhappy with it. Still distant from her source, she had at least come to hope that she might yet connect with who she was.

Ironically enough, the play was called *American Bagpipes* and in some ways contrasted disturbingly with her voluntary exile. The scenario was of a grown-up, hate-filled son returning home to Scotland after a ten-year stint in America, seven of which were spent in prison. During those seven years he had written a book entitled *Family Atrocities* which, understandably enough, made her even more reticent to speak of her own family.

After the play Hugh took her to Oriel, the busy restaurant in Sloane Square.

They ordered spaghetti bolognese and a salad and a bottle of Chianti and settled back to talk.

After agreeing that it had been an excellent play, brilliantly directed, with talented actors, she carefully changed the subject. 'This is the first time I've been to a restaurant since I left the States,' she said, thinking aloud.

'Then I am doubly honoured to have you with me,' he said swiftly. 'How long have you been here?'

'About four and a half months,' she replied. 'Your aunt is very proud of having a clinical psychologist for a nephew.' She gave a thoughtful sigh and added, 'It must be very taxing work, trying to sort out other people's emotional problems and tragedies.'

486

'It is that,' he said.

She noticed a slight scar on his chin and wondered how it could have happened. She liked his looks, his too-long greying hair, his firm, unflinching gaze. Why, she even found his stooped posture attractive. But she loved his voice, loved the tenderness and the music in it.

'You work at a wonderful hospital, your aunt tells me. She told me that she could never have been to a better place when she had her cardiac surgery.'

'They took very good care of her,' he said soberly. 'St George's has one of the foremost cardiac surgery units in the world.' He broke a piece of bread in half and began to nibble at it. 'What are you doing in London?' he asked casually.

'Me?' she responded, at a loss for a reply. For a moment she silently flirted with the temptation to say: '*I do nothing. But I do live for the moment, and that takes a lot of doing.* Giving way to temptation, she said: 'I do nothing. But I do live for the moment, and – let me tell you – that takes a lot of doing.'

'I see,' he said. 'You are convalescing.'

'I *am* convalescing.'

'Convalescence leads to recovery.'

'I hope so.' She sighed. 'Tell me about you.'

'What sort of thing would you like to know?'

'Oh, whether you are married, have children – that sort of thing.'

'I was married,' he said slowly. 'I married when I was thirty, shortly after I got my doctorate. I married one of the loveliest women in the kingdom. She was called Davinia and she was barely twenty-one when we married and barely thirty-one when she died.' He fiddled with his ear. 'She died five years ago, when I was forty. She was expecting our son, but he went with her.'

'Your son?'

'She had a scan. We knew it was a boy.'

'So you were born during the war; in 1945, right?' she said. 'So was I.'

'I thought women didn't like to discuss their age.'

'Yes,' she said. 'I thought so too.'

487

'Were you born in America?'

'Yes. Why?'

'You're not a typical American.'

'I don't know what a typical American is,' she replied. 'But my mother was born in Italy. She only came to America the year before I was born.'

'That must have been unusual, travelling like that during the war.'

'It was,' she agreed.

So she told him what she knew of her mother's life in Italy, and he told her about his mother, a stern woman who had been a lawyer, and suddenly it was past midnight and he took her home in his ageing Volkswagen.

The whole evening had been an entirely new experience for her new self. 'Which is the real me?' she wondered. 'The blonde or the brunette?'

Over the following four weeks all three saw each other several times. Gina loved being with them, loved being with the sort of people she would never have met in her previous incarnation. When Christmas came it seemed only natural that the three of them would spend it together. It was decided to have Christmas lunch in Hugh's tiny mews house in Chelsea Square. Brian Hitchman, one of Margot's former students, and Polly Cunningham, one of his former patients, were to join them.

Again Gina found this a strangely new and infinitely uplifting experience. And again she was at a loss to know why. But stranger still was the fact that she did not miss either her daughter or her mother.

Nor did she miss her business.

Why?

Perhaps Hugh could explain.

She considered asking him – he was, after all, a psychologist. But even if he had not been a psychologist, she would have been reluctant to expose herself to him.

A saintly, unmaterialistic sort of man, the reality of who and what she was would – she was sure – both alienate and isolate him from her.

The following day, Boxing Day, Polly Cunningham took Margot to the country to have lunch and to spend a few days with her father and stepmother. Christmas lunch was reserved for her stepmother's children. Watching them leave, Gina felt not so much lonely as empty. There's no need to brood, she told herself. She would return to the beautifully bound volume of *Wuthering Heights* Margot had given her for Christmas. She would lose herself in the world of Cathy and Heathcliff. She had, of course, read *Wuthering Heights* before, when she was at Radcliffe. Flicking the pages quickly, she came upon the phrase that had so moved her all those years ago, to the force of Heathcliff's: '*How would you like to live with your soul in the grave?*'

Was her soul in the grave, too? she wondered.

Feeling suddenly sleepy, she took the book to her bedroom and was about to change back into her Marks & Spencer cotton pyjamas when the door-knocker sounded. Still holding the book, she went to the door to find Hugh brandishing a bunch of carnations.

'It was all I could get,' he said apologetically. 'I wanted roses or tulips.'

'Thank you. These are beautiful.' She smiled. They were still standing at the doorway. 'Would you like to come in?'

'I was hoping you'd say that,' he answered, unbuttoning his heavy overcoat.

'A drink?' she asked.

'Gin and tonic, please,' he said. 'I've come to take you out to lunch.'

'Wouldn't you rather have a good, old-fashioned American brunch?' she asked. 'I've got no grits, but I've got bacon and eggs and mushrooms and sausages.'

'Sounds more like a good old-fashioned English breakfast to me,' he laughed. 'And yes, I'd love to have a scrumptious English breakfast at noon.'

Rising to help her, he saw her book. 'Ah, *Wuthering Heights*. I see you're pleased with Margot's gift.'

When everything was ready and the inviting smell of bacon filled the tiny flat, and the Albinoni tape was playing, they sat down to eat at her coffee-table. Looking around the room as he tucked into his food, he said, 'It's a pleasant enough room, but there's nothing of you here, is there?'

'It's furnished accommodation,' she said defensively. 'But you're right, there is nothing of me.'

'You're a very mysterious woman,' he said. 'And a very lovely one.'

'Thank you,' she said.

'Whenever you're ready to talk, I'm here.'

'Thank you, I know that,' she said softly. 'Believe me, I am grateful.'

'How is the convalescence going?'

'It is no worse,' she said.

The Albinoni came to an end and she hastily switched the tape to Beethoven's Emperor.

He rose to help carry the plates to the kitchenette.

'I always leave the dishes to soak,' she explained. 'There's no room for a dishwasher, you see.'

'So I see,' he said. As he took the dishes from her hands, he brushed against her. She was aware of his body touching hers but thought it might have been an accident. But when both their hands were free of dishes, he put his hands about her waist.

'You've a slim waist,' he said, looking deep into her eyes.

She lowered her eyes but otherwise made no attempt to remove his hands. Slowly he moved his hands from her waist, letting his fingertips travel teasingly slowly over her breasts up to her neck and around her chin until they reached her lips. She felt a ringing in her ears, and she smiled inwardly. She had thought Hugh unworldly, and yet she had never experienced anything as sophisticated – or as skilled – as the pass he was making.

Still they stood together in the kitchenette. She felt her whole

490

body quiver with longing. Now the edge of his fingernails lazily traced the outline of her lips.

Suddenly her need became an insistent frenzy. 'Let's go to bed,' she said. 'Please, let's go to bed.'

'I wanted you to be the one to ask,' he said.

Chapter Seventy-Six

So far all the changes in Gina's appearance, life-style and attitudes since she had been in London had been wrought by herself. Now, under Hugh's excellent and extravagantly gentle tutelage, she felt herself utterly transformed. His values, his standards and his expectations were everything she had not known she wanted. She had thought that people like Hugh were losers. The fact that he neither coveted riches nor considered material wealth to be of any relevance to his own life was extraordinary to her. It was also fiercely comforting.

By now she and Hugh had been together for three months. They saw each other every day and every night; sometimes she stayed with him in his mews house and sometimes he stayed with her in her basement flat. Just as long as they were together, it made no difference to her where they lived.

In the New Year, only a week after he had first made love to her, she began training as a volunteer for a hot line for FAMFRI, the organization that had been established to help and inform the family and friends of drug addicts. She enrolled for the one-afternoon-a-week, ten-week course, and became one of a group of eight other would-be telephone counsellors. She could not but apply what she had learned to her own life. For example, she learned that choosing not to die is not the same as choosing to live. Had she come to London because she had wanted neither to live nor to die? A sort of hibernation that might or might not result in a rebirth? She had not expected to meet the likes of Dr Hugh Jenkins.

So far she had disclosed very few details of her own life to him. He knew that she was widowed. He also knew that she was the mother of a grown-up daughter who had an exceptionally

492

close relationship with her maternal grandmother. But she had never told him that she was one of the empresses of the cosmetics industry and he knew nothing of her international reputation as a woman whose genius at merchandising had made her a legend in her own lifetime. She had told him that she had had a high-powered job in New York which had paid her enough to take a sabbatical for a year.

However, although she felt safe enough with herself to spend the whole night with him, she did not tell him any of the particulars of Morgan's death. She told him that she had had a falling-out with both her mother and her daughter. She openly said that because she had been the victim of a terrible betrayal as a young girl, a long and cruel vendetta had resulted. Later, her best friend, Kate, had betrayed her with her own husband, Morgan. That, too, had resulted in a bitter and unresolved feud.

Meanwhile, she found her volunteer counselling work at FAMFRI more and more rewarding. She now manned the phone every day from 10 a.m. to 6 p.m. She had been well taught about cocaine and heroin, the hard drugs. She was no longer shocked when she heard herself explain to distraught parents, the husbands, the wives and the children of addicts, that some forms of cocaine were so soluble that they could be drunk, injected, snorted or smoked. Calmly she would go on to inform them that cocaine can be so soluble that it can be introduced into the body through any mucous membrane: the eyelids, the mouth, the gums, the anus and the vagina.

In almost no time at all, callers specifically asked for Gina. She had rapidly acquired the reputation of being the most competent of the counsellors. When additional funds were needed for advertising the services of FAMFRI, she told every-one that she would write to the American company for whom she had 'worked'. Within ten days FAMFRI had received a grant substantial enough to include a much-needed repainting of their dingy offices.

*

On a Thursday afternoon in March, after a particularly taxing day at FAMFRI, she returned home to her basement flat to find an anxious Andrew Walters, her London lawyer, waiting among the garbage cans. When she saw that he was holding a letter, she felt a jolt of real fear.

'What's happened?' she said, her voice high with fright.

'It's good news, I'm told,' the lawyer said confidently. 'But I've had several faxes asking me to deliver this into your own hands.'

'Thank you,' she said, taking the letter. 'I am relieved.'

The lawyer left at once and she rushed in and opened the letter.

Gina, *mia cara* [she read]

I have to hope that this letter will not go unanswered.

I do not reproach you for your nine-month-long silence. I do not reproach you for keeping your whereabouts secret from everyone. As your mother, I respect your need for solitude. As your mother, I respect your need for silence. From the very beginning, I understood your ambition for power. I now understand your ambition for peace.

Come home to my wedding. In four weeks' time I am to be married in St Patrick's Cathedral.

I am going to marry the American major who gave me chocolate forty-five years ago when Rome was liberated.

How different our lives might have been if I had known that surname at that time! How much endless suffering you, *mia cara*, would have been saved!

But regrets for what cannot be changed are as useless as they are painful.

The surname of the man who saved me was Cartwright. The Marco I always told you about was none other than Mark Cartwright, the grandson of the founder of Cartwright Pharmaceuticals.

Remember your surprise when I was able to help you and Morgan raise the funds to take over Keene Inc? My darling Mike's insurance policy was not remotely as much

494

as I encouraged you to think it was. I had a small trust. I
was never told who the donor was. I thought it was the
American officer who had brutalized me in Rome. But I
was wrong – the trust had been set up by Marco . . . More
on this when I see you again.

I say again, in all the world you have only two blood
relations. Come home, *tesoro mio*, come home.

But whether you come home or not, I shall love you till
I die.

Mama

Chapter Seventy-Seven

Gina's head spun. Though short, her mother's letter was too much for her to absorb at once. For all the emotional distance between herself and her family the news of her mother's remarriage would have been enough to jolt her out of her comfortable present. As it was, however, the shock was further aggravated by the fact that her mother was to marry Rufus's father . . .

Half furious, half despairing, she made no attempt to put the letter out of her mind but decided to go ahead with the evening's plans. She and Hugh were to dine with one of his former patients, Trevor Lockridge, an accountant who had only recently overcome the disabling condition of agoraphobia, the fear of crowds that had prevented him from leaving his home. Tonight was by way of celebrating his huge achievement; he had braved the supermarket to shop for their meal.

It was when she took her green paisley Laura Ashley dress from its hanger that she realized she was not yet ready to return either to New York or to her family. She liked her uniform of sweaters, skirts and jeans, and the occasional dress, like the one she was wearing tonight, and did not relish the thought of returning to the world of *haute couture* and its accompanying competition. She was comfortable. She was content with her new life where – unlike her former life – the challenge was to help rather than to defeat. Now, here in London, working with her colleagues on the hot line, the whole challenge was in co-operating rather than in competing.

Over dinner that evening in Trevor Lockridge's surgically neat, mirrored dining-room, watching Trevor's grateful eyes follow Hugh's every movement, she experienced pride of a kind that was entirely new to her. Once again, she could not help comparing this calm, gentle sort of pride with the ferocious, exciting kind of pride she had known in New York. Scrupulously fair, she recognized that if she had been in the business world of London it would probably have been the same.

She longed to tell Hugh about her mother's letter, but needed time to decide what she would do.

Sleepless all through that night and the following two nights, she wondered how Hugh, a socialist whose father had been a staunch card-carrying Communist, would react to knowing what she had been. Since notions such as wealth or success or power were not a part of his vocabulary, she had no way of knowing how he felt about tycoons. She had been known for her magical aura of perfumed power – an empress who had built up an empire. How would he feel about that? Would he see her as a fraud, who had given it all up on a whim? Or would he understand that her close encounter with death had stripped her values down to the raw bones of survival?

Well, she had survived, and in surviving she had learned humanity.

And how would her mother and Scarlett and everyone in her previous world respond to the person she had grown into? Would they look upon her new and naked persona at worst as an aberration and at best as a temporary, phoney eccentricity? Did it matter what they thought? Perhaps the strangest thing of all was that she was entirely at peace with the naked face with which she had been born.

Once or twice she had used a pale pink lipstick.

'You are too beautiful for artifice,' Hugh had said in his lilting voice. 'A classic Roman beauty like you has no need of make-up.'

Perhaps it was just a phase. Even so, it was gloriously simple to wash her own hair, towel it dry and then run a comb through it. Instead of being distressed by the streaks of grey that had become more numerous, she found them curiously distinctive. Sometimes, staring at her new self in the mirror, she thought she resembled her old headmistress at Talbot Hall, Miss

497

Armstrong. She would smile then, and the three dimples would dance, and though she had not forgiven her father (and probably never would) she no longer resented his dimples.

On the fourth night she told Hugh that she had had a letter from her mother telling her about her plan to remarry.

'Are you going to the wedding?' he asked. 'Silly question,' he added with a chuckle. 'Of course you're going to your mother's wedding.'

'Of course,' she replied, realizing that she had actually decided that she would go as soon as she had read the letter. 'Of course I'm going.' She hesitated and then said, 'Only—'

'Only what?'

'I can't bear the thought of leaving you.'

'Nineteen days is a very long time, I agree.'

'Nineteen days?' she repeated, mystified.

'The nineteen-day excursion, of course,' he said. 'The company you worked for used to pay for your air tickets, so you don't know that a nineteen-day excursion costs little more than half an ordinary ticket.'

'You're right,' she said. 'I didn't.'

'When is the wedding?'

'In about three weeks. April 20th.'

'Good. We've got time, then,' he said, hugging her. He kissed her ears with those beginning kisses of his which drove her mad. 'Don't think about the trip for twenty-four hours,' he said. 'I have some leave due me, and Cunningham and I have a deal about our leave, anyway.'

'A deal about leave?' she asked, her business instincts rising automatically to the fore.

'We swap sometimes,' he said. 'Let's make love and forget about everything else.'

Making love to him, all her worlds receded and she and he became one wildly whirling world of their own.

Gina used to joke that she knew many males but very few men. Hugh, however, was sensitive and kind and intelligent and the most masculine man she had ever known. His power was a quiet power and it came from within and owed nothing to the usual trappings of success. So that when he presented her with two return tickets to New York, which included a stay at the Holiday Inn Hotel, it was far more meaningful and far more precious than any of the most extravagant gifts she had ever received.

'Cunningham agreed, you see,' he said.

'Cunningham?' she echoed faintly.

'Dr Cunningham,' he reminded her gently. 'The chap who swaps leave with me.'

'I'd forgotten.'

'It's a ten-day round-trip ticket. It's a special promotion deal from my travel agent,' he said proudly.

'I don't know what to say,' she said, meaning it. Shouldn't she tell him who she was right now, this very minute? But she lacked the courage. She, who could take on the fiercest competition, she who had even taken on Wall Street, lacked the courage to tell the truth about herself to a man on the sort of salary a garage mechanic would get! It was not that she was ashamed of who she was; she did not want to tell him the truth because she was afraid it would distance her from him.

'Write and ask your mother if you can bring a friend to her wedding,' he teased. 'Do you know the man she is marrying?'

'I met him once,' she sighed, 'but only very briefly.'

'And it was not a happy meeting?'

'No, it was not,' she replied. 'How did you guess?'

'You sighed.' He stroked her cheek. 'You sighed very deeply. Is he not a good person?'

'From what my mother tells me in her letter, he must be an exceptionally good man.' Go on, an inner voice screamed. Take your chance. Tell him now! But she held silence.

Realizing, later next day, that she had not yet acknowledged her mother's letter, she hastily sent off a telegram:

CONGRATULATIONS MAMA STOP WILL BE IN NEW YORK
IN TIME FOR YOUR WEDDING STOP LOTS OF
LOVE   GINA

That done, she knew in a flash what she would do.

She would fly with him to New York.

She would make some excuse about her mother not wanting any strangers at her wedding . . . He need never know who she had been.

Too soon they were on a flight to New York. They both wore jeans, sparkling white Adidas shoes and matching windbreakers. He stacked her hand luggage and fastened her seat-belt for her. Then he went to the back of the plane to fetch some American magazines. She had never known the luxury of being looked after like this . . .

'I always pick up a few magazines before the plane takes off,' he said with his shy smile when he gave them to her.

She smiled up at him, and took the magazines. She had never flown economy class in her life, and when you travelled first class there was no shortage of magazines . . . And yet now, squeezed as she was into a narrow seat, she realized she had never felt more cosseted in her life. At the same time she knew that she was cherished for herself, and not for her achievements. Once they were safely back in London, she promised herself, she would tell him all about Gina Gibson Inc. And then the ball would be in his court . . .

As the plane took off he held her hand tightly, and she his. They shared things, she thought, nestling her head against his shoulder. Moments later, she was asleep. Two hours later, when he awoke, she discovered that the meal had been served, but that he had skipped his dinner so as not to disturb her. How privileged she was to be loved by such a man!

'There's no need to go hungry,' he said, pulling his case out from under the seat. 'I brought bread and cheese and a bottle of red wine for just such an eventuality!'

Not much longer after they had polished off their bread and cheese and drunk all the wine, he fell asleep.

Half reluctantly and half fearfully, she picked up a copy of *Town and Home*, a magazine she had not seen since she had been in London. There was a time when she had gone out of her way to be interviewed by *Town and Home* because it reached the 'right' sort of people. Idly turning the pages, she skimmed articles on movie stars, recent brides and recent books, until she came upon a full-page photograph of herself. Trembling, she turned the pages back to see what the article was about. *Great Parties of the Eighties*, she read. *Spain Comes to Gina Gibson's Glorious Park Avenue Apartment* . . . She could not bring herself to read further. That was the time she had flown in an entire orchestra from Madrid. As if they had a will of their own, her eyes returned to the page. *Mrs Gibson is wearing her ruby and diamond necklace that once belonged to the Russian Princess Eugénie*, she read.

But the full-page photograph was in black and white, and there was no caption to it. Taken by the illustrious photographer, Loewe, that photograph in stark black and white had cost 25,000 dollars. She studied the image of herself, of a timeless classic golden beauty, as if she were studying the image of someone she knew, a dear friend of whom she had demanded too much, and therefore had not seen for many months.

Yet there she was, on the page, standing tall in her long, flowing velvet gown, its jet black in perfect contrast to her blonde chignon, gazing unashamedly into the camera, her closed lips curved in a secretive smile so slight that her dimples did not come into play.

That it was the only black-and-white photograph in the whole magazine made it all the more dramatic. Remembering now how she had stamped her foot and fought for that black-and-white photograph, she could only shake her head in wonder. Why, she was light years away from the creature in that magazine.

Just then Hugh awoke, stretched himself and smiled tenderly at her.

Impulsively, she took her life in her own hands, tore the photograph out of the magazine and handed it to him.

'What do you think of her?' she asked casually.

He glanced at the photograph. 'Not my type,' he said, handing it back to her.

'Take a serious look at it.'

501

'I already have.' He grinned. 'Too glamorous for me.'

'You don't like glamour?'

'No.'

'Why not?'

'It's too synthetic for my taste. The exterior is everything, usually because there's nothing inside.'

'You're generalizing.'

'I know I am,' he said, kissing the tip of her nose. 'With an authentic beauty like you, I can afford to generalize.'

'Thank you.' Then, her heart pounding in her ears, she said, 'That is me.' Thrusting the photograph back to him, she went on, 'Well, it used to be, I guess.' In response to his quizzical look she pointed to the headline: *Spain Comes to Gina Gibson's Park Avenue Apartment for One Night.* 'See?' her voice shook. 'That's me. Gina Gibson.'

And then, the words tumbling from her mouth, she told him everything. She told him how tough it had been to be the daughter of a seamstress at a school like Talbot Hall; she told him about her terrible meeting with her real father; she told him about Rufus and the planted brooch. In short, she told him almost everything, including having paid for a man to pretend he'd fallen in love with Scarlett.

'I was right not to tell you earlier,' she sobbed. 'I knew you didn't like the synthetic type! You wouldn't have as much as looked at me.'

'That never was the real you,' he said easily. 'I'm in love with the real you, remember?'

Weeping against his shoulder, she was unable to speak.

'You're afraid your family will see the real you as an affectation,' he said, slipping unconsciously into his professionally reassuring voice.

Still weeping, she nodded.

'You believe they will not credit you with having had a genuine change of heart.'

She nodded again. His shirt was soaked.

'Will you let me handle them for you?' he asked quietly. 'Can you trust me enough to let me do that for you?'

502

She stopped crying. 'Yes!' she said clearly. Then she fell into yet another fit of weeping.

He smoothed her hair and she began to feel safer.

After a long while, she said, 'But you must tell them that you found me like I am now, without make-up and all that stuff.'

'Of course I'll do that,' he said staunchly. 'They have to know that you had come to your moment of truth for yourself. It's not as uncommon as you might think, my darling.' He half smiled and half sighed. 'Several of my patients have found that there is nothing like death, or a close encounter with death, to transform their existing value-system. You've been through your own private revolution,' he continued. 'And revolution without pain is no revolution.'

'Some revolution,' she murmured.

'New York is your town, I know,' he said, smoothing her hair again. 'But for the next few days, if you agree, I'm going to take care of you.'

With the tears still wet on her cheeks and her defences in ruins about her, she looked deep into his eyes and knew that she had reached the point of no return. Her life was no longer under her own control.

Chapter Seventy-Eight

Dazed, Gina was in a yellow cab speeding through the fading dawn light to a New York Holiday Inn on the corner of Broadway and 49th Street. After her long bout of crying, and having let go all her defences, she was understandably exhausted. With her head safe on Hugh's shoulder, she slept all the way to their hotel. Dimly feeling that she had earned the right to be passive, to be taken care of, she submitted to being firmly tucked into bed at breakfast-time.

Satisfied that she was sound asleep, Hugh went down to the lobby to make a phone call. He knew only that Gina's mother's name was Cecilia O'Connor and that she lived in Monk's Bay, but that was enough for Information to find her number. Moments later, Cecilia answered her telephone.

'Mrs O'Connor?' he asked.

'Yes? Who is this?'

'You don't know me,' he said swiftly, 'but I bring you greetings from Gina.'

'Is anything wrong? I hope—'

'Gina is wonderfully well, Mrs O'Connor,' he said, reassuringly. 'I've just flown in with her from London.'

'Gina's in *New York*! And she hasn't—'

'She hasn't called you because she's only just arrived,' he said placatingly. 'Let me explain myself.'

'I certainly wish you would explain yourself!' Cecilia protested. 'Who are you?'

'My name is Dr Hugh Jenkins, I'm a psychologist, and I'm a friend of your daughter's. She told me she wanted to attend your wedding, so I managed to get a package deal—'

'You got a *package deal* for *Gina*!' Cecilia exploded.

'I got a package deal because I had no idea who Gina was. She has been living very modestly in London, you know.'

'I didn't know that. We have not been in close contact for a while.'

'Gina told me about that,' he said earnestly. 'It might seem strange to you, but I only found out who she was a few hours ago. She showed me her photograph in a magazine called *Town and Home*. We had found a copy in the plane. I didn't even recognize her in the photograph!' he said, with a low chuckle of bemusement. 'She's much more beautiful now that she's not a blonde.'

'Where are you speaking from, Dr Jenkins?'

'The Holiday Inn on Broadway and 49th Street.'

'I'm on my way.'

'Wait one minute. There is something I have to tell you.'

'Go ahead, I'm listening.'

'Gina had changed her life-style *before* she met me. She's now an excellent counsellor on a voluntary hotline for the families of drug addicts.'

'Gina! A *counsellor*?'

'Gina is happier than she's ever been,' he said firmly. 'I phoned you so that I could give you some small warning of the change that has come over her—'

'Gina's happy?' Cecilia said doubtfully.

'Yes,' Hugh said resolutely. 'Gina is happy.' He paused for a moment to recover his composure. 'But she wears no make-up, her hair is a little grey in places, she is not one of your social X-rays, but her natural loveliness makes her an exceptionally beautiful woman.'

'I'll be with you in an hour or so,' she spluttered.

'She should be awake by then.'

'Thank you, Doctor. Thank you.' The phone clicked off.

Almost the next second, Cecilia had Scarlett on the line. 'Your mother's here,' she bubbled. 'Gina's here in New York.'

'*What?*'

505

Quickly Cecilia explained all that she knew, and finally concluded, 'I'll pick you up in fifteen minutes, okay?'

They arrived at the Holiday Inn five minutes short of one hour after Hugh's phone call. Because he knew it would be easy enough to recognize them, he was waiting in the foyer to welcome them. He watched them approach the concierge and ask for him, and then he introduced himself. Both Cecilia and Scarlett hugged him, and there was laughter and tears, and he took them to see Gina.

Then he left them to be reunited in private. He waited in the coffee-shop and tried to imagine their reunion.

Upstairs, in room 515, as the three women hugged one another, the laughter and the tears continued. It was a long while before any of them could speak. At last, Cecilia said, 'So my middle-aged daughter turned into a teenage rebel!'

'You look beauiful, Mama,' Scarlett said, her voice low.

More laughter, more tears.

'I'm glad I stayed alive,' said Gina soberly. 'There was a time when I didn't want to—'

'Tell us,' they begged. 'Tell us what happened to you.'

So, lying on the bed between her mother and her daughter, and while her mother stroked her burgeoning grey hairs, she told them.

When she had done, her mother said: 'He seems a wonderful man.'

'But I had changed before I even met him!'

'I know, *tesoro mio*,' her mother said. 'He told me.'

'You'll never believe this, Mama,' Scarlett said simply, 'but I've been going in to Gibson–Keene.'

'Scarlett overheard your marketing director, Ed Johnson, talking about Gibson–Keene chartering a plane to have a weekend in Hawaii,' Cecilia put in proudly.

'Ed Johnson? I never would have believed it.'

'Ed admitted it, and we had to let him go,' Scarlett said

506

sternly. 'I'm kind of an assistant to your assistant.' Looking directly into her mother's eyes she added nervously, 'I hope you don't mind.'

'That's great news,' Gina replied. 'You couldn't have a better teacher than Monica Martins.' Then, with a crooked smile, she added, 'But I can understand why you would be nervous about telling me.' She looked away, and then, taking an obviously firm grip on herself, continued, 'But you will find me greatly changed. It hasn't been easy, you know. But then, as Hugh says, a revolution without pain is no revolution.'

Moving to more comfortable matters, Scarlett broke in, 'You should see what Grandmama is wearing to her wedding,' she said. 'She made it herself, wouldn't you know.'

'I bet she's used lace,' Gina grinned.

'Gina knows her mama, huh?' crooned Cecilia. 'It's a frivolous little pink jacket, crisp with white ribbon lace, flaring over a tiny peau-de-soie skirt.' She giggled. 'Well, that's exactly what the magazine said.'

'You'll be going to your office, of course?' Scarlett asked.

'Not this time,' Gina said gently. 'Next time, perhaps.'

'It's a good thing Gibson–Keene is privately owned,' Scarlett said sharply. 'Think what would happen to the stock if it were known that you were in New York and didn't even pay a visit to your office!'

'Perhaps that is why I have always gone to such lengths to keep it in our own hands,' mused Gina. 'Who knows?' Then, turning towards Scarlett, she said, 'Perhaps you're a born businesswoman, darling.'

'Well, I didn't know I was even interested in business myself,' said Scarlett. 'But when I overheard Ed Johnson planning on taking Gibson–Keene for a ride, I just saw red. I felt I had to do something about it, so I called Monica and we had a meeting, and she set up another meeting for me to see Clay Wright. So I saw him a couple of times and he suggested I call on a couple of drugstore accounts, because they were giving us a hard time, and things kind of snowballed, I guess.'

507

'And then Clay, as financial director, said that since you now owned 51 per cent of Gibson–Keene, you should take an ative interest,' Gina commented with a wry smile.

'How do you know that?' Scarlett asked, suspiciously. 'Who told you?'

'No one needed to tell me. I always knew Clay was a good man,' Gina answered smoothly. 'Tell me, how does Theo feel about your commitment to Gibson–Keene? It has to be full-time . . .'

'He's pleased, of course,' Scarlett replied quickly.

'It's a new generation of husbands,' announced Cecilia solemnly.

'Thanks to feminism!' proclaimed Scarlett.

'Thanks to feminism!' chorused Cecilia and Gina, looking at one another over Scarlett's head.

Then, as if following a signal, they were in one another's arms again, and again allowed their tears to flow as freely as their laughter.

'I behaved badly over Theo,' Gina said softly. 'I'm sorry.'

'Grandmama told me how hurt you had been over Rufus,' Scarlett said kindly.

'I'm the luckiest of women,' Gina said. 'I've got the most wonderful daughter, and the most wonderful mother.'

'We are blood relations,' Cecilia pronounced. 'And blood relations are born to one another.'

'Since we have no other blood relations in the whole world,' said Gina, 'we are an exclusive club of three.'

'In about six months' time we'll be a club of four,' said Scarlett shyly.

Cecilia opened her arms, and her daughter and her grand-daughter came into them, and they were in total harmony and in perfect unity.

Four days later, in the glory and dignity and peace of St Patrick's Cathedral, Cecilia O'Connor and Mark Cartwright were married. Although they had decided not to have a reception, they had planned on a small family lunch at the Four Seasons. Now that Gina and Hugh were with them, and by way of honouring Gina's need for anonymity, they decided on Primavera, a quiet Italian restaurant famous for its cuisine.

Even at seventy-three, Mark's face dazzled with unconcealable joy. It was as if his own happiness had taken him by surprise, and could not therefore be hidden or dimmed, still less controlled.

'People are not supposed to fall in love at my age,' he told Cecilia. 'So I guess when they do, they fall harder.'

'Love is more valuable when we grow older,' Cecilia said. 'We are more vulnerable, I guess.'

They were in a luxurious Italianate suite at the Grand Hotel in Rome. They had left New York as soon as their wedding lunch was over. They had thought it right and proper to spend the first night of their honeymoon in Rome, where they had met so long ago.

In the background the bells of St Peter's pealed. Cecilia had waited for this moment. 'Listen,' she said. 'Listen to the bells of St Peter's.'

He listened. 'I remember,' he said.

Handing him a neatly wrapped gift in maroon paper, she said, 'This is for you.'

After quickly unwrapping the package, the maroon and silver colours of a Hershey bar were exposed. 'Why, it's Hershey's,' he said. 'What a memory you have!'

'They say history repeats itself,' she said lightly. 'Only this time – forty-six years on – it's the other way round. I'm giving you the chocolate.'

Overwhelmed by the emotional memories of how they had first met, they said nothing for a while. Then he said, 'It's comforting to know that some things don't change.'

She broke off a piece and put it in his mouth. 'Just for once we are going to forget about cholesterol.' She laughed.

He hugged her to him.

509

Later, as so often happened these days, he read her mind. 'I'm glad Gina came to the wedding,' he said, between mouthfuls of chocolate. 'I like her young man.'

'He's hardly young, he's at least fifty,' she said, smiling in the dark. 'I love you, Marco. You're ageless.' Her thoughts returned to Gina. 'Did she tell you she's going to London University to become a psychologist?'

'Yes,' he said. 'And she'll be a good one, too.'

'Hugh explained her decision to me,' she said. 'He told me that she's not turning her back on Gibson–Keene because she's ashamed of what she's done. She's very, very proud of her achievements.'

'She's an empress of an empire. Why shouldn't she be proud?'

'Hugh told me she's giving it all up because—' Here her voice broke, and she could not continue.

'Because?' he prompted gently.

'She needs to save others,' she said simply, 'because she needed to save her own soul.'